TABLE OF CONTENTS

TROUBLE THE WATERS:
TALES FROM THE DEEP BLUE

Edited by
Sheree Renée Thomas
Pan Morigan
Troy L. Wiggins

Published by
Third Man Books

Cover art by
Stacey Robinson

http://thirdmanbooks.com/troublethewaters
password: water

Trouble the Waters: Tales from the Deep Blue
Copyright © 2019 by Sheree Renée Thomas, Pan Morigan, and Troy L. Wiggins

For more information:

Third Man Books, LLC, 623 7th Ave S,
Nashville, Tennessee 37203
A CIP record is on file with the Library of Congress

FIRST USA EDITION
ISBN: 9781734842272

Cover Art by Stacey Robinson
Design and layout by Caitlin Parker

For the Love of Ama Patterson, Liz Roberts,
and Mrs. Cornelia Bailey

INTRODUCTION

There are those who claim to know the ways of water. They have listened to its many flowing tongues and watched its comings and goings in an effort to achieve some form of mastery. They have watched its promises of calm be broken by mercurial moods that swiftly change from tenderness to the rage of dismembered ships and boats splintered, homes swept away to disappear in the horizon.

What binds those who claim to know to those who know better than to claim, is the undisputed fact that water, all water, is life. It is the water around our blue-green world that sustains us, and yet it is also water, troubled waters, that can lead us into danger, or, as the spiritual "Wade in the Water" suggests, intervene to protect and save us from ourselves.

This collection of tales from the deep blue has multiple origins, like the many shifting forms that water on earth knows. Perhaps the first was when I had the good fortune to hear poet Linda D. Addison perform "Mami Wata, Goddess of Clear Blue" at the 2005 World Horror Convention in New York where Linda was the Poet Guest of Honor. Her reading of this fine work was held only a few months before the devastating impact of Hurricane Katrina. With grace and power, Linda visibly stirred the audience and her evocation of the West African water goddess remained a beautifully haunting memory.

Four years later, art historian Henry John Drewal and guest curator David Driskell helped visitors to the Smithsonian National Museum of African Art gather a framework for viewing the extraordinary exhibition, *Mami Wata: Arts for Water Spirits in Africa and the African Atlantic World.*

My daughters and I traveled from New York City to see this rare exhibit in Washington, D.C. Created by the Fowler Museum at UCLA, the exhibit displayed breathtaking altars and various creative celebrations of the powerful water goddess whose unmistakable mermaid persona can be seen throughout Africa and the African diaspora.

Between Linda's New York poetry reading, Hurricane Katrina, and the Mami Wata water spirits exhibition in Washington, DC, the first droplet of an idea was born. My dear friend, the late author and literary patron, Ama Patterson, a co-founder of our Beyond 'Dusa Women's Writing Group, agreed to co-edit a collection of tales around Mami Wata and various water deities. We were excited about the possibility of diving into works that centered water spirits, mythology, and lore. We exchanged writers wish lists, bookmarked stories and articles, and dreamed about what might be. Unfortunately, Ama's health took a heartbreaking turn, making her work on this project impossible after a time. It is our great loss that dear Ama, a brilliant, gifted writer and a true goddess in her own right, is no longer with us, writing her stories, telling her tales in that wonderful voice that evoked a true sense of wonder.

In hindsight I realize that *Trouble the Waters* was also inspired by the multitalented dynamo, Liz Roberts and Mrs. Cornelia Bailey, an invaluable voice in the Sapelo Sea Island community. It was in her home, overlooking the Atlantic Ocean, where we ate Mr. Julius Bailey's delicious shrimp and grits, and witnessed firsthand the beauty and magic of storytelling as a natural force. Trouble the Waters is dedicated to these three amazing women. I am also truly grateful to have the opportunity to continue this project with four of the most talented editors and artists I know, Pan Morigan and Troy L. Wiggins and our cover artist Stacey Robinson and designer Daniel Coates, friends and comrades on this aquatic journey. The twenty-nine short stories and three select poems collected here represent water spirits, gods, monsters, and the unclassifiables from around the world by writers from voices you are going to love.

The works explore many themes and tones, evoking water in its myriad moods and modes. "Mami Wata, Goddess of Clear Blue," the opening poem by Linda D. Addison and "Dance of Myal", by Maurice Broaddus, examine **Myths and Deities: Present, Future, Past**.

Tales such as "All of Us Are She" by Jasmine Wade, evoke primordial womb waters and remind us that sometimes we must birth ourselves, while "The Ancestor Abiodun Tells Me About the Time She Forgot Osun" by Maria Osunbimpe Hamilton Abegunde, and the poem, "Maafa to Mami Wata" by Heather 'Byrd' Roberts, reimagine **The Middle Passage and Other Histories**.

"Deep Like the Rivers" by Christopher Caldwell, "At the Opening of Bayou St. John" by Shawn Scarber, "The Sea Devil" by Susana Morris, and "Hagfish" by Rylee Edgar recall the transformative power of water and offer us intriguing takes on **Shapeshifters**.

The **Water Creatures** in my own story, "Love Hangover," "Seamonsters" by Ama Patterson, "Lilies and Claws" by Kate Heartfield, "Mother of Crawdads" by Betsy Phillips, "Against the Venom Tide" by Henry Szabranski, and "Mississippi Medusa" by Elle L. Littlefield all remind us that while the earth is round, her waters are vast and deep. We may never know all the strange, wondrous lifeforms teeming below.

Other works such as Jacqueline Johnson's poem, "Green Symphony", "Portal" by Mateo Hinojosa, and "A City Called Heaven" by Danian Darrell Jerry, capture **The Power and History of Water Itself**. These works remind us that water lives. And no volume on water can be complete without **Watery Legends, Fairy Tales, and Lore**. "Salt Baby" by Nanna Áradóttir, "Numbers" by Rion Amilcar Scott, "The Weaver's Tale" by Cecilia Quirk, "The Stone" by Naila Moreira, "Spirits Don't Cross Over Water 'Til They Do" by Jamey Hatley, "The Half-Drowned Castle" by Lyndsay E. Gilbert, and "Follow Death" by Story Boyle, cast their own spells, creating haunting tales of characters that operate within their own systems of magic and logic.

There are also works that offer us **New Worlds**, **New Wata**, such as "Andrea Hairston's "Seven Generations Algorithm," and "Water Being" by Pan Morigan. We are reminded to be good stewards of earth's many waters and of ourselves in works that explore **Eco-Justice and Environmental Change**, including "Hoʻi Hou e na Pō" by Gina McGuire, "Juniper's Song" by Marie Vibbert, "Whimper" by Nalo Hopkinson, "Call the Water" by Adrienne Marie Brown, and "Ghosts" by Jaquira Díaz.

In the old days, Pliny the Elder and others described an ancient practice of water divers and seafarers pouring a bit of oil over troubled waters, to ease the path before them and ensure a safe journey ahead. We hope these tales from the deep blue recesses of these talented writers' imaginations will soothe you at times, frighten and unsettle you a bit, make you laugh, and nod your head in wonder, reveling in the fact that our world is indeed round and water, sweet, deep, life- sustaining, transformative blue water makes up most of it.

Sheree Renée Thomas
Memphis, Tennessee
Mississippi River

WATER DREAMING

Underwater dreams, a child's permeable flesh, I become lake. In emerald murk, sipping heavy metals, I track alewives floating dead on the surface of Lake Michigan, my refuge. For years I swam all weathers in an old t-shirt and sneakers. A solo, girlish thing, I wasn't so safe on that tide or on the cold, grey shore. But I imagined myself a child of water and felt the lake watching over me. Many would call this notion fantasy. *Yet we're all born of water.*

The stories we tell become truth, rise up and wander, go swimming. Remembering that time, that deeply-felt affiliation, I reflect on tale-telling, *thingification*, and ancient treasures like the Great Lakes. Our tottering, Western hegemony calls water voiceless, devoid of rights. We can do any ole thing to rivers, streams, wetlands, lakes, and seas. No need to ask water. That would be *unrealistic*.

When I was little, many American waterways were declared dead. Some rivers were so polluted, they were flammable. The 1972 Clean Water Act helped fix some of the mess. At least the rivers stopped catching fire! But loopholes in the act permitted continued damage, leaving the veins of Earth in peril. Currently, lax regulation of factory farming, clear-cutting, fracking, and mining allow agricultural run-off, pesticides, mining, and industrial waste, (including *forever* chemicals) to be dumped into our waterbodies. From Pittsburgh to Reno, Calgary to Houston, folks have awakened to find their water unsafe, stolen, in need of protection. Environmental racism, classism, and colonialism make water dangers even worse. Abandoned mines, military and industrial sites leak unchecked. *If* there is running water, failing sewage and water treatment plants and lead-leaching plumbing poison water a second time. The people of Flint, Michigan; the Navajo Nation; East Chicago, Indiana; Neskantanga First Nation; Centreville, Illinois; and Grassy Narrows First Nation have nightmare stories to tell of water injustice. This list could be pages long.

Meanwhile, Wall Street trades in water futures.

We have a notion that we can flush bad stuff *away*. Just toss it! Watch the nasty drift downstream or sink beneath the ocean waves, as if water was some zombie thing, keeper of our dead ideas. But there is no *away*. Away is someone else's home, someone else's water-pitcher. Earth's water is like the veins in our bodies. All waters connect, surging in, out, through one another, circling the atmosphere, and flowing over us as mist, rain, or snow. What we send downstream lands in our cup and in us. If not today, tomorrow.

Water is life, said the water protectors of Standing Rock as they risked their lives and liberty to protect Lake Oahe and the wide Missouri from the Dakota access pipeline. *Water is alive,* said Josephine Mandamin of Wiikwemkoong Unceded Territory as she walked 25,000 miles and more around the Great Lakes and other waterways, telling us of water's sovereignty. Many across the world follow in the footsteps of these water-teachers. In 2017, after generations of effort, the Whanganui Nation of New Zealand had the Whanganui river declared *ancestor, person,* with rights, by law. They also changed the conversation, demanding that another reality rise to the surface of the world's mind. Shortly afterwards, a court in Uttarakhand, India granted personhood to the Ganges and Yamuna rivers.

Line 3, a Canada-based, tar sands pipeline may be thrust through sensitive wetlands on Anishinaabe territory in Minnesota. Temporary jobs are dangled at struggling communities, dividing neighbors. Meanwhile, the project endangers one hundred ninety waterbodies and the cultures that flowered beside them: uncountable generations of history, language, belief, creativity, and scientific knowledge. Such value can't be squeezed onto a spread sheet, unless rendered *thing*.

Our blue planet is miraculous. Its watery ecosystems are treasure troves, irreplaceable preserves of sustenance and biodiversity millions of years in the making. With our burning, extracting, dumping, plundering addictions, we may drain that treasure in decades. The primordial can't be reconstituted or remade. *Realistic?*

Who is your beloved water?

Speculative fiction at its most powerful asks us to question master narratives; imagine another mind, path, or world. What we call real, realism, realistic is only an agreement about a particular perspective among specific affiliations. In the West, that slant has crowned itself the only perspective on the block, i.e. reality itself. *Trouble the Waters* offers new-ancient ideas and fresh, clear realities, helping us feel water and other beings in revelatory ways. May water sing on in us, and we, become water's song! Drink deeply reader, swim long.

Pan Morigan
Lake Michigan
Connecticut River

WE ARE CALLED TO THE WATER

I wasn't born near the water, but I was called to it very young, mostly by ancestry and need. My ancestral connection is one that matured in the Mississippi Delta but maintains an umbilical current clear across the Atlantic Ocean. My need-based connections to water are more simple: without it, my life would not be sustained. As a child, I watched men in my family reminisce about the impassive Wolf River, how it looked and smelled before human interference made it almost unfishable. I enjoy the privilege of hailing from an American city with a legendary water supply made possible in part by that same river, called the "Neshoba," meaning "Wolf," by its indigenous Chickasaw inhabitants, and I honor that blessing by making snobbish remarks about the taste and quality of other cities' tap water whenever I'm able to travel.

If I'm honest with myself, I know that the urge to be near, or return to water is a deeply human one. Far beyond serving merely as the sea spray on our lips, we recognize our planet's waters, interconnected and seemingly endless, as a life-giving divine being. Humanity has watched the water since we emerged from it. Its depths fuel our dreams—and our nightmares, and we've created countless water mythologies that inspire us to seek understanding of water's power and caprice, while helping us to situate our base needs in memory.
Water and storytelling have always been connected.

Still, we must look out on our times with eyes as clear as the Mother Waters. We are removed from the humans that built our first civilizations around ancient waterways by stretches of time that are miniscule when compared to water's lifetime, and our planet's waters have often been the victims of the ravages of technological advancement and all of its associated horrors. Corporations have deified profit, and now use water to fossilize markers of oppression all over the planet. Declaring their right to price humans out of access to water, using legal precedent to destroy waterways in search of crude, or contaminating the planet's lifeblood with chemicals and heavy metals.

As we sense in our bones this planet's call for a reckoning, we know that our species must get in right relationship with water and return ourselves to reverence of its power and its shaping of our existence. Over a long year in the mid-aughts, the Water Protectors at Standing Rock brought their powerful imaginations to bear, shouting Mní Wičóni—Water is Life to try and halt this destruction in the name of progress. Mari Copeny, better known online as "Little Miss Flint," bore the weight of Flint Michigan's water crisis on her then-pre-teenaged shoulders, broadcasting to a global audience how the state of Michigan had neglected Flint's residents. And in my own city, in the current moment, community members in historic South Memphis and North Mississippi defended themselves and our city's aquifer from industrial construction that could devastate Memphis' aquifer, the source of its incomparable water. These water crises, and many others like them around the world, are persistent, nefarious, and ongoing.

This is when the human drive to recall memory and share the fruits of our boundless imaginations are most powerful. Each of the stories in Trouble the Waters is a testament to the transformative power of the human imagination, a clarion call to readers to remember that human connection to water, and the memories, and mythologies that it continues to hold for us. Trouble the Waters authors use their global perspectives and connections to water to complicate our understandings of our water-based histories, myths, ideas and futures. I encourage readers to take time with Trouble the Waters, to satiate themselves with the stories and allow themselves a dip into these collected imaginations, that they may emerge changed, cleansed, and renewed.

Troy L. Wiggins
Memphis, Tennessee
Wolf River

MAMI WATA,
GODDESS OF CLEAR BLUE

LINDA D. ADDISON

Worry sings bright in your neurons, your light so blurred I could barely taste you
      while I was sleeping, dreaming of the time before
      I melted down two galaxies making my way here
      why you wait so long to call for me, baby?

Your pain is clean and clear in the thickening tattoos on your back
      you no longer hunger for us in your dreams
      silence has softened your soul, eaten at your aspect
      you rest in my arms now, it's going to be alright.

I used to visit the vodun pantheons when you gyrated in dusty courtyards
      back when you came to us free and open in your sleep
      Mami Vishnu and I introduced star maps to the faithful
      crowded your dreams with tomorrows full of luminosity.

Bought your children to my lap, just like you now, let them look through my eyes
      into the darkness to see nothing is empty
      leaned their head against my belly
      so they could hear the purr of the Never-Born.

What took you from us is the hard things you build so you could forget the soft things
      but hunger for a way to live without bruised outstretched hands
      don't just go away because you fill the night with bright lights
      making the moon and stars blush away with neglect.

You always hungry for things to fill your hands and pockets, shiny unneeded things
        I stayed with you because with all that wanting you made an opening for me
        couldn't resist your eyes rolled white upward and inward to me
        you know how vain we can be, it's vanity hurting you now, baby.

There's always a way to heal – you got to know where to look
        what matters is the sharp edges behind your closed eyes
        I savored the small wounds unhealed in your heart
        even when my name laid dead in your mouth.

SEVEN GENERATIONS ALGORITHM

ANDREA HAIRSTON

"I know you all loved the future, but…"

Cinnamon Jones stood at the graves of her ancestors, making excuses. Dead clover skittered across her boots—ghostly lace dissolving into the rubble of wildflower stalks. The sun struggled up over battered hills. Low-riding clouds made a purple and orange carpet of first light. Tomorrow was becoming today.

"Your future was where dreams folks fought and died for finally came true. I'm stuck in some other jacked-up future." Cinnamon winced. "I know you don't want to hear that. Sorry."

Granddaddy Aidan, Miz Redwood, and Great Aunt Iris were buried in a grassy Amphitheatre on their heirloom-vegetable farm, right off the bike path. It was Cinnamon's farm now, and she was lucky to have it, even if she couldn't farm worth a damn. Blessed be the Co-ops! No crops in the amphitheatre though. Semi-circles of smooth rock formed tiers of seating on a hillside overlooking a crabgrass stage. Star-magnolia bushes and oak and maple trees provided backstage and wings. Maple sap was running. Buckets were stacked in the prop shed waiting to be deployed. Upstage center, three memorial stones carved from pink granite nestled in dead clover and wildflower stalks: Thunderbird, Dragon, and Mami Wata with snakes curling around her scaly tail—the elders' favorite Carnival masks.

Cinnamon's dark eyes welled up and plum colored lips quivered. She was wheeling toward sixty and still felt like a child.

"Your little scientist-artiste is all grown up."

She snorted at herself and popped homemade licorice suckers in her mouth—Miz Redwood's tonic for unruly stomachs and cranky moods. Granddaddy Aidan wrote her hoodoo conjure recipe into a song. Great Aunt Iris said Cinnamon should sing and suck for maximum effect, but she forgot the lyrics.

"I'm supposed to be cruising the good life, carrying your spirits with me, until I hand a better future over to someone else."

Was Cinnamon a big disappointment to the ancestors, a broken link in the chain?

Bruja licked her hand and whined. A mutt with a good measure of Border Collie, Bruja would be trying to herd Cinnamon soon. They needed to get going. People at the Ghost Mall were hungry, itchy, twitchy. Showing up late for the rehearsal breakfast would make a tense situation worse. Still, Cinnamon had to clear her head before she could finish the sunrise ritual and head out.

"I don't want to give this future to anybody."

The asphalt bike path snaked from the amphitheatre at the farm's edge through flood rubble and across gated roads nine miles to the Ghost Mall. Refugees, squatters, and former desperadoes were pitching tents in dead big-box stores, hoping for miracles: jobs, food, electricity, a plan, a vision—maybe just cheap cell service. An Afro-Deutsch hipster, wearing fibre optic sneakers, hoody, and winged cape, crashed Carnival last year and handed out free burners with solar chargers. Ghost-Mallers cheered the faceless, glow-in-the-dark figure calling for hope. Cinnamon wasn't impressed with the fibre optic kicks or Euro-trash accent, but Ghost-Mallers were waiting on the second coming. All they got in tent city was tap water, compost toilets, and Co-op volunteers pedaling in whatever they could spare. Nobody in the hill towns could spare much. Folks who could were locked up tight down in the valley behind a flood wall and megawatt gates. Electric Paradise was on the other side of the Mall—a waste of power and good river valley soil. Cinnamon had gates around her farm too, but no lethal current and no guards, gun-bots, or patrol-drones, mostly just urban myths keeping desperate people in check. A good horror-rep was cheaper than hiring thugs and electrifying fences 24/7. Still...

"I'm afraid of the future." Cinnamon hated to admit this to her grandparents and great aunt. She'd sworn on their graves never to be like the old farts in gated communities ranking on jacked-up humanity and waxing nostalgic for glaciers to ski, rain forests to plunder, and only two genders to love. Yet here she was, stuck on the past too. Bruja nipped her elbows and stared, one brown eye in black fur and one blue eye with a pink lid in white fur. An unblinking challenge. "You're right. Lying to myself or feeling sorry won't help."

Cinnamon had wasted her one hour on the net watching news for Granddaddy Aidan. He'd insisted, after the elders were dead and buried, Cinnamon had to come out to the amphitheatre every sunrise and do a story storm on the future, starting with yesterday. Aunt Iris wanted her to sing about the future too. That's why the elders were buried in a natural amphitheatre, to come back as weeds, as yellow dandelions and purple lupine, and enjoy the shows. Cinnamon hadn't felt like singing in years. Miz Redwood told her to do headlines with funny commentary if she couldn't put up a production. I can always do that, Cinnamon promised her grandmother. But the news was old and tired. The elders were long dead. Their ashes had dissolved by now. Would they notice if she missed a day?

The hunk of junk circus-bots lurking in the wings grumbled and farted a smelly discharge on magnolia buds. These unruly bots would get on Cinnamon's case later if she didn't keep the promises she made to the elders. Erasing memories of her grandparents and great aunt would be too cruel, maybe even impossible. The ancestors were all through Cinnamon's circus-bot algorithms. She might have imagined the farting and grumbling—projecting her bad mood on innocent machines. In sentinel-mode, the bots were mostly silent, just a faint buzz now and again.

"I'm two months behind paying my access bill." Cinnamon wiped schmutz off the memorial stones. "I spent my cash on spring planting and Carnival supplies, on rehearsal treats, taxes, and bribes. Virtual Living costs more than brick and mortar rent." She sighed. "No telling when Consolidated might cut me off the net."

Some digital divide algorithm decided how much grace period was profitable for the coalition of providers aka the net monopoly. If Consolidated cut Cinnamon loose, this morning might be her last news report for a while. She refused to hack random Wi-Fi. Consolidated hunted down hackers with vengeful AI. Who needed that static?

Giving up on gentle nips, Bruja rammed Cinnamon's butt then ran to her pedal-people bike with the hefty six-trashcan trailer. Bruja barked and wagged a spotted tail, a command gesture. Do the damn ritual.

"OK. OK. OK. Granddaddy Aidan, Miz Redwood, and Aunt Iris, this is for you: Polio Comes Roaring Back in the South and the CDC Stumbles. Funding got gutted in 2025. Coming back from that, well, any response is a miracle. I mean, last week it was nasty tropical diseases wasting Nova Scotia to Maine. Water Wars In The Wild West Are Getting Ugly. Were there pretty water wars? They're burning up in Texas, and in Massachusetts, we got nowhere to put the rain. Scattered Brownouts Cripple The West Coast. A government spy agency in China or the USA or Brazil launched shapeshifting digital weapons at power grids by accident. Maybe it was Russia. Nigeria insisted it wasn't their fault. Nobody believes anybody. Suicide Soars. Not Just On The Rez Or In Black and Brown Ghettos. Yeah. It's never APOCALYPSE until rich white men are jumping from bridges. Everybody living in the third world now."

Not funny. Even Bruja looked hangdog. Cinnamon couldn't get any comic relief going.

"Crime Soars! Hormones. Young folks need more than gangsta hype or booty calls."

Nobody said booty call anymore. Nowadays it was a riff on sex-bots and slits that Cinnamon felt on the tip of her tongue but couldn't remember.

"Reboot Your Bright Young Mind. Let It Soar! Soar is the word of the morning. Genius doctors swear they'll not only cure Alzheimer's soon, but engineer drugs and enhancements to clear all the mist."

Hadn't Ready-Med already done that six years ago? Something must have gone wrong with those treatments. Or maybe it was recycled wishful thinking. No matter. Designer drugs and cyborg apps were out of Cinnamon's price range. And forget trusting her mind to chemical or electrical engineers working for the company store.

"Well, that's what I got." The memorial stones glittered in the sun: Dragon, Thunderbird, and Mami Wata, mythical wonderworkers expecting more out of her than she had. Cinnamon sank down in damp weed stalks, blinking tears. "It's hard to keep going. I get tired. Everywhere is a refugee camp… Too many people out of work and on the run. It's like we're spitting in the ocean!"

"Only seems overwhelming," one of the circus-bots whispered in Aunt Iris's intrepid adventurer voice, powering up a bit for the end of the sunrise ritual, "just follow your intuition. Do what you do."

A murder of crows burst from oak branches up into the sky, mobbing a hawk that was trying to be slick. Cinnamon wiped tears and gaped at the squawking black mob. "Good luck catching a single crow in broad daylight," she shouted. The hungry raptor glided by, glancing at her with disinterest before taking refuge in a magnolia bush. The crows didn't follow.

"Almost forgot. AI Caught Lying! Big fancy Artificial Intelligence shouldn't do that. Surprise! Must be a creative one." She grinned. "Maybe this AI knows better than to trust people with straight truth, if it's going to get us to do what we want to do, what we need to do. Got to hoodoo us!" She laughed full out. "A lying AI is funny. Had me writing a song, words and music, right before dawn—now that's something." Bruja threw back her head and they howled together. "Temperatures Soar! Warmest February 29th On Record. Leap year might be jacking the statistics, but the Weather Wizard says another fury storm coming up the coast." Cinnamon scratched Bruja's ears. "The coast is closer than it used to be, and all the storms are furious with us."

Bruja knew weather was the end of the ritual. She wagged her butt and tugged Cinnamon's sleeve, but then turned into the wind sniffing and huffing.

Cinnamon scanned for danger. "What?" A skirt of mist from the Mill

River clung to forsythia bushes—unusual up here at the amphitheatre. "Water spirits checking on us?"

Bruja flattened her ears and yelped.

"Talking to other dogs? Is Spook out there?"

Fangs bared, Bruja crept downstage left to the circus-bots and tried to herd them upstage to safety.

"Don't worry." Right now, the bots looked like heaps of bug-eyed junk. When deployed, they became the mythic creatures carved onto the memorial stones: an Anishinaabe Thunderbird with fire eyes, a wingless Chinese Dragon, and Mami Wata, African queen mother of waters. "We always take the whole crew to the Mall."

Cinnamon hoisted Dragon and Thunderbird—lightweight, yet unwieldy despite handles. Bruja herded them to the bike-trailer then chased Cinnamon back for Mami Wata and her snake coils of LEDs. Mami Wata's scales looked wet lit up, like the kicks on the Afro-Deutsch hipster. Solar panel seashells covered her head and the locs cascading down her back. The broken glass tail housed a generator. Cinnamon lifted the heavy light-bot, and nerves in her back zapped out a warning, as if sturdy leg muscles couldn't handle the load, as if special effects weren't worth the weight. She wavered. Bruja nipped her heels, impatient, unsettled.

After three nasty nerve-zaps, Cinnamon staggered on. "Happy?"

Bruja growled. Cinnamon scoped the trees and allowed herself a shiver of fear. Danger was everywhere. The farm was due for a raid. Horror stories had to be recharged or folks stopped believing they were true. Keeping up a danger-rep without doing real damage was hard work. The old African living in the treehouse helped with that, doing an African Amazon thing when fools tried to raid the farm. Instead of moping around in the oak branches, Taiwo should start the growing season with a magic act for Carnival—the one show Cinnamon still managed every year. "If I'm gonna sing, Taiwo need to come down out the trees. Maybe we'd both feel better."

Bruja barked agreement.

Cinnamon hopped on the bike saddle and shouted over her shoulders to the ancestors. "Good news. I actually wrote a song and I'm inviting the Ghost Mall and Paradise Valley for Carnival tomorrow! Taiwo too. Get that old African on solid ground. That's as far in the future as I go. The day after that is not my fault."

#

The bike path wound up and down through the hill towns, crisscrossing the Mill River. A danger-ride. This forested route was maintained by the Co-ops and preyed on by desperadoes. After pedaling hard for four miles, Cinnamon felt a twinge in her thigh. She hoped it would stay a twinge and not turn into a week off her feet. A fit fifty-something, she regularly hauled two hundred pounds of instruments, tools, bots, and oat and apple treats. Ghost-Mallers depended on her reliable Co-op delivery system. Cinnamon pumped the pedals and got up to ten MPH. Fearless, Bruja circled her three-bot and bike-person herd, ears erect, nose wide. Rustling bushes and snapping branches followed them across a wooden Mill River bridge. Not Spook. That dog was silent as a ghost. Only newcomers would be foolish enough to attack them, or folks who hadn't heard or didn't believe the horror tall tales about cyborg dogs, aliens in the trees, and demon spirits swimming the Mill River. Actually, the Mill River was more like a stream, and most of the dark lore was true.

Mist on the river could have been a parade of haints, dancing. Cinnamon squinted. Naked women with seaweed hair and rainbow waist beads stomped across slippery pebbles, fading in and out of shafts of sun. Cinnamon blinked, and they were gone. Mist evaporated in the warm air. "I should invite water spirits to Carnival too. They could do an act with Taiwo. That would be something, right?"

Bruja cocked her head, non-committal. Water spirits weren't in her herd yet.

Cinnamon slowed to six MPH as she approached the cavalry checkpoint where the bike path crossed the road to Electric Paradise. Valleyites living behind high voltage gates hired a thug brigade to monitor the gun-bots and patrol-drones that kept the refugee deluge at bay. Gun-bots were chill and hard to hack. Tampering set off an attack mode, followed by a self-destruct protocol that took the hacker out. She pinged the gun-bots and they ignored her: no threat. Underpaid thugs, however, had a trigger-happy rep. Skittish, macho, and bored, the Valley security force had been promised superhero tech and game-world adventures. Instead, they were maintenance men polishing chrome widgets, shooing mice away from wires, and cleaning up squirrel turds. Shooting at a homeless refugee or wayward desperado broke the monotony.

Up ahead, a guard stepped from the bushes near the bike path. Cinnamon waved, cheery as always. A skinny new kid in a bulletproof helmet and vest snarled as she pumped up a heartbreak hill (which last week seemed like a modest incline). The kid was hollow-eyed, sallow, and hungry—as lost as kids at the Mall. He might have been camping there yesterday. The cannon on his hip looked too big for his hands. Cinnamon halted five yards from him to massage her thigh and tossed a greasy paper bag. He caught it without thinking. It could have been a bomb. Might not last long. A crumb apple treat tumbled out. He clutched it quickly, good reflexes. "What's this?"

Bruja wagged her tail, not really friendly, but fronting.

"An apple surprise." Cinnamon shook her leg cramp, and a story storm took over her tongue. "Made with special biker spice, Aunt Iris's recipe. She could make anything taste good. I mean nasty weeds from the woods. Every dish was a surprise. Born the end of the nineteenth century, Miz Lady boogie-woogied into the twenty-first. A hoodoo conjurer with a PhD— cultural anthropology. She spied your spirit wherever you roamed. Nobody got lost around her. She could find anyone's heart." The kid shook his head at Cinnamon's motor-mouth blather. "Eat!" She used director voice. "It's free and tastes as good as it smells. Better." He sniffed the apple surprise. Enchantment overwhelmed skepticism. He nibbled a corner, grinned, and stuffed the whole cake in his mouth. "How old are you?" Cinnamon asked.

"Old enough." He dug in the bag for more. Instead of joining the cavalry, this kid should be up at the colleges filling his mind with dreams.

Pain shot up to her lower back. "Shit!" Lingering made the cavalry suspicious or worse. Her muscles didn't give a damn. She stepped off the bike and powered the circus-bots up to active, for cover, for security. Compact trash unfurled into a Dragon with bike-reflector eyes and cellophane and aluminum body. Funkadelic legs splayed into rotors and whirred to a funky beat. Dragon lifted up and hovered over her head. Thunderbird unfurled trash-bag wings, stepped out of the trashcan, and let loose loon-like calls. Tap-dancing talons turned bumpy asphalt into a drum. Mami Wata's eyes lit up. A waterfall of light surged from her mouth down green tennis-ball breasts, over a basketball belly, and across a broken glass tail. The kid gawked at theatre magic, too stunned to wolf another treat or pull his gun or worry why Cinnamon dropped onto the bike path in dead-bug pose—back flat on cold asphalt, legs and arms flailing. Dragon breathed a cloud of colored glitter over her: cool fire, a spirit tonic.

"I've heard about you," the kid said, awe-struck.

"Have you now?" Special effects were a good shield. Cinnamon also wore a bullet-proof bike helmet and vest.

"Hola! Cinnamon! Out here putting on a show." A burly older thug she'd seen often charged from the tollbooth/guardhouse. A survivor. His sun-burnt bald head gleamed. Barbed wire was tattooed around his throat with a trickle of blood down each side. "Where's my bag of goodies?" he shouted. "What I tell you?" He pounded the kid.

"Stop thinking of folks as thugs or Euro-trash," Dragon whispered so only Cinnamon could hear, her grandmother's voice—a Georgia Sea Island scold.

"Aren't you on a fitness kick, Rob?" Cinnamon jumped up. Maybe too soon.

"It's Diego," Dragon muttered.

"I mean Diego." She threw him an apple—Macintosh, sour and crisp. His favorite.

"Would you believe this fine woman is in her fifties?" Diego attacked the fruit.

"Pedaling around, outside the gates..." The kid chewed the third apple surprise from the bag and scanned her ancient breasts and muscled thighs, unimpressed. "That's dangerous, isn't it, for an older lady alone?"

"I'm never alone." She scratched Bruja. "And I look forty." Dark satin skin from her mom didn't crack and not much gray in her braids like her dad. "Forty's feisty, too much trouble."

"You look thirty-five." Diego lied and leered at her. He rubbed his bald head. Where was his helmet? "Good trouble."

"None of that." She wagged a finger. "Nobody wants my drums and shovels."

Diego turned serious. "Some new crew sweeping the hills. Rough characters. Doing a lot of mischief. Valley-Security put out a warning. Bonus if we catch anybody."

She sucked her teeth, disgusted. "That might mean random travelers picked off."

"What about your drones? I'd steal them." The kid sputtered at green-eyed Dragon hovering in his face. "And apple cakes. Those are good too."

Cinnamon sneered. "Maybe I'm a poison trap."

The kid stopped breathing and dropped the empty bag.

"A joke, Tyrone," Diego said. "Cinnamon's a clown. That's a dragon from her Carnival circus, not a drone." Mami Wata rippled her ocean cloth, a wave of tiny lights, like the sun reflected in an unruly sea. She added whale song and water crashing in a thunder hole. Tyrone gawked at her, in love. "They're all circus-bots." Diego laughed and punched Tyrone again. "Watch out for ghost-dogs, materializing out of nowhere and ripping your throat, if you get out of line." Diego was sharp and no-nonsense, good for boosting Cinnamon's horror-rep, but witch-dog Bruja was more likely to take out predators than Spook. "Ghost-dog can catch you anywhere."

"Not possible." Tyrone licked his lips, eyeing Mami Wata—a realist, lusting after a circus-bot! Diego sniggered, and Tyrone shoved him, shouting, "People say demons lurk in the Mill River and a Rambo-alien lives in the oaks on her farm. You buy that?"

Diego shrugged.

"Well, actually it's a homeless Eshu from another dimension, not

Rambo." Cinnamon chuckled at truth stranger than fiction. "Built the treehouse after the last flood and called up a water-spirit brigade."

"Eshu? That old African, suffering from PTSD?" Diego scowled. "Fought in Viet Nam, Iraq, Syria. Somewhere. I thought his name was Taiwo, not Eshu."

"E-shoo—sounds like a sneeze." Tyrone laughed at this tired joke.

"Eshu is the trickster riding Taiwo's spirit, a powerful Yoruba deity, from Nigeria." She glared at Tyrone. "Standing at the crossroads, the laugh is always on you."

"Tyrone meant no disrespect. We know war does a number on you." Diego shuddered. "My father fought in Syria. Taiwo—he's got scars inside and out."

"Taiwo is not a he or she," Cinnamon said. "Oun in Yoruba."

Tyrone rolled his eyes. Diego groaned. "Right."

T-bird played a groove from a mega-hit by that Yoruban rapper and her Korean blues-singer husband. Cinnamon chanted her Carnival jam on top of the infectious melody. Diego added a bass-drum voice riff:

Dark days
Just a flash
Love be on the run
I ain't waiting
For some freedom to come
I'ma be my own sun
And rise

Diego nodded and grinned. "Nice pipes."

"You too." Cinnamon leaned into him. "I'm putting together a show tomorrow. You two should come, do my song, astral-bop."

Diego and Tyrone exchanged glances, shifted their weight, and scratched stubbly chins. Weird macho display. "We got to work," Diego muttered and rubbed his bald head like it was a crystal ball—a tell for sure.

"Ain't felt like singing in years, but the news was so bad, I had to write a song. At four AM, got my bots rocking." She winked at Diego. "Call in sick."

"Captain will fire you for that." Tyrone looked panicked.

Diego nodded. "Captain George has nobody to spare, hunting that rough crew in the hills."

"Just a morning off. I'll call George, offer him a ghost-dog scout. Spook." She had a few chits with Valley-Security, for clearing desperadoes from the hills last Christmas and debugging their grid last week for free. Captain George wanted to hire her to be a tech scout. He'd settle for Spook in the woods. "Come on," she pleaded, suddenly close to tears, "a Carnival with circus-bots, you all backing up my astral-bop. Everybody rocking out." Her voice cracked. She sniffled and sneezed to cover the gush of sentiment. Dragon sang BaMbuti rainforest music from the Congo: clicks, trills, and whistles, rustling wings, branches, and cricket legs in a soft rain. A finale. Diego groaned as Dragon tucked limbs away and dropped in the trailer, a silent wad of compact trash again. T-bird offered a machinegun flourish against hard plastic before also collapsing in the trailer. "Sunrise in the amphitheatre." Cinnamon cooed. "I got roles for everybody and lots of food."

"You mean roles? In the show?" Diego sputtered. A closet thespian!

"Food? Any meat?" Tyrone tried not to look eager.

"Sure. We'll do it." Diego declared.

"I'll call Cap George." She jotted down their names. "You two can be fire spirits."

Tyrone scowled. "What's a fire spirit do?"

"Burn bright like there's no tomorrow, but never go out 'cause the spirit's eternal." Cinnamon did a few steps with Diego. Her leg felt fine, her back too. Diego broke out, dipping and twerking, old school, but good moves.

Tyrone eyed their old folks' antics and licked a crumb from his lip. "We get costumes?"

"What's a show without the right rags?" Cinnamon had a barn full of costumes.

Mami Wata swallowed the waterfall of lights, rolled ocean waves into a thin staff, and clutched this between tennis-ball breasts. In sentinel-mode, blue-black eyes smoldered, aluminum teeth glinted.

"You'll work with Mami Wata," Cinnamon said. "She likes you."

"Me and the mermaid?" Tyrone saluted her. "Fire and water. Yeah."

Cavalry in the show was a first! Maybe all she had to do was ask. Bruja nipped Cinnamon to get her pedaling. They were really late. "See you tomorrow. Five AM, to get suited up and rehearse." In a better mood, Cinnamon sailed down the other side of heartbreak hill. Four more miles to go.

#

The Ghost Mall had never opened. Big-box tenants went bankrupt, as business migrated on-line or to community boutiques. The cost of mall demolition was hefty. Nobody wanted to pay property taxes or deal with waste water runoff from so much asphalt and concrete. The non-profit Co-ops promised to renovate for public use and flood control and got deeds for a song. Ground level was community workshops—maker spaces. Cinnamon and the pedal-people had helped turn the second floor into temporary homeless shelters. Refugees kept pouring in. More people, more trouble, more challenge—a security nightmare.

Two years ago, during a raid on Co-op workshops, a rough crew fell out, like somebody yanked their plugs: every bad boy crumpled on the ground, unconscious for no apparent reason, except the leader, Game-Boy. White dude with dreads, he choked on his gangsta-rap threat and dropped his gun. Co-op doctors couldn't explain the comas and told Game-Boy to prepare for the worst. Nobody locked him away—what's a gang boss without his boys? He hung around the Mall doing workshops and security detail while his crew was laid up. Then Taiwo and the water spirits blew in, did African hoodoo, and called the crew back to themselves. Game-Boy had videos of the resurrection. He also caught the Rambo-alien eating bullets, and misty haints patrolling the Mill River—impressed every badass for miles. Gangs declared the Mall a neutral zone. Stealing Co-op tee shirts and food that was already free wasn't worth the aggravation. The Back-From-The-Dead Crew became secret Co-op members, patrolled the neutral zone, and boosted Cinnamon's horror-rep.

They threatened to do a Carnival act this year, but had chickened out last year. Cinnamon wasn't holding her breath for tomorrow.

Bruja jumped up, barking and wagging her butt at Back-From-The-Dead patrolling in the bushes near the Mall. Cinnamon waved. "Almost there."

The circle of squat concrete buildings holding back weeds, rain, and wind resembled a bull's-eye. An optimistic parking lot receded to infinity. The Co-op built a bioswale, a marshy wetland that curved around the perimeter and filtered runoff. Skeletons of cars, buses, and SUVs caught in the last flood hulked and groaned in the wind. Alarms used to blare for no reason, till they ran out of juice or something. One die-hard security system split Cinnamon's ears as she trundled by, the last delivery person to arrive.

"Radio-wave ghosts," she muttered. "Damn!"

Bruja leapt on the hood of the rusty vehicle, and the alarm fizzled out. A crowd of pedal-people, Co-op volunteers, and Mallers of all ages and sizes cheered. A few thin folks, raggedy as their last high, hung at the edges ready to bolt. Actually, everybody looked rattled, even Back-From-The-Dead stoics. They had worried about her!

"Sorry for holding things up," Cinnamon shouted, sheepish. "Recruiting for Carnival."

"You didn't answer your phone." Shaheen, pedal-people chair, smothered Cinnamon in a fragrant hug, lavender and basil. She also hugged Bruja who wouldn't tolerate that from just anybody. "They wanted to cancel the work detail and send out a posse. I said no. Not yet." A resilient, muscular woman as bouncy as her salt and pepper curls, Shaheen anchored the Ghost Mall community. "Here you both are, safe and loaded down!" She began unloading Cinnamon's trailer. Commands in her posh Mumbai English got everybody psyched for patching leaks, recycling junk cars, and rehearsing tomorrow's Carnival. Cinnamon marveled. Shaheen put her hands on her hips, smirking. "What's good, girl?"

Cinnamon chuckled. "Nothing like a practical visionary to reverse engineer tomorrow."

"Is that all you have to say? You're looking a little bejiggity."

"Bejiggity, huh?" Cinnamon laughed and took off the bullet-proof helmet. "Something's not right. No real data though. It's all vague."

"You hate that, but don't worry. Things are looking up." Shaheen was a good friend, a glass half-full girl. How Cinnamon used to be.

The breakfast buffet was set up in the old food court: hydroponic greens, tomatoes, and cucumbers piled on corncakes with last year's potatoes, onions, and beans. The work detail guzzled chai and inhaled apple surprises before heading out. Back-From-The-Dead tagged along for security patrol. Gazing at excited faces, Cinnamon wondered what had depressed her so this morning. Too much time alone talking to dogs and circus-bots. Do what you do. Act how you want to feel. That's what the elders always told her. Cinnamon hugged Bruja and patted the bots. They made sure she got where she needed to be. Pinging her solar rig, she fired the pizza parlor oven to 600° for crispy crusts. Tomato sauce bubbled on the stove.

"Breakfast always zooms by." Shaheen offered Bruja a link of Valley sausage. "Don't give me the stink eye. Dogs require a meat ration. She's part Rottweiler, right?"

Bruja turned to Cinnamon, wagging her tail. "You can eat it," she said. Bruja gobbled the treat and curled up by the circus-bots. "I like to keep her poison-proof."

"You're in a mood." Shaheen kneaded pizza dough and rehearsed a Bollywood hit for Carnival. She preferred astral-bop, but the pedal-people wanted movie hits from Shaheen's youth. Cinnamon chopped mushrooms in the groove. Shaheen tossed dough with the high notes. A twenty-four-incher landed in a cloud of flour on the counter by a scrawny desperado. Several filthy coats hung from his drooping shoulders and it was warm today. Puffy red eyes scanned the pizza parlor kitchen. He had a wispy beard, reeked of months on the road, and waved a handgun. Lucky for him, Back-From-The-Dead was out on patrol. Maybe catching Cinnamon and Shaheen alone was the plan.

He threw down a vast knapsack. "Put the tablet, mini-generator, solar rig in there."

Shaheen ducked into a utility closet. Bruja growled. He pointed the gun at her.

"She's friendly," Cinnamon lied. "Outside Bruja. Al mal tiempo, buena cara." Bruja trotted out reluctantly.

"A Spanish witch dog?" He hissed. "What you tell her?"

"Bad times, good face."

Mami Wata's third eye glowed in the back of her shell-covered head. Dragon activated sensors to high alert too. T-bird burped up darts and edged toward the backdoor but froze when the desperado jerked that direction.

"Plain cheese or veggie?" Cinnamon played calm, a good actor.

"I will shoot you." His gun-hand trembled. "Those gadgets worth dying for?"

"Asking me or yourself?" She splashed tomato sauce on dough then covered the bloody-red with soy cheese. "Black market never touches my tech."

He snorted. "Is that so?"

"Ask around—I got viruses and worms that lay waste to anything. Valley engineers say it ain't worth the devastation." Liars. Cinnamon knew two creeps who'd kidnapped a circus-bot and were trying to hack it. They'd find nothing.

"I got a client." He sniffed and salivated. Hungry.

She stirred up steam from the tomato sauce. "In Electric Paradise?"

"What do you care?"

"I can't pay ransom."

"Maybe they just want to piss you off or take you down or steal your mermaid."

"Mami Wata's a heavy load." She scattered onions and mushrooms on the cheese. "Don't I know you? Fred from University IT?"

Fred put the gun to her head. "I don't know me anymore." He stared off, probably at a bleak future. "I used to be more than this."

"Put the gun down. You're not a killer."

"Nobody's a killer till the first time."

"I'll give you some food. Tastes as good as it smells."

IT-Fred backed away. "Got to eat three times a day. What can you do about that?"

Spook, a feral husky/wolfhound mix, materialized from the shadows and chomped Fred's wrist. Gun flew one direction; Fred raced the other, shrieking and scrambling out the back. T-bird spit a dart in his neck. Spook retrieved the pistol and dropped it at Cinnamon's feet. Her heart was a machine gun rat-tat-tatting in her mouth. One desperado was nothing, could have been a gang or the cavalry on a rampage or...

"You were following us this morning." Cinnamon tossed Spook a hunk of soy cheese. He wolfed it down, licked her face, and disappeared into the shadows, trailing IT-Fred. A few of Mami Wata's blue scales flew off with him. Cinnamon lifted the pistol and turned to Dragon. "It's empty."

"Everybody's out of bullets, darling." T-bird used Granddaddy Aidan's Seminole/Irish lilt, trying to soothe her.

Cinnamon shuddered. "You knew that?"

"Spook knew too."

"I don't speak dog." Nerve pain burned up her leg. "Why didn't you tell me?"

"Don't be breaking your shin on a stool that ain't in your way." T-bird chuckled.

"Think, child," Dragon roared like Miz Redwood.

"Does Fred need to hear us talking?" Mama Wata was Aunt Iris.

"Shut up." Cinnamon swallowed tears. "You're not them."

Shaheen raced from the closet. "I'm such a coward. Sorry." She hugged Cinnamon. "Nothing rattles you. I wish I could do that."

Me too. Cinnamon's knees were watery. She couldn't get a breath. Shaheen held her up, talking 'bout how brave, how beautiful she was.

#

The open-air food court was warm in the sun and jammed. Families, drifters, teenage posses, and volunteers stuffed their faces, laughed, and carried on. More people than Cinnamon had ever seen were hunched together on benches around concrete tables—like a picnic on flying saucers.

Lunch was pizza and horror tales about Mill River water spirits, Spook, and the Rambo-alien. Surviving this morning's attack had to be celebrated with all the dark lore.

"I want a ghost-dog bodyguard!" Game-Boy jumped up on a table.

"Spook's got cyborg eyes, telephoto lenses," Shaheen said, eating the last piece of pizza. "Never a sound and he's on you."

"Witch-dog's badass too," Game-Boy said. Back-From-The-Dead chanted Bruja, Bruja. She wagged her spotted tail. Co-op volunteers and pedal-people grinned and cheered, like fans at a concert. Game-Boy hopped from table to table and waved his phone at the crowd. Teenage boys threw burnt pizza crusts at him. "You see Bruja coming, but Spook appears and disappears. I got video." Gameboy displayed blurs that could have been Soot and the water spirits.

"Don't post that. What I tell you?" Cinnamon shouted. "They're always watching." Consolidated probably sent IT-Fred after her, maybe blasted a bounty on the darknet and hired a rough crew to terrorize the hill towns. "Trying to make me stumble."

"Who?" Game-Boy sucked his teeth. "You're paranoid. Nobody cares about us."

"A disappearing dog might trip some algorithm." Cinnamon lowered her voice. Folks felt too safe inside these stories. Nobody was safe. The horror-rep could also work against them—too much attention. "We're on the radar."

Shaheen rubbed Cinnamon's shoulders. "No one believes hoodoo-voodoo mess."

"Shit looks real in my videos," Game-Boy insisted, proud. He held up a naked water spirit running on ripples of water and dissolving in sunlight.

"Please." A teenager in slash rags rolled her eyes. "We have to rehearse." Black and blue eye shadow, vampire chalk foundation on brown skin, and bruised-blood lipstick completed the look. "Hawk and I ain't making fools of ourselves in front of the Valley." The vamp and Hawk moved in on Cinnamon for a teen sulk attack, graceful, in sync. "Tomorrow's sneaking up on us and most of y'all don't know your shit."

"Right. You two are cyborg amazons." Cinnamon waved at the bots. "You and T-bird will dance everybody into the dust." T-bird flashed flame eyes and fluttered trash-bag wings. Talons tapped a polyrhythm.

Hawk smirked. "Beryl and I been dancing together since we were four. You think you can keep up, bird?"

Cinnamon grinned. "I'll teach you how to write code for this bot."

"Deal!" Hawk twisted her hips and let her feet fly. Beryl acted reluctant for two seconds, then joined in. T-bird echoed Hawk and Beryl's moves elegantly. Other sullen teens applauded. Dragon hovered above their heads, a funkadelic drum machine.

"Does Thunderbird invent steps or just mimic?" A familiar voice made Cinnamon's heart do another rat-tat-tat. The bots curled into themselves, in sentinel mode. The kids groaned, Cinnamon too. The vague trouble that had trailed her all day stood by a busted Cherokee Jeep, sporting a giant afro wig and Texas dust make-up.

"Tatyana?" Cinnamon croaked.

"It's Francine," Tatyana said. A fake nose almost fell off as she sneezed. The only thing she'd fool was a stadium back row or a dumb satellite.

"Francine," Cinnamon stammered. "It's been awhile since—" Tatyana stole Cinnamon's life work and sold out to Consolidated.

"What's up?" Tatyana scoped giggling teens. "Rehearsing the future?" Bruja poked her crotch. "You were just a puppy."

"That was another dog. Spook."

"Hard work tracking you down." Tatyana scratched a sweaty neck. Back-From-The-Dead shifted into macho mode. "I'm unarmed," she told them.

No weapons they could see.

"It was you crashing through the bushes this morning." Cinnamon's smile failed.

"You won't answer your phone." Tatyana scolded her.

Shaheen smiled a welcome, glass full and overflowing. "She never turns it on."

Cinnamon left the damn thing home in the microwave so Consolidated couldn't track her. Tatyana strolled toward her, scowling at a patrol-drone swooping overhead. Not a Valley device, corporate issue. "Still paranoid, Cinnamon, or are you a Luddite now?" She halted at arm's length.

"Luddites got a bad rep." Cinnamon sighed. "Fake history. Luddites fought the bosses, not the machines."

Tatyana stepped close. "So are you fighting the bosses?" She blew sour breath in Cinnamon's face. "Turning off and tuning out?"

"Instant access is a ball and a chain. Why waste power on that? I'm living the moment I'm in." Why had Cinnamon ever ditched Jaybird for Tatyana? Jaybird was a good man. Tatyana was a hot mess. Cinnamon tweaked the fake nose.

Tatyana groaned. "Can we talk somewhere? Private?"

#

Cinnamon had a million questions. Curiosity overwhelmed caution. She left Hawk and Beryl in charge of rehearsal and gave Tatyana a spare pedal-people bike. They headed out with Bruja and the circus-bots for the old theatre, a brick fortress on the Mill River, not far from the Valley main gate. Cinnamon kept a breathless pace for half an hour. Tatyana was hauling Mami Wata but didn't complain. Twilight turned the path to misty grays and blues. Cinnamon refused to waste the batteries in her headlights. Somebody in a bear suit stepped beside a honeysuckle bush and looked both ways.

"Getting ready for Carnival?" Cinnamon yelled. Bruja huffed and growled. "It's OK," Cinnamon reassured her.

"No. Fuck!" Tatyana hissed as they raced by. "That's a bear, an actual bear!"

Cinnamon gasped. "You're right." She torqued her spine to look back. The bear loped across the path. "A black bear. Up early." She sniggered. "We get coyotes too and other creatures." Cinnamon bit her tongue. Why tell everything she knew?

"Great," Tatyana grumbled, unnerved.

Bruja halted at the concrete bike bridge just before the theatre. Dark green ivy snaked through the red railing and into the trees. Bunches of blue-black berries had escaped the birds all winter.

"Beautiful," Tatyana mumbled. Sweat streaked her makeup. "But why are we stopping here?"

Cinnamon put a finger to her lips and pointed. A woman ambled below them, along the rocky edge of the river toward a waterfall. Shadowy limbs, bare feet, and bare breasts glistened in frothy mist. A water spirit, she was clothed only in rainbow waist beads. Braids on her scalp looked like seaweed caught in coral. She faded in and out of view. IT-Fred and a motley gang of armed desperadoes crept from the woods behind her. She turned to face them. A shot rang out. The bullet passed through her belly, ricocheted off the rocks, and grazed Fred's arm. He yelped. Not everybody was out of ammo. The water spirit shook her head and bared her teeth—a grin or snarl. Fred punched one of the desperadoes and cussed him out for wasting bullets and almost killing him. The water spirit sang like rain in the trees and beckoned the twitchy, grumbling men to follow her. One by one they disappeared into the rush of water. Still cussing and moaning, Fred was the last to run into the falls.

"What am I seeing?" Tatyana demanded as she and Cinnamon pedaled across the bridge to the theatre. "Smoke and mirrors?" She was more rattled by the water spirit, than by the bear or armed desperadoes shooting at innocent spirits. "Holograms?"

Cinnamon unlocked a stage door. "Come inside."

"What was that?" Tatyana pedaled into darkness.

Cinnamon walked her bike in. "Is somebody after your ass?"

"Yes." Dismounting, Tatyana tripped over something. "Can we get lights?"

Mami Wata powered up. A geyser of light shot from her head and illuminated a black box theatre. Plush purple seats at a steep rake looked ominous. Props from the final production littered the stage—broken animal masks, shields, a dented drum. Bruja chased a hapless mouse.

"Did you hack another girlfriend and steal her shit?" Cinnamon's voice trembled.

Tatyana shivered even though it was hot in the theatre. Stifling. "Worse."

Cinnamon wanted to smack her. "You sent me a message: AI Caught Lying?"

"Hacked your news feed. You need better security." Tatyana ditched the afro wig and fake nose and wiped streaky Texas dust onto towelettes. She was brown, but not that brown. Her aunt was a Cherokee medicine woman and Cinnamon's godmother, a force in the Indigenous Water Warriors. Tatyana grew up fighting the power, till she stomped Cinnamon and joined it. "Explain what happened at the waterfall." Tatyana fluffed her matted hair, shoulder length and streaked green. A grin creased her craggy mountain face. Majestic, beautiful, still. "Come on. Tell me."

"One of Taiwo's water spirits—fashioned from mist, dust, and light and—"

"Taiwo, the old African? Carnival magician with PTSD?" Tatyana was relieved at a reasonable explanation—always jumping to easy conclusions. "Taiwo could do fabulous tricks. Old. Hasn't died yet?"

"What do you want, Tatyana?"

Tatyana took Cinnamon's hand. "A sustainable future. Ethical machine learning, cracking deep time and plotting a course, seven generations out and more."

"You? Going for Artificial Intelligence with ancestor-wisdom?" Cinnamon fell out on the stage floor laughing. Bruja rolled and barked with her. Spook nosed in the doorway. He dropped on his haunches and cocked his head to one side at the spectacle.

"I want to make amends." Tatyana slammed the door tight and rubbed Spook's ears. "The AI said trust my intuition."

"Oh?" Cinnamon sobered up. "The lying AI?"

Tatyana paced upstage and down, twitchy as a Ghost Mall rat. "We borrowed a few of your ideas, for SevGenAlg."

"Stole. Seven Generations Algorithm was my team, my idea, from our ancestors to the future." Cinnamon was suddenly seething. "I can't believe you came here."

"Your team was so close to a solution, but YOU wouldn't collaborate."

This truth stung Cinnamon. "Collaborate with Consolidated? They want to swallow the world." She was an ace at building gadgets and writing code, but the tech world had been too toxic—not enough women or colored folks, too many predatory capitalists maximizing profits and monetizing spirits. When Tatyana did a hostile takeover of her SevGenAlg team, Cinnamon quit and came back to the elder's farm. Everybody was shocked, disappointed. Cinnamon was supposed to be a fire spirit, a cyborg amazon inventing the future. How could she quit?

"I completed your research," Tatyana whispered, "and I missed you."

"Took you ten years to realize that?"

"I brought SevGenAlg to you for safekeeping." Tatyana held up colorful data cubes. "Nobody will look here." She danced around a battered demon mask.

"You cracked the code and then stole it?" Cinnamon snorted. "Why bring it to me?"

Tatyana bumped into Mami Wata. LED snakes on her tail pulsed. "Was the mermaid a weapon? And the other bots—drones, spies, repurposed?"

"Carnival-bots for shows I promised the elders. We imagine a future we want and try to reverse engineer it."

"SevGenAlg would be perfect for your Ghost Mall!" Tatyana's voice was shrill. "A virus wrangler, a Weather Wizard problem-solver, looking seven times seven generations backwards and forwards, and I've made it transparent, able to explain itself." She held out the cubes. "Go on. Take it."

Cinnamon smacked Tatyana's hands away.

"Don't!" The data cubes flew in the air. Tatyana caught them before they hit the ground. "What's wrong with you? Loaded in your bots, SevGenAlg could get community experience, talk to folks, gather wisdom. Do the Carnivals."

"You could be a spy from Consolidated."

"No. After the last water wars... I've changed." Tatyana wrapped an arm around Cinnamon's waist and rested her chin on Cinnamon's shoulder—an old move, slick and sweet. "Let SevGenAlg help you do what you do at the Ghost Mall."

"You stole from Consolidated, from me." Cinnamon broke free. "You stomped my heart. Why trust you?"

"I had to run. Consolidated was greenwashing and perverting SevGenAlg's code."

"They've been doing that from the beginning."

"They launched a digital weapon at us, their own dream-team." Tatyana sneered. "SevGenAlg redirected that worm to a power grid on the West Coast, blamed the CIA, China, Brazil, and Nigeria, then got caught lying." Tatyana stroked the cubes. They sparkled like amethysts and diamonds in Mami Wata's lights. "Consolidated wiped the neural nets and scrambled to rehab their optics."

Cinnamon gasped. "All my code, gone too?"

"SevGenAlg had warned me, said, Steal me. Scatter me where they won't come looking." She took a choked breath. "My aunt used to talk like that."

"If you found me, Consolidated can too." Cinnamon snatched the cubes and smashed them on the floor. Splinters of colored glass cut her cheeks.

Tatyana screeched and slumped down. "How could you do that?" She fingered the broken pieces, cutting herself. "I risked my life to bring SevGenAlg here."

"Give me proof you've changed, not stolen goods." Cinnamon pulled IT-Fred's pistol on her. "Then we'll talk."

Tatyana sputtered. "Are you threatening me?"

"Leave and take your bugs with you." Cinnamon released the safety. "Nothing more to say."

"What about the thugs outside?"

"Your thugs, aren't they?" Cinnamon pressed the gun to Tatyana's temple. "Take the bike. Leave the trailer."

"OK, OK." Tatyana unhooked her ride and pulled a hood over her face. "I can see why you wouldn't love me again right away." After this lame sop, she pedaled out the door and disappeared into the hills. Soot and a couple blue scales from Mami Wata trailed her. Green scales swept the stage for bugs, melting anything from Tatyana. Cinnamon's heart ached—maybe not love, but close to it.

"Love will come back in style." Mami Wata used Taiwo's voice. The old African was deep in the circus-bots' neural nets too. "We let Tatyana find us.

Nobody else."

"Why?" Cinnamon prodded the shattered data cubes with her toe before a green scale zapped them.

"In a pinch even the devil eats flies." Dragon did Grandma Redwood's drawl and dodged a reasonable question. "You quit Consolidated after finishing the code too."

Cinnamon shrugged. "So?"

"So, you didn't tell Tatyana that SevGenAlg has been with you all along." Dragon hovered in her face. "Ain't that like lying?"

"Well..." Cinnamon picked up the demon mask, perfect for her tomorrow—a forest for hair, lightning bolts on the cheeks, fibre optic eyes like burning coals. "You lie too."

"Promising the moon." T-bird hooted at her, Granddaddy Aidan. "And the stars!"

"Yeah," Cinnamon groaned. "I thought you'd be a magic wand, make everything easy."

"Easy is overrated," Mami Wata murmured, Aunt Iris now. "So is convenience."

"OK, OK, OK." Cinnamon groaned. "Just because it's impossible—"

"Doesn't mean you get to give up!" The bots did the elders' words in three-part harmony—an old move from when Cinnamon was six. Bruja wagged her tail and hooted. They were ganging up on Cinnamon.

"I'm not giving up, all right?" She activated screens at the stage manager's station—feeds from Mami Wata's scales and Spook's eyes. Cyborg dog was an excellent tracker. Cameras captured Tatyana meeting IT-Fred and the desperadoes by the Mill River. They were soaked and looked dazed, jumping at every twist of mist. The filth and blood had been washed away. Cinnamon zoomed in on the men's vulnerable faces. They glanced from the falls to Tatyana, uncertain. After a water-sprit encounter, desperadoes were always born-again, never quite who they were before. Look at Back-From-The-Dead-Crew. Blessed be Taiwo! "We'll see what Tatyana and her crew do. Y'all know girlfriend got another copy of SevGenAlg somewhere, right?"

"Gotta love her spirit." T-bird declared.

"Consolidated kept a copy too, don't you know!" Dragon played a jazz code. "'Stead of getting bejiggity, let's get this show on the road!"

Lights flickered overhead, a kaleidoscope of colors. Bots trundled in from the shop with costumes and solar panels for tomorrow's celebration.

#

The air in the amphitheatre was heavy with a spring scent. The stars faded, covered over by a purple canopy. A geyser of sparklers from Mami Wata lit up the last of the night. Sunrise over the hills was always a grand spectacle. Bruja herded Tyrone and Diego across the grass over to Shaheen at the feast table. Orange and yellow flame robes snapped in the wind. Tyrone stopped at Mami Wata as she unfurled her sparkling ocean waves. He boogied around the fibre optic ripples, fire in the water. Hawk and Beryl, brandishing light spears, danced the cyborg amazons through Valley elite dressed in hiking gear. Game-Boy and Back-From-The-Dead came as themselves doing Karaoke-rap. Captain George from Valley-Security tramped across the grass in a winged cape and whispered new horror tales on Cinnamon to anyone who'd listen. At Carnival, everyone was performer and spectator.

The sun sprayed gold across the sky. Thunderbird and Dragon lifted off. Spook barked up a tall oak tree, and the old African stepped out on a limb wearing robes and top hat that were red on one side and black on the other. A long red and black feather nestled in cowry shells at the hat's crown. Eshu, not Rambo was riding Taiwo—Cinnamon cheered the Yoruban trickster of the crossroads. Taiwo jumped down from the oak near a bush that had burst into bloom overnight: fragrant star magnolias as big as your hand. Water spirits ghosted in naked forsythia branches. They sang a river rumble, tumbling in and out of harmonies. Rainbow waist beads scattered the sunlight and then the spirits dissolved with the mist. The crowd applauded Carnival magic.

Cinnamon hugged Taiwo to her heart. "Here we are at the end of the world, thinking up what the next world will be," she whispered.

"Thank you," Taiwo said, "for calling me down."

"Good News." Cinnamon stood at her ancestor's memorial stones offering a full production. "Co-op volunteers will tap more maple trees after the show. Right now, we got a song." Everybody joined in:

Dark days
Just a flash
Love be on the run
I ain't waiting
For some freedom to come
I'ma be my own sun
And rise
I'ma be my own rain
And drink
I'ma be my own poem
And think

Dark days
We know that
Truth under the gun
I ain't waiting
For justice to be done
I'ma be my own light
And shine
I'ma win my own fight
Surprise
I'ma be my own sun
And rise
I say
Dark Days
We got that
I'ma be my own sun
And rise

WATER BEING

PAN MORIGAN

1

There are limits to science and silence and I'm convinced we've reached both. Yesterday, the Bureau of Scientific Purity dragged me in for questioning. What a farce! None of my interrogators, those mighty merchants of silence, wanted to say dangerous things. We talked streams of nothingness, our words dead water circling a drain. Afterwards, without warning, I was extracted from my world-class research lab and imprisoned in a dingy, half-lit, secure wing. "For your protection," Smith said. Traitor.

Apparently, the B.S.P. had another captive here as well, one who simply agreed to experience the experience. How else to keep a Water Being in custody? In whispered tales, they appeared and disappeared at will. No Water Being had ever been sighted on Corporate Island before. Too smart, I suppose, to relish sterile, bio-tree adorned, suburban sprawl parked on an armed barge in the middle of the Atlantic. I was informed that our strange guest would be brought to me for study. We'd best hope the elusive creature continued to agree, and that the B.S.P. returned me to my maudit lab!

These days, my country, my profession, even my thoughts have been colonized by delusionists. Two years ago, when Niviliat disappeared, the B.S.P. forced everyone to take an oath. Nobody would leak news of the vanished isle. We must forget the tiny country and its people, famous for orchestras of conch trumpets and gourd mandolins. But who could forget that Zeus, with three-hundred-mile-an-hour winds, had ground Niviliat into the sea forever? Search parties were not sent out. Funding was not allocated. Maps were scrubbed. Any mourning or protest, however submerged, was smashed with swift finality.

We swallowed tears and shoved panic into a dungeon of forbidden thoughts. Two months later, the Water Beings emerged. The Bureau of Scientific Purity announced that speaking of them would also be forbidden, even if one appeared in our house! We had to look away, stay silent. Otherwise, Code Indigo—soldiers smashing the doors down, detaining the talkative.

The world changed so fast—our thoughts, emotions, and ideas went obsolete instantly. Worldwide, Water Beings strolled up out of seas, lakes, rivers, and swamps or dropped from sewage pipes and kitchen faucets. They emerged from puddles, sending pedestrians into cardiac arrest. How could a six-foot creature slide out of a half-inch of water? They burst from toilets at inopportune moments, causing incurable SASS, Sudden Alien Shock Syndrome. Folks took to using outhouses from an excess of caution, but was that a real solution? Most of the population was afflicted with a pathological fear of puddles... but kept quiet.

This keep-mum mess became the answer to all things. Silence, that beleaguered word, was weighted down with odious tasks and ominous definitions. Desperate, I became a collector of words, a witness to the dimming of their natural glow. I wept as words were turned from jewels to junk. I believed that each time a word died a spirit also died. My heart rebelled against our lying, malevolent silence. Yet, I kept my mouth shut like everybody else. Hypocrite!

Meanwhile, people without regard for wonders shot Water People, sliced them up, bombed them. They changed shape and carried on! Citizens poured concrete down wells, bricked up lakes, sucked wetlands dry, and buried rivers in rubble. The Water Beings just turned up elsewhere and went about their business. Nobody understood what their business was.

2

Dawn breaks hard. I've been awake all night. Smith storms into my new, worse office without warning. He brings no greeting, no bad coffee, zero jokes. "You really ticked them off at yesterday's interrogation," he snaps. "Said not one damn thing of substance!"

"They order us silent, then complain we don't talk. You see how management threw me out of my own lab, right? Mon Dieu, I was in the middle of a hundred important projects."

"There's no they, just us, and I'm only here to warn you." He lights a roll-your-own, knowing I detest smoke in quarters. This place is a holding tank though, so, c'est la mort. Ha, ha.

"You'll die hacking." I gnaw an end of stale bread. "Poof! Just as life starts to make sense."

"Shut up and listen. The director is saying Water Beings are your fault!"

"Oh, please!"

He squints through smoke, not laughing with me. "They'll use torture if you don't come up with a cure for your rogue research."

I snort. "Have the good souls at B.S.P.'s corporate wing forgotten that they funded said research? Snatched plenty patents off it too. So, who's the rogue? Anyway, using pain as a first-contact tongue, we'll learn exactly nothing about Water Beings."

"I'm not talking about learning or even about Water Beings, dammit." Smith jams his spent cig into my soup bowl. "They'll use waterboarding or worse on you, if you don't find a way to halt this invasion."

"You are joking, right?"

"Don't play stupid."

"Stupid because I don't believe colleagues torture one another?"

Smith rifles through the folders on my desk. I barely register the intrusion, intent on defending reason itself.

"After a decade inventing bacterial meds for dead oceans, hoping to resurrect a cleaner rain, something may have gone off. I admit that, however..."

"Oh, so you do admit to poisoning the primordial stew." Smith fingers my calendar, cracks my personal diary.

"Sacré bleu!" I snatch the diary from his hands and stuff it in a drawer. "There's zero chance my experiments have anything to do with the Water People! How idiotic."

He smirks. "I'm just the messenger."

"Since when?"

"Since I was promoted, and you weren't."

"Congrats, Smith. You get to do their dirty work now. Let the good times roll!"

"Oh, be serious for once. Mass panic spreads worldwide. We apes are losing our minds over those lizards."

"They're not lizards." I hated it when he called them lizards.

"All you need to know is, the Bureau of Scientific Purity let slip that terror may make you think faster. So, get to thinking."

"As if I alone can explain the overnight appearance of a new species!" I yell. "As if I'm the maker of the Water Beings and can unmake them? Their presence here is a wonder."

Smith paces the tiny distance between desk and wall. He's sweating. "Your wonder is breeding mayhem."

"We can't handle miracles anymore? Look, Smith, tell me exactly what the Bureau of Scientific Lunacy expects me to accomplish sans staff? They've fired my assistants, bolted my lab, and moved me to this dump. I'm defunded. Nights, post-curfew, while I try to sleep, somebody creeps into this closet cum office and rifles through my research notes. These very pages are smeared and greasy, as if some flatfoot, maybe you, perused my equations while slurping tomato soup." I rattle a fistful of pages in his face. "Something fishy is going on here."

"No kidding," Smith snaps. "Be afraid. Find a solution, fast. Think of your family."

I get in his face, furious. "Is that a threat?"

"I'm speaking as a friend." He sucks hard on another ashy butt while messing with his phone. "Guard!"

Popovski unlocks the door, holds it for Smith, and bolts me back in.

I fall into a chair, rattled. Smith and I were colleagues once, sort of friends, even. What have I lost here? Maybe something. Camaraderie and mutual respect have become rare commodities. Silence is always brewing. And we do think of everything as commodities... I signed a contract when I was hired. Buried in reams of small print, if I recall, incarceration was mentioned. I ignored the ominous detail, rushing to join the anointed. Like Smith, I've got nothing left to sell.

I pound the door.

Popovski enters looking weary, wary. "Problem, Ma'am?"

"They've confiscated my phone. Can I use yours?"

"I'm not supposed to. They're solely for Code Indigo emergencies."

"I have to call home, talk to my kid. I'll make it worth your while." A lie.

"Just this one time, if you're saying I have to."

"I am."

I call home six times and reach no soul. My heart falls to my feet and I walk on it. Phones off-island are archaic. You try a hundred times to reach someone, praying for luck. Desperate, I ring Smith. I'll apologize, grovel. Maybe I can trade privileges for the commodity our so-called friendship has become.

He doesn't answer, just his stupid bot. "Bonjour, Hola, Jambo, Merhaba..." Frustrated, I yell, "I need my phone back, you fascist! Also, your story doesn't add up! Why am I still locked in? What do the guys up in the big office really want?" The bot answers. "The means to eradicate said threat from mind and world. No memory, news report, gossip, or dream shall be left in the wake of the Water Being-disaster or its remedy. Full stop. However, I am only a bot. Nobody said these words. Ciao. Goodbye. Thank you. Dhanyavaad. Gracias. Xié Xié. Disconnecting now, disconnecting..."

"Ah, an extinction mission." I laugh, near tears. Sentient tech, surveillance, officially mandated delusions... Such paltry responses to life's great mysteries. Gingerly, I hand the hectoring phone back to Popovski.

Taking it, the guard gazes at me a moment too long. Black eyes shimmer with green dampness. Bright, hot light glances across ebony cheekbones. I must be on the verge of a migraine. Popovski locks the door behind him. The bolts shrill thrice, sounding final.

3

Time laughs. The clock spins backwards. Days dissolve. Sunsets, barely visible out a porthole in the drab green wall, linger hours-long, filling me with delirious longing and screeching impatience. Insomnia nights die on vines of feverish self-recrimination and desiccated half-dreams. I subsist on cold tomato soup spooned from dented cans I find in a utility closet.

Why does the B.S.P. leave me here, awaiting the sight of a Water Being? My guess is they're bluffing, lying about having trapped one. I'm lying to myself too, about what I'm capable of. No redemption in denial. Of course, we don't know all that the Water People are capable of, either. We've heard no reports of violence from them, just from our own. Exhausted, I prepare for an encounter that may never occur. The more time passes, the less sane I feel. Are these final days? Can it be we're a mere droplet in the sea of life? Then again, aren't entire universes born in a drop of rain or sip of dew?

My guards refuse to lend me the emergency phone again, but agree to deliver an urgent summons to Smith. He shows up days later, looking tense, exhausted, grey. The man needs sun, a laugh. Even his freckles have faded. "What now," he sighs. "I told you, find the damn cure. Nothing more to say."

"Oui, your multi-kulti bot informed me of everything. Listen, I must speak with my family before the Water Being arrives. After all, I may not survive that encounter with strangeness. C'mon Smith, be the friend you say you are."

"I have news." His grey eyes are raw, bloodshot. "The Water Being vanished from a vault with walls a mile thick!"

"I knew it."

"Top brass went nuts, threatened to have me arrested. I prayed like mad, and the lizard reappeared."

"Huh?"

"I prayed."

"C'mon, Smith. we both know there's no controlling the circus. You're a scientist, no?"

We gaze at one another a moment and something authentic transpires. I was going to say, something human transpires. But lately I've lost trust in the supposed superiority of the human hegemony.

Smith looks downright hangdog. "Fuck. You're right."

I feel bad for him, a bit. Who doesn't long for magic or easy answers?

"The point is, we're a go." He puts an arm around me. "I'll be with you every step of the way! We'll get to the bottom of this disaster."

"Sure, Smith. Like old times, in the lab together." We slide back to lies so easily. "So, when do I meet the Water Being?"

"Soon."

"Merde! You have no clue. You're still praying. How about my calls, then? You confiscated my phone. Nobody has collected my letters home in weeks. Look at this stack. Why would you do this, Smith? Gran' Maman works too hard, and she's getting on. My girl, Red, has nightmares. You know this!"

Smith looks away. "No communications to or from detention. No phones. No mail delivered Off-Island. Security first." The man quotes orders like an automaton—as if our connection of two seconds ago was fairytale stuff.

"Furthermore," he continues grimly, "if you use Popovski's emergency communications device again, he'll be terminated immediately. That goes for his shift-partner, too, what's-her-name."

"Lucia. And you'll burn in hell for this, Smith."

"It isn't me."

"Yeah, right. It's never anybody. Le diable made you do it. Now that we've got that cleared up, do I get anything to eat besides tomato soup?"

"No need to be bitchy."

"Because I ask for food, I'm bitchy? And how about a shower?"

"No water allowed at this level. Just prepare yourself, dammit!"

He slaps the wall exceedingly hard on the way out. He'll have a bruise. Am I supposed to be grateful he hasn't slapped me?

"How do I prepare myself? And when did you go all floating island?" I shout at the door. "Corporate lapdog! Tool!" I get locked up, and Smith basks in the glory of his promotion to head asshole. Amazing what a few extra bucks will do to a person. And he's an Off-Islander, just like me—grew up in scabby bare feet and hand-me-downs. I can still hear his fancy patent leather shoes clicking down the corridor. "Hurry on, traitor!" I cry. "Go join the silence!"

4

My room is drab but luminous. As of yesterday, my electricity is cut, and my tiny window is locked shut. but I'm allowed candles for lighting, like ancient times. Apparently, I'm imprisoned in a labyrinth of capricious illogic. My overlords demand the moon but offer no means to work or live, per usual. They work all sides of every story, and I've played along for the paycheck. I feel no shock at my insights, only dull. Is this how the spirit dies? I pace the smoky gloom, worrying over family, my daughter. Hours later, candles sputtering, I fall on the narrow cot, wrapping a quilt around me. Lucia collected it from my former quarters and slipped it to me, a bold kindness.

A lifetime ago, Gran' Maman sewed the quilt from fabric scraps she'd collected, years-long. It was a name-day gift. Off-Island, home in the swamps, we get a new name for each decade we survive. Very, very few are the six or seven-name elders. My Gran' Maman is one. I miss her so.

Tearfully, I embrace the threadbare keepsake, a scent of home—my fast-fading histoire. "Nice digs," I shout at nobody. "Nice way to treat your top scientist! Your Nobel laureate! Am I surprised? Non, sacré bleu, I'm not." But maybe I am, to be perfectly honest.

Gran' Maman appears before me as I drift off. Her white braid gleams. She wears a necklace of hand-carved beads. "Don't wait on others to be what you must be or speak your peace. Does earth wait for say-so to bear its fruit? Does a river ask, can I run to the sea?" She gave me my first science lessons, declaring, "just you listen at the world, ma petite fille." The memory sooths me. I sleep hard but am wakened by electronic locks squealing.

Popovski and Lucia rush in, sweaty, jittery.

"Leave the quilt," Popovski mumbles, removing it from my shoulders with a gentle touch and laying it on the cot. "Today we escort you to another place."

"We wish you very much luck." Lucia is from the swamps like me. Her brown skin is ashy. Her lower lip trembles. "And we're sorry."

Emotions laid bare give me strength. I appreciate them, like fugitive words offered on the sly. "Ça va, Lucia?" I ask. "You alright?"

"Can't talk much with you." She looks away. "Orders."

"Is this my big moment? To meet the...you know."

She blindfolds me, whispers. "Le cocodril has ways!"

"Water finds hidden valleys." Popovski murmured his own non-sequitur, holding the door wide for us. Hall lights flicker. I've forgotten if it is day or night.

Lucia handcuffs me, leads me out. "Green birds migrate..."

Is this poetry-talk a code, sign of an underground resistance? Or is it more hallucinatory nonsense? Hard to know these days, but I can hope. "I'm ready," I say. "Especially for the green birds."

The two guards urge me down long, cold, ill-lit hallways, round and around through endless wings. The research complex has hidden twists and turns. Many layers to this life that I've ignored. Or are we wandering in circles?

"Much longer, Popovski?" I'm thirsty, hungry.

"Don't ask things," he murmurs. "These halls see, hear. I'm sorry also."

Finally, my blindfold is removed, and I'm pushed into a chill, barren room with harsh lighting. "Another holding tank?"

"They try to capture water," Popovski hisses, locking the door.

Legs giving out, faint with hunger, I topple into an orange, plastic chair. Why orange? I'm duly wracked by the question and spend a good hour meditating on it. Without warning or ceremony, Lucia and Popovski burst back in, shove a Water Being into the cell, and retreat in stumbling panic. I stagger backwards, stupefied, overjoyed.

Swathed in laser chains, the creature squats down upon the floor, legs arranged in double-jointed elegance. Devoid of pupils or lids, green eyes wander past me to a tiny, dark porthole set high in the wall. The eyes emit light, like floodlights. Simian ears change directions, tracking soundwaves I can't detect—or so I infer.

I stare, my chest throbbing. The Water Being is magnificent beyond measure. Why are we all so afraid? Long moments pass. Neither of us moves. Footsteps echo in the halls.

"Sign here." I jerk at the sound of Lucia's voice. She's shoved paperwork and a leaky fountain pen through a meal-slot in the door. I give a cynical glance at five pages of self-righteous, Corporate disclaimers, delivered in the most archaic fashion, as if this place were not wired to the inch. Naturally, I must agree in handwriting that I'll never speak of my experience here, and furthermore, that my employer is devoid of responsibility if I die today. They won't pay for my burial. Any costs will come from my final check.

In this awesome moment, my heart rebels. I shout, "Water People, Water People everywhere. Talk about them. Let them come. I, Doris Belakwa, refuse silence!"

The alien does not respond to my fit but continues gazing at the porthole, despite there being no view that I can see.

"You're not supposed to admit Water Beings exist," Popovski growls through the meal slot, mauve lips drawn tight. He speaks for other ears.

"Ha! Even now, while observing one," I laugh. "I declare that Niviliat drowned in the storms of our idiocy, and Water People are glorious." It feels good to speak unfettered truth.

"You mustn't call them people."

Lucia's mouth joins Popovski's at the narrow opening. "Calme-toi. Please. I was ordered to use a syringe if you act up."

"But le cocodril has ways." I laugh. "No?"

"Ah, she'll get us in a mess," Popovski sighs.

"Les experts don't much care about us water-bearers." Lucia sighed. "Always, they pinch the tail and suck the head."

I pull myself together, shamed. "Sorry." All we do is apologize, nowadays. For our helplessness, our cowardice, our acquiescence, our cruelty. What does it matter to me if I sign or don't sign? I glance at the Water Being who remains pacific.

Signing the disclaimer with a jaunty flourish, I add a sun, moon, tree, and flower for good measure—all the things I never see. My fingers are stained with indigo ink. Emergency!

"Hurry!" Popovski pounds the door. He and Lucia will return to Off-Island starvation if they get fired. Me too. Dutifully, I shove the papers back through the slot, worrying over Red and Gran' Maman. What are they eating these days, with me in detention? "All signed and sealed," I say. "Good luck."

The two guards make a hasty retreat, armaments clanking as they go. They've not had luck. Still, I hope that "green birds" really are "migrating."

"Your kind are a story we tell beneath the waves, not the other way around." The Water Being speaks up, wielding perfect Swampland Français. Startled, I automatically translate for whoever is spying on us. I'm an automaton too, I suppose. It'll be the top dogs listening in, the nameless, impervious, powerful jerks, pretending they're good and very clever. Seated somewhere cozy with wine and fine cheeses, fortified by bottomless bank accounts, surrounded by gleaming weapons of mass destruction, they'll toy with our lives. No harm in a little clarity, eh?

The Water Person's voice has a warbling resonance, soft, yet penetrating. "You are our invention, our mistake, our miscalculation. We must find a cure. If not, the tale will be retold, remade."

I feel a vibration within, a mind-quake coming on.

The Being's bright eyes dim, perhaps for my comfort? "Could be your kind will be written dark until we find a solution. You may be returned to substance afterwards, depending how dreams unfold within the ellipsis…"

We gaze at one another.

I hear water trickling somewhere, deep in the walls, or perhaps inside me. Anxious, I babble. "We're an invention of yours, you say. And we will be written dark." I latch onto that last line, not the mysterious, ellipsis one. "Do you mean my kind as in female humans? Black scientists? Us being written dark wouldn't be news. Maybe you mean rebellious throwback scholars, raised barefoot Off-Island? Or state-U trained, Nobel-prize-awarded, ocean-biologist, single mothers with a taste for bourbon lemonade, wild broccoli, and yam fries?" Finally, an encounter with a Water Being, and I pop off!

The alien remains quiet, still. The lamps of its eyes have shifted to silver-black, a smoky luminosity that takes my breath away. Its chest is translucent as early witnesses described. Behind a delicate, damp membrane, the rose-colored, jellyfish heart pulses in iridescent fluid. Actually, we haven't proven the thing is a heart. After all, we've never successfully trapped or examined a member of the species. I'm pretty sure we haven't got one trapped now either. Can't say the same for myself.

Without warning, the Water Being transforms, becomes me: from the insomnia bruises around my brown eyes to neglected, ash-grey locks jammed into a rusted barrette, and even the gap between my front teeth. It's got my jeans, the beat-up sandals on scarred feet, my torn, unkempt toenails.

Observing self, I tremble all over.

The Water Being trembles all over.

"You know my emotions, my thoughts?" I feel ill. "Clearly, you know my cells, bones…"

"Oui, Doris Belakwa. I feel you." the creature says. "I am you."

I'm reminded of octopi, able to melt into any environment. I never melted. Never quite belonging here nor there. Why do I think of this now? "Please don't do that!" I cry, despite being fascinated by the sight of my own double. I can't calm down, even with deep, heaving breaths. This must be the most powerful experience of my life, similar to that vivid moment when Red and I locked eyes, sensing the undertow of destiny. I rescued the child from the Foundling Home for Weather Flotsam. Now I've abandoned her. That's what she'll think.

The Being returns to its first face. Silver-blue skin glints with rainbow bioluminescence. Of course, this look may not be its for-real either. I chuckle at my creaky thinking, teeth chattering. Isn't life change, water-natured? For sure, matter and emotion are not strangers...

I'm filled with a sacred feeling.

"Do you mean all earthlings must be eradicated?" Ruining the mood, I resume the interview my superiors expect. "Isn't that what you're saying? For the record, you're here to wipe us out, destroy us all."

"Such hostile formulations." The thing responds in perfect, standard Earthish. "Simply, you land ones must be changed. You can't change yourselves. Like petrified wood, you've lost the moisture of your being. You'll relearn the waters. Or your youth must. We depend on them. We've begun the process."

"Process?"

"We teach them. They learn schooling. Like sardines, as an example."

"Sardines?"

"As an example, only. Sardines. We've already begun—with your young."

"Our what!"

"Your offspring." The creature regards me tenderly. Surely, the expression can't be trusted any more than the face.

I jerk away from the lamp-like eyes, panicking. Thoughts flood, yanking earth from under me. *You believe you're the observer, the one to say what's real and true, believable. You're sure you make the world, tell the tales. Fool! And yet, I've known what it is to be written into the story or out, to be slandered, scapegoated, and forced, raging, into some stranger's alternative factoid. Thought I'd escaped such a fate the day I set foot on Corporate Island, three degrees in hand.* "Leave my kid alone!" I screech. "Monster!"

The Water Being flushes gold, emitting a fresh scent of pine needles. Like flickering stars, it changes face: once human, twice reptilian, presenting last with rabbit ears. "Worry not!" Giggling, it tosses a necklace of hand-carved beads into the air and disappears.

"No!" I leap to my feet, trembling. The orange plastic chair tips over, hapless despite its virulent hue. I gape at state-of-the-art laser chains scattered across the floor, flashing Code Indigo. An alarm shrieks. I contemplate the high window, dim and dusty as a closed mind. The Water Being doesn't reappear. Instead, a dozen soldiers rush in, jostling, cursing, and shouting. I know none of them, and they ignore my pleas for calm. I hope Lucia and Popovski are safe, or better yet, riding le cocodril down some river to freedom.

I'm dragged through endless hallways that all look the same, down uneven steps plunging narrowly into frigid darkness. We descend so many flights, my legs nearly give out. I'm shoved into an airless dungeon. The soldiers hurry off, panting, cursing in multiple tongues. I'm alone. Heavy stone walls drip moisture. Moss smears the cold, worn floor. Rats rustle in shadowed corners. Rusted bars mock my sense of reality. Are they meant to keep me in myself or force me out of myself? Is the idea of self an irrelevance in such circumstances? Anyway, it is zero surprise to learn we've got medieval dungeons at corporate. But I don't understand. We're only a floating island, a ship of fools. How many lower levels have been hidden from us here? How deeply can we descend?

Somewhere a door clangs shut. Silence looms. Yet a scent of moving water soothes me. Kneeling, I squint through a rusted keyhole. Quaint. Real keyholes, I muse. A green eye with neither pupil nor lid appears in the narrow opening. I gasp at the brilliant stream of light illuminating my solitude.

"We've stirred many imaginings, sipped timeless thought-streams." The Water Being whispers inside my head, a gentle drip, drip, drip. "We've sung, merged, swum new distances, through wet, young narratives. We will collaborate with you at world-spinning for a season, as an experiment, though we're wary of your malevolent makings. We'll be rivers, rolling backwards, forwards, up, down, all at once. Space-time, the waters of the sky will be our lab. Now... listen with your blood. Oui, just so. Breathe my voice-substance deep into your belly-fish. Ah, oui, ma chérie, mon petit poisson. No fear. I bring you a gift, complex and fragrant, full of possibility—a beautiful darkness. You Dirt Ones constantly slander the word, using it as a hammer.

Stop that now."

I collect darkness, a word newly reborn, and store it in my heart.

The word, silence, I release through the rusted bars. It becomes a green-feathered bird with quick wings and a raucous song.

Bare bulbs set into dungeon walls pop all at once, expelling last lightning. I'm plunged into a freshly forged night, no longer able to feel the stone floor. The air smells of salt and seagrass. I hear my child, Red, calling from fathoms deep.

"Where are you, Maman! I've found a sacred lake behind barbed wire!"

My heart leaps and breaks all at once.

The Water Being murmurs on and on in rumbling tones, reminding me of a trillion captive feet shuffling through primordial mud. The water in me bubbles, swirls. My hands go numb, become mist, and disappear.

"Oh, holy fuck!" These last words are garbled, as if I choked on thousand-year flood-tides and raucous, unfettered rains,

rising fast

rising high.

LOVE HANGOVER

SHEREE RENÉE THOMAS

That night disco records weren't the only things that burned. I lost someone irreplaceable, a creature that lived off blood and music, the lifeforce of a people, but a creature that was also my friend.

Delilah brings it, and I mean she brings it one hundred percent! Delilah Divine! Sang, girl, sang!

Delilah teased death the way she teased her fans. Her voice, an odd constellation of sound.

She had tasted death and knew she would always live, in one form or the next, like the singer resurrected in the record's groove. Every night was a different club, one after the other. Sixteen on a hi-hat, four on the floor, two and four on the backbeat, that was the sound that announced her arrival and all of Disco. Like Delilah Divine's voice, the music was sweet water finding its own way home. It was going to get through, just a matter of time. The challenge was finding a way to listen and not get drenched. With Delilah you drowned.

The first night I met Delilah, she danced on a speaker box. Bianca Jagger rode by on a white horse, her black locks shining ebony waves, but all eyes returned to Delilah. To say she was a vision is to insult the very nature of sight. Beauty is internal and eternal, and Lilah's beauty came through in her songs. Motown, funk, soft Philly soul and salsa. It wasn't what she said. Not the lyrics nor the music with its lush orchestral arrangements, her soaring vocals with reverb. It was the story that was beneath her words and music, the message she carried within.

The message was about freedom. That's what the sound was and the movement. We danced to be free. Candi Staton sang from her heart and that's why we loved her songs, too. I had no idea how true her lyrics would be.

Self-preservation is what's going on today. Delilah started off singing jazz, top 40 hits. When deejays arrived in clubs carrying crates between sets, she and the other vocalists sang for their own survival. And sing she did. I loved the way I moved when her music was on, the way we dove and split from our old selves into something sensual and new. The way the dance floor took us in, wet and holy in its mouth. We were all glitter and steam, blurred blazing bodies spinning in the music's light. If I turned away from the hypnotic rhythm and the beats, from Delilah's seductive song and dance, I could have saved myself and a lot of dead people a whole lot of trouble. Heartache was Delilah's last name. Nothing else was fitting.

Young hearts just run free. Delilah only had time for the young and none of us, not a single soul could run away or leave her embrace. She was like Diana's song. *If there's a cure for this, I don't want it, I don't want it.* I thought about Delilah all the time and she gave me and all her fans the sweetest hangover. When Delilah got into your bloodstream, she controlled lives, heartbeats. I practically lived in the clubs to just to see her.

The club's appeal was that the ultimate rocker lifestyle was available to anyone who could manage to get in. When I first met Delilah, it seemed like she was always in the club, as if she emerged from beneath the parquet floors fully formed. Dressed in slinky, silk dresses that wrapped her curves in silver-tinged moonlight, Delilah was a vision. You could not turn away from her and believe me, many tried, only to find themselves in her thrall.

Music was her spell. Deejays played with minds. Stories told with songs seeped into your soul. Walk through a door in the forest. No confidence at all, but in music spirits take shape. I became who I wanted to be, what I needed. Dancing with Delilah Divine was like that.

Five a.m. when the club was closed, most others would stumble their way home or fall into the faded booths of a diner. Delilah wouldn't want rest or breakfast. She wanted to be near water. Delilah would sit next to the ferns and bulrushes. She said unlike the clubs, the green life formed a wall of kindness. She would bend her ear to the waves that lapped up against the shore, whispering to voices I could not hear. I tried to reach her with a joke, some laughter, or a bit of gossip, anything that might hold her attention, pull her from the faces, the arms I could not see. But she was lost in the waters, in search of depths where she could drown her weight of years. What she sought to drown was not a name but her history. Sometimes she spoke as if she lived beyond her twenty odd years.

Lilah lived for the rust of songs, for the scars and cutting parts of choruses, the hooks that dug in your soul and made you cry from recognition of depths. She wanted to laugh with the joy of it, and dance and dance until she could reach the gray vaults of sea. She said her sisters waited for her on the other side, but she could not swim her way back to them. Said she was already drowned. Each night at the club I watched her struggle to breathe. They played her songs before I knew they were hers. String sections and synthesizers, syncopated baselines and horns, and that voice, that incredible voice. She danced as if the music was a stranger. As if the songs were notes that came out of another's throat.

"Where did you learn to sing like that?" I asked. She looked at me with dead fisheyes that should have run me away, but I was already hers before the first time we even touched or danced.

"From the throats of a thousand, thousand men and women. But the children," she said, closing her eyes as if the memory pained her, "their voices are too sweet. I cannot bare the taste of their songs."

I thought she was high. I'd seen her with blow and biscuits, poppers and whippets—whatever made the music and lights, the dance and the tempo last longer.

"What do songs taste like, Lilah?"

"Like ambergris and champagne."

She spun around, eyes staring straight up. "They've come back." She pointed. The disco ball was the largest in the studio. It reflected the jewel tone beams of the strobe lights. "We used to party with these in the 20s, back in Berlin."

"Berlin? Lilah, you are only twenty, if that. How would you know how flappers partied then?"

She stopped spinning with a shrug. "Saw it in a movie?" she asked. "Mirror balls. *Die Sinfonie der Großstadt, Die Sinfonie der Großstadt!*" she shouted, then repeated her spinning top dance. Her nipples brushed the sheer fabric of her teal, jewel-toned dress. I forced my eyes from staring. Instead I watched her sleeves flutter and float, gossamer moth wings. Lilah favored dresses that made her look as if at any moment she could fly away. She was always so restless, like a hummingbird, a kind of lightning flowed through her, even without the drugs. She was never fully present. Her eyes, her mind, the random stories—her memories, she claimed—would burst from her at any moment. And the voices no one heard but her. I thought she was schizophrenic and mentioned it to a doctor friend, a shrink who frequented the clubs. "No," he said, after chatting with her, drink in hand. "Frankie, that one's very clear."

Lilah was like standing on a hill with the weeds and the wildflowers. The wind blowing through me. If I wasn't so determined to pretend that I didn't imagine her breasts in my mouth, the soft curve of her belly beneath the silk skin, I would have seen the tell-tale signs of the monster she really was, the creature she hid.

#

The garage on 84 King Street became our paradise. The club was like church. More than gospel piano riffs threaded through twenty-two-minute extended versions of songs. There we had chosen family. Delilah was mine. I didn't know who I was until I came here. Then I found out I was everybody. Everybody was me. No judgments, everyone enjoying themselves. Love, peace, unity, unforgettable happiness, and then there was blood.

Though I wanted her more than my own disappointing life at the time, Delilah never wanted me. She said there wasn't enough music in my blood to sustain her, not enough firelight and smoke.

"You've made up your mind to die young, Frankie," she said one night, after we left the dance floor, having spent hours studying the power of sweat. She would dance with other bodies, take one or two back into the VIP rooms, but she always found her way back to me. When she returned she was uncomfortably clear, her edges more precise. Before she disappeared with her various lovers, she was like a channel on the television or radio dial that you can sort of see and hear but doesn't quite come through. You would try to turn it left or right, experiment with various degrees of movement, but there was always a kind of distortion, a slow rupturing of meaning, of sound—and feeling.

Lilah was mercilessly blunt.

"It's your choice, of course," Delilah said, no judgment or pity, just straight no chaser with Delilah the Divine, "but if you do, you'll never find your song then, Frankie. They've run out of music on the other side," she said. "And I ought to know." The sadness that shadowed her eyes deepened as she spoke. "Sorry, but you've got to live a while longer," she said, throwing her head back. "Until then, there's nothing there to take from you."

She didn't want my heart, so I offered my body. She laughed.

"No love, I like you fine, Frankie. There's just not enough song in that stream of yours to make it worth the while," she said slowly, as if explaining to a very small child. "As they say, you couldn't carry a tune." She stroked my collarbone. Her touch felt like red streaks of fire. I wanted to kiss her and never, ever stop but her eyes were a warning. I thought her obsession with musicians was weird but nothing my musical inability couldn't allow me to overcome. "Ironically," she told me later, "your lack of talent, my friend, saved your life that night and every night since. So, don't feel so bad about rejection. It's a blessing in disguise."

Mother said I looked sad in childhood pictures because I was an old soul.

I looked sad because I knew what lay ahead.

#

The first time I saw Delilah's true form was an accident. It was the only time I was grateful I'd stayed conscious during those dry bone English lectures

51

in college. It was Ovid and Hyginus who said the original sirens were friends of Persephone, the poor soul snatched up by Hades, forced to spend a season in the underworld. Ovid assumed they were good friends, loyal women turned into halflings. Transformed, they wore the head of a woman and the body of birds. The wings were gifts to help set their abducted friend free.

But Hyginus had a darker vision. He said the transformation was a punishment. That the grieving mother, Demeter, cursed the jealous girls for not protecting their friend, her daughter during the abduction. She blamed them for the rupturing of her family and cursed the women to spend their lives as half human, half serpent or fish. From some craggy island in the middle of the Mediterranean, halfway between Africa and Europe, the legend of the sirens was born.

But I was following the wrong legend. Delilah was something else, something more ancient.

Delilah wanted a drink. When I returned to our spot under the balcony, she was gone.

I went searching. I know it's not attractive to be possessive of what was never yours and never would be, but that night I did not feel like being evolved. I wanted to find her, so she could drink the bourbon before the ice melted, the drink I stood in line to get. I wanted to find her so she could bless me with a smile, approval, any kind of sign that I would be in her company again.

When I stumbled into the storage room, a wet, panting sound drifted above the music's dull thud.

"Delilah?"

I walked in and a sharp iron scent assaulted me. I strained to see. The walls bled red. Claw marks covered them. His or hers, I could not tell. The strange metallic scent I smelled was that of someone dying. There is honesty in murder.

"It doesn't have to hurt," she said. The bearded man was slumped beneath her, his eyelashes twitched until they stopped. Lilah's lips were stained as if she'd been eating strawberries. "Doesn't even need to be blood." She stared at me. "I just like the taste." Horror must have flickered in my eyes. She offered a wry smile, a lifeless explanation. "My sisters would not approve."

Fear gripped me. I concentrated to slow my breathing, to make my vocal cords work.

"Is that why you don't see them anymore? Why they went away?" I managed.

"Creative differences," she said. Her voice steely. "You could say we broke up. Like the Supremes. I'm the star now."

I had the feeling that she always was. Even as she drained whatever melodies and harmonies she could from the man's throat, the deejay played her song. She finished wiping her mouth then joined the chorus, adding impossible runs that no record label had ever recorded.

"You can't give them everything," she said, smiling. "Got to save some for you." A berry-sized crimson stain rested above the mole on her chest. She sniffed. As far as anyone knew, could have been a nosebleed. She rose and adjusted the glimmering halter top. Her golden harem pants shimmered around her hips.

"Don't look so mournful, Frankie," Delilah said. "Yes, Simeon was talented, but he was on his way out." She held up his limp arm. Track marks and cuts like jagged railroads all along the stiffening flesh. She reached for me and I recoiled. I couldn't forget the young man's face. She took the drink instead. Blood and lipstick stained the high ball glass.

I watched her, frozen. Unsure if I should run or stay.

It was not the blood that killed them. It was the heartbeat, the life force in it. Delilah took their first music, the heart drum, that unique rhythm we are all born with, and then, she took the last. All of it. She told me later that she had stopped stalking churches and choirs. "Too much practice," she said. "Neverending rehearsals. Hollow hallelujahs." She stalked amateur nights, but they brought too much attention, so she settled on nightclubs.

Satiated, Delilah's face switches textures and tone. First she is a diamond, now her face is the shape of the moon.

"I need water." She doesn't wait to see if I will follow her.

Looking at the budding singer's lifeless body, I knew then why nightclubs were her favorite haunting grounds. Anonymous hook-ups and no real-world connections. She could feed and still have time to dance until her feet went numb. And of course, vanity. The deejays played her record on constant rotation with the most popular beats, Donna and Diana. They called her the *Never Can Say Goodbye Girl* because Delilah could dance all night. She shut the club down with her rhythm and song. Killed it every time.

Hers was a visceral music. The kind of hard-won grace that came from speaking across elements, living across time. She opened the door. When a cone of light revealed the second body slumped in the corner, I knew I needed to get away. After spending most of the night with her, I was running out of time. But she leapt on me. The glass crashed to the floor. My arm felt as if she had wrenched it off. Her breath was overly sweet, the opposite of rot.

"Just because I can't feed from you doesn't mean I won't kill you," she said.

I could feel her hunger across the stale cigarette air. Her angled bones pierced the darkness, paralyzed me where I stood.

She was on my throat before I could cry out. Her hands burned me. She released her palm, leaving me rubbing the slightly blistered flesh. "We will get along fine, Frankie, as long as you do what I say. I don't want to hurt you. Let's keep this cool." She nodded her head toward the door.

"What about them?" I stammered.

"A bad trip. Won't be the first."

It wasn't the last.

We walked past men grinding in the strobe and black lights. Their hips were all shadow and sound. The whole scene was raw and delicate. Pressed bone to bone, each breathless body swelled into a wave of desire. Red lips, eyes pretending to be flowers. That night on the dance floor, she held me like I had never been held, as if my every movement was necessary. She made me forget the dead eyes hidden in the darkness. We danced on until I was delirious. Her laughter rang through me. Finally, Delilah hurried out of the club, just a few steps from sunlight. I avoided my reflection in the mirrored hall. Guilt betrayed by my own ravenous glare.

After that night the mood was different. It wasn't about dancing but feeling the energy of the place so it could stay with me forever. The sound that could not be replicated, the lights. Being with Delilah, as dangerous as it was, became its own intoxicating drug for me. She made me feel powerful, glamorous, seen, needed in a way I had never been before or since.

But some friendships eat you alive. Some love is stolen by water, carries you away except for the bloodied hands that held you.

Avenues emptied hours ago, the sidewalks wrapped in secrets, we skulked along in silence until we reached the great steps that led to the water. We were in Battery Park, the southernmost tip of the island. Delilah said the Atlantic was a gray bowl of sound and need. That there were layers of want and memory. She said if she wanted she could strike its rim like a singing bowl, call her sisters and they would return to her. Said she could still hear them singing, not through blood but in water. The sound of grief made her wish they never came here.

"Where did you come from?" I asked. The air was cold against my face. Her eyes look tear-stained, scabs falling from a wound.

"A place I am not sure I can return to."

"Why don't you want to be with your sisters?" I asked again. She usually dodged this question. Her answer surprised me.

"I'd rather die than meet their judgment," she said. "They take the joy out of this cursed life, what joy there is."

"Can you die?" Delilah did not answer. She took so much from life. I wondered if death was something she even feared. The white bolero on her shoulders trembled like moth wings. She ripped the garment off and leapt into the ocean.

"Lilah!"

She disappeared under the water. Moonlight stripes raked the ocean's surface. I held myself, shook, my jaw locked from shock. Her absence triggered a strange withdrawal in me, a separate grief that broke free. Who was I without the shroud I wore, the bodies I carried? Delilah was the shadow who walked with me, the valley I feared and could not escape. I called her name a few more times then turned to go. I had no destination in mind. Wherever I was going I had already been.

Behind me a keening sound erupted, water churned. Something burst from the ocean's floor.

If it wasn't for the expression in their eyes, defiance, oblivion, I would not have recognized the creature that rose from the waters. Stories tell of ships and men dashed against the rocks, but what I saw that night was the nature of stone itself. Hard, iridescent metallic scales covered what used to be toned brown skin. Gone were the delicate bones under soft flesh. Water droplets dripped from long golden feathers. Neither an angel nor a demon, they were another creature for which I had no words. The wind howled as they rose. Wings, scales, the twin-tailed serpent, not fully dragon, not fully fish.

I knew it was Delilah from the way the creature hovered over me. I wanted to scream but no sounds emerged, just the choked silence that comes when fear takes over your body, even your breathing. When she surfaced from the waters I wanted to look away, but she was like a sun forever rising. She reflected her own light. There was a wholeness in her irregularities. The oddness was better than beauty, how she chose traits from species found on land and sea. Her bird-like mouth was shaped as if she wanted to say something but there was nothing to be said. I knew Delilah was a monster. I saw her monstrous appetite for reaping talents she never sowed. But when she took another shape, so did my fear.

I watched her circle the air, the night filled with music culled from the centuries, from the lives of other humans I could never know. She sang as if she had ten throats instead of one. I covered my ears. The weight of what was stolen crushed me, the songs these long dead voices never sang, the strings never plucked, the drums of gods forgotten across time.

Delilah wanted a witness, an accomplice, but her eyes told me that she wanted something else, too. She had revealed her face to me but not her real motives. She came from deep ocean or dark cosmos. There was no way to be sure and she would not tell. It wasn't until later when I realized what Delilah wanted was a stooge.

#

Radiant plumage full and thick, she extended powerful wings. She still wore the guise of a woman's body, but her arms and breasts were tattooed with golden symbols I could not read. She held each of the two-serpent's tails up in her hands as if they were long braids and hovered over me. Her eyes flashed, daring me to follow, then with an impossible note, Delilah screeched and disappeared behind the clouds.

Terrified, I was afraid to move. I waited, my whole heart in my throat and wondered how she lost—if she had ever known—the meaning of kindness. She took so much. Generous isn't a word anyone would use to describe Delilah Divine. But she had a seductive charm, charisma. Being with her was like being all the things you knew you would never be.

How did I ever believe that she cared for me? But believe I did. My thoughts churned, chaotic as the first waters. Frozen in fear, I waited for her to emerge from the clouds. Waves upon waves crashed against the walled park, the sound ominous. I shivered. No sign of her disturbed the parting clouds, the moonlit sky. I exhaled, hoping it was safe to go. When my mind gave my body permission to move, I ran.

Dancing shoes aren't made for marathons, but I didn't care about that. I pounded the pavement as if my whole world depended on it. Remembering the look in her eyes, I knew it did. I tore past the huge gray granite pilons that dotted the plaza. I never spent much time in that part of the city, and I knew if I survived that night, I wouldn't want to return again. The park was deserted. The wisps of trees made strange shapes across the night, but when I ran headlong into the shadow of giant wings, I nearly had a stroke. Unlike Delilah, this bronze eagle remained still, perched on its huge black granite pedestal. I wiped my eyes and continued running out of the lonely park until I finally reached State Street. Gasping for air, my lungs burned in my chest. I stumbled past an overturned trash bin, looking for the subway when I heard a familiar voice up ahead.

"Don't move. Sing for me."

Naked, her body glistened, still wet from the ocean or her transformation. I could not tell which, but the fear on the suited man's eyes was unmistakable. Delilah held him by his throat with one hand. Her hair dripped down her back. A briefcase was tossed on the street. Another man, his companion, held onto his arm, weeping.

"We don't have any money!"

"Did I ask for money? I said sing." Delilah's voice was low, menacing. The skin on her back rippled, remnants of the golden fish scales shimmered in the night. I tried to will my breathing to stillness. It was the first time I did not want her attention.

"But I can't sing. I don't know any songs," the suited man said, coughing. He struggled to speak over Delilah's iron grip.

"Then you better think of something quick," she said.

The poor man began to hum out of tune. "What a fool believes..."

"Please don't," the weeping man cried.

"...no wise man has the power..."

Delilah's fingers tightened around his neck, press at his windpipe.

"No!" the other cries and sobs. "... to reason away what seems to be ..." The sobbing one's voice was frightened but sure. His notes more solid and confident than his lover's.

Delilah pushed the suited weeping man away and held the sobbing one's throat. "Tolerable but ..." He faltered, stops, tries again louder this time, the notes crack under Delilah's crushing vice grip.

She takes his neck and squeezes it until his voice is a sieve. All the pain he feels, and his lover's, seeps into the air. There was no music worthy enough for Delilah to take, but she took this man's life anyway. I want to close my eyes and unsee the way his body crumples to the ground, a lifeless doll. Unhear his lover's scream. I want to walk through the shadows and streetlights to a night that is all mine. A night without Delilah.

She takes the dying man's jacket from his body, even as he lay in his lover's arms. The sobbing man keeps rocking him back and forth. "Why? Why would you do this?" She strokes tears from his cheek. He cringes. She loosens his tie. Unloops the dark, silk fabric from around his neck. Takes it. Ties it around her throat.

"Because I can."

When she rises to walk away, she turns and looks straight at me. Hidden in shadow, behind thick undergrowth and bushes, my heart stops.

"Time to go, Frankie."

The sound of my name on her tongue made me recoil. I stumbled out of the darkness and left what remained of my courage in the night's mouth.

#

Night after night I returned. From 54, the Garage, GG's Barnum Room to the moving sets of Xenon and my pre-Delilah favorite, Infinity, where it all came to a fiery end. How could I have known? When she returned from feeding, her mouth slick, eyes glazed, almost giddy, she never questioned what I did to take my mind off the murders. As long as I helped cover her tracks, made the straight lines look crooked, the zigs zag, I thought she didn't really care about what I did. So, I danced with many partners and took more drugs than I ever had. She wasn't the only one wearing a tiny canister on a ring of gold around their neck. I needed a little more each time I cleaned up after her "bad trips." I had no idea how much music was stolen from our world, how many futures. I did not have the stomach to count them. I wondered how long Delilah had plundered the world, stealing the songs that might heal whole nations. And for what? She sang beautifully but why should her voice be the only one? Wasn't the world room enough for multitudes?

With each new rising star snuffed out by her insatiable appetite, her voice became even more astonishing. She had depths that came from having lived and devoured many lives. I found myself seeking solace elsewhere. New partners to erase the horror I witnessed. Each night we danced as if time was our servant. Like Lilah's beauty, I knew it was a lie. Tomorrow morning could never save us.

I had just tucked a number in my back pocket when I heard her unmistakable voice behind me.

"So, this is who you've been hiding."

Thierry, my dance partner looked confused. Just another lonely soul looking for absolution. I knew Delilah did not love me, yet she had begun to watch me as if she did.

"Let's go," she said.

"But I'm just getting started." I didn't want to be alone with her. Not now. Not anymore if I was honest. She frowned. I returned the hat I'd borrowed from my new friend and watched them escape to the dance floor. There was always another dance partner waiting. Everyone looked happy except for Delilah and me, locked in a dangerous dance.

She watched Thierry disappear in a cloud of smoke.

"This place is dead. I need some air, water."

I hailed a cab and we rode in silence all the way down to the river. Traffic was light, still early yet. The sky over the Hudson looked foreign on the other side of the dark window. Sirens swept by but Delilah didn't even blink. We'd all become numb to them. As she leaned against my shoulder I tried to disappear into the corner of the cab. The cool glass felt good against my skin.

Clearly I had listened too closely to her music and yet not close enough. The night she found me lost in another body's symphony, her interest shifted. She knew I had once loved her, as inexplicable and unrequited as it was, but the monotony of murder had dulled that ache.

Was it now Lilah's turn to wait for the words that end affairs, break hearts? She knew better than most that speeches begun with words of love ended in heartbreak. How many times over the years had she pretended? Like any killer, Delilah needed to feel good before she tore your heart out. But a monster like Lilah didn't need a ruse to be let off the hook. She was the hook.

Anger sliced through the cab's cigarette smoke-filled air.

"I'm just here for the music!" I cried, fear and shame rolling down my cheeks.

"The music I gave you," she sneered. We stepped out of the cab and walked along the boardwalk, beyond an abandoned pier that had collapsed in the river. The Hudson rolled silently past us. On this side of town, the piers were our only beaches. There was no other major place to get sun. Now the normally crowded boardwalk looked deserted. The few lights from the Jersey side twinkled faintly, muted like distant stars. Lilah kicked off her heels and sat on the weathered planks, holding her knees. I couldn't tell her how I hated the curve of my own back, how I could barely hold my head up now that I had felt the weight of bodies, devoid of life, the ones I carried and tossed in the dumpsters, in the waters that she sat, meditating by. One day the truth of my own crimes would wash back on shore to haunt me.

I thought I could dance with a demon, that the only thing that would burn would be the hot music branded into skin. Now my skin bore the mark of the damned. Old and new pains stained my face. I didn't have any more music inside me than when I first met her.

A fetid scent of decay and mildew blew across the waters. My foot slipped on moss-covered, rotten timbers.

Delilah rose without looking. I knew what this night meant. Goodbye.

I resolved that whatever rage she contained, whatever music I hid within, she would not steal my soul's last song.

Human muscle gave way to ancient inhuman bone. Skin stretched and twisted, turned into scaly flesh and shimmering feathers. Eyes steely, I waited for the rip of flesh, the acrid scent of my own blood. But without a sound Delilah leapt into the darkness. She flung herself into the wind and was gone.

Heart pounding, the veins in my neck strained from tension. After that first deadly night with Delilah I'd started grinding my teeth. I trudged toward the street. I almost made it when I heard a ghost-like whipping sound, its source felt more than seen. I looked up. A fedora hat floated down in a spiral and landed on the cracked sidewalk before me. My new friend's hat, Thierry's.

I doubled over, sickness filling me. When I opened my eyes again, Delilah was bending down to pick up the hat that was still spinning like a top.

"I feel like dancing," she said and placed the fedora atop her head. The brim dangled at a rakish angle, covering her eyes.

I grabbed her elbow, forced her to face me. "Where did you get it?" I yelled.

"Want to come and see?"

The thought of seeing Thierry tossed away in some alley as if their life never mattered... I wanted to scream, wanted the sound to be more than hurt rising to the surface. I wanted Delilah to feel some of the pain she only expressed in song. Defeated, I shook my head 'no.'

"I didn't think so," she said. "Aquarians make the worst companions. Come."

"Where are we going?" I asked, my voice hoarse.

She smiled showing all her teeth. "Infinity."

#

The 600 block of Broadway in Soho was home to a few warehouses where artists could live and work without needing a trust fund. 653 Broadway had an old, vaulted reputation. Originally Pfaff's Beer Cellar, Walt Whitman and others descended a set of stairs to drink pints. Later it became an envelope factory and then a nightclub. Like Whitman's unfinished poem, the weekly parties at Infinity were more intimate and never seemed to end. With its black walls and ceilings covered in neon lights, banquet tables of fresh pears and ice-cold water, the atmosphere in the block-long nightclub was for true-blue partiers, those who came strictly to dance and release.

But Delilah wasn't there to dance or to see *the bright eyes of beautiful young men* as Whitman had penned. She came to teach me a lesson, something about possession, about what it means when you can't—or won't—break free. Engaged in our own battle of wills, neither of us had any idea that hundreds of miles away a mob would gather in a baseball field, intent on breaking every Black record they owned. A bonfire had been set up, a disco demolition, by a twenty-four-year-old disgruntled rock deejay. He was angry that the music we loved, pioneered by mostly Black and Latino gay artists, had taken over the air waves. His airwaves. The music provided a powerful platform for those who were often invisible.

We, the misfits, the invisible would-be superstars, and all those in-between were drawn to its irreverent rhythms and pulsing beats, the hypnotic cymbals and sounds. Disco even changed the way we moved. The dancefloor was no longer restricted to just couples, straight or otherwise. Stemmed by a series of epiphanies and communities, the experience became en masse, a group high where love was the key. It was all about love in the beginning, being in love, spreading love, the very act of creation, breathing new life into something that did not exist.

That last night offered its own epiphany. It was already crowded beyond belief when we walked through the club's infamous black double doors. The last shift was in full swing. Both the front and back bars were packed. Vincent, the bartender flowed back and forth behind the long oak bars as if he was rolling on skates. Blondie's "Heart of Glass" blared from the sound system, and I had no idea it was Valentine's Day until I saw all the pink neon and red-clothed dancers crowding the floor.

Delilah took my hand and I flinched. She offered one cutting glance as she led me past the giant white columns that guarded the dance floor, ancient sentinels from a forgotten era. Even Debbie Harry's icy vocals couldn't pierce through the deepening sadness I felt. The revelers danced on, oblivious to the threat that threw her head back, lipstick on her teeth as she swayed among them. Non-stop energy pulsed through the music and the lights. The neon illuminated the heart-shaped confetti that suddenly rained down from the ceiling.

"Come on, dance! Frankie, you used to be fun." She pulled me close but the thought of her kiss, the same mouth that drained my friend and so many nameless others, repulsed me. What I once thought was inner beauty, her incredible energy was just endless hunger, a gaping hole of want. She had all the makings of a god but none of the love, no mercy. Whatever light drew her to our world was snuffed out long ago.

She stroked my face. Her touch felt like hot razors against my skin.

We navigated the mass of bodies that danced around us as if they feared no tomorrows. Under the confetti shower, her body poured into mine. Squeezing ever tighter, her fingers made it known she could snap my neck and spine at a moment's whim. Time passed under the flickering lights. Nothing was the same as it was before. Infinity was the place where I came to know myself, the club where I once felt most free. Lilah took that. She made me a stranger to myself, a witness and accomplice to terrible deeds. What I knew now was loss. Whatever music I once had was drained out of me.

"You ... make ... me feel .... miii ... ighty real!" Delilah sang as she spun around. As soon as Sylvester's falsetto pumped through the speakers a roar went up. The crowd came alive, lit beneath the swirling constellations.

"When we get home darlin' and it's nice and—"

Delilah froze. Sweating bodies swayed around us. Spinning colors, beautiful fabrics, shimmering lights. Something was different about her. An emotion I hadn't seen before. Fear.

"Frankie," she said, her voice low. She turned me slowly so that my back now faced the back bar and her back faced the front doors. "Do you see that one there?"

"Who?" I asked, confused. Who was Delilah hiding from? Infinity was a New York City block long. The club was packed, a throng of fashionable bodies dancing each other under the tables. You could get lost just going to the restroom. Too bad if you were new and got separated from your friends. Might drift in the void for a while. I peered over Lilah's shoulder, unsure who I was looking for and then I saw her.

A woman so serene, she exuded radiance. She walked with a kind of assured calm and peacefulness amidst the pheromones, chaos, and noise. A being so ethereal she could not be from this world at all, a being so magnetic that it could only be one of Delilah's infamous sisters.

Dressed as if she had just arrived from the equator itself, she danced her way through the crowd, the copper beads of her braided hair bounced and shimmered across her shoulders.

"Yes, I see them," I said, matter-of-factly, trying to mask the satisfaction in my voice. Delilah had once said that the only thing she feared was her sisters' judgment. I didn't know who Delilah had once been, but I did wonder what this long, lost sister would think of her now.

"Where is she going?" Delilah asked, her voice a whisper. Her nails dug into me. Could she actually be afraid? I had seen Delilah emote before, a persuasive performance to lure her ill-fated lovers, but I never thought fear was within her range. The novelty of the moment got the best of me.

"I think she's heading this way," I said. "Third column."

Delilah's eyes widened. Sweat beaded on her forehead. "No." She pulled away. "Follow me!"

She pushed through the crowd without looking back, weaving in and out of the jubilant dancers. I watched the mysterious woman stop at the DJ's booth. Heads bent, she and DJ Animus, the latest phenom passing through, were deep in conversation as the music swelled. Surrounded by vinyl-filled crates, they held each other with the warmth and intimacy of old friends. She kissed him, her wrap dress hugging her curves. Clearly seduction ran in the family, but there was a genuineness about this other sister. She held her friend with a sense of caring that showed in her slightest movements. There was no malice there.

Adrenaline with the ever-present sadness filled me as I turned to shadow Lilah through the nightclub. A few of her fans greeted her, but she waved them off.

She ran all the way to the back, stilettos stomping past the couples hidden in darkness. Concealment was key in places of nocturnal revelry. The ends of cigarettes burned in the shadows, unblinking red eyes. When she reached the off-limits area, a bouncer moved to stop her. She fingered the canister on the gold chain around her neck. With one hand on her high-slitted dress, she smiled at him. I knew that smile.

"Oh," he said, recognizing her. "Miss Divine, go 'head." She didn't have to whisper a code name like the patrons from the past. He frowned at me but waved me through. She didn't wait for me as she strode down the dark narrow hall. We descended a rickety flight of stairs, down a ramp. Here, the four-on-the-floor, constant quarter note bass beat was muted. I had never been in the club's labyrinth. I half-expected a minotaur to emerge from the shadows, but the only real monster there was Delilah.

We walked past several old dusty oak barrels. The hoops were rusted, the lettering on the heads faded. She sidestepped the barrels outside a wide, heavy door and ducked into a vault-like room.

"What is this?" I asked. She shrugged, visibly tired, tossing Thierry's fedora and taking a seat on a velvet couch. In the time it took us to get downstairs, Delilah had aged ten years. "Back room deals need back rooms, no? This used to be a speakeasy." I frowned. It looked like a tomb. "Speak easy," she said, whispering with a pitiful laugh. "Like the basement clubs in Mississippi." She adjusted the strap on her dress. I moved to sit with her. "No," she said. "I need you to go back up. Return when she's gone." For the first time her voice was shaky. None of the dazzling diva confidence that fueled her flight. She looked weary, pensive. The room's primeval green walls cast murky dark shadows over bronze skin. My mind reeled. I had never seen Delilah ill. "Light?" She held a skinny joint up.

I pulled a lighter out and lit it, eager to leave. Fragrant smoke floated in the air, a halo around her face. She closed her eyes, not offering me a hit. She sighed and tossed the roach on the floor. I watched as she opened her canister. Whatever family reunion lay ahead, Delilah wasn't ready.

"And Frankie?" she said.

"Yes?"

"Bring some ice."

I left her fingering her necklace, the canister empty now as I wondered what awaited me outside. No sooner than I reached the top stair than the stench hit me.

A scream rose from black clouds as I stepped out. "Fire!" The guard that waved us into the labyrinth was gone. Panic-stricken dancers reached for each other, knocking over the swivel-back chairs and stools.

"What happened?" I screamed at a passing couple. They shook their heads. I couldn't see the flames at first, but I could feel the heat. On a good night the club was smoldering. This was hellish.

As the giant neon lights that spun around the columns began to flicker, the overhead lights dimmed. Instinctively I ran back through the hall, down the stairs. When I made it to the vault, the image of Thierry's fedora hat haunted me. Delilah had taken a life she didn't need. She did so to punish me.

I had been a loyal, faithful friend, never revealing her dark secrets, even when loyalty and faith were the last things Delilah deserved. Going back down into the maze beneath the club could cost me my life. Did I still believe being with Delilah was worth it?

I stood outside the heavy door, silent, thoughts lost in the corners of the past. Labyrinths were designed to generate chaos and confusion. Like magic, this labyrinth manifested clarity.

"Frankie?" Delilah's voice on the other side of the door was a tentative question. I held a barrel by its spigot and awkwardly rolled and wobbled it over, propping it under the door's handle. "Hello?" I kicked the other oak barrel on its side and rolled it to the door. The handle shook slightly under its weight but did not move.

"Whose there? Open this door!" she cried. She pounded but the door held.

I backed away. My feet felt heavy as iron, as if I was bolted to the ground.

"Hello? Is anyone there? I'm stuck. The door is stuck. Let me out!" she screamed.

Panic set in but also resignation, and now the screams reached a fever pitch.

I could run or I could unroll the stone sealing the tomb, but I knew this was no messiah coming back.

I ran, running into one of the other barrels that lined the hall. "Damn," I cried out, my knee throbbing.

"Frankie?" she screamed, incredulous.

I ran but two partiers emerged from the narrow hallway, startling me.

"We've got to get out," I said, breathless. "There's a fire."

"What?" Confusion flashed across their faces, then panic. We fled as fast as we could, up the ramp and the rickety stairs. When we re-entered the main floor, the room was plunged in total chaos. Black clouds of smoke filled the air. I tripped over a high heel shoe, coughing up half a lung. Even in the panic, the tears and fear, my ears strained. I could hear Delilah over the din. That voice, that incredible voice, the throat that sounded like ten. The sound was a keening, weeping. I paused in the darkness, shame and guilt knotted in my chest.

I was the monster now.

Then I heard it, not weeping but laughter. Her voice, that remarkable otherworldly voice rising above the echoes of terror and dismay. Faced with being burned alive, Delilah Divine laughed.

A chemical, plastic scent began to fill the air. Smokey fingers reached for me. I bolted, banging into a cocktail table, tumbling over an upturned chair. Whatever grace I once had was gone, too. Vinny from the bar waved me on.

"What are you waiting for, get out! Drag anyone else you see. Infinity's going to blow!" He pulled up a man who had fallen down, his ankle twisted. They hobbled away.

As I ran, slipping over the slick, drink-stained floorboards, the piles of pink confetti, I couldn't tell if the pounding I heard was the pounding of my heart or the pounding of the music's beat. No one stopped the music. The deejay booth was empty. Crates of vinyl sprawled across the dance floor. If Delilah's sister had come looking for her, she was gone now.

I reached a bottle neck near the fourth column. Neon pulsed and flickered above our heads. An explosion from the left then a screech somewhere behind us sent us scrambling.

"¡Ay bendito!" someone cried. "What is that?" People shouted, pointed.

Just like Orfeu, I knew I shouldn't look back, but I had already stared into the abyss. Only a narrow strip of sky separated us, so I turned to see.

Golden scales, impossible wings. One, no, two serpent's tails bursting through the flames. A song so loud and wretched, it sounded as if the whole sky's throat opened to sing. Then, another joined it. Mournful, like every sorrow song I'd ever heard erupting from the night.

For some, cautionary truths, though known, must be lived. Others can see the signs before the symbols emerge and still they fall head in. I was the latter. I saw but didn't want to see. I wanted the dream. When we look in the sky to watch the stars, we are seeing them as they once were. But bright suns give the most light when they are leaving you.

Transfixed we watched as the creature circled the high, vaulted ceilings of Infinity. Brilliant flames, great flickering tongues of fire and heat, rushed through the nightclub engulfing the black walls. The crowd moved, eyes wide, coughing, wailing, mouths flung open, but it was as if all the sound was turned off. It felt like I was running against a great, hot wind.

Then something spun me around so fast, I lost all sense of myself. It was as if my sight had shifted. The vision of my right eye moved to my left, and my left moved to outside my face, beyond flesh and skin. But a voice brought me back and it wasn't Delilah.

"What did you do to my sister?"

The eyes that held me were a beautiful terror. I could see the pain and fear, the kind that comes when you might lose something you only just realized you have. Delilah never shared any details about her sisters, but it was clear that their relationship was complicated. The way her sister stared at me, her coppery skin translucent, shimmering as if she vibrated on a different frequency, was unnerving, like a soul facing oblivion, alone.

"Please don't hurt me," I said, coughing. "I...I didn't mean—"

"Sister!" she yelled and cut me off. She was staring into the clouds of smoke above. Heat spread from where she had touched me. I felt as if I'd been burned. Panic set in but before I could back away, I was shoved from behind.

"This way!" The guard from earlier guided me and a few others out of a side door that led to an alley. Relieved, we bumrushed the door, one person getting jammed before the screaming crowd pushed us all through.

"El fiesta se fue al garete!" a woman in a glittering emerald gown yelled. "The party went to hell!"

Standing outside shivering in zero-degree weather as firetrucks descended, I had to agree.

The night Infinity burned was the night Disco nearly died in me. But even though the nightclub burned, the fire couldn't burn my memories. I had gone to the discos in search of strangers, anonymous partiers who on the dance floor became my friends. Instead of love and solidarity, I left with unclean hands, a stained shirt, and enough disparate memories to haunt me for years.

I could hear the last notes of Delilah's song, a scream as if every star in the night was afire. The notes scatter like broken teeth across the smoke-filled air. What was tender in the notes, the soft, the thrumming, came from a thousand other heartbroken souls like me. That night I stood in the crowd with those who were still in shock. We watched as the firemen worked to control the six-alarm fire, grieved for the loss of our shared home. I blink back tears and shame, grief covered in ashes, but when the day rises and the sky clears, there is only the burned-out building, its gaping windows, and the outline of the sun. I walk away, my throat sore, mind reeling with memories of Lilah but only make it a few steps when something falls from the sky and drops in front of me. A melted canister. I pick it up. Misshapen, it's still hot to the touch. Like her love, a smoldering wild thing.

SEAMONSTERS

AMA PATTERSON

I

"Damn. Ain't she *never* gon' drop that baby?" Shirl's voice drips into the thick, midafternoon air and pops like spit in a hot greased skillet. Makes me wanna jump back 'for I get burned. It's too hot to be startin' shit. It's too hot to be sitting on this red plastic couch Miz Lucy got on the porch; gotta put a towel under your butt to keep from sticking to the seat. I don't know how Shirl can stand it with them braces on her legs. Twelve- and-a-half pounds of metal and leather just so she can stand between two crutches, when she ain't in that wheelchair. Heat lingers, fingers bags of BonTon chips and boiled peanuts, sets a spell on a crate of Orange Nehi, makes conversation with a few flies humming lazily in and out. Heat, like me n' Shirl, just be passing the time. Even the hands on the wall clock are droopin' in the heat, tho' that clock ain't kept time since time began. Even in the shade of the porch at Miz Lucy's, with that clackety black metal fan slapping at the heat from up on top of the Frigidaire, and the front and back doors of the store propped wide, it's damn near too hot to turn my head. Air full of salt, and not the slightest hint of a breeze. I turn anyway, and see VidaMac making her usual slow, waddling progress down Marsh Road. VidaMae turning the corner puts you in mind of a big diesel truck trying to twist itself down these little streets between the highway and the docks. Sweat makin' her face shine like chrome and the rest of her is all hip fenders, butt bumpers and a big ol' payload—'cept hers is in the front.

"'Oman been pregnant long as there's been dirt." Shirl toss her head, whippin' them long, Indian straight pigtails 'round her shoulders. "'Least since...since after..." she kinda crunches up her face, and her voice trails off. Shirl do have a tendency to sort of drift out on you sometimes. I give her a minute to let it pass. "How many kids she got?"

"None livin'," I say, resisting the urge to remind Shirl that she knows this already. I get up to see if Glory and Honor done drank all the lemonade, or if there might yet remain a trickle for another mouth. Them two boys are a plague of locusts in any kitchen, and a pain in the ass on any given day, but they sweet and they mine. "This be her firstborn," I say.

"Hmmph," is all Shirl say, which is a powerful improvement over her usual: a slew of conjecture with a double helping of condemnation. Who does VidaMae think she is, anyway, walkin' to an' fro everyday, and what's she doin? Ain't swimmin', fishin' or meetin' no boat, but there she goes without so much as a good afternoon for anybody, not that anybody in their right mind gon' speak back 'cos something 'bout VidaMae just ain't right. And so on. And on. The more Shirl talks, the more riled up she gets. Her big hands are hard and knuckly from grippin' those crutches or bumpin' that wheelchair over these cart tracks we got for roads; look like crab claws and she wavin' 'em in my face.

Shirl's my sister, so I gotta love her, but she stays confused and her tongue got more barbs than a sticker bush. Heartbreak don't have to make a body hateful.

There's no lemonade to be had. I know Miz Lucy wouldn't mind if I helped myself to an RC or somethin' but I got a taste for lemonade. Shirl still runnin' her mouth. I say a quick prayer for VidaMae and her babies, and for me an' mine, 'cos if some syrup and lemons don't walk themselves up in here before Shirl gets done ranting, it really *will* get hot.

II

VidaMae shuts and double-locks the door of her small apartment, drops her heavy backpack, breathes in dust and quiet, tips silently past drawn shades and covered mirrors. Once she liked her rooms open, sunlit and shining, but glass surfaces are a source of terror these days. She knows she just walked in from the concrete, asphalt and steel of the city, but beyond her windows green trees border on a narrow dirt road. Instead of her own reflection, a strange woman, light-skinned with a face as lean as a blade, stares mockingly through her mirrors, hissing tempting insults. All in all, it is easier not to look. Her bedroom is all in green, a cool glade of pine, ivy and mint, shaded by fern sheers.

There is a chitinous tapping within the floorboards. Or maybe it's just the building settling, releasing the day's heat.

Mama? It's Tyco. Tyco, he's a good boy. Good to his mama, in spite of everything.

We home now, Mama. Take off your shoes. Gratefully, VidaMae toes her scuffed sneakers off her swollen feet. Pretty soon, all she'll be able to wear is her house shoes. That's better, but not good enough. VidaMae stands, undoes the drawstring on her pants, and shrugs off the blouse, long and generously cut, that conceals her belly. Both garments settle around her ankles in an indigo puddle. VidaMae steps out of it in relief, stretching her arms above her head, lifting her heavy braids off her perspiring neck. She looks past her belly to the floor and squats to retrieve a white business card from the spill of fabric. The card is bent at the corners from much handling and heavy with the weight of impending decisions. VidaMae has been carrying it around for what feels like forever.

Oakcrest Clinic, PA
Abortion Services to 20 weeks
Reasonable fees. Sedation available.
Pregnancy Testing. Birth Control. Individual Decision Counseling.
Appointments Monday-Saturday

VidaMae flips the card over, scans the address she has already memorized: 7 Marsh Road, Waterside....

VidaMae blinks. Reads again, slowly: 1212 East 68th Street, Suite 70...

The lime green muslin covering her dresser mirror ripples sinuously, like a water snake crossing a still pond. VidaMae freezes, waiting for the mirror woman to start hissing in her ear.

Okay, now get you something to eat. Tyco breaks the tension.

"It's too hot," murmurs VidaMae, feeling suddenly sick, thinking of the quiet oblivion of her bed.

"...lemonade..." Kaycie's cravings nudge VidaMae from the inside like tiny fists. VidaMae licks her lips, tasting tart, cold sweetness.

The green muslin slaps the mirror glass.

Mama. Mama!

Her baby boy. VidaMae sighs. "Yes, Precious?"

Mama, did you see, in the water?

"See what, baby?"

Me! I'm in the water, Mama. I go like this. Sound of babybubbles kissing the air, breathy little pops. A pause. Precious laughs mischief and malice. *Come down to the water, mama.* Splash of needy greedy fat little arms open wide. *Maaamaaa...*

You betta shut up, warns Ty. *Always talkin' some mess. Kaycie?*

Silence.

Kaycie!

Shhh, said VidaMae, finally, patting her belly. She just don't feel like talkin'.

She gon' be like Shirl, Precious sing-songs. *Shirl never talks to you.*

There is a long, green silence.

Well. You can't blame her, says Tyco, finally. It is worse than any casual cruelty. VidaMae closes her eyes.

From Precious, a bubbling, watery laugh: *You gon' make Kaycie _swim_, Mama? She'll be good at it. It runs in the family... Bet _you_ can swim, Mama. Can't you...?*

Shut UP! Tyco snaps.

MAKE ME!

The boys plunge away, leaving the dust to settle into silence once more.

Lemonade forgotten, VidaMae lies down on top of the ivy patterned coverlet, on her left side, just like at that other clinic that first time: marooned on a narrow cot, pierced and deflated, leaking seawater while the nurse searched the waiting room, found no one waiting for VidaMae, and finally sent her home in a cab with prescriptions and meaningless advice.

"I wasn't ready," she reminds them all, "to be nobody's momma." VidaMae hugs her eternally swollen belly.

"... ready now...?" Kaycie twists within her mother's embrace.

But VidaMae is already asleep.

III

Near dark, Miz Lucy's back from wherever it is she goes, and Shirl's gone down to The Bucket, where she sings most nights while Moss Robinson or Ben Rayburn's son James picks the box. Singing is the only thing that seems to smooth ol' Shirl out. I 'spect she got that voice to balance out her nature. Even sticker bushes gotta bloom sometime.

It's been too hot to even think about cooking. I sent Glory and Honor off to Briscoe's for fried fish sandwiches, and gave them extra for ice cream, since they had pooled their bait money and brought me back lemons and syrup. A mite later than I'd wanted it, but right on time, nonetheless. Sweet boys, like I said.

"How were things?," asks Miz Lucy, like she's expecting to hear something new and different. She heads straight for the Frigidaire, though there's not a drop of sweat on her narrow, high-yellow face. I shrug.

"Mister Mimms came 'round for his BC powders and Ballentine."

"You could set a clock by that man's hangovers," say Miz Lucy, prying the cap off her own bottle of cold beer.

"Janecee's kids came in for breakfast again. Little Debbies and Seven-Up. She owes you a nickel."

Miz Lucy chuckles and smothers a burp. "Hate to be their mama. Love to be their dentist."

"Corliss picked up for the Bolito Man. 397 straight and combination?

What you dream last night?

"Fish." Miz Lucy spreads her own towel and settles herself on the red plastic couch. "Dead baby fish, swimmin' all 'round the ocean."

That ain't in your dreambook, I think. That ain't even your dream. Out loud, I say: "And of course, ol' Shirl sat up here 'most all day. "'Oman could talk the ears off a brass monkey."

"Don't I know it." Miz Lucy lights one of her nasty cigarettes, huffing out the match in a thick grey cloud. Nobody else's Lucky Strikes smell like bad eggs. I cough, move to the far end of the couch. "Who she bad-mouthin' today?"

"Who else? Wish she'd just let it be."

"Don't know why she should," say Miz Lucy. "'Oman yank *you* out by the roots and throw you away, you might have a different feeling on the matter."

"Shirl don't know 'bout all that," I say.

"She don't remember, but she do know."

I roll my eyes. "'Zat why she so spiteful?"

"I 'spect so," say Miz Lucy matter-of-factly, draining the last of her beer. Much as I hate to admit it, Miz Lucy's right. I don't wanna end up like Shirl.

"You might not," say Miz Lucy, as if I'd spoken aloud. I hate when she does that.

"But you don't know that fo' sure," I say. This is not a question.

Miz Lucy look sharp at me. "So you rit t' make a deal?" I study the warp of the boards in the porch floor, say nothing. Miz Lucy blow another stank puff in my direction. "We all get what we settle for, Kaycie. You just took matters into your own hands. Can't say as I blame you. Where would you be if you hadn't? All at sea, that's where. All y'all." Miz Lucy chuckles at her own joke, but it ain't nothin' funny. *Taking* a place, a place to be, a place you can't get tore out of is one thing, but *keeping* it is another. I think about never seeing Glory and Honor come whooping 'round that bend in the road with a string of porgies, never hearing them laughing together at night when they 'sposed t' be 'sleep. There's compensations for the extra washing and the empty icebox. I think about wiggling through briny, blood-dark depths, crippled, discarded and disowned, washing out on the flats at low tide, mad and mean like Precious or half-crazy like Shirl. I shiver, despite the heat and try *not* to think about that conch shell Mister Briscoe found tangled in his fishing nets and let me keep. I got buried in the dirt beneath Miz Lucy's porch with seven new pennies. Safe. For right now, anyhow.

Miz Lucy still staring at me. "So do we have a deal?"

I shrug.

"Mind the store for me again tomorrow?"

"Okay." Why not? I'm just waiting. Holding on as long as I can 'tween Miz Lucy and VidaMae. As they say, 'tween the devil and the deep blue sea.

IV

VidaMae, seeking forests, dreams oceans instead: dark, craggy caverns and grottoes beneath the tides. She tugs frantically at urchins and anemones anchored to moss-colored walls; she has to pull them out or else the cave will be filled with grasping fronds. They are stubborn and hard to uproot. The harder she pulls, the more firmly they attach, and once they bloom, it's forever. She struggles as the floating tendrils caress her insistently, wrap themselves lovingly around her waist, tighten around her throat, insinuate themselves between her legs and sprout deep within her. Panicked, VidaMae flails out and up, up, up...

The air is harder to breathe than the water, and her legs ache beneath her weight. Lights visible between the trees, illuminate painted wooden signs:

THE BUCKET. COLD BEER. MUSIC. OPEN EVERY NIGHT. COME ON INN.

VidaMae drifts toward them like a moth.

The Bucket sits on a curving dead end dirt track about half way between Miz Lucy's and the bluffs, a tiny shack with two tarp walls and a big, wrap-around porch. The bar, a small stage and a few tiny tables are inside, but the real spot is the porch. The front porch is where folks stand, drink, tap their feet to the music, or dance when the beat gets good. The back porch is where you take your business if you got no business doing it. A big, old oak leans over the back rail, dropping acorns like good gossip and begging for an excuse to fall.

VidaMae stands among the trees, invisible to the anonymous souls out back. The evening air is full of cigarette smoke, the clink of beer bottles, scraps of conversation, laughter, and the occasional angry shout. And Shirl. Her Shirl. It is the first time VidaMae has heard her sing.

Somebody's working that slide guitar, urged on by handclaps and hollers. Shirl's voice swoops up, rasping at the crest, a burr caught under an angel's wing.

...Got no one to love me, no one caaares if I live or die

Won'tcha take me hoomme Momma, if I go dowwwwn to the water side...

I love you, thinks VidaMae, but the laughter from porch sounds like derision. Shirl's voice is as insistent as a pointing finger. Forests, thinks VidaMae, desperately. Oaks like old sistahs; dark, sheltering arms wrapped in shawls of pale moss. Support. Refuge. She finds the marsh instead, the road, the porch, the voices receding to a border of solemn, stately trees, then a sea of tall, golden reeds parted by the inlet. The ribbon of black water reflects the silver moonlight. Bullfrogs singing to whippoorwills herald the night. VidaMae inhales the fragrance: pine and sweet honeysuckle, the tang of salt.

A splash. Something broods just visible beneath the waterline. The reeds rustle.

Mama? Tyco sounds happy and surprised. *Mama!* VidaMae turns. Tyco is stretched full length on his belly, propped up on his elbows, just his head and shoulders visible between the parted reeds like he'd crawled there playing soldier, smiling up at her, the day's mud and sunshine smudging his cheeks and forehead. VidaMae wants to kiss him and brush the twigs from his hair, wants to hold him to her and—something. Tell him a story? She can't tell. His face is hard to fix on—like a baby one minute, and a grown man the next, like grandmas always say kids do.

"You alright, baby?"

I'm glad to see you. Tyco ducks his head like he's shy. *You don't never come down to see us.*

'Cos you're always with me, thinks VidaMae, but doesn't know how to make it not sound mean. Her oldest, her big boy, always kind and loving. She sits beside him in the gritty mud and slips her hand in his. Wouldn't hurt him for the world. Or so she'd thought.

At the time, she'd thought she was doing right by all of 'em.

Unbidden, Shirl's tune slips past her lips. She lets it. Don't mamas sing to their children?

I know that song, says Tyco, laying his head on her knee. *Don't know the words, though.* His soiled shirt rides up above where brown boy skin gives way to rough, dark, rectangular scales. He wriggles, and there is a swishing in the reeds too far away for boy feet. VidaMae looks, but can only bring herself to touch his hands, his hair.

"Y'all come down here to play?" An honest question for all that, VidaMae does want to change the subject.

Sometimes. Well, not Shirl. But me and Precious, most times we stay in the water. VidaMae looks questioningly at the marsh, the inlet, the black ribbon eddying under the silver light.

"This water right here?"

Tyco's small hand lingers shyly on VidaMae's belly. *Water,* he says. His other hand makes an expansive gesture, the seas of the world in the curve of his palm. He laughs delightedly at the restless movements beneath VidaMae's belly skin.

"...ask her..."

Hi, Kaycie.

"...ask..."

Tyco sighs. His hand pats VidaMae's stomach, keeps his eyes there. *Mama, what you gon' do about Kaycie?*

What you THINK she gon' do? VidaMae jumps at the familiar, bitter sing-song, but too late to avoid the teeth tearing at the tender flesh of her ankle. VidaMae screams, crawls, stumbles away from the pain, from Precious' savage laugh, from Tyco's sad *"bye, Mama,"* running blind, blunders through haints and shades, trips over knotty roots. Snakes dip from low branches, hissing like the mirror woman. VidaMae lands, sprawling, in a circle of trees. She hugs the earth and sobs with relief. The sistah oaks bend to inspect her, rustling their mossy shawls, murmuring *shhh* and *here nah*, their ruffled heads inclining gracefully toward one another as they confer.

Cousin, one says gently, *this not your place.*

Vida Mae wakes gasping. The clinic card is crumpled in her left fist. Her ivy bed smells of the sea.

V

"Where them two rag-muffin children of yours?" Shirl fumes into another morning of heat and salt funk. Her legs stick straight out in them braces, taking up the whole red plastic couch – not that I mind.

"They 'round," I say, keeping words to a minimum. This morning I got 'em up early, fed 'em corncakes and molasses, and allowed as to how since I'd be minding Miz Lucy's again, this would likely be a good day to go help Mister Briscoe with his nets. Ain't seen 'em since their plates were licked clean. Times when I'm tempted to judge them solely on legs and appetite, they do show a glimmering of common sense. More than I got, sometimes, 'cos after all, where am I?

I'm hoping Shirl ain't on her usual evil stick, 'cos today just ain't the day. Woke up this morning feelin' wrung out, like I'd spent all night fighting a battle that weren't mine no how. There's a low cloud malingering over Waterside, holding the heat tight. Miz Lucy done give me the keys to the store, which ain't been locked up in a month 'a Sundays, and when I asked her why, she just smile sideways and slide on off 'bout her business. Look more like a snake every day. I stashed two pitchers of lemonade in the fridge, though. I'm ready for Shirl's ass today. Or at least her mouth. I pour a big glass for myself, and an even bigger one for her, hoping to keep her lips fruitfully occupied, at least part of the time.

I hope in vain.

"How you just let them boys run loose 'round here? Ain't you 'fraid?" Her tone lets me know that if I had any sense, I would be.

"'Fraid of what, Shirl?" I ask.

"Some ol' somebody snatch 'em up, and you wouldn't even know they was gone."

I have to laugh. "Anyone snatches them boys won't last an hour, 'specially not if they have to feed 'em. And since when you seen somebody 'round here that you *didn't* know well enough to talk about 'em like a dog?"

"Hmmph. Ain't funny. Gots to be careful even of folks you do know. Plenty of folks 'round here, I wouldn't put it past 'em to try something. That VidaMae—"

I can't stand it. "Shirl, why you hate VidaMae so much?"

"I just don't trust her."

"Naw, this is past don't trust. Hell, I don't trust Miz Lucy. VidaMae do something to you?"

"I...she...," Shirl scrunches up her face. "Why you ask me that?"

"Why you so down on VidaMae?"

"Selfish heifer."

"You talk about her, but you ain' never talk *to* her, so how you know?"

"She just is."

"Why?"

Silence.

"Shirl," I say. "Who's your mama, Shirl?"

"I ain't got one," she snarls.

"Okay. Shirl, who's *my* mama?" Maybe my mama, I add, silently.

"She... you..."

I wait. I'm good at it.

"You..." Shirl's voice breaks apart. "You gon' be like the rest of us," she whispers. Naw I ain't, I think.

"You *s'pposed* to be." Shirl's as bad as Miz Lucy. Her whisper's edge could cut glass. "How come you get to walk 'round here all regular, and we gots to be... to stay like..." Them crab claw hands wavin' in my face again. I snap.

"Y'all the ones all the time hangin' round VidaMae."

"I ain't. I hate her!"

"Fine, but don't hate on me. I tried. I can't fix... everything, but I did try."

"You didn't do *shit.*"

Stung, I holler back. "I got us a place."

"This ain't our place!" Shirl screamin' now.

And we both just shut up right there, 'cos it's true. VidaMae and me and Shirl and Precious and Tyco; even Glory and Honor. We don't really belong here. And Miz Lucy...well, she's got her own agenda and I 'spect it ain't in nobody's interest but her own. Life ain't supposed t' hold still.

"You don't have to stay," I say. "You could go. We all could."

"But... but then... how you know what Vida—what Mama gon' do?"

"I don't," I say.

"I don't..." says Shirl after a bit, " I don't want you to end up like us." It's the nicest, softest thing I've ever heard Shirl say.

"What you wanna do, Shirl?" I ain't even stressed no more, and it's like floating. Shirl twist up her face at me like she mad again. Then all of the meanness kinda wash out of her. I understand. It takes too much energy to hold all that hurt.

"Go h-h-home..." Shirl cryin' like there ain't already enough salt in the world, but she makin' sense.

I drag her wheelchair down the steps and help her get settled before crawling under the space beneath the porch. It's almost cool under there, and the dirt between my fingers is as soft as cake flour. Shirl still cryin'. It sounds almost like music. I haul myself out 'fore I'm tempted to stay. The conch shell feels warm and heavy in my palm, and uneven, like somethin' sloshing 'round inside it. I toss the shell and Miz Lucy's keys over my shoulder as I walk back toward Shirl. Hear a clink and a crack. Don't even look back.

"You don't haf' t' push," Shirl sniffs. I do, anyway.

VI

VidaMae walks heavily through the late afternoon, heart and womb full up, leaving tracks in the softened tar and dirt past the road to the docks, all the way down to sandy curve of deserted beach. White foam washes over metal slats threaded with leather straps and a wheelchair abandoned on its side. VidaMae kicks off her shoes and walks right into the water, relishing its coolness against her ankles, her thighs; shedding her blue jacket and white blouse now soaked and indistinguishable from water and foam.

Mama!

Mama's here.

"Mama's sorry. Ty? Precious? Mama's so very sorry."

I know, Mama. I know, Tyco, mannish, comforting.

VidaMae hears singing from far off, and down deep, but can't make out the words. "Shirl?" She calls. "Baby girl?" VidaMae dives in the direction of the song, glimpses a flash of silver scales and landlocked legs that have found their purpose, surfaces smiling with her hair streaming and shell-encrusted, water droplets beading like pearls, the blue drawstring pants drifting off below.

Look at me, Mama. Look! Precious arcs up out of the water, splashing like a dolphin, naked, glistening brown, and laughing. VidaMae laughs, too. Baby boy! He wheels and lunges, a bloody raw stump mudpuppy with a screaming mouth and glistening teeth. *See me, Mama? See me? SEE ME???*

"I see you. Come here." VidaMae leans into the rending embrace of soft, angry flipper arms. Precious' teeth tear at her breasts; blood flows like milk or the tears leaking from the corners of VidaMae's eyes, brine dissolving in brine. Shirl's voice is closer now, crooning in VidaMae's ears as rough scales abrade her skin, claws and pincers grasp, pierce, rip away flesh to make space for the anemones and seaweed to root. VidaMae closes her eyes, turns her pain into a harmony hummed deep in her chest, rocks in wave rhythm as she pulls her babies close.

I love you, Mama. VidaMae squints up into Tyco's eyes. The sun behind him makes a halo of light around his wet curls. His lips are rounded, protuberant. VidaMae raises her chin, offers her face fully to jellyfish stingray kisses, poisonous and sweet. Tentacles wrap around her, attaching with persistent suction. VidaMae clamps her legs together and they fuse, lengthen, her feet turning outward, expanding and unfurling like wings. VidaMae slaps her broad tail against the water's surface, sending up a shower of sparkling droplets. Laughing, she sweeps her children into a crushing embrace and dives them down together, moving with the tides, streaming life in her wake.

VII

I'm left here to wait. Like I say, I'm good at it.

The sun is a big orange ball falling down behind the water. Mr. Briscoe's boat is a grey-blue silhouette against a sky the color of ripening peaches. The chug-chug of its motor makes its own kind of music, but I can still hear Mama and Shirl singing.

I smile, picturing Miz Lucy's store unminded, my towel folded neatly on the red plastic couch, the blades on the black metal fan and the busted clock spinning to themselves; Miz Lucy coming along, finally, to find the key ring and the cracked shell on the steps. For a minute, I swear I smell them nasty Lucky Strikes. Then a quick breeze fills my nose with the smells of machine oil, salt and sea flesh.

I see my boys on deck, pullin' in the nets, workin' hard. I wave just in case they can see me. Glory and Honor, comin'.

SALT BABY

NANNA ÁRNADÓTTIR

The Fishwife crouched over Salt Baby, hands sinking into the straw mattress. Her engorged breasts swung like pendulums, brushing the infant's lips. The milk had come down, forming sweet creamy droplets that clung to her nipples. Salt Baby rooted and snorted, poking at the Fishwife's teats. She suckled at one dark nipple, then the other. But she was not satisfied.

The Fishwife looked about the dark cavernous badstofa where she and her husband The Fisherman slept, ate, and kept company. Perhaps she might see some sign and know what to do. She gazed at her spindle and basket of wool crammed in the corner, at the blackened hearth, over which hung glass floats attached to gill nets awaiting their next trip to the sea. She listened for the waves lapping the shore outside the shack. But no solution, no vision came to her.

"What now?" asked The Fisherman, shoving a pinch of tobacco under his lips. His teeth were stained, and he had only a few oily hairs left on his head. He sat repairing a net in their only chair, set at the end of the bed. His face was lit by a single oil lamp, ruddy and textured as a cliffside, worn by wind and winter. "She's hungry, sure enough."

The Fishwife's bosom sagged, as sad as she, that Salt Baby couldn't suckle. "She doesn't like the milk. I suppose it must be sour, at my age."

That very morning, the couple had created their Baby from salt harvested from the sea. They scooped mounds of it from a sack, pouring it onto the table. They moulded the child's nose, toes, and spindly bow legs. They made her in the image of their friends' babies, born decades ago. Then, all things had seemed possible. But time passed too swiftly, and the pair were never blessed with a child of their own.

Standing over Salt Baby's inanimate, salt-white body, the couple studied their handiwork. They acknowledged the magnitude of their want, running their fingers over her face. Even after all these years, they still longed for a child. Too shy to share their joy openly with one another, they smiled inwardly as they gazed at Salt Baby. Their tears bathed her little face. The Fisherman wiped his wife's withered cheeks with his calloused hands and she returned his gesture. "Enough of that," she said, and he grunted in agreement. They straightened their backs to return to Practical Matters. But Salt Baby stirred, shuddering in the cold. She gasped to breathe yet made no sound. Her face twisted in pain, shocked at entering life, like any new-born.

"The tears!" The Fishwife flopped her breasts back into her shirt, tucking them away. She re-swaddled Salt Baby in the woolen blanket she'd knitted especially for her and cradled her. Gazing down at Salt Baby, The Fishwife - moved by her own love for the child - began to cry. Tear-drops slid down her cheeks. She let them drip into Salt Baby's heart-shaped mouth. Salt Baby snorted and purred, so the Fishwife continued weeping into the child's mouth. Satisfied at last, the little one slipped into sleep.

"Jæja," The Fisherman said. Well now.

#

Fed by her parents' sweat and tears Salt Baby grew into a charming young Salt Girl, the pride of the village. A good omen. A gift from the sea. With no pupils, she could not see, so a retired sheep dog was tasked with keeping her safe and taking her from place to place. Dog had a shaggy fur coat, brown as dirt, white as snow. Above his soft eyes, two black markings gave him a look of surprise.

Salt Girl's birth brought a time of abundance, seasons upon seasons of great hauls. For that reason, she was welcomed into any home. She was even allowed to explore the creaking wooden ships docked in the harbour and sit with the women weaving new nets. She was mute but kind and unimposing, with her quiet good humour and her pleasant white face, with skin the texture of sand and salt.

Drifting through the harbour one afternoon, Salt Girl found rows of crates stacked high. She felt the rough splintered wood of the crates, slipping her hands about among the fish packed tightly inside. Haddocks with their sharp pointy fins, lumpy flat flounders, and wide mouthed monkfish with needle teeth slithered through her fingers. Their eyes were slimy, like soft-boiled eggs. Salt Girl moved from crate to crate, plunging her hands into each one. From the cold sea water coating the fish, she drew salt to help her grow.

Finding the thread of The Fisherman's scent, Dog huffed and snuffed, tugging at his leash to pull Salt Girl along. Salt Girl smiled, understanding without words. She allowed herself to be dragged up the plank to her father's trawler.

Seeing his daughter, The Fisherman knelt, opening his ropy arms wide. His oiled canvas trousers creaked, and his fleece-lined rubber boots squealed against the deck. Salt Girl wriggled happily in The Fisherman's embrace. His beard tickled her face. The Fisherman kissed her cheeks. Once. Twice. Three times.

He reeked of chum and wet, coiled ropes; sweat and sweet, rich tobacco; of sour old age and robust tenacity. But Salt Girl couldn't smell him any more than she could see him. She could only feel the warmth of his breath and the steadiness of his heart beating in his chest, thudding against hers. Ba-Boom. Ba-Boom. Ba-Boom.

#

When the Fisherman's trawler was lost at sea, The Fishwife locked the doors and sank into her loss. Endless tears poured from her eyes. She cried until her head pounded. She cried until she floated in a pool of her own grief. Dog paddled around the badstofa, straining to keep his head above the rising water. As always, his little eyebrows showed his surprise.

Salt Girl stood on the single, wood chair, ankle deep in the lagoon of her mother's bereavement. She used the leash to help Dog swim to her, then grabbed him tight.

With Dog out of immediate danger, Salt Girl's panic gave way to understanding. The Fisherman would not come home after all.

She became untethered from herself, began disintegrating. The Fishwife, afloat in the pool of her tears, finally took stock of her surroundings.

Her spindle, baskets, and oil lamp floated about, bumping the walls. Salt Girl's legs melted away, and the rest of her threatened to follow. In her tired arms, Dog wagged his damp tail slowly, side to side, dipping closer to the water with each heavy swing.

Dread beat in The Fishwife's throat. She struggled to find her footing, staggering, splashing. The lake of her mourning reached her waist. The Fishwife ignored the painful bones grinding in her old feet, and waded to Salt Girl, wrapping her arms around her daughter. She was smothered in Dog's muggy fur. "Please," The Fishwife pleaded. "Don't leave me, child. Don't be foolish now, don't die!"

Salt Girl's knotted forehead relaxed, the forcefulness of her mother's embrace reassuring her. She gripped the Fishwife's sleeve, nodding to Dog and handing him over. Hands freed, she felt for what was left of her body, then ran salt-white fingers over The Fishwife's puckered face. She opened her mouth and sucked, drank down gallons of her mother's tears. She grew and grew, salt crystallizing, forming a grown woman before The Fishwife's eyes - a fine woman, a Salt Woman. She had long salt legs, heavy salt breasts. On her soft, round belly, she had a little dent where a navel might have been.

The Fishwife stumbled backwards until she hit the wall. "Jæja," she croaked, as salt woman finished forming. Her voice was hoarse with surprise. "Did you see that, Dog?"

He snuffled in reply.

The spindle lay on its side near the door. The oil lamp lolled on the wet bed. Dawn light streamed into the room through the small circular window, bouncing off wet surfaces.

Salt Woman stretched out an arm, searching the air for her mother, but found only the chair. The Fishwife put Dog on the floor and grabbed her daughter's hand. She was surprised at the strength in Salt Woman's grasp. Her arthritic joints melted in her daughter's strong arms. Her heartbeat slowed in her chest. Ba-boom... Ba-Boom... Ba-Boom. Salt Woman stroked her mother's thinning white hair and kissed the top of her head. Slipping an arm around the weary, limping Fishwife, she wandered into the early morning, Dog shuffling behind them.

Knowing her way after years of roaming the village, Salt Baby led Mother and Dog through stacks of rough-hewn fish crates and dull metal anchors bumpy with barnacles, down to the black sand beach. Fat kelp squelched under their feet, popping like bubbles, spilling brackish water on sand. The sea wind whipped them, cutting the flesh of the Fishwife's withered cheeks. Shivering in her wet clothes, she fell to her knees. Salt Woman caressed her mother's face, and the Fishwife kissed her briny palms. Once. Twice. Three times. "Jæja," the old woman sighed. Well now. "That's enough of that."

#

Salt Woman picked up her mother's body easily. Beside her, Dog panted, the heat of his breath rising over her naked thighs like waves. She strode to the water's edge. The tide was meek, rolling in and out, gently. She dropped the leash and nudged Dog's head lovingly with her hip before wading into the sea.

The water didn't bother her, but Dog gasped as he followed her past the breakers. Trembling, he paddled beside her until his heart gave out. The further out to sea Salt Woman swam, the lighter her mother's corpse became. She held on as long as she could, Dog and The Fishwife floating beside her. She was not afraid. She was not cold. She heard nothing. Saw nothing. Smelled nothing. But she remembered.

Dwindling, melting, returning to frothing seafoam, Salt Woman's limbs dissolved. An old couple's wish bobbed up and down in the rhythmic grey waves. The family had surrendered themselves to the sea. A favour repaid. Ba-Boom. Ba-Boom. Ba-Boom.

JUNIPER'S SONG

MARIE VIBBERT

It was in the asteroid field we call Dinner's Leavings, in our fourth year without a whale singer, that a stranger came into our midst.

Dinner's Leavings was not a good place. It was too far from its star to be useful, and the planets near it had a habit of war, but we had traveled long in cold space from more prosperous grounds and needed to rest before we moved on again. The whales were grumpy, bumping noses and not forming an orderly pod. We had no singer to calm them. The tribe of Ginevra promised us an apprentice singer but we had no rendezvous planned. I hoped she would be a woman, and beautiful, and fond of short men with star-lines growing early around their eyes from too much time in the unfiltered light of different suns.

My name is Jacques. I am a herdsman. I was minding the inward edge of the pod, keeping them from wandering deeper into the system, which of course they wanted to do. They were hungry from the scarce grazing of interstellar space. I had to maneuver up, down, side to side, firing the small jets on my herdsman's suit, to keep in front of them. Lillian, one of our largest whales, had calved three times that year and was tireless in seeking a weakness in my guard.

A shadow appeared on Lillian's side. I looked up to see a ship low above me. It was not a tribal ship. It's often that way in space: stillness for ages and then sudden disaster. I had my back in-system; the ship must have come from there. The whales scattered out-system. I had to leave the inconsiderate spacecraft for others to deal with and chase after my herd. I thought nothing more of it, except to curse the system-dwellers and their ways.

Old Martin was the last caught, despite his advanced age. I found him behind a far-flung asteroid, green with agitation and trembling with his song, which I could not hear, nor, alas, answer. There is no sound in space, and only whale singers can hear the whale song despite this. The other whales would be picking up his tune and his agitation. I stroked his side and extended my staff until it was long enough to reach his tail. Martin was a biddable beast and knew to move in the direction I urged him. Moving a large whale alone is a beautiful, meditative task. Up close, their markings become mysterious, like the surface of a planet.

A glint of light shone from the surface of the asteroid behind Martin. I paused in my urgings to take a look. Martin would not wander far, now that he was no longer frightened, and a sparkle like that could mean wealth for the tribe.

It was the spacecraft. It had landed on the asteroid, and none too well, for a plume of atmosphere was leaking from it. I realized Martin had not been merely hiding behind the asteroid; he had been snacking on the free oxygen.

I was irritated with the stranger, but I went to see if he or she were alive and could be rescued. I did not expect, as soon as my hand touched the rocky surface, to have a gun pointed at my face.

She was in a slender environment suit, of a sort we do not have the means to make, and her helmet was completely clear, giving her an excellent field of vision. Her left hand clutched the opposite side of her torso, and her right held the gun, which was, frankly, the feature I concentrated on the most. Her lips moved. A pause, and she spoke again, and then the signal came through on a band my suit could pick up. She spoke in two dissimilar languages before speaking a third time in the parlance of the herdsmen.

"Who what intent?"

"My whale found your craft." I pointed to Martin; though a whale is not a thing one can call one's own, it was easy shorthand.

Her eyes widened and her jaw slackened. She lowered her gun. "Good. It is good. Help."

"Are there others?" I gestured toward her craft. She shook her head. I kicked off toward the craft anyway. There would surely be something I could take.

"Leave it," she said. "Please. Us leave now quickly fast."

She held onto me and I carried us to Martin. She leaned forward as though it would speed us, but once we were in the whale shadow, she relaxed. She was strong, holding onto me with only her muscle strength—there were no hooks or anchors attached to her suit. She must have been a fearless person. After a moment, she leaned away from me, trusting one hand to keep us attached, to run the other over Martin's flank.

When we approached the pod, Martin took off, speeding his return to his family, color flashing happily, song evident in his movement. The whales did their dance of trouble having been passed safely. I collapsed my staff to its carrying size and slipped it into its pocket on my arm. I then held onto the stranger with both hands. It seemed presumptuous, like I had taken her to dance without permission, but she eased the strength of her grip on my arm and let me carry her by her waist.

I brought her to the home-ship. We landed in the large guest airlock, for she was a stranger. I alerted the elders that I had rescued a crashed outsider, and sent the co-ordinates back to her ship, which could make valuable salvage.

She watched me remove my herdsman's suit, but did not release her helmet nor crack any seal on her own suit. Her left hand finally dropped from her side. In the lights of the airlock I could see bright rubies of crystallized blood. Still, she stood tall and ready like a person uninjured. Her gun rested at her hip. I did not like bringing an armed stranger into the home-ship, but she did not react to my entreaties to remove the weapon, pretending not to understand me.

She spoke well enough when the protectors met us inside the airlock. "I want sanctuary," she said. "I am a friend."

And so she was taken to the elders, and I was not privy to their conversation, but it must have gone well because she came out of the elder chamber and approached me directly. "Thank you," she said. "Where sleep I?"

I took her to the quarters for those without children, where I stayed as well. No one had ever liked the pallet by the intake ducts because of the draft, and so it was empty for her. She sat down and opened her suit by an almost invisible seam in the neck. It parted smoothly, like unseen razors were cutting it. Her skin was mottled with purple and red along her left side, and the suit stuck to her wound. "Do you have..." she mimed scissoring with her right hand. I nodded and went to fetch a healer.

When Ealdred, our chief healer, reached for her side, she flinched. "No," she said. And after a stream of outsider language, she added, "I do. Me."

Ealdred sat back. "Oh, it's like that, is it?" He handed her the surgical scissors. "Let me know when you've had enough."

It must have hurt terribly, but she cut her flesh to save the suit and pulled it away bathed in fresh blood. Free of her garment, she handed the scissors back. "Cloth?" she asked.

Ealdred took over, pushing aside her objections with a gentle wave of his hand. There are tricks to the healer's art, like the tricks to guiding whales. He knew when to turn aside and when to stand firm. The stranger let him clean and bandage her wound.

I fetched her a gown of my sister's which was in need of mending but better than nothing. The stranger did not know what to do with the shoulder-drape and I had to set it for her.

We gave her broth to drink and expected her to sleep, but she sat against the wall at the head of the pallet, watching us warily.

"Please rest. You are safe," I said.

She laughed without humor and her gaze turned harder. "They will come. We need leave."

"You are safe," I repeated.

After a long time, she blinked. She touched her own chest. "Juniper," she said.

Juniper is a scent, a flavor, and a wood. I was confused. "You need medicine?"

"I Juniper," she said and patted her chest.

It was not a hand extended in friendship, nor did she put off her gun, but she gave me the gift of her name first. "Jacques," I said.

"Jox," she said.

My sister, Colette, pushed through the gathered protectors. She was still in her environment suit. "Ships are coming from in-system," she said. "And I hear we have a guest." She looked at Juniper as one might observe a weak point in the ship's hull. "That's my dress."

"You've not worn it since it was torn."

"I'd have mended it. I've few enough." She shook her head. "At least you got the shoulder-drape right, man that you are, but a stranger should not be in family-dress at all. Strangers are to be delivered to their own people, hopefully for a reward."

"Talk with her and make her less of a stranger."

Colette turned her helmet in her hands. "I have to go straight back out, to salvage her ship. You talk to her, if it means so much, but hold your heart, brother; she'll be gone ere tomorrow."

Juniper watched us with amusement. I did not know how much of our conversation she understood.

As Colette had warned, other strangers came, numerous larger craft, looking for Juniper. They saw our crew dismantling her ship and asked where she was. Eldest Alys told them, "We do not salvage the dead," and nothing more.

The whales were moving chaotically, wanting to go in-system, wanting to kiss the nutrients off the stranger's hulls. They bumped into each other and trembled and flashed every color. I had to go out again, all the herdsmen were needed. At least the stranger ships had dragged invisible shrouds of atmosphere with them, rich detritus from in-system.

Colette radioed me the news that Juniper's ship had food-packs and an oxygen generator and good solar cloth. Not long after, I saw our sails extending, like a spider stretching her legs one at a time. The repair crews eagerly took advantage of our windfall and our stagnation.

It was a wearying, endless night. We took spells resting in the herdsmen's airlock. But when Juniper came out, I was instantly awake and alert. She wore a herdsman's harness over her black suit. A thick patch of our tribe-fabric covered the rent in her side. I did not pause to tell my companions I was moving from my spot, but flew directly to her.

"Jox. I want see whales," she said.

"Come with me and I will show you," I said.

She followed me back to my post. Guy, the senior herdsman, sent me a few words concerning my behavior, but I hardly heard them. I took Juniper to Lillian. The calves always stayed near to their mother's tail, and it was a sure way to be close to more than one whale at a time.

"Your whales sing," she said, touching Lillian's side.

I stared at her. She frowned at me through her glass helmet. "Did I not speak correct?"

"No. Yes. You spoke well. They sing, but you should not be able to hear them."

"They sing in microwaves. Your radio... no hear?"

"Only the whale singers can hear and transmit whale song, and they know the songs and their meanings."

She laughed and spoke something in her own language, quick and staccato. She then said, "Someone lies. Holds power. Waves don't need special people, only proper radio."

I didn't like what she implied. "Let me show you how we tell the whales to move." I extended my staff to its full length, and that interested her. She asked to try it herself.

She was studious and careful. Soon she had Lillian turning in circles. She collapsed the staff and extended it again to half-length. "This is... weapon, but not weapon."

"It is not a weapon," I said, uncertain of her meaning.

"Why do you not... give... me give..." she groaned. "Them me give?"

"Give you up?"

She nodded.

"It is not our concern." She turned, confusion clear on her face. "We do not care what world-dwellers want."

"But... I may do bad things."

"You wear a weapon. This bothers us. But if one of our own were adrift, we would want a stranger to see them to safety, so that is what we do."

She flew away from me, toward one of Lillian's calves, the larger one. She tapped her tail and urged her back to the in-herd side of her mother. "Why this whale is red?"

"She is happy," I said. "She thinks you are another calf, playing a game." Juniper stroked her side and the young one spun around to expose her belly.

"The young are often red," I said. "When she survives her third year, we will name her. I think this one should be called 'Joy'."

"Color is always..." she waved my staff impatiently. "Happy sad?"

"Moods? Some of it. But they also turn greener when close to a sun, for nourishment. And they express their mood in motion, too. They dance frustration."

I fired my jets, making an agitated little sidestep to demonstrate. She copied it, and then the whales near us did as well. The young one turned a loop, still thinking this was a game. Juniper and the calf rolled in tandem, and Juniper laughed.

She flew in front of me, so we could see each other's faces. "These animals... value much. The milk and... um... scent. We value. Not as you value. I—"

One of the stranger ships came closer, a shadow over us, and she halted. She let out a slow breath, brows knit in frustration. Without looking toward the ships, she handed my staff back to me and flew calmly back to the visitors' airlock.

I had rescued Juniper; I had flown across distance with her arm around my waist, but I could not follow her.

Some hours into the next day, when the whales accepted the strangers and we had at last been released to our normal work schedule, the elders announced that the whales were fortified enough to withstand another journey. We would head to the Shining Twins system, which was not very far, and closer to where Ginevra's tribe was currently grazing. Everyone was pleased with this announcement, because Shining Twins had no human colony around it, and we would be able to bask in the fullest light of its suns without risking some property line. We were all feeling restless and cramped under the watch of the stranger ships. The elders broadcast our intention to leave.

The stranger ships shifted, more of them on our out-system side now.

"We will not allow you to leave the system. You have a dangerous fugitive on board," they said. "You will turn her over or we will open fire."

Eldest Alys called a full-family council in the great chamber where meals are eaten. Her white hair was disordered and she fidgeted with a repair in her shoulder-drape. "Never in all my years has someone threatened to fire on a home ship for any reason."

All eyes in the great chamber turned to Juniper, who sat quietly in the circle of traders. She had gotten better at hanging her shoulder-drape. She raised her eyes. "I will go," she said.

We had not asked, and would not have asked, but neither did we argue against it. I wanted to, but what would I say?

In the echoing silence, Juniper stood. "I go. Tell them that it is me who goes, myself. I ask to keep this dress, and for a herdsman's staff. I will go."

Her speaking had improved, but I did not feel pride in her but jealous of the traders with whom she had practiced.

The elders conferred quietly in their circle. Alys turned to face the rest of us and nodded. "The elders approve if the tribe approves."

Around the room, hands rose in the signal of assent. I covered my face in dissent, but it was not a decision that required unanimous approval, and most were eager to put world-dwellers with world-dwellers.

I gave Juniper my staff before anyone else could offer. I kept it always with me, as herdsmen do. She smiled at me, then. It made my heart ache.

"Thank you," she said.

"Don't go," I said, foolishly, and took her wrist as she turned to leave.

Her expression changed instantly to that of a warrior and I felt a stab of fear. But she smiled again, and lifted my hand from her arm. "I will give staff back," she said. "Jacques."

"I don't care about the staff," I said.

She turned her back to me and was gone.

The hour was arranged for her leaving. I went to be alone with the whales. The youngest of Lillian's calves was small enough that you could hold her, one half of her circumference, at least, in your arms, and I did so, taking comfort from the gentle motions of the whale as I hung from her and watched the stranger ships. Juniper would leave from the family airlock, as a parting honor for her sacrifice. Two traders would go with her, carrying ambergris perfumes, milk, and jewelry made from wreckage. We took all opportunities for trade, even ones as tenuous as this.

The four figures floated away. Juniper was hard to see in her skinny black suit next to the bulky, grey-tan suits of our people. They became one little rock of grey as they neared the stranger ships.

The calf was restless beside me. She bucked. I did not have my staff to direct her. She lunged, she flew, and all I could do was hold on.

The entire pod was racing toward the stranger ships, leaving the other herdsmen behind.

Their color was vibrant, fluctuating joy-resolve-protect, their tails moving in time. Though I could not hear it in the vacuum of space, not without a whale singer's special gift, I knew: They were singing in unison. I had never seen that deep blue flash with red and purple before. What were they singing?

Juniper extended the herdsman's staff. The whales fanned out around the stranger ship and our radios echoed with the confusion and displeasure of their crews. Juniper met our largest whale, Old Martin, and took hold of his tail, letting him pull her to the front of the ship. I heard her shouting in her own language, loud on my radio.

The whales danced to her direction. They lay against the ships' airlocks, closing them off. I floated, still with shock. Juniper was singing the whales.

Juniper placed my staff against a particular spot on the hull and extended it, inward. The rending of metal was silent but clear. She twisted the staff and the panel drifted away. Escaping atmosphere blurred around her. She entered the ship of her people on her own terms and in a place of her choosing.

Her broken words came back to me. Weapon. Was her admiration of the whales, likewise, just as tools for her plan?

I waited with the traders outside the stranger ship, unsure what to do, until Juniper sent us a message. "Leave! Go!"

The whales turned toward home-ship. I had to rush to catch hold of Joy so I could ride her. After us came the traders, still laden with their wares.

"But what must we do?" The traders asked.

"Come in," sent Elder Alys. "The strangers will signal if they require us, and this day has been long enough."

"We don't know if Juniper is still alive!" I said. "She may need our help!"

"She is in the world-dweller's ship. She is beyond our reach," Alys said.

From the stranger's ships we saw a bright point of light expand to engulf all of them. The sphere of light dissipated, leaving behind twisted remains of metal, like a popped bubble. I looked in alarm to my fellow herdsmen, but they only shook their heads. It was a matter for strangers, and not for us to know.

I cried, before my sleep, and Colette came and slept with her arm over me like when we were children.

When I woke, everyone was in motion; the home ship was in motion.

I joined the herdsmen, driving the whales ahead. I looked back at the system of Dinner's Leavings, at the pieces of stranger ship hanging in the sun like sequins.

We turned our backs to the light and urged the whales on. After so long in the same picked-clean space, the whales were eager to go.

I was glad for the work and solitude. I could not turn my thoughts away as easily as my back. I should have been angry, horrified at the terrible wrong of destroying a ship—had Juniper done it? With our tools and whales? Or had the strangers caused their own destruction somehow?

All I cared was if Juniper still existed, somewhere in the darkness behind us, and if so, did her smile still catch the light of that sun?

Two days into our run, we were hailed by a trading vessel, which sparked talk. It was unusual to find at this point in a journey, and the vessel itself was unusual. No bigger than an out-ship, it could have no large cargo and no crew over five persons. Still, trade in small things is still trade. The rendezvous was set for another day ahead, along our path to Shining Twins.

Though we were early in our time between systems, there would still be a small festival for trade. We could not feast, not knowing if our provisions would see us all the way, but we could dress in our best and dab perfumes and sing the festival songs.

The cheer was false to me, but I let Colette drag me through it. She tore up an old wall hanging to make new leg-wrappings for me. I stood before the polished wall as she adjusted them.

"You are handsome enough now," she said, tying my tunic a little too tight, "that I should have a niece or a nephew by the time we reach Shining Twins."

"You have been beautiful for years," I countered, "And where are mine?"

My eye caught a figure in black behind my reflection. The figure walked toward us, and still I could not move. I could not move because I recognized her and her sleek suit.

Juniper smiled and held out my staff. "I say I return," she said.

Not thinking, I pushed past Colette and wrapped my arms around Juniper. She stiffened a moment, but then her arms were firm and strong around my own. When we parted she pressed my staff into my palm.

"Thank you for staff."

"Stay," I said, holding the staff with both hands.

"I... do bad things." She gestured to the side, as people do to indicate the past.

"You destroyed the stranger's ship."

"More. Before. I do bad things."

"They are forgiven."

There was a soft look on her face, so tired and grateful. I dared reach for her, and she leaned into my touch, as though she needed support to stand.

"Stay," I said.

"Foolish." She glanced shyly around. "But... you need a whale singer?"

And so it was when we entered the system of Shining Twins, with a woman no longer a stranger in our midst, that we began the first year of Juniper's Song.

PORTAL

MATEO HINOJOSA

Author's Note

In the Andes, we celebrate the dead each year on November 1st. Families gather to honor and feed their ancestors with food, song, and stories. Today, I invite my ancestor Puquio to take part in healing our world through story. I've been dreaming about her, and about her life between worlds in the 1500s. I like to think that she dreamt—or perhaps even dreams—of me, and of us.

A *puquio* is step-well, a spiral staircase leading underground, where it connects with vast networks of subterranean aqueducts. This technology was largely lost when the Andean world was upended.

The world is being turned upside down once again. Teachers in Bolivia have told me that the last major *pachakuti*—when the world is inverted, shaken to its core, utterly transformed—was 500 years ago, right when my ancestor Puquio lived. They say we are now living through another pachakuti. When the glaciers on the mountains finish melting, they say, this world will end. I believe them.

This story is set 500 years in the future, during the next pachakuti. From this present, I invoke my ancestor into this future time, to ask for guidance in what we need to build now to survive and maybe even—we might dare to dream—thrive.

Mateo Hinojosa
November 1st
Ohlone Territory
Turtle Island

Portal

Puquio opened her eyes in the darkness. She hadn't been sleeping for well over an hour, her mind wrapped in visions of the day to come, her arms draped awkwardly around Roa's feverish body. On the other side of her fitfully dreaming granddaughter, Agapito slept soundly, his deep breath even and calming. *Chachawarmi… everything balances out. He rests as I stay wide awake imagining dreams*, she thought with just a tinge of bitterness. Just enough bitterness, she hoped, to make it all more digestible.

Through their one-room home's skylight, the bioluminescence of the undermountain's roof began to glow dimly as the veins of inti algae channeled the sunlight from the mountain's surface. Puquio sighed, knowing that this was her last moment of stillness before eternities of movement stretching out before her. She gazed for a moment on the networks of branching and braided warm yellow filaments as they lit up, undulating, brightening by the moment. She closed her eyes again and imagined the visible structure of woven energy flows that she knew was repeated inside, on the nanoscale: pathways for the algae to swim their daily life cycle between light outside and clean, humid air inside. She visualized herself leaping into one of the luminous tributaries, swimming through the currents. She did a little imaginary backflip just for kicks. *If you can dream it…* she thought, smiling.

"Is it time?" Agapito whispered. She opened her eyes, startled as she often was at his uncanny ability to keep time, even in sleep. In response, she carefully kissed Roa's 13-moon-young head fuzz, extracted herself from the baby's embrace, and rolled away and out from under the soft warmth of the alpaca furs. She walked around the bed and leaned down to wrap her arms around Agapito. They held each other tightly, grounding themselves in each others' bodies before they flew separately into the day's storms.

30 of my 54 years together, Puquio thought. *Feels like a single moon. This body is not so very old, not compared to all the lives I've lived in it.* She walked over to the oneirogram on the bedside table and picked it up in her left hand. The three bands of minerals each had their own temperature.

The top tiger eye projection band was cold; the middle blue control quartz band was cool, neutral; and the bottom deep green andesite recording band pulsed warm with the night's activity. With her right hand she grazed her fingers over the control crystal, and the projection band hummed to life, filling the air above it with colorful images, landscapes, figures. She zipped through the holo of her latest dreamed life. She remembered the night's activities perfectly—the flights, songs, dances, meditations, and ur-memories—but she wanted to make sure the machine was functioning perfectly. Even with the sound off, she saw there were no glitches, no blur, no interference from other dreamwaves, her night's lucid dream vividly displayed. *This might just work,* she thought, *and these decades of preparation won't have been for nothing.*

She struck a match and lit a fresh stick of palo santo, letting the smoke rise from the resinous wood, praying a silent blessing as the solidity of the wood—grown in real above-ground soil—turned to smoke. She blew on the ember, sending some wisps of the blessings to Roa and Agapito, some to Pachamama, some to Tata Cielo far above the undermountain, some to the mountain itself as their home and guardian. Then she deactivated the oneirogram, which purred to silence.

She braided her hair with her special occasion tassels, which were her mother's—who received them from *her* mother. She had to remind herself that she wasn't sure how many generations of women had worn these llama hair pendants as adornment and reminder of the duty of a weaver. As she wove the sections back and forth into two long braids, she noted more bright streaks of age in her night-black hair. Next, she slipped into her favorite boots, which she had recently resoled for the umpteenth time. The uppers of the boots were of real Spanish leather, ancient and wonderfully worn, their skin still alive, pliable and breathing from the cuerophilic biota she had woven into their tissue. She looked at herself in the mirror, and flexed her feet into place, as she had seen her father do with these same boots. *Chachawarmi,* she thought again. *They are still with me. From tip to toe... as above, so below.*

She walked to the door. She paused in the threshold and looked back at Roa, who stirred, whimpered. *She won't last long now*—the thought came unbidden. Puquio felt her stomach clench, her teeth begin to grind. Agapito nodded to her, and hummed a three-note tune: the first line of the Weaver's Vow. Breathing deeply, willing her body and mind to release, she smiled at him in gratitude, then opened the door and walked out.

≈ ≈ ≈

The Great Hall of the Ayllu, her community, was stirring to life. At one side of the central plaza, the large Bioweaving Dome was the one space already in full activity, and it had been humming for hours already. As they put the final touches on the day's community food bundles, the smell of roast potato, toasted kañawa and stewed corn met Puquio as she walked up. Her stomach grumbled—she had fasted 3 days now, in preparation, and would not eat for another day yet. She had spent much of her life in the Dome, as had much of her lineage of weavers on her mother's side; she had cooked in the food side of the Dome for only 9 years before she proved herself capable to learn bioweaving, which was the fastest anyone had ever advanced. It was a good thing, too; with all the traditionalists questioning her half-breed lineage, she had to be better, quicker than anyone else just to be allowed to stay. The painstaking crafting and cultivating of layer after layer of terraced nanoscapes for life to grow was a joy to her, and she built medicinescapes for three decades. Then her daughter, Roa's mother, died of the Fevers.

That was when she moved from weaving medicines to weaving doors into dreams. And now, here she was, on her way to step through doors no one had ever even seen before, for Roa's sake.

So now she walked past the bioweavers with just a quick peek through the window to see a handful of the masters busy at their luminous looms, weaving projected holos of infinitesimally small worlds, cultivating beauty and usefulness. They all knew her mission today, and had almost all already given their blessings and support—or asked her to assist in some last-minute task. She left before they might see her, stepping onto the pathway that led winding away from their village in Uju Pacha, here where they dwelled, up towards Kay Pacha: the middle world they had left behind, the world they were now dreaming of reclaiming.

The walk was fragrant, full of muña in flower, and she breathed in the sweet scent to settle and center herself as she climbed. The terraced undermountain hillsides of Uju Pacha were full of food and medicines, animals and plants. They had co-evolved with the Ayllu. She wondered at all her ancestors had managed to achieve with the help of their plant and animal relatives and the apus, the spirits of the mountains. *Could it be,* Puquio thought, *that just as we nurtured and developed and cultivated millions of generations of alpacas to give us warmth, and countless generations of inti algae to give us light, could it be that we have been cultivated by the mountain to keep its icy heart beating?*

It still amazed her to see all they had managed to preserve, to defend from the pillaging and chaos by making their land above appear worthless and their water appear non-existent. Puquio grimaced as she remembered Kay Pacha from her travels, as she and her companions pretended to be fools wandering with insane religion, a few more of the dumb starving masses, all while eating the tightly knotted nanonutrition of dense almost-nothings which bloomed and expanded in their bellies. With these they travelled great distances healthily, undetected by gov or corp. Foraging at the dumps, they found the metals they needed to weld their nanotek for visioning and cultivating back home. And even this was not enough, for the Fevers wracking the world above were here below, too. Puquio herself had almost died during her last bout. She knew they needed a portal to the world between and within all worlds; a portal they could enter together; a portal from which they could return with allies. And so she built one.

She stopped, suddenly, realizing how far her mind had strayed from here and now. This distraction could be deadly where she was headed, and she was distressed to notice it. She had gone into the dreamworld many times alone, had entered her own dreambody, and even there generally she felt her own presence in space with the vivid intensity of a journey with Grandfather Achuma's medicine. When she was fully present, she could fly and float along the rivers of her own energy, the pulsing memories of old healing songs, and even unlock ancestral knowledge long-forgotten, hidden deep inside her own bones. But the few times she had entered her dreambody uncentered, the journey had been chaotic, dangerous, terrifying. She'd almost lost her mind once. She had blundered into a kamasal flow full of ancestral memories of unimaginable horror. Rape, genocide, incest, and rage had overwhelmed her, and she'd barely found the nodal valve that allowed her to redirect the ur-memories back into contained isolation.

That nightmre had been a gift: now she knew how the repressed trauma was stored, and that it might be redirected. She knew she could not do it alone—she would need her community. Today she could not risk a careless blunder—she needed full presence now.

Puquio's stomach clenched, her knees weakened. *I'm not ready. I'm not worthy.* Just as she was beginning to gasp under the weight of fear and anxiety, just as her panic felt like it was turning to fever, a single drop of water landed on her forehead. She looked up, holding her breath. The dripping inti algae looked back at her, as it drew liquid sustenance from the rivulets running down the undermountain's patchwork stone roof. Puquio's eyes followed these rivulets up, all the way to their source: the glacier at the very top of Uju Pacha. She watched the ice send down its mineral-rich, life-giving essence. She felt her own essence well up in her eyes, then spill down her cheeks. *That any of this exists at all is a miracle. That miracle won't be the last.*

She looked down now and saw her tears land on mosses at her feet, where she stood on one of the wide stair-step terraces. The mosses covered ancient stones that had been crafted into the terrace's walls, and their bright green almost glowed on top of the slate. Single-cell mosses had taught humans to be small, the value of humility and lowliness, hiddenness, how to cultivate microscopic environments, how to drill their homes into stone with microexplosions. The Ayllu, and indeed all the people, owed their very survival to the mosses. *This won't be the last miracle.* Puquio sank down. She touched her fingertips—the same color as the earth—to her tears, and blessed the moss with a soft caress of her wet fingertips.

When her breath had returned to steady, Puquio stood up again and continued walking. As she walked, she passed community members working the Allyu's plots that they were stewarding. Some were lively, tending the fields and singing, intent on their tasks. Others moved slowly, clearly battling their latest bout of Fever. She smiled at them all on her way by. They smiled back, for of course they all knew her; everyone in the Allyu's corner of the undermountain did. Many of them currently had coursing through their bodies medicines evolved from biospheres she'd cultivated years ago.

Inside, she grieved. They were not getting better. The Fevers that had scourged them for generations were intensifying. Even llamas and alpacas, too many of them, were ill now. All reports from outside in Kay Pacha, gathered on their regular excursions, suggested that things were as bad or worse—in some cases much, much worse—throughout the entire world. She tasted bile in the back of her throat, and her jaw clenched.

"Puquio!" She turned at the call, knowing the voice and wishing it was another. "I see you are going through with it after all we've told you." Yawar walked up behind her on the path, sweat glistening as he caught up.

"Yes," Puquio responded, softly. "As I told the Council, I've seen it, the world within. I have seen the unhealed wounds, heard the voices of the Others, and tasted the shared medicine. I now know how to show everyone what I have seen. Today I will invite my sisters in, and we will record it all, in full transparency. Soon we will invite you in, too."

"I know what you said," Yawar spit angrily. "I was there for the Council meeting. But I wasn't given a voice then, so I am telling you now: you play with forces you don't understand. You will all go mad. You shouldn't even be in the sisterhood—"

Puquio's anger flared, and she shot back "I only remind you because you seem to have forgotten the decision of the Council, backed by the sisters of the Guild. They know it: this is our best and only chance." She suddenly felt very tired. It felt like she was five years old again, still being taunted by the other kids, their scorn at her overmountain father still stinging. "Yachay knew it, too... she chose to make this journey with me. She told me to continue. We have nothing to lose, except more generations of sickness and death."

Now it was Yawar who was stung, touched in his still-raw, aching core. For a moment, he seemed about to cry. And just as quickly, fresh anger flared, smothering his pain: "We have the sanity of all your sisters to lose, six of our finest. We can't afford to lose any more of the great weavers. You do what you have to do with your own sanity, but leave them out of it."

Puquio leaned back, took a deep breath, and whispered, "I'm sorry, Yawar. I loved her, too. This won't bring her back. But it might save your daughter." And with that, he stood silent, his face stone. She turned and walked on, up the undermountain.

The walk was a full hour, and by the time she reached the Transition Zone, she was feeling real hunger. The Zone had only humble plants, mosses, lichens and dwarf bushes, the extreme altitude forcing them to lowliness. Direct sunlight had crept up the overmountain, and the inti algae was channeling it inside, progressively blazing to life in the undermountain's roof. The brightness would soon reach the Portal, where Uju Pacha met Kay Pacha at the convergence of the undermountain and overmountain peaks. The slope she walked up grew closer and closer to the stone roof, and she could now make out the pools and veins of multihued green and gold above her: epiphytes, mosses, illuminating algaes.

As she approached the glacier at the peaks, she saw that her six sisters were already assembled. They stood in a semicircle around the door set into the ice, their colorful ceremonial cloth a rainbow against the glowing azure of the glacier. She approached them, and they greeted her with smiles, nods and concerned looks, all in complete silence. They looked as simultaneously terrified and determined as she felt. All words had already been said, and they all knew what to do. Breathing deeply, she took out 3 leaves of coca, breathed on them, and offered them to the ice. Her sisters, in response and in unison, made identical offerings, their hands fluttering up, the leaves sailing on the light breeze, down to the foot of the glacier.

Puquio walked to the doorway and gave silent thanks to the lineages of thermophilic bioweavers and to the thermoproductive bacteria themselves. Without them they would all bake, freeze, suffocate, or die of thirst; the balancing of temperature was also the moving of air, and of course the glacier was the source of all their water, and so their life. The Portal lay deep inside the ice, and she and her sisters would take the same route their people took when they passed through Uju Pacha's peak to reach the overmountain and Kay Pacha: through the ice caves.

Puquio opened the door and entered the caves, her sisters behind her. As they walked straight into the ice mountain, the cold heart of the apu, the bright light from the undermountain roof began to fade as the blue ice filtered it out. Her sisters at the front and rear held up carrier crystals full of inti algae, and as they activated, a warm glow met the deep blue walls. They ascended steadily and gently up the ice tunnel.

As they traveled the veins of the glaciar towards its heart, their footsteps fell into rhythm, syncopated by the faint echoes of the icy passage. Quietly at first, increasing slowly in intensity, together they intoned a very old song:

Pacha, world without end, turn end to end,
Kuti, shake quake burn freeze transform send
Ice into water from apu peaks—liquid seed seeks womb
In the valley below, till the iceflow slows to stop,
Pachakuti, this world ends and a new one begins

After what seemed like an eternity in this timeless place, they saw their destination ahead through the translucent ice, the heart of the two mountains: the Portal. A five-layer chakana chamber—a three-dimensional stair-stepped cross—at the exact convergence point of the peaks, the very threshold between Uju Pacha and Kay Pacha, the meeting of underworld and overworld. Here, like an iceberg from water, the huge glaciated peak of the undermountain emerged as the overmountain glacier, a tiny chunk of unremarkable ice. This was the secret passage where their forays into the wider world began. *Now this place will be our passage into a new world inside,* Puquio thought.

As they entered the Portal, the curved deep blue walls of the passageway shifted suddenly, dramatically, as the walls, floors, and ceilings of the Portal's chakana shot out, above and below, nearly transparent, in perfectly straight planes, meeting at impossibly precise right angles. At the exact center of chakana, suspended in mid-air, hovered the dreamsphere. Puquio smiled.

Then her smile faded. *I'm too old for this,* Puquio thought. *I need Yachay.* Still, she walked into the central chamber as her sisters took their places, sitting in their respective corners, each one entering one of the farthest extruding blocks of the chakana. *Have I not done enough for the clan, for the world?*

Indeed, she had already done plenty. Her perfecting of the oneirograph was a phenomenal achievement, and ever since she had been revered and honored. Too honored for her taste, since all honors brought responsibilities—and interminable speechifying. All she really wanted was to play with her granddaughter all day, enjoy a good holokhipu story in the evenings while drinking a gourd of chicha, and dream deeply and adventurously at night. But of course, her granddaughter hardly played anymore. If Puquio failed, Roa would do little else but cry and suffer for the short remainder of her life.

Her head was pounding as she approached the dreamsphere and reached her fingertips up to touch the surface. The seemingly metallic surface liquified and elongated into threads floating in the air. Her fingers did not shake as she wove the knotted password patterns in the airborne threads. The threads responded like old friends, twirled about her arms, and lifted her gently into the orb. As she passed through its permeable iridescent surface, she felt a surge of pride at this true beauty and power which they had woven in community.

Inside, she was suspended in the center of the dreamsphere, and with a thought she turned around to look at her sisters through the translucent surface. She nodded at them, and they all lay down, covering first their bodies and then their eyes with cloth. Then, they took out their own oneirograms, each with Puquio's new cyclical networked retrofeedback modifications, and placed the three-banded crystals on their chests.

More mercurial threads extended from the walls of the dreamsphere. Adeptly, she wove the pattern to trigger the animographic scan of her own body. Her final movement was to remove her oneirogram from her pocket and hold it up to her heart. After weeks of ritual and fasting, decades of planning and building, years of training, and her granddaughter's infinitely excruciating and fragile lifetime wavering at death's door, she was ready to begin.

She lay back and closed her eyes as the threads gently brought her to a horizontal position, cradling her body. She felt the energetic activation of the sphere as it received and re-transmitted the signals being sent by each miniscule movement of her every cell, mitochondrion, and kamasal node and thread. She felt the almost electric prickle of her sisters' kamasal networks beginning to weave their ways into her own.

The seven sisters lay quiet.

Slowly, one by one, they drifted into sleep, then slipped into dream.

≈ ≈ ≈

DEEP LIKE THE RIVERS

CHRISTOPHER CALDWELL

I loved my boy, but I never understood him. Momma would have. They would have taken to each other like bees and flowers. Sometimes it felt like her old eyes were staring out of his little face. He'd make me so mad. That calm. Insisting he knew so much I didn't. Insisting he knew things he had no right to know.

When I was a little girl, momma told me if I ever lost someone I loved to write his name in red ink seven times on a piece of onionskin paper. Wrap the paper around John the Conquer root and a rock as big as my fist. Tie the whole thing up with a bright red ribbon, then bury it in the sand. Low tide under the next full moon. If I found that ribbon-wrapped rock after seven days and seven nights, the lost one would come back to me. I found out too late that the sea takes all things.

Momma was what they called back home a root-worker. Used to say she could *conjure*. When I was seven, angry at the boys who chased me across the playground and threw my books on the cafeteria roof, angry at the white teachers for not caring, angry that I didn't have soft yellow hair, I came into Momma's kitchen. I slammed her screen door, tracked in dirt from the outside. And she must have known, because she didn't scold. Her hands didn't stop moving. She continued chopping garlic for the big pot of red beans simmering on the stove.

"So?" She said, the question cut off by a chop.

"It's not fair. It's NOT fair. When am I gonna get power like you to make bad people stop hurting me?"

She clattered the knife down on the chopping board. She swept me in her arms. She smelled like starch and onions and pound cake batter. "Baby, it don't work like that. It ain't in the *blood*. It chooses who it chooses. And ain't nothing can stop not one of us from being hurt."

"Then what good is it?" I wailed.

"I can teach you to set a bone with a kind word and cool water. To keep an enemy from your door with graveyard dust. To bring back home a lost loved one. To sing to rest a heart full of grief. But can't nobody stop you from being hurt. Not while you're living."

"Teach me, Momma. I want to learn."

She slid me to the floor, gentle. She smoothed the flyaways from my pigtails. "You go along and do your homework first. Then we'll eat supper." She rested her hands on her hips for a moment then turned back to chopping her garlic. I sniffled.

"And then *maybe* we have a little time for you to learn what I know."

Momma was a good teacher, patient and exact. I was a bad student.

\#

When Isaiah was five, his teacher, a nervous white woman with oversized glasses and Lucille Ball red hair suggested to me and Roderick that maybe he should be held back in school another year. "I have concerns that little Izzy isn't able to keep up with the rest of the class." She pressed her thin lips into a smile. "Particularly in reading."

"Excuse me, Ms. Cowan?" I used my business voice. "*Isaiah* has been reading since he was three."

"We've had him tested—" Roderick said.

That thin smile again. "Mrs. Daubert," she pronounced it *dob-bert*, "I know every parent wants to believe their child is exceptional, but—"

"As my husband was saying, we've had Isaiah tested by a psychologist, and there's nothing wrong with his intellectual development." I scooted upright in the metal folding chair. "The psychologist did suggest that sometimes *bright* children can be bored by rote exercises."

I took a mean bit of pleasure in her expression.

That night, we took Isaiah out to McDonald's. He ignored the toy that came with his happy meal and drew pictures on the border of a napkin. Tiny precise figures in blue and green. Women with shark fins and hair billowing up like kelp. Men with twisted mouths and eyes on the same side of their face, like flounders.

"Your teacher says you're not paying attention in class when they do reading," I said.

"I can read." Isaiah said, not looking up from his drawing.

"Buddy," Rod said mouth half-full of fries. "Sometimes you have to do stuff you already know how to. It seems silly, but it'll help you be what you want to be when you grow up."

"I want to be a mermaid when I grow up." His face was fierce, solemn.

Rod laughed. "Scooter, you're a boy. Boys can't be mermaids."

"I can *too* be a mermaid." Isaiah colored in a figure with a foam green crayon. "I can be anything."

#

By the time Isaiah was twelve, I figured out he was what Momma would have called "sweet." Rod would have had a problem with that, if he could have bothered with being around. But Isaiah was still just my boy. My smart, serious little boy.

One Saturday I was doing laundry and was in his warren of a room looking for whites when I came across a spiral notebook wedged between his headboard and the wall. I opened it, thinking I'd find drawings of Atlantis. Instead there were drawings of other boys in impossible sexual positions. The name Jason written on three different pages with hearts around it. My heart sunk. The world was already hard enough for a little black boy who would be seen as nothing more than a nigger. Now he'd be seen as a faggot, too.

When Isaiah came home from music practice, I was waiting in the living room with the notebook on my lap. He bounced in carrying his violin case in one hand and a sheaf of music in another. "Mom, you'll never guess what—" He trailed off when he saw the notebook.

"Isaiah, honey. I found this in your room. We have to talk about this."

"Mom. Those were my things. They were private things." He stared at the wall, blinking back tears.

"There's no privacy when you're living under my roof, you hear!" My face felt hot. I remembered the betrayal I felt when Momma read through my diary and found out I kissed a Bobby Jenkins from down the street. *Not gonna be with them no 'count Jenkins.*

His voice was raised, not quite a shout. "You had *no* right. You had no *right.*"

I don't know why I didn't take him to my chest. Didn't stroke his hair and tell him things will be fine. I had to protect him, didn't I? How could I protect him if he hid things from me? "I think you forgot who here is the parent. You don't use that tone with me. You go to your room until you can talk to me right."

The look he gave me was his father's, measured and cold. I loved my child, but I wanted to slap him across the mouth just then. He said quietly, "Yes, ma'am."

There was a tightness to his walk, a way of squaring his shoulders that brought out the spite in me. "And don't think you can slam my doors. You don't pay any bills around here!"

The deliberate care with which he shut that door was his silent rebuke.

#

He took up surfing. It started with boogie boards, but as he grew more confident on the water, he asked for a surfboard. Things were tight, but I'd saved up for driving lessons for him and he showed no interest in driving. I got him that surfboard for his sixteenth birthday. He was growing up. Dark like his father, and already taller. He had my suspicious mouth and Momma's old, weary eyes. I used to drop him off in Malibu for surfing lessons and pick him up after. Uncle Freeland had left me his big ugly Buick station wagon in his will, and we put a rack on top for the surfboard.

One of those hot and cloudy Southern California days when the air feels heavy, I decided I'd stay out on the beach while he surfed.

"I was thinking that today I might get my ankles wet and lay out on the sand instead of heading up to IHOP."

Isaiah didn't look at me. "Okay."

"You're not embarrassed by your old mother, are you? I'll wear a floppy hat and those big sunglasses and you can pretend you don't know me."

He kissed me on the cheek. Quick. Hard. "I love you, little ma. Of course I'm not embarrassed."

The drive out was quieter than usual. He made a comment that the chaparral reminded him of seaweed as we drove through Laurel Canyon. I rolled down my window. An old smell of woodsmoke. The salt tang of the ocean we could not see.

I watched my boy out on the waves. He seemed so confident and loud and carefree. He was different on the water. After his lessons he splashed around with some of the other boys until they drifted away into whirls and knots of two or three.

I saw him talking to the only other black boy on the beach. High yellow and pretty, this strange boy rested his naked chest against a rocky outcrop. He kept his legs under the water. It was overcast, but that boy's skin shimmered. This boy looked at my son like he was something good to eat. My boy looked back at him the same. My palms itched. I wanted to pull my boy by the car away from him. I turned my attention back to my true crime novel.

I got so engrossed at how some white man killed his wife and almost got away with it that I didn't hear Isaiah tromp back across the sand. His lanky shadow striped my torso. I looked up from my book. "Who's your friend?"

He ignored the question. "Ma, did you know all the waters in the world are connected?"

I looked over at the outcrop. The pretty boy was no longer there. "I did not know that." I rose to my feet, pulled my beach towel up.

"Well they are, and I don't just mean how lakes go into streams that go into rivers that go into the sea. They're all really the same thing. I feel like I'm touching the world when I'm out there on the waves." His smile was unguarded. My heart hurt a little. I knew how rare those little boy smiles were.

"Hey, you know when you were little you told your dad you wanted to be a mermaid when you grew up? And he said—"

The smile faded, like a cloud crossing over the sun. "I remember."

We both stood there looking out at the rocky outcrop and the waters beyond it.

#

He started staying out late. Strange men would call the house. His grades got worse. He wouldn't tell me where he was going. One night he came home soaking wet, smelling like the ocean, with hickeys all along his neck. The Perry Ellis pullover he'd worn out was gone.

I roared at him. "You still are under my roof. You think you're grown? Where have you been, Isaiah Baptiste Daubert?"

He smirked. His voice cracked into song. " If you go out on the sea today you're sure of a big surprise. If you go out on the waves today—" he spun in a circle and pointed at me. "—*you* better go in disguise. For every fish that ever was will gather there for certain because today's the day the mermaids have their picnic."

I grabbed him by the wrist. His skin was slippery and cool. "Have you been drinking? What do you think you're doing?"

"Only the nectar of the deep. And I think I'm falling in love."

I'd never raised my hand to my boy. I'd wanted to, but I'd never done it. I slapped him. "You will not disrespect me or my house."

"My father's house has many rooms." He reeled back. He steadied himself on a kitchen chair. "Most of them are sunken."

Momma would have known what to do. She would have seen what was happening. Momma would have given him a broth stinking of sage. Would have slipped the right ribbon under his pillow. Would have whispered a charm. *I* slapped him again. "What you are not going to do is go out with strange men and come home stinking of seawater and drink. You are not going to have whoring ways and nasty manners. I am not breaking my back working for you to do whatever the hell you want."

His shoulders sagged. He crouched down so we were the same height. "I'm sorry Ma. Let's not fight. I'll take a shower and we can watch T*he Five Heartbeats.*"

His breath smelled like rotting kelp and raw fish. My stomach turned. "Go to your room. I don't want to see you again."

I meant to say I don't want to see you again *tonight.*

#

They told me he drowned. Nice Latino policeman and his blonde partner who looked at me like she smelled something nasty. There was no body. They found his board cracked in two, floating on the waves. Found his board shorts on the sand.

"Those shorts were shredded, ma'am," the blonde said. "Probably caught on a rock, or maybe some sort of sea animal—"

Her partner nudged her. "Mrs. Daubert? I know this must come as a terrible shock. I'm afraid I have to ask you a few questions."

"It's Baptiste, actually. Hasn't been Daubert since the divorce. Do you mind if I sit?" Before waiting for an answer, I sunk into the blue and white la-z-boy that was Isaiah's favorite seat. It smelled faintly like him. "He is … was … *is* an excellent swimmer, Officer."

He looked sheepish. "We're not going to stop looking, but I need you to know in cases like this, the outcome is most often not the best."

#

I sold most of my things except for Uncle Freeland's Buick. I sold the little bungalow where I'd lived for 15 years. I moved back home to Louisiana with my sister. Couldn't stand to be anywhere near the Pacific. After we had the funeral with its empty casket, Rod kept calling me until I blocked his number. He wasn't there for Isaiah when he was here, no point in him trying to be a father after my boy was gone.

Two grey years passed. Each day ate a little into my savings. My sister kept trying to get me to do something, anything but miss Isaiah. First good-naturedly, then cajoling, finally exasperated. I decided to clear out the crawlspace. Momma had left all sorts of debris up there.

I was crouched over and aching from pulling out cardboard boxes with old report cards and yellowed newspapers when I found a little notebook. It used to be red, but was so covered in dust and cobwebs that it was now the brown of old photographs. I opened it. In fading ink in my own shaky childish hand I'd written, "How to bring back lost love."

There was still some Great John De Conquer root in the back yard. And red ribbon couldn't possibly be difficult to obtain. I thought to myself *why not*?

#

On the seventh night of the seventh day I drove myself down to the river in the Buick. I took a good strong flashlight. I knew I was in the exact place I'd buried that rock. I shone my light across the mud. There was a hole a little bigger than my fist near the gnarled cottonwood root I'd used as a marker.

A wind blew across the water and showered me with cottonwood fluff. In one of the tree's branches I caught a glimpse of a swallow-like bird with shiny black feathers. It had something red in its beak, like a ribbon. I set to with my spade, stabbing at the mud, plunging my hands in and feeling for rocks. Knowing all the while that the hole I'd left it in was empty. I kept at it until my hands cracked and bled. Until I was out of breath. Then I leaned against the cottonwood and wept.

The surface of the river looked greasy under the moonlight. I heard Isaiah's voice clear in my mind, "All the waters of the world are connected."

I wiped the snot from my face with the least muddy part of my sleeve. I walked back up the bank to Uncle Freeland's Buick and sat behind the wheel. Thought about all the times I should have listened more. Should have been more patient. I thought of how I should have just watched the Five fucking Heartbeats. Then I gunned it.

The Buick loped down the riverbank, slipping in the mud, losing traction but not getting stuck. The splash as I reached the water was horrendous, and I thought it just might crack the windshield. The river was fast and deep, and the Buick and I sank like a ribbon-wrapped stone.

#

The headlights lit the murk outside the Buick, but the headlights gave out all too soon. I'd left my flashlight in the mud. In the dark the Buick and I kept falling, and I couldn't tell if I had hit the bottom. I was suspended upside down in my seatbelt. I heard the glass crack, then a cold spray of dank river water hit me in the face. Great glugs escaped the car, and I knew it would soon be filled with the river. I groped in the dark for the steering wheel and pulled my head up as far as I could. "Please," I shouted. "I just want to see Isaiah one last time. I need to tell him I'm sorry."

The glass cracked again, and this time the water flooded the car. I took one last panicked breath, and then reached up to unlatch my seatbelt. It was stuck.

I hung there for a moment in the dark and cold, trying not to scream, my lungs already pounding. A ghostly blue light filled the car's interior. Was I going to heaven? The light grew stronger, and I counted the seconds before I would have to gasp again, and then swallow river water and silt.

I could make out a figure. The boy from the shore. He was the blue light. Rather than legs he had a long flat fluked tail, like a dolphin. The light radiated out from his shimmery skin, green now under the murk instead of golden. He opened his mouth and rows of small, spiny teeth gave out the same light. He swam up close. His eyes were black with pinpoint pupils. He reached out a long-fingered hand and I saw webs between those fingers. He grabbed my throat. Clutched it tight. I screamed, thinking I was going to be choked, then noticed I could breathe.

The sea creature spoke. "You can't stay here."

I looked at him. Only I was no longer sure the creature was a *him*. *They* shimmered iridescently, and their form seemed in flux. One moment his face was square and masculine, and another it seemed that small tender breasts budded from her chest, and her gaze was girlish and tender. What I thought were dolphin flukes suddenly expanded out to octopus arms with gripping suckers, and then collapsed into long, human like legs. I looked into their face, into shark eyes fringed with thick black eyelashes, and said without accusation, "You took my son."

They shook their head. "No. Isaiah chose to come with me. Willingly and of his own accord. It *has* to be that way."

"I drove him away."

The mermaid, and I believed that I now understood what mermaids really were, stroked my cheek. "No. A part of him always belonged to the sea."

"Can I talk to him?"

"There isn't much time. My power to keep you breathing won't last."

"I need to say goodbye."

The mermaid smiled. Those terrible sharp teeth with their blue glow shone between pouty lips. He grabbed onto my wrist. "I can give you that."

A warmer current buffeted me. Threatened to tear me away, but the mermaid's grip was strong and he stayed with me. Another blue glow, weaker this time, from behind me. I turned. Isaiah was there. He was changed. His fingers were longer, webs between them, his legs ended in flippers instead of feet. He smiled at me. His teeth were still human but had already begun to glow blue.

"Little Ma!" He gave me a look like he'd woken up on Christmas morning. He furrowed his brow, jutted out his jaw. He looked a wild thing. "I tried to tell you. I knew Daddy wouldn't get it, but I thought you—I *told* you I could be a mermaid!" He bit his lower lip. Then squeezed his eyes shut. When he opened them, the wildness in them was calmed. "You shouldn't look so sad."

I pounded my fists against his chest. "I thought you were dead!"

He held my fists in one hand – when did he get so strong? Then leaned forward to kiss my cheek. "I don't believe Grandma Lou never told you about us people."

I looked at my boy and the mermaid. "I never believed."

"You found me. You must have believed some." Another unguarded smile.

I began to weep, my tears warm on my cheeks. "I wanted to say I'm sorry. I wanted to say you deserved better as a mother. I wanted to say that I love you and—"

Isaiah embraced me. His skin felt rubbery and cool. "Ma? Mommy. You did the best you could. You were the best mother you knew how to be. I'm grateful for all you've done for me."

"Are you safe?"

The mermaid moved closer to my son. "There isn't much time, beloved. Say your farewells."

"Safe? Ma, there isn't any safe on the land, or under it. I'm not safe. But I'm happy." He let go of my hands. He did look happy.

I said, "I love you."

The water churned and swirled and I rocketed upwards. The blue lights shrank away into pinpoints. The water which I had been inhaling without thinking turned thick in my nose and mouth. I broke through the surface, coughed and sputtered for a moment. The moon was bright, and all the stars were out. I wasn't a strong swimmer, so I drifted with the current and made my way to shore. Not safe but happy was the best that any black boy could hope for.

HOʻI HOU E NA PŌ

GINA MCGUIRE

Puna, Hawaiʻi Island, November 1, 2100

Facing increasing levels of radiation, food scarcity, nuclear peril, and threat to their cultural survival, Puna's Hawaiian community has decided to return to their ancestral source of life deep beneath the surface of the sea to find safety. The community has been planning for years for a day that has become known as *hoʻi hou e na pō*. Today is that day.

*

Uliana took a deep breath of the humid jungle air. She would miss the green taste of the forest, would miss looking up at the vast heavens' stars on a moonless night. She didn't look up at the sky now though, she kept her eyes down, on the soft flesh of the earth beneath her feet.

"Uli! Where's the box with the regs?" someone called, bringing her back to her sad reality.

"It's under the box that has the *maile*," she answered back and turned to help offload the truck. They had been moving supplies to *Kaipaliuli hale*, the house under the sea, for months. But this would be the last time, her last time, in this world of soil and sun. She slid the plastic box of regulators off the back of the truck and moved it over towards the tanks. For setting up one of the most advanced underwater residencies, it seemed backwards, in a way, to have to dive to reach the *hale*, the house. She pulled out her reg from the top of the bin and moved towards her tank and vest where they waited. She latched the regulator on with a few strong twists, and felt the air fill the tubing as she cracked the tank. She could feel someone crouch down beside her but still she kept her eyes on her checking the pressure gauge, on her last lifeline to the world above.

Ikaika crouched next to his little sister. She was fiery and fierce, trapped inside a small sturdy body. She didn't look at him right away and so he busied himself by setting up the regulator on the tank next to her. Around them were all the members of their community, the elders chatting on the back of pickup trucks, the children clinging to mothers and fathers or running around screaming, depending on their personalities. The young adults moved briskly, with purpose, to prepare their departure. Everyone was kinder, gentler with their words; they all knew that this was it. The heaviness of finality hung in the air despite the blue sky and gentle sunlight. He had been meaning to tell her for many days but each time he saw the concrete trust in her eyes he had told her a joke or offered to help her pack instead.

"Hey," he finally said as she continued to fidget with her BCD vest, purposefully not acknowledging him.

"Oh, it's you," she said with relief, meeting his eyes immediately and punched him gently on the shoulder. She looked her brother over. He was tall and muscular but she could see the dark rings under his eyes and the grey cast to his skin that showed the tell-tale signs of one of the many illnesses that had claimed her family one by one.

"Avoiding good-byes?" he asked lightly.

She looked back at the ground. "If I don't say goodbye, I can pretend I'm going to see them all tomorrow." She paused for a moment before she added, "I'm really glad you're going to be there."

A chill shot through his heart like a worm crawling through an overripe mango. It was now or never. "About that…"

"Did you forget something at the house?" she asked, too quick for him. And that was when he realized that deep down, she already knew.

"No. Uli, there's something I need to tell you."

She looked at him for a long moment, her eyes blurring against her will. She knew what he was going to say. It was written all over his face. It had been for days; she had just been trying so hard not to see it.

"You're not coming." It wasn't a question.

He shook his head slowly. "I can't."

"What do you mean?" Uli said, standing up suddenly. "You have to!" She felt her stomach churn. What was there left for him to stay for? She had been able to face this with a good face because she had known she would face it with him beside her.

Ikaika rose too. "Uli, don't be mad at me. I can't go."

"You can. And you won't," Uli said. The earth was dying, the sea rising. The forests overtaken with invasive plants, the water too acidic. The air, even on their island, in the middle of the Pacific: tainted. He wouldn't live for long. No one who stayed would. And they all knew it. Only the strongest would move to Kaipaliuli. The elders would remain, would rejoin *honua* so that the young might live. The guarantee of death was not what drove her anger, for that was to return to many generations of *kūpuna*, of ancestors, who had come before. To feed the earth. She was not running from death, she reminded herself. But he was choosing the spirits over the years of life they might share together.

"I need to stay," Ikaika said.

"You're being selfish," Uli countered, shaking her head again and again.

"You're going to have a better life. You're going to save our people. Our culture." He paused, looking up at the sky that was still so blue, so deceivingly hopeful. "Someone needs to stay, to feed the *kūpuna*, to seal and protect the cave entrance. Until the end."

Ikaika watched the tears stream down Uli's face in their slow rivers.

"I'll stay," she whispered.

"You're going to have a better life. Away from," he waved his hand, indicating the dying island. "all this... despair."

"Please, come with me."

"How could you love me if I ran now?" he asked with short laughter and pulled her rigid body into a hug.

"We're not running," she said into his shoulder, now hiccupping the tears she wanted to swallow.

He couldn't leave, the way you could never fully uproot one of the ancient tree's roots in the deep forest. A part of him would always belong to the old-growth-flesh of the island. He would always be drawn to the surface, always wondering, not knowing what had happened to the land his ancestors' bones belonged to. For him, knowing your *mo'okū'auhau*, your genealogy, was everything. *Mo'okū*: your backbone, what keeps you standing tall. *'Auhau*: the appendages of all of those that have come before you. What held you to the land, allowed you to walk in their beauty. He held his sister tighter.

"You have to let me go."

The sound of a *pū*, a conch shell, blew in the background, signaling that it was time for the elders' ceremony. Uliana let go of Ikaika and moved towards the circle of people that was forming. She kept her back on his figure for she did not want him to remember her with tears.

Two circles formed around each other, those who would stay in a larger ring around the smaller group of those who would move to their very own Atlantis. She latched hands with the two boys next to her, as everyone in the circle joined together. She searched the wrinkled faces around the half of the circle for Ikaika but he was not there and so she knew he was behind her, watching her back as he always had and would even as she left to join *pō*.

The soft murmuring of the community died down slowly and several moments of silence floated among them before a single strong voice rose over them and up to the sky. The voice was male and elderly, but despite the undulating vowels spread throughout the chant, his voice did not break. Uliana knew that the singer was Uncle Kaipo. He was the eldest, but also the strongest of the kūpuna that remained. Dependable and kind. He had taught Uliana all of the chants and songs that held her upright when she felt weak.

His voice gradually faded back into the world around them. Uliana swallowed hard for what was to come next. She prepared her voice to join their voices together for one last time.

"*Ke lei maila 'o Ka'ula i ke kai ē...*" she began. She felt a great surge of hope as the voices of all those surrounding her joined in. As they repeated the song for the second time Uliana felt the soft rain of Puna tickling her eye lids despite the blue sky above. It seemed that Kāne would bless them with one last gift.

The ceremonies carried on with prayer and individual songs until again it was silent. Uliana knew there was just one person left to speak. Uncle Kaipo walked to the middle of the inner circles, directly in front of Uliana. She wondered what he would say, of what kind of speech he would give.

He didn't say anything, however, but kept moving until he was within an arm's length of her. He stopped for a moment, looking into her eyes for a long second before reaching around his neck to take off his necklace. Uliana looked at the boys on either side of her, making sure this was really meant for her.

"*Alakaʻi e*," he said in a low tone, yet loud enough for all to hear. *Lead them*. He draped the shark tooth necklace she had admired for so long around her neck.

Uliana shook her head. She couldn't accept this. She was not the oldest, nor the strongest of those that were moving to Kaipaliuli. "I can't," she whispered.

Uncle Kaipo pulled her into a tight grasp. "You can. You are the last *aliʻi*," he whispered in her ear.

When the ceremony ended, the community returned to the urgent activity, loading the last boxes of materials into the rail carts at the lava tube's mouth. Then the tears and hugs of final goodbyes. Uliana sat next to Ikaika at the cave mouth, watching the heart being torn from each half's chests. Still, she did not say her goodbyes. *I'll see them again*, she lied to herself.

Slowly, one by one the young moved into the tunnel mouth, beginning the long walk to the ocean entry. Uliana thought of what Ikaika had told her as she faced the dark descent into the lava tunnels they would now enter. She willed herself not to look back despite the ice flooding her veins that willed her to stay.

You are my heart walking around outside my chest, he had whispered, handing her a small *ʻiliʻili* rock. She rolled it around in the palm of her hand now. It was pitted and yet smooth all at the same time. It would be her reminder of a childhood playing in streams, of the trickle of freshwater under rippling sunlight. Of the boy who would linger in the dying world above.

She had made the trip before: through the hollow, damp tunnels, past the burial caves, past the underground hospitals of her ancestors, and to the sea. But this time when she would greet the gods of the deep: *Nāmakaokaha'i*, goddess of the depths and *Kamohoali'i*, shark brother, it would be to join their realm. Until her bones would be given to the sea.

Uliana did not look back as she moved into the cave opening, but Ikaika's eyes never left her retreating figure. All of the dinners he had made her, her cheerful face in the passenger seat of his car, picking flowers for *lei* together, it all ran across his heart. His little sister. But he did not wonder if he had made the right choice. And when he slid the stone cover over the tube's entrance, sealing them from the world above, he did not cry.

It was a long, twisting path through the lava tubes to the final place they would enter the sea. The damp, soft dripping walls arched in a large protective tunnel, allowing seven people to walk across at one time. The center of the tunnel was lined with a rail road track, the cart system they used to move their building materials, and today the last gear they would be bringing, to Kaipaliuli. It was not dark, however. The walls shown with the soft light of bioluminescent worms. It was not light to see by: the small bodies lined the walls, alone amongst the engulfing darkness. But it was light to hope by. To whisper your greatest fears and trust that there was something, maybe some conscious energy listening. Every so often as they walked, they would come across a spot of light, where the ceiling had cracked, allowing the sunlight to trickle in through a violent beam. Rather than linger in these bright reminders of the world above, Uliana would notice a slight increase in the pace. Each spot of sunlight was an uncomfortable reminder of what had now been left behind.

She walked beside different people as her pace waxed and waned. They weren't in a hurry, and so they slowly spread out as a group, each lost in their own thoughts, committing to memory their last tastes of pollen, the last words of their elders. Uliana found herself drawn to a soft sniffling sound and she took the tiniest of steps until she leveled with the crying behind her.

Uliana came to a stop beside a young boy of about six years old, she would have guessed. She had seen him before but she could not recall his name. He was bony, thin and tall for his age with the dark tanned skin of someone who spent a lot of time outside. But at this moment he was shaking, his shoulders hunched in on themselves and his body quivering with tears. He was old enough to walk by himself but she was still surprised to see someone so small on their own.

"Hey little man," Uliana said, crouching down beside him. "Come here," she said and opened her arms. She half expected him to do the six-year-old-boy thing and to act like he was fine but he flopped into her arms in a rush.

"Hey, shhhh, it's gonna be ok," she whispered, rubbing his back. "Where are your parents?"

His body shook several times before the crying subsided slightly. "They're dead," he said matter of factly.

Uliana felt the familiar sting of her own parents' passing. "Who takes care of you?"

"My Tutu *kāne* and *wahine*," he said, sniffling again.

His grandparents, Uliana thought. They would have had to remain behind. She wondered what you were supposed to say to someone who had just left everything they knew behind. Usually her policy was, if she didn't know what to say she said nothing at all. But you couldn't do that with children. She racked her brain for a moment before coming up with something.

"What do you think your Tutus would say right now?"

The boy scrunched up his face as though he were thinking really hard. "They told me to be brave. To take care of my Aunty."

Uliana felt relief that there was one family member down here somewhere, even if she had let him fall behind the group. Probably just too many kids to watch.

"And they said they'd take care of my dog for me."

"You miss your dog?" Uliana asked, her heart lifting slightly.

"What if she doesn't realize I'm gone?" he said, crying harder.

"Oh honey," Uliana said, scooping the boy up and hoisting his thighs onto her hips to carry him. "Of course, she's missing you. You know, I think, you could probably tell her your secrets and she'd still hear them. Even down here."

"Even when we're under the ocean?" he said, drying his eyes and snotty nose against Uliana's shirt.

"Even then," she said, listening to the echo of the many footsteps in front of them and the soft rolling sound of the rail carts in the far distance. *The ones we love are never really that far away*, she thought to say but she kept it inside, where it was safe.

The boy grew silent for several minutes and she felt her arms ache but she kept carrying him. She knew that they were nearing where the tunnels met the sea by the constant sloshing sounds of waves getting louder. She vaguely wondered how far ahead the others were and if she shouldn't be further ahead, helping everyone with the ocean entry.

"Can I sit on your shoulders?" the boy said.

Uliana's arms sighed with relief. Just as she put him down on the ground to shift him, the earth started to vibrate in violent pitches. She lost her balance for a moment and fell to her knees.

"Get against the wall!" She grabbed the little boy's arm. She didn't know if it was the smart thing to do or not but her immediate thought was to find something to hold onto as their world rocked. This was not a small tremor and she couldn't think of anything except for the adrenaline-fear that ran through her body. It felt like it went on for minutes, although she was sure that couldn't be the case.

Small chunks of the ceiling and tunnel walls fell to the ground like rain on concrete, splintering into tiny pieces about them for many seconds after the ground stopped pitching beneath their feet.

The world fell still and Uliana slowly let go of the small boy.

"Is it over?" he asked, gazing about the tunnel.

"I don't know," Uliana said, rising to her feet again. "I know we gotta get to the ocean. Soon." She pictured the tunnel collapsing on itself and she felt like hyperventilating.

"Get up," she said, hoisting the boy onto her back. His legs wrapped tightly around her waist and his arms around her chest.

She moved as quickly as she could down the tunnel, now avoiding the obsidian shards that had fallen to the floor. She kept her ears wide open for the sea, for the sounds of the others but it was as though the world had fallen silent.

After several minutes of her heart thumping wildly inside her chest, Uliana paused, just around the tunnel corner that she knew hid the ocean entry from view. She was afraid to turn the corner for some reason. It was all so close, her people, their path to the sea. It was all so fragile.

She turned the corner and gave a sigh of relief: they were all there. Slumped against the tunnel walls: sitting, snacking. She could see the bright turquoise glow of the tide pool mouth to Kaipaliuli and her heart leapt. It looked like everything was ok.

"We waited for you," her cousin, Manakuke, said. "Hoo, crazy 'dat shake huh?"

Uliana smiled about his name. It was an inside joke. Manakuke. Mongoose. He was chubby, tall. Slow. The opposite of a mongoose: sneaky, quick, and darting. She gave him a grateful look. She had been doubting herself, wondering if she was up to the responsibility that had been laid at her feet. She needed all the help that she could get.

"Go find your aunty," she said and lowered the boy to the ground from where he still clung to her but he remained by her side.

"We've got the *maile* ready and tanks lined up," Manakuke said.

Uliana looked around at the rail cart that still held the *maile* garlands and at the SCUBA tanks neatly lined up against the tunnel walls. *Maile* grew as winding vines through the Hawaiian canopy, filling the forest with its sweet fragrance. At one time it had grown abundantly, but under the combination of over-harvesting and acid rain, it had become difficult to find. This was to be their final offering from the land. Uliana was excited for this part of the journey. She looked around at the group surrounding her; she was proud of them, that they had come this far.

"Great! Let's get ready for the *lei* ceremony," she answered.

No sooner had the words left her lips than the sea roared to life before them. No one had been paying much attention to the ocean, and the water suddenly moved into the tunnel mouth in a sweeping, sudden wave. Uliana remembered what her father had said to her growing up: *Don't turn your back on the ocean.*

"Grab the tanks!" she yelled desperately but it was too late, the world thrown into a rolling mass of liquid confusion. The rail carts were knocked off of the tracks and thrown backwards into the tunnel, the scuba tanks and *maile* floated about wildly, and the people swept off of their feet. At first, they were pulled forward, deeper into the tunnel, but then dragged out towards the sea in a swirling confusion of bodies. The sea had come to take what it knew was already its own.

Uliana had one moment to grab onto a tank next to her or onto the boy and after a strange shuffle in both directions grabbed the boy and held him to her chest. Her one thought before she remembered to hold her breath: how would they make it to Kaipaliuli now?

Glossary, in order of appearance

ho'i hou e na pō	return to pō
pō	night, ancestral darkness, associated with deep sea
maile	fragrant Hawaiian vine, Alyxia stellata
hale	house
honua	earth
kūpuna	ancestors
mo'okū'auhau	genealogy
pū	triton conch shell, used as a trumpet
Ke lei maila...	opening line of Oli Lei, the lei chant
Puna	southeastern district of Hawai'i Island
Kāne	Hawaiian deity of sunlight, freshwater, forests
alaka'i e	call to lead
ali'i	chief
'ili'ili	freshwater pebble
lei	floral garland
Tutu	grandparent
kāne	male, man
wahine	female, woman
manakuke	mongoose

AT THE OPENING OF BAYOU ST. JOHN

SHAWN SCARBER

It's usually the midwife who leaves the letter. I find it scrawled on the faded front page of the *Times-Picayune*, or written on The Arlington's fine stationery, or scribbled on the back of a receipt from Antoine's. I'm not sure why the authors won't use a fresh sheet of paper. I guess it's the nature of my service. Nothing comes to me fresh. The letter is never addressed. The author doesn't want to know my name. Those from outside the city, the real Crescent City, don't want to think about what I do, until they need me. If they do talk about me, then I am the bayou woman, or the woman in the boat, or the thing that takes the *ordures* away to the luminous ones. There are no words on these letters. There's a date and a time. The date is never far off, usually it's the day I receive the letter, or a couple of days after. But the requested time is always at night and always in the latest hours.

The letters arrive in my lamp box. The lamp box won't accept the type of letters one finds in a postal box. No, these letters don't require a stamp and they'll never leave the city. The lamp box has a singular purpose. Hung under the Orleans Avenue Bridge that crosses the Bayou St. John, it's as black as coal and the letters that arrive there are from desperate women seeking a second chance. I only open the lamp box at twilight. There's no point checking it earlier. Today, it gives me a single letter. It's as though the lamp box knows to only schedule one journey a night. Such an enchantment wouldn't surprise me.

I read my letter. Its message is drawn on the back of a cloth cottonseed bag. For a change, it's not the date, but a sketched picture. With much care and beauty, with the clumsy tools of thick chalk and charcoal, some poor soul has drawn for me the moon. It floats wide and bright and on its surface I see every mountain and crater. Around it float the clouds of night, and below it, a view of the city from my bridge over the bayou. If I'm not mistaken from the position and phase of the moon, the letter means for me to meet my artist tonight, near the eleventh hour. I turn in my letters to the master, every one. They account for my services. They are how I shall claim my final reward. But I will not turn this one over. This one I'll save in my private trunk, with all the other treasures I keep for when my service is complete.

#

My gondola swims through bayou waters like a swamp moccasin, lacquered black as deep night, with red velvet seats and comfortable pillows. Minor enchantments keep the rats, roaches, and biting flies away. Because my cargo isn't always fresh, the passenger cabin is perfumed with roses. Lanterns hang at the risso and ferro, lighting both my path and wake with blue fairy fire.

As I near my bridge, I see a woman in a sharecropper's dress, her hair disciplined under a scarf tied like a bonnet, and in her arms held to her chest in the unmistakable embrace of a loving mother is the stillborn gift. She sees me and I know what she's thinking. Not because I've any art in clairvoyance, but because I've been in this spot, meeting this same type of woman, for so, so many years.

She wonders, in that first moment she sees me, if she's made the right choice. This is a decision she's fought for. A husband, father, or lover has probably lectured her, yelled at her, beaten her, and then pleaded for her to change her mind. A member of her family—likely an aunt or a sister with strong religious convictions—has told her the sin of this choice, the evil of this path, and the hellfire awaiting any woman who would consider my boat an option. Her whole culture and community has roared up upon her like a hurricane wave from the ocean and in her time of greatest mourning it has doused her in torrential waves of rebuke, scorn, and judgment. Yet here she stands. A country woman, a creature born in a barn, condemned to work the field until her fingers can no longer feel the cotton she plucks from the hard shell. That is her home nation. Coming to the Crescent City to seek out the woman on the bayou is a betrayal to that nation, but when she sees me pull the gondola to the walkway under the bridge, she stays still like a rabbit, holding the gift and searching my empty eyes. These frightened women, they are the only ones with the strength to meet my gaze.

I anchor the gondola with my pole and hold out my arms to accept the swaddled gift. The woman doesn't move until she speaks, and then her breathing is fast, as though she hasn't breathed for days.

"I come to understand from what some folk say, that if I want, I can go with you." Her voice is lilting and her cadence rhythmic. "I brought paper bills. I know you like coin, but paper bills is all I could find."

"You've confused me for someone else, my love," I say. "Your gift is payment enough. It's true, if you wish to accompany me and your gift, you're welcome. I must warn you, though, what you see may be harsh. More than one woman has leapt from my boat believing she will recover what was lost. I will give you three chances to abandon this journey. You may take them and their consequences will be yours. If you stay to the end, you must promise me you will not leave the boat."

She says nothing for a time, and I find that comforting. It means she thinks on what I've said. The drowned and devoured tended to answer quickly, without thought.

She nods once, and I offer her my hand, and guide her to the passenger seat.

The journey from the bridge is easy for the gondola. The bayou is straight and wide. The water flows from Lake Pontchartrain to the city, and tonight the moon is as bright and alive as my passenger had captured it in her message.

"Your letter," I say. "It was drawn by you?"

"Yes, ma'am," she says. "I never learned no reading or no writing. My daddy learned me to sum, you know for the farming, and my grand learned me to memory all four of the gospels when I was a little girl, but when I take to the sending messages, it's easier I put the pictures in my head down. Folks say I can make a picture like one of them cameras, they says maybe I gots a fairy's glamour in me somewhere, but I think that's just porch talk."

"You draw beautifully," I say.

I cannot see her face, but I think she smiles.

#

Life along the bayou does not die at night. The ports and portals of the Crescent City are open to many worlds, and it's not unusual to see the Fae walk among the mortal. On this particular night, there's a dance in a courtyard near a home built by the settlers who flew the first flag of the seven to fly over the city. The attendants of the dance gather in the yard under gaslit chandeliers hung from trees as tall as the mechanical cranes that move cargo on and off steamboats in the harbor. As they pass into and out of the courtyard's gate, the celebrants are changed from humans, elves, and goblins, into wolves, sheep, and bears. They waltz on hind legs.

"I never been to no ball," my passenger says. "All them, even as animals, is more beautiful than me."

"Untrue," I say. "The elves and goblins are glamoured. They are eternally beautiful to the eye of the beholder. The humans are simply in finer attire. Should I stop here? You could enter through the gate, turn into someone new, someone different. As long as you don't pass back through the gate, you can stay in the form of a beast. You could be a wolf, or a cat, or even a bear. Shall I stop?"

She bows her head to the gift swaddled in her arms and says, "No ma'am. It's best we move on through."

"Are you certain?" I ask. "Turning into a beast isn't your only option. If I stop here, and you attend the ball, there's a chance you could walk back through the gate and discover you're no longer a sharecropper. Maybe your clothes will turn from sweat-stained rags to shiny silk or satin. At the ball, you may meet a baron or a prince. He'll adore you, and steal you away to his castle, where you will never want for anything ever again."

When she glances up, there's hurt building in her tense eyes.

"No prince or baron can return to me what I want," she says. "I won't go to no ball, and I won't change to no beast or beauty. I got my path decided."

"I understand," I say. "But know this. We won't return to the bridge on this bayou. Additionally, I've never seen this ball before and though I cannot swear it, I doubt it will ever be seen again. This is your last opportunity."

She nods and says, "My mind is made."

#

As we continue past the ball we arrive at the St. Louis Cemetery where the caskets are placed in cement tombs that must rest above the ground or they'll sink so far into the earth that they'll eventually fall into the underground river and wash out to the lake. The monuments jut from the ground on all sides of the bayou like horse teeth in dark fields, and upon the smallest tombs sit children of all ages and in all the various periods of dress from the time of the first settlers to today. When the children see her, they hold out their arms, and in their own tongues they whisper my passenger's true name, repeatedly.

"What cruelty is this?" she asks. "Don't they know I'll never hear that word from mine? Don't they know what that stirs in me? Are these ghosts of children or are they real?"

"They're not cruel," I say. "These are the forgotten children. Sons and daughters of Cain. It's said that God has a place in heaven for every child who dies, but this isn't true. 'Tis above as it is below', and if a child is unloved by his mother and father here, so is he unloved in heaven. There is no room for imperfection in the throne room of God, and there is none so imperfect as an unloved child. They are the monsters of the Earth, the sowers of hate, the enforces of cruelty, it's them to thank for plagues, and it's them to blame for the God's harsh judgment."

She gazes again at the gift and shakes her head. "It was for that I wanted a boy or a girl. I'd a thought for what love was. I'd heard some stories, fairytales, and in them was this idea of love. I wanted, when my time came, I wanted that I would love."

She laughs, and its sound is both terse and hollow, and then she says, "My own grand slapped me three times when I told her I would never strike my child. She called me a liar, she told me only the devil never hit a child, because the devil don't like fear. But I don't know why the fear's so important. It's in every part of me. I eat, drink, and when I can sleep, I sleep in a cold puddle of it. I know I could have loved. I know I could."

"Of course you can," I say. "I can stop the boat here and you can go into the cemetery. You'll find a thousand souls desperate to be loved. You could pour forth a fountain of unending love and these children will take it. They'll take more than any mortal child ever could. They'll whisper your name for all eternity."

Silence rests between my passenger and myself, but the bayou and its offerings don't relent. She covers her ears and says, "No, no, we must not dally. For all the love I give, will it ever quench their thirst?"

"No," I say. "I'm afraid not, but you'll always be needed and you'll always be wanted. You'll not die alone and you'll not suffer the sadness you feel now."

"No, no bayou woman," she says. "I don't mean to misspeak my place, but I think you can't know the weight of my sadness. It's heavy enough to rip from my soul, and fall through Earth, and then through heaven, and right through the heart of God, like that arrow loosed from Nimrod's bow. Don't stop. Please, please continue."

#

She hugs the swaddled cloth to her chest and rocks until we pass beyond the graveyard. The whispering voices of the ghost children blend into the soft music of the wind flowing through the cattails. My passenger sobs. I do not have tears, but I carry a handkerchief. I offer it to her.

"I cannot," she says. The piece of cloth is likely finer than any clothing she owns.

The gondola arrives in the cathedral district, the final section of the Crescent City.. Here the spires of temples and churches reach into the night sky like the claws of some starving beast, grasping for what little sustenance God will feed it. A crowd has gathered outside the great doors of The Holy Trinity Cathedral of All Saints and in the church's yard they have built a tower of old broken furniture, dirty rags, and rotting wood. A stake extends from the wood and tied to the stake is a woman close in age to my passenger. The crowd's cries fill the night:

"Burn the sinner, burn the witch, send her to Hell, the filthy bitch."

"What're they doing?" she asks.

I don't answer. There's no point. It's clear what they plan. I know my passenger must speak because she needs to hear herself question the spectacle.

"Is there nothing you can do?" she asks.

"I am doing all that I am able, at the moment."

"They'll kill that woman," she says.

"Maybe she deserves it," I say. "Maybe she's done something wretched and terrible like dined on fish on Monday morning instead of Friday. Maybe she went to confession and mispronounced the name of God's mother. Maybe when the parson's sister asked for sugar, she gave her salt."

Now her face is a mask of scorn and indignation as she says, "Beg your pardon. I know you are a thing made, like a machine or like Adam, created from mud and breath. I can't believe even a thing like you wouldn't know this is wrong. Is it because of your mast—"

"No," I say. "I've allowed you to join me on the journey, I've answered your questions, and I've shown you many paths, but you shall not mention my master. In the Crescent City we are all servants. Even these people about to commit a barbaric act. The woman tied to the stake, she too is the master's servant. And you, my love. You're as much the master's servant as I. Don't question the springs and gears, only be glad the clock does tick."

She watches as the pile is lit. As the orange light of the blaze reflects off the bayou, she mutters, "Just wish there was something I could do."

"Oh, there is. I could stop the boat and you could join the crowd. Your voice could blend into their voices and together you could call down the holiest spirit of them all, the spirit of righteous indignation, and that righteousness will fill you with a fire so powerful your mind will grow numb to empathy and sorrow. All who you have hated for the injustice they have done to you could eventually find their way to that stake. They too could lick the cleansing flames. That is an option. I could stop the boat, if you like."

"No, no bayou woman," she says, barely in a whisper, "don't stop, do not, but please tell me we're reaching the end soon. I have reached the place where my daddy's beatings take me. That place where I don't feel nothing and I can be all, completely alone. If we don't arrive soon, I'm sure I won't ever come back."

"We are close now," I say.

#

I row along the bayou until it opens to the wide Lake Pontchartrain. I anchor my boat to the roots of the lake grass that grows in the murky depths. A paddleboat chugs to the canal leading to Lake Borgne and in the far distance the gaslights from the only bridge leading into the heart of the Crescent City reflect off the water.

"What now?" my passenger asks.

"When they reach toward the boat, you're to put your stillborn into the lake. No matter what you see, you mustn't go in the water. No matter what you've heard, there's no life for you there. Do you understand?"

She nods.

"I need to hear that you understand," I say. "What you release this night is no longer yours. You are giving it a new life, but not one you can ever be a part of."

"I understand," she says. "But you don't have some other offer? Some other path? Some choice?"

"None that you would want to take," I say.

After a few minutes the sound of water lapping against the gondola is joined by a chorus of soft voices. The chorus volume increases from a light whisper to a choir of men and women singing, "*A-a-a-men. A-a-a-men, amen, amen, and amen. Glory, glory, days. A-a-men. Glory, glory, days.*"

As this song builds, under the dark water, bright beings lit by luminous skin gather near the shore. They've come as family, as friends, holding the hands of their children, some of them are young, and some of them are old, and they have the eyes of frogs, the mouths of fish, and feet like fins. There's happiness to their song and the way they swim in one another's company. They are a congregation held together by love.

Around the boat they form a half circle, like an audience about to bear witness to the holy word of God from a traveling evangelist. They finish their chorus of song and let it die down to a light hum, and a young couple swims together to the boat. A young male and a young female. They have no child with them. They hug one another, and this gets a few cheers and shouted *hallelujahs!* from the crowd, but then they turn to the boat and offer up their hands to the surface.

My passenger glances up at me, there are tears in her eyes, and though I've no gift for seeing such things, I'm certain there are tears in her heart. I nod to her.

She rocks her swaddled gift once, twice, three times more, brings its tiny head to her trembling lips, and in a whisper so faint I barely hear it, says, "Goodbye."

She leans over the gondola and hands the stillborn to the luminous beings in the water. They accept the gift, remove the swaddling that floats away like a puff of smoke, and each takes turn breathing into the dead baby's mouth. After a few tries, the baby twitches. Then its arms and legs kick. Its skin fades from a chalky gray to a bright, shining green. The couple passes the squirming child between them, holding it to their bare skin, kissing it on its tiny head.

"She's alive," my passenger says. "She's alive."

And she turns to me to give me the expression that so many other women have in the past. There have been times I've let a woman go without warning. It's petty of me, but if she was especially cruel or judgmental towards me, I'd let her jump into that water and I'd watch as the lake people devoured her flesh.

I don't allow it this time. I grab the sharecropper by her dress and hold her. She fights to break away from my grip, but I am no woman. I may appear as a woman. Many a man has foolishly approached me as though I am eligible for their affections. But I am a thing. I am made of the swamps and dead sparrows and all the sorrows that wash up on the bank of the Mississippi. I know a thing or two about holding onto rage, and holding onto a powerful sadness, and so I grasp this woman despite the fact it breaks every sparrow heart that's ever beat inside me until she has fallen to the boat, covered her eyes, and cried out all of her tears.

When all the luminous families and friends have returned to their city at the bottom of the lake, I row the gondola to the head of the bayou. The first stop before entering the Crescent City is the road to the countryside. I pull my boat over and give my passenger two paths.

"This road will take you to the place where you came from," I say. "The place that gave you your sorrow. You may leave the boat now, take that road to your destination, and live your life as a woman who has survived this night. You say you want to give love. Well, there will be plenty of chances for you to give that love if you take this path. Or you can stay in the boat, take this gondola's rod from me, and then return to the Crescent City to discover what the master with the skull's face and the big top hat will make of you."

My passenger doesn't say a word. She gathers her skirting, and without taking the offer of my burden, steps from the gondola to the road. I watch her march, almost run down the dirt path with her skirts held tight in her hands. The moon hangs high and bright, as beautiful as the image in her letter, and its reflection lights her path.

#

I return to my quarters, my master's servants feed me, bathe and perfume me, and before I retire to the dream world to meet with him, I open the window to my apartment. It overlooks the entire city, and in the distance slithers the mighty Mississippi, and along with the wind I hear the joyous singing of the luminous lake people, celebrating the birth of a brand new baby girl.

I wonder what fate awaits her mother. Before I drift to sleep, I think on the night I made the choice to remain on the boat. What would my life be, had I taken the country road?

MOTHER OF CRAWDADS

BETSY PHILLIPS

It probably goes without saying, but you don't want fifty crawdads up your cooter. No matter how small they are, those bugs are coming out at some point and you gotta think about things like claws or that feathery tail.

But here I was, spewing tiny lobsters all over—the toilet, the floor, the crotch of my panties—and here's how you know you're at a Walmart and not a Target. You birth fifty crawdads at Target, someone's got their phone out and you're on the cover of the Weekly World News. At Walmart, no one wants to get caught up in someone else's weird-ass shit. They all act like they can't see.

"No, no, no, I need them crawdads!" I reached down into the toilet, which you got to know is the lowest moment you can have, fishing something valuable out from your own toilet water. But I got them, most of them, I think. "Lily Bell, bring me a bag," I hollered and I don't know what everyone else in the bathroom must have thought was going on. When I was a girl, you could buy bait at Walmart—small, silvery fish, fat ole nightcrawlers, crickets, and, sure, even crawdads—and back then, if they found you in the bathroom with your drawers full of them, they would have said you were a shoplifter and called the po po on you.

Lily Bell came back with a bag and we scooped up as many crawdads as we could find and put them in it. Have a Nice Day. That's what the bag said. Well, we'll see.

My sister married a creek. This ain't the strangest thing she ever done, but a creek don't make meth in your car or sell your baby's toys for money or shove you into the door when he's drunk, so whatever, marry a creek, Flo. You done worse.

The state called it Jenkins Branch and the state knew a lot about it, because it tended to flood. When they ran the new state road through, they put it high up, on a long bridge, where the water couldn't touch it. That was fine with us. Rather a road above us than next to us, I thought.

But Nashville's spreading out this way, like a tick on an artery. Lub-dub, it's bigger. Lub-dub, it's bigger still. Eventually, they were fixing to put up a big new subdivision on the other side of the state road, right along the creek. Well, we're neighborly, so we didn't think nothing of it. Until the backhoe showed up. Then the giant concrete pipes.

"They running sewer out here?" Flo asked.

"I don't think so," I said. I was afraid to say what I though, afraid what she might do. They was going to bury that creek. Put it under ground. Flo was going to bury another spouse. She'd barely lived through Rodney dying. I didn't see how she could make it through losing someone good for her. And the creek had been good for her. She put on some weight, stopped drinking, found some dance lessons for Lily Bell. It's a wonder what being loved will do for some folks.

We did what we could do to stop them. We pulled out all the wires we could reach in the backhoe. We slashed the tires of the construction workers' trucks when they wasn't looking. We found some dynamite Rodney'd left in the shed and we blew up three of them concrete pipes.

The sheriff came out and asked us about it, but mostly, they considered us too dumb to find our ass with both hands and thought dead Rodney was the only one with any ambition, so they settled on blaming environmentalists.

One day, I was at Foodland and I could tell the girls in front of me were not from around here. They was wearing windbreakers, which is not a thing any of us would spend money on. Just put on a sweatshirt. And one of them had a notebook and they were talking about the Clean Water Act.

"Are you environmentalists?" I asked. I didn't really know for sure those were a real thing and not just something the sheriff made up, but the world's big. You got to be prepared for all kinds in it.

"Kind of. We're grad students," they said. "We're studying the Nashville crayfish."

"What's that?"

"Well..., see..., there's... a... special... kind... of... crayfish...," The red-headed gal was talking so slow, like I needed five seconds for each word to settle in my brain. I get that, when people look at us, all they see are ignorant rednecks, and there's a lot I don't know, but I'm not dumb. "And... it... only... lives... in... Mill... Creek..., as... far... as... anyone... knows. ... It's... protected... so... we... have... to... be... very ... careful... with... the... creek..., so... the... crayfish... can... thrive.... We're... checking... other ... streams... in... the... area... for... the... Nashville... crayfish... or..., maybe..., some... other... species... no... one's... found... before."

"So, you got a special crawdad, and nothing can happen to the place it lives?" You can see what I was thinking. But how the hell do you get a crawdad that don't live nowhere else if there's not already one in your creek?

I packed up Flo and the kids in the truck and we went in to the city to try to find Mill Creek and some of them crawdads so rare you can't fuck with their creek.

Swear to God, it probably took us an hour to get through Nashville, but we had an easy time getting into the creek, scrambling down the bank, pants rolled up clear to our knees. The kids were overturning rocks and Flo and me were poking in holes with sticks, though Flo was also screaming and yelling "Oh, snake! Snake!" But it never was a snake. She just likes shrieking.

"Ask this creek where we find them bugs," I said. "Save us some time."

"Oh, no, they don't like it if you talk to them without someone to vouch for you," Flo said. This was stupid as shit. How's a creek end up with a bunch of friends with opinions on people? There some kind of creek Rotary club?

"Well, then, next time, I guess we'll just bring a jar full of your spouse with us and let it tell everyone we're okay," I said.

"Don't be stupid," Flo said. "How's a way-up-north creek know a creek clear down here?"

"Got one!" That was Lily Bell. She held up a crawdad, 'bout as big as my thumb, with red-tipped claws.

"Yep, that's different than regular," I said. "Let's grab a bunch and bring them home. Flo, go get the cooler out of the truck."

Well, she wasn't halfway up the bank when them two environmentalists from Foodland show up and they're confused and then pissed.

"What are you doing?" the one with the high ponytail said. "These are protected waters. You can't fish in them. I'm calling the police."

"Now, now," I said and then I think the red-headed one did recognize me. "We're not looking to eat these crawdads. We're just trying to see if these special crawdads are the same as the ones in our creek. But they ain't."

The red-headed one narrowed her eyes at me. "What do the crawdads in your creek look like?"

"They're a might bigger, with sky-blue claws."

Them girls looked at each other.

"Are they all blue?"

"That could be the Florida blue crayfish."

"But just the claws? That could be a variant of Orconectes shoupi. We could name it after ourselves!"

"Orconectes shoupi HaileyandJen!"

"Where do you all live?" the ponytailed one asked. Flo told her where Jenkins Branch was. No, no, no! But she told them to come on by, give us a call before they came clear out there. Damn it, Flo.

How was I supposed to get a big crawdad with sky-blue claws in our creek in, like, no time? Wishing? Magic?

Aw, crap. Yep. Magic.

I was gonna have to go see that witch, Miss Ruby. Rodney's grandma.

She let me stand outside her trailer for fifteen minutes after I knocked. I heard her in there, rummaging around, looking for a gun to shoot me to death with.

"Come on, Miss Ruby," I said.

"You had no right!" she hollered back, her voice cracking on the high notes. She found the damn gun. Threw open that aluminum door and pointed a big old Colt .45 right at my face.

"How many times did Rodney steal from you?" I fished the gun out of her hand and set it gentle on the front step. "And that winter, when you fell and broke your hip? It wasn't some stiff breeze knocked you off your feet."

"I raised him," she hissed at me.

"That's on you," I said. We both stood there, waiting to see which one of us was going to break first. She's evil, but I'm stubborn. She let me in.

I told her what I needed: a brand new crawdad. Not just one. I needed a creek full of them and I needed their line to continue.

"Sure," she said. She pulled a cigarette out of her housecoat. Held it to her lips. It lit, on its own. Or Satan gave her a light, without showing himself. Either's possible. "I can do that."

"That's it?"

"Just tell me you did it," she said. "And tell me how." She pulled a small tape recorder out of another pocket, slid it across the table, and hung her finger over the record button.

"You already know," I said.

"Tell me."

I stared in her beady black eyes as long as I could, then I watched out the window at the orange cat sneaking through the tall grass toward a mockingbird. Mockingbirds are tough sons-of-bitches. I couldn't say for certain who was going to come out ahead.

Here's the thing. Flo's my baby sister. Her and me, the kids, and that scrap of dirt we live on that Momma left us when she died. That's my world.

Rodney always was a piece of shit. But when he kept it to speeding around, running over stray dogs, drinking, and squabbling with his own family? Fine.

But he's punching my sister? That's different.

I turned back toward her. I nodded. She hit 'record.'

"You remember when me and Rodney was little and you had that black cat, with the white patch on her tail?"

She nodded. Now it was her turn to not have the guts to look me in the face.

"You remember when she had kittens? You remember what Rodney did to the little calico? I still hear that kitten screaming. Thirty years, I still have nightmares. And what did you do, Miss Ruby? You took the rest of those kittens to the creek and held them under water 'til they died."

She snapped her head toward me, her lips curled into a growl. "And what would you have had me do? Keep them around so he could torture them all?"

"You know, he don't breathe any better than them kittens under water," I said, licking my lips, daring her to pass judgment on me. "Easy enough. Would have saved us all a bunch of misery, if you'd had the guts right then."

"Say it. Say it!" she screamed. "Say what you did to my boy. Say it and let me show your sister what an evil, vile piece of trash you are."

I sat back in my chair, propped my arm up over the back, and I looked at her, realizing for the first time, her, too. Thinking we was stupid.

"She knows." I said. Flo wasn't too happy with me at first, but she's come around. I shrugged. Maybe Ruby'd start to feeling the same way. Hard to tell.

"Get out," Miss Ruby said.

Sure, I left, but that old witch and me were at a stand-off. I didn't have my crawdads. She didn't have her confession. I wasn't too surprised when I saw the ghost of Rodney standing at the four-way stop down at the end of the road. I'd rattled her. She's gonna rattle me.

Took him most the afternoon to make it down the lane. I sent Lily Bell a couple of times to ride her bike out to see how far he was and, for being the one folks thought was ambitious, he sure was taking his time getting to the house. I didn't know what would happen when he got there, but I figured it would suck for me.

After dinner, I got on Lily Bell's bike and I made my way up the dirt lane, past Rodney. I stopped a ways up the road and turned back toward him. He wasn't easy to see in the sunset, but he was there, turning and turning, back toward me. I rode that bike across the pea gravel, over the gullies the rain had washed into the road, slow up the hill and too fast back down the other side, until, once it was good and dark, I ended up back at Miss Ruby's.

I sat on her front step and waited. Come about eight o'clock, she started getting ready for bed. I didn't see no sign of Rodney yet, but I knew he was out there, making his way to me, just like she'd set him to. By eight-thirty, all the lights in her trailer were out and, after a while, I could hear her soft snores.

I went through a bad spell in my younger days. I did some shit I ain't proud of. A lot of it with Rodney. I can't tell you why. I reckon it was seeing that thing with the kitten. It screwed me up. But it's like I tried to make Miss Ruby see: he was a kid. She was an adult. My granny was an adult. Everyone else who heard that poor kitten and came outside, they were adults.

And they were all afraid of Rodney.

No one spanked him or took a switch to him. No one smacked him with a hairbrush or an electrical cord. They didn't make him stand in the corner until his legs burned and his feet ached and the bruise on his cheek throbbed like a bass drum. They kept their hands to theirselves.

Which meant that Rodney scared the shit out of me and I hated him, but, holy Sweet Jesus, I wanted to learn what it took to make grown folks leave their hands off you. So, Rodney was also my best friend.

We broke into Miss Ruby's trailer more times than I can count. You could pick the lock with two pieces of bailing wire easier than you could rummage for a key.

That's what I did right then. Sat myself down at her kitchen table and waited for Rodney to join us.

Soon enough he lumbered into the trailer and began to toss shit around. He threw a lamp across the front room, knocked over the recliner, and shook all the pictures off the wall. He came into the kitchen and he looked like hell. I don't know what afterlife Miss Ruby had drug him out of, but Death did not sit easy on him.

When he saw me, he howled like someone had run sandpaper across his nuts.

I heard Miss Ruby behind him before I saw her.

"Well, go on, kill her," she said. Rodney turned toward her, his head revolving clear around first, then his body, then his legs. It was creepy as fuck. He reached out to her and I think both her and me thought he was fixing to hug her. But he slipped them ghost hands around her neck and started to strangle her.

It took me longer to jump up than it should have, I admit. I was so tickled by how shocked she was that he turned on her. But I did get up and I did go over to him and whisper, "You promised me you was done doing things that would hurt Lily Bell. Losing her granny would hurt her."

He dropped his hands. I put my arm around Ruby and led her to the kitchen table. Rodney turned the lights on and, like ghosts do, he vanished in the electric light. I looked around for some tea and put a cup in the microwave.

"What are you doing, Miss Ruby?" I handed her the cup, and she let it sit, watching the steam rise up out of it.

"He was my whole life," she said, the corners of her mouth turned down so far I almost couldn't understand her. "I raised him. I thought I could do better with him than I'd done with his daddy and I'd have at least one good thing to show for this dumb life. He could have changed. You don't know. He could have." Now she was crying. I handed her a half-dirty napkin from the pile of dishes by my elbow.

I can't tell you how long I hoped he'd change. I hoped being with me would change him. I hoped me dumping him would change him. I hoped jail would change him. I hoped, well, after I was done being pissed, I hoped Flo could change him. I hoped having step-sons would change him. I hoped Lily Bell would change him. I hoped right up until the end.

"Promise me you'll change." Those were the last words I said to him.

"I promise. I won't never hurt Lily Bell again. I swear." Those were the last words he said to me. I was about to let him up, but I got a vision in my head of that kitten screaming, its arms limp at its sides, and I saw again in my mind Lily Bell's arm yanked out of socket. And I knew he meant what he said only until he didn't mean it no more.

We had fought. He'd beat the shit out of me, but he was drunk and I wasn't and I got him upside the head with his own whiskey bottle. He fell into the creek and I lept on top of him. I held him under. I pulled him up. We said those words to each other and I leaned forward and he went under and that was that.

I told the Sheriff that, after Rodney'd beat me up, he stumbled off drunk and had an accident. No witnesses except the creek and it kept quiet on the matter. Which I respect.

"Miss Ruby, you help people every day." I patted her arm. Her skin felt like dry leaves. "Folks can't afford doctors or divorce lawyers or social workers, you're here for them and you fix 'em right up. That's a life to be proud of. You done good. And look at Lily Bell. You got her. Straight As. You know that wasn't our side of the family." It was, but whatever.

She nodded and blew her nose into that dirty napkin.

"You killed him?" She turned her head so she was watching my reflection in the dark of the window. I turned so I was watching hers, ghostly, hovering over the black night.

"Yes, ma'am."

She shut her eyes. She was real quiet and still. I counted the seconds. One Mississippi. Two Mississippi. Twenty-seven rivers later, she spoke.

"Hearing you say it didn't change nothing." Her scratchy, defeated voice made me sadder than I could stand. For so long, you build your life around, "if only..." and you get that "only" and it don't fix nothing. I guess I knew that. About myself anyway. I was hoping it was different for her.

"Sorry."

"Well," she took a deep breath and then a long sip of her tea. "Let's get you those crawfish. Any special requirements?"

"I told them environmentalists that they were big and that they had sky blue claws."

She stood up and began rummaging around the kitchen. She got out some Tony Chachere's and a jar of small eyes. I want to say 'newt' but that seems too obvious, don't it? She went in the other room and came back with a light blue crayon. She dumped all the spice mix, the eyes, and the crayon into a cereal bowl.

"Go out in the yard and fetch me a crawfish," she said. "You just tell them it's for me and they'll send someone out for you."

I got out into the back yard just as she started to mumble into the bowl and stir it with a dirty spoon that came out of the sink on its own and rested itself in her hand.

"Hey, y'all," I called, squatting down in the dim light from the kitchen window. "Miss Ruby needs a crawdad." I waited maybe a minute or two, and out of the darkness there came the biggest crawdad I ever saw. A lobster would have looked at it and been all "Is that my baby?" I reached out my hand, and it crawled up onto me.

When we got in the house, it went right into her hand.

"Thank you," she said. I thought she meant me, but then she cracked that thing in two and added it to the bowl. She stirred some more. Said some more words in some foreign language and then she said, "Ta-da!"

I looked in the bowl. There was fifty brown crawdad eggs.

"Wow," I said. "Now what?"

"Momma, you have to shelter those eggs under your tail and kept them moist."

"Oh no I don't!"

But you know I did. I put them all in my cooter and I regretted every decision in my life that had brought me to this point.

I went home and I sat myself in the creek and I waited. The environmentalist girls called a couple times, but I told Flo to tell them we was all sick. Lily Bell came out to the edge of the water and read me stories to help me pass the time. But mostly, I just sat there, and I was growing more and more bored. So bored, that soon enough, I could even understand the creek.

It was telling me stories about how the holler had been before people lived in it, how the bison would come through, and before them, bigger, stranger things. How mastodons babies would splash in the water, just south of where we was and how humongous wolves drank standing on its banks. It told me that, for a long while, a family of beavers as big as me lived here and during that time, the creek was a pond and a marsh and a tiny, tiny brook.

It told me that it had siblings up in the hills and that they all considered the Cumberland to be like a grandparent in some ways, old and wise, but also like a child they all parented, since they all went into making it and keeping it healthy.

I asked if there was ever jealousy among creeks and quick as can be, it laughed and said no, but then it paused and said, well, it had heard that the Mississippi and the Ohio can be told apart, one brown and one green, for miles past Cairo, sometimes clear to New Madrid. Two rivers, laying side by side in the same bed, refusing to mix. The creek didn't know if that was jealousy, but it was very strange and the creek thought that wasn't how folks should behave unless there has been some kind of betrayal.

I learned a lot about creeks and waters in general, though I don't know that I'll ever need to use that learning.

Now you may wonder how I ended up popping them crawdads out at the Walmart, if I was spending all my time in the creek, but it was simple enough. Flo started hollering out the bathroom window that she was having a tampon emergency—she needed one and there weren't none—and I yelled for her to use a pad and she said we was out of those, too, and I yelled, well, who's the dumbass who didn't pick some up at the store last week?

But it was me, busy sitting in the creek.

Which I guess brings us back to where we started. Me and Lily Bell came back home with our sack of crawdads and the stuff to free Flo from the bathroom. I sent Lily Bell inside with the supplies and I went down to the creek. I dumped most of them in the water right behind our house. The creek did the rest. Some it spit right back into the warm wet dirt of the creek bank. Some it carried farther down and tucked in under the big rocks by the four-way stop. I didn't see where the rest of them went.

Flo and Lily Bell came out of the house now and the three of us followed the creek up under the road and past the empty, treeless spot where the new subdivision was supposed to get a playground, and on into the area where the backhoe had already carved out a big chunk of dirt. I took half the crawdads I had left and I put them right where the backhoe had been digging in the creek.

"I'm sorry," I said to them, because if any of the crawdads was gonna die, it was probably gonna be these guys. Still, I hoped they might make it.

Then we walked further still, through the subdivision, up into the hillside, and past the blackberry bramble and the line of sumac, up where the creek was a damp spot and a dream, just a small trickle hoping to someday make it to the Cumberland. We left the final five there.

We watched one, his little blue claws still so soft, his tiny tail curling and uncurling in the shallow water. He clung for a while to a leaf and then he dug himself into the dirt and we didn't see him no more.

"Live," I whispered. "Please, just live."

More than a month later, after Lily Bell was back in school, those gals came out to look at the construction site. Low and behold, right in the path of the next concrete pipe, there was a crawdad nobody had ever seen before. Flo reached over and squeezed my hand as those gals' eyes got wider and they started taking pictures and sending those pictures to their scientist friends.

After lunch, the construction site was jammed with people—the contractor, the backhoe guy, some gal from the developers, more lawyers than you could shake a stick at, a guy from the state who kept telling people he wasn't there on official state business, but that, yes, this did look new, unknown, rare.

"Endangered," the gal with the high ponytail said. They all went dead silent.

"You can't do anything else to this creek," the red-headed gal said. "You probably need to put it back how it was."

"Not without our oversight," the guy from the state said. "No one touches anything or moves anything until we have a chance to get up here and look around." The guy from the state was pissed, Flo and me could tell that. He came over to us and shook our hands. He was sweating.

"I remember y'all," he said. "You live downstream. I did the environmental impact survey when they put the road through here. I documented all the wildlife and I cleared this stream for a road to come through. I could kick myself. I totally missed this. Biggest find of the year, of the decade, even and I missed it."

"Don't feel too bad," I said. "We never saw them before the bridge, either. But you think this ol' creek will be protected now?"

"Yep," he said.

Flo and me shared a grin.

The other day, I took the truck into town and I stopped at Miss Ruby's. She stood in her front doorway, wearing her house coat, smoking on another in a long line of cigarettes.

"So you saved the creek," she said. "You and all your crawfish babies."

"We saved the creek," I said. I shoved my hands in my pockets. "Thank you. Really and truly." I squinted into the late afternoon light, trying to see the look on Miss Ruby's face. I couldn't make it out. "We all had about all the grief we can stand, I figure." She nodded. "You want to come out for dinner this weekend? We got them college girls and that dude from the state coming. Lily Bell would like to see you."

"What you having?"

"Crawdad boil." I waited as long as I could, watching her face go from shocked to horrified to angry to shocked again. "No, I'm just teasing. We're doing pulled pork."

DANCE OF MYAL

MAURICE BROADDUS

The ghosts of home smell like curry. The aroma fills the house as I stir the small saucepan of chicken, and with it being almost ready, I turn down the heat on the giant pot of rice and peas. My neighbor grew the red beans in her garden, as a favor to me. It seemed only fitting that I try my mother's recipe. I even soaked the beans overnight with the ritual solemnity of reciting liturgy. This is what home is supposed to smell like: a living room with a faint hint of lemon-scented furniture polish and a dash of the aroma of moth balls emanating from the closet; meat marinating in a thick gravy; a bubbling bowl of rice and peas; and tea brewing, but not too long or else it gets bitter. The smell of my childhood home.

Sometimes I worry that I'm a broken story. That could be my title: "The Broken Story of Faren Sims." The kind where you can be reading along and you know something's not right. You can't quite put your finger on it, you just know it's not working, you lose interest, and you quit reading. Some stories pass from parent to child, like an inter-generational game of telephone, the parents and grandparents hoping that the story will be remembered the right way by the time the great grand-children hear it. If it is remembered at all.

I once toyed with the notion of becoming a caterer. I guess I still do, late at night when I toss and turn, unable to commit to sleep, my mind racing with ideas, could-have-beens, and dread. As if one story of who I am, or was supposed to be, was overwhelmed by another. I portion out a serving of food on a jade-colored Fire King dish from a set of dishes my grandfather used to own. I was never the best at plating food, probably another reason I ought to let the dream of catering go, but this wasn't about presentation as much as it was about respect.

I back out of the patio door, careful to not let the door clatter shut and risk jarring the precariously balanced plate. The house belongs to my grandfather—we called him Pap—a two story home in our little corner of the Riverside neighborhood in Indianapolis. When Pap lost it, a slumlord owned it and nearly ran it into the ground before he skipped out on the taxes and took off to Florida. I bought it last year in a tax sale. Its façade is cracked and chipped, but the bones remain intact. The backyard opens onto a trail.

The air smells of rain-soaked logs. A wan breeze barely flutters the leaves. The trees hide the path, crowding the little used trail. A gate concealed by bushes blocks the route to the canal from the other side, not that it has ever stopped the occasional shortcut taker. The walk to the canal used to remind my mother of her home in Jamaica. She said that every morning she, her brothers, and sisters had to walk five miles to collect water from a cave for the day's use. I never envied my mother's stories.

All manner of foliage presses in until it finally relents at the clearing. A bank of exposed roots, a conspiracy of tree limbs and tall weeds, ring the canal near the concrete bridge. Brackish water feeds the dark earth. A fraught silence freezes the air, as if I've interrupted an ancient argument between stream and earth. A large rock shaped like a raised fist juts from the water. A neighborhood group had received money to erect a statue of a long-time elementary school principal. The base is as far as they got. The River Mumma rests upon it like it's an altar in her honor. My mother, now another ancestral spirit waiting to be remembered in story and passed along, whispered of the River Mumma's impending arrival to me in a dream.

The River Mumma follows the river. By the noon day sun, their ilk are the most radiant of women, and this one is no exception. Her flawless skin is a delicate shade of mahogany. Black hair falls to the small of her back. She presses her hands against the cold stone, her body perfectly poised, waiting with a regal air as I attend her. She shifts. At her waist, her body morphs, her skin fractures like crystal petals, and the scales of her fish form glisten. She tucks the rest of her tail under her, eclipsing it from view.

She runs a gold comb through her hair. I never quite meet her eyes. Her eyes see truths.

"In days gone by, we would come and dance *myal* for a River Mumma, but you don't know about that," my mother once said to me, but the words hung in the air between us like a question. Or a test. She wanted to know, without asking directly because that was never her way, if I were born with the gift. Too? Another word that went unspoken because perhaps she also had the gift and hid it within her practice of being a nurse. *Myal* speaks of the old ways and runs even deeper than the science, *obeah*. People think of obeah and voodoo as the same thing. Close enough, I suppose, as far as outsiders need understand. But those who practice *myal* call on spirits and they dance. Lord, how they dance. Everyone joining in, both a community practice and the practice of community, bridging the spirit and the physical worlds. Bringing healing.

I dip my toes into the water, about as much of me as I trust in the canal's current condition. Abandoned and mistreated, its presence taken for granted when all it wanted to do was do good. Or at least be. In peace. Safe in its own home.

I sense eyes watching me. I'm fully aware of how prey feels being stalked. My palms sweat. My thoughts become an inchoate jumble, driven only by the impulse to run. To hide. Packing up my things and heading back to the house, I retreat to safety in the nearest cover. When I glance over my shoulder, the River Mumma has abandoned her perch.

#

A man knocks at my door. A few tremulous heartbeats later, my cell phone chirps. Groceries have been dropped off. I have the delivery people text me when they arrive. The first time they knocked on the door, the sound filled me with a gnawing dread. My mind drifted off. I don't know how long I stood at the door before I moved to answer it. I didn't recognize the man on my porch. He turned and stared right at me. I ran to the far corner of the room and refused to open the door. The hollow erratic beat of the knock threatened to consume me. I left the groceries out there until someone took them that night. At night, things are always taken.

So many weeks later, that dread hasn't improved much. I sleep with the lights on. In the dark I swear I hear things moving around in the room.

Still, I've gotten better. A baseball bat cants at an angle against the door frame, like it fell asleep on a friend's shoulder, within easy reach. I steel myself. I always have my tennis shoes on now, always prepared, even sleeping with them on. I'll never not be ready again.

When I swing the door open, Kevin Paschal–known as Pass within the community, a part time drug dealer as well as would be real estate mogul—paces my porch as if he owns the place. He certainly wants to. He's made it clear that my house would make a fine addition to his collection of properties throughout the neighborhood. He calls himself one of us, but he's no better than the slumlord who ran down our neighborhood. Pass lives on the border of the Golden Hills neighborhood which sits next to ours, but on the border nonetheless. Golden Hills represents old money, the family names of mayors and governors and executives. Kevin represents hood money.

"Nice necklace, Faren." His half-shut eyes, as if perpetually bored, focus on my exposed cleavage. Suddenly uncomfortable with his level of scrutiny of my neck, I cradle my necklace—an eye of Horus on a gold chain—in my hand, blocking his view.

Kevin is bald, the rest of his face completely clean shaven. A lone skin tag protrudes next to his left eye. He carries his stocky build in the manner of a firefighter wrapped in a lab coat. His bearing is familiar. Not in the face, because I never look him in the face, but in his lumbering swagger, both brutish and confident.

They all move the same way. Though, I know in my head that he couldn't have been the same man behind what happened to me because the police caught that man the same week, less than a mile from Pap's house. His fingerprints and DNA matched, and he was ready to plead out without too much of a fuss, as if part of him secretly wanted to go back to prison. Kevin slips sunglasses onto his face, an irritating affect meant to hide—for those that see—that he comes off like a once bullied nerd not used to playing tough.

"What do you need, Kevin?" I can never bring myself to call him Mr. Paschal because I know how he runs his rental properties. Nor did I presume to call him Pass, as I wasn't part of his clientele's world. A pair of glasses aside, it was like recognizing Clark Kent as Superman but pretending not to notice in order to maintain the veneer of civility and avoid making things awkward.

"I wanted to see if my man installed everything," he said.

"Q does good work if you let him." Q was an old head around the way. The neighborhood handy man who Kevin didn't use nearly as often as he should. "Thank you for the recommendation."

Kevin pretends to inspect the locks, an excuse to cross my threshold. He's the kind of person you quit inviting to cookouts. All to-go plates, cutting in line, and spreading drama wherever he went. My grandfather impressed upon me that we should never criticize our own in front of outsiders. Outsiders didn't know us, didn't understand us, and had no connection to us. They searched for anything to reinforce their backward beliefs. Still, Kevin's a blight on us by any measurement. "No problem. I always liked this house."

"Can I help you?" I lean against the edge of the door, preventing him from seeing any more of my home.

"Just wanted to see if you'd thought about what we talked about."

"I'm not interested in selling."

"I know this place means a lot to you and your family. I just thought that with your recent trouble, you might want to be free of the neighborhood."

"Thank you for your concern." I continue to hold the door open. A stinkbug buzzes in, equally unwelcome, but it takes the hint of the opened door and flies back out. "I'll let you know."

"Faren, I saw you by the canal." His voice thickens, suddenly serious.

"That must've taken some doing."

"There are no easy roads in life, but if you're determined enough … " He bends close to my ear, perhaps attempting to intimate a threat. His presence pales in comparison to my mother, so I remain unmoved.

"I handle my own business." I pad my voice with steel, both hard and unimpressed. "I suggest you leave things be."

Back in Jamaica, River Mummas guard each of the great rivers. Since places are sacred and have a history to be respected, they are terrible water spirits, protectors of the sources of the rivers. Some people whisper that if one was captured, the river would dry up. Few dare risk fishing near where a River Mumma might rest because the fish of that river are thought to be her children. Fewer still dared to anger her. The water whispers its secrets and guards them fiercely.

"We'll talk soon." He turns to leave. "Oh, by the way, someone left this on the rock."

He hands me the River Mumma's comb. The glint in his eye says that he's not finished with me.

#

There were many stories of the River Mumma in Jamaica. One time an owner of a great estate stumbled across the River Mumma. When she vanished, the owner rushed to the waters to find any trace of her. He only caught a glimpse of something bobbing just beneath the surface. It was like a table of pure gold, with intricate drawings carved onto its veneer. The inscriptions spoke to him in a language before words, stirring his heart. Its image filled him with its terrible beauty. His pulse quickened with lust, excited by the fire of the dark obsession possessing his mind. His thoughts collapsed into a singular desire: he had to claim the table as his own. When he disturbed the waves, the table sank, taking its mesmerizing beauty and story and secrets with it. The only evidence he had of her presence was a gold comb. On it he vowed that the golden table would one day belong to him and him alone.

No one encountered a River Mumma and remained unchanged.

#

Pap lived in Indianapolis his entire life. When he was young, the canal bridge served as a boundary. He used to catch fish from the canal before companies started dumping their wastes in it. The owners of Riverside used to live over on Harding and 28th Street, big time politicians, and businessmen. No black people crossed 28th Street back then. All my grandfather knew was that he and his family and anyone who looked like him couldn't go to Riverside Park because it sat on the other side of the canal. Signs that read "Patronage Whites Only Solicited" barred them. On several evenings, he and his family would line up along the bridge and watch the lights of the Ferris wheel go round and round. They listened to the laughter and shouts and sounds of enjoyment with a mix of expectation and envy, like the ancient Israelites unable to enter their Promised Land.

One day a year, Polk's Dairy company sponsored a "milk top" day to thank customers for collecting their milk-bottle caps. His mother collected the milk stoppers—with the face of Elsie the Cow plastered on them—washed them off and made a necklace of them for each of her children. On that blessed day, the children would rush into the park with the guarantee that one milk top meant one penny meant one ride. One day a year, they were allowed to feel equally human.

#

Momma used to wash our clothes in the canal. She'd hang our clothes on a line in the backyard to dry because she had no use for dryers, except in the winter.

#

The land fell under a great drought. The workers of the land grew worried. Some met with the land owner in hopes to persuade him to make

*sacrifices to the River Mumma so that she would renew the land with her
healing waters. The owner had little patience for their superstitious nonsense,
but he withdrew from them and began to scheme. Within their plea he saw
an opportunity to approach the River Mumma. He could bring workers to
accompany him to confront her. With so many marshaled before her, she
would have no choice but to surrender whatever treasures she guarded.*

#

I quit my job not too long after the Incident. The Incident is as close as
my mind allows me to frame what happened. I can't put any more into words.

Only once the court heard his plea—ironic since he paid no
attention to any of mine—did my nightmares lessen. It took months
before I returned to something resembling routine, allowing me room to
cling to the hope that my life might return to normal. Some part of me
secretly knew that couldn't be the case. That the neighborhood took a
piece of who I was. Friends advised me to never return to this place, this
pain, but I had to come back.

Now I work from home. I wake up and head downstairs to fix a cup of
coffee. Drinking it while checking my e-mail, that's the time I wrap my head
around the work I am going to do that day. I can provide tech support from
anywhere. I shuffle from kitchen back to the bedroom to get dressed and back
down to the living room. Rather than remain in pajamas and tennis shoes, I
get dressed so that I feel like I am going to work. This is my life. I can't help
but feel like I am doing penance.

#

There was an eclipse not too long ago. In Indianapolis we had 91%
coverage. Most of the sun's light was blocked by the moon. The day was still
bright, but the world seemed off. The remaining light was eerie and lonely
and sad, like it knew it wasn't what it was supposed to be. But people put on

their eclipse glasses and stared at what remained.

#

My memories of my father amount to a mound under blankets on the couch or on his bed where he stayed between working double shifts. No match to the portrait of the young adventurer painted by Momma. The man who wooed her from across the globe, two distant stories finding each other. The only other image I have of my father is at family reunion picnics. He and my uncles would assemble around his car trunk where he kept a minibar. "Grown folks' Kool-Aid" they called it with a knowing wink, as if we children didn't know what they were doing. I couldn't wait until I was old enough to join in with the secret rituals and conversation of being grown.

I avoid the cabinet above the sink. I know that Vodka, Jamaican rum, gin, wine (Riesling only), and amaretto bottles line up inside it like soldiers awaiting inspection. I used to joke that they wouldn't drink themselves. When I drank, I didn't begin to feel okay, but I did feel less and that was a start. I never saw myself as being happy. Even the word "happy" was so abstract that it lost all meaning for me. "I am happy." "I could be happy." My imagination fails to figure out what happy might look like for me. So I sit and flip channels watching nothing in particular.

I'm not very good at drinking. Or being grown, I suppose.

My father passed away nearly ten years ago. For some time my mother and I moved past each other in the hallways like *duppies*—the shadows of people left behind—haunting our own spaces. We lived in the echo of memory, of hurt not dimmed by the passage of time. Momma reminded me that stories were built on conflict and we were forged in pain. I missed the lilt of my mother's accent, even the sharp pitch of it when it was raised in the heat of anger, which usually happened when she was telling me how I was living my life wrong. I hated to agree with her. A part of me knew, even then, that her raised voice erupted from a place of wanting a better life and more opportunities for me. A vocalizing of *myal* pouches, a healing poultice filled with herbs and earth, hair, nail clippings, and fluid, maybe an article of clothing tucked within. Her death interrupted the fraught, delicate dance of mothers and daughters.

I haven't touched the bottles since I began tending to the River Mumma.

#

People sought out the River Mumma when they wanted to make a change in their lives. Only she could coax me outside. I'm here now. Tending to the Canal Mumma like a nun in a convent. The soft edges of her shape blur as if cloaked in the heat mirage of the noon day sun. Her head is big as a cooking pot; her hair a tangled mess. She hugs her shoulders and stares at the dark swirling eddies as if lost in a dream about the water. She invites me to her.

I am broken. Broken mind. Broken heart. Broken spirit. Broken self. I am tired of fighting. I am worn out by the struggle to be better. I am a pocket watch with missing gears, the pieces lined up almost correctly, but with enough absent that there is no hope of being repaired and working. Storytelling is a part of the healing process. It allows opportunities for others to speak truth into your life. To walk alongside you and break through the loneliness. To access our hearts and end the dance of disconnectedness. I just had to learn to listen. The River Mumma tells me a story.

There was a couple. The man used to go away and leave his wife home alone. Eventually she began seeing another man. One night the husband came home unexpectedly while her lover was still there. The husband knocked at the door. Tap-tap-tap-tap-tap. The woman picked up their baby and began to sing.

"My baby's in my hands and my husband's in bed

Go back and come tomorrow night."

The husband knocked again. Tap-tap-tap-tap-tap. She sang the song again, a bit louder, but not enough to rouse their child. The man banged again. Tap-tap-tap-tap-tap. So she sang a different song.

"What a damn foolish man you are, can't understand,

Go back and come tomorrow night."

So her husband left her alone.

Like with most of my mother's stories, its point eludes me. The River Mumma combs my hair. I rest along the thick coil of her tail.

"Keep your stories to yourself," I say without the heat of anger. I never feel the stories, not deep in my bones like I suspect I was meant to. I brace for the lashing that usually accompanies Momma's roused temper. But the River Mumma just shakes her head. She speaks with certainty, every suggestion having the mettle of command to it. But she pauses—the space of considering the sum of choices made, the little decisions that made her who she is, her own collection of stories—and lowers her voice. Thick with regret, maybe even sorrow, the River Mumma tells me how, as a girl, she repeated the stories of her people, our stories, and wants to pass them down to me. The stories make us strong, tell us who we are. Storytelling is a part of the healing process. But soon the stories and songs will be lost to television and cell phones, she fears.

Without realizing, I looked into the River Mumma's eyes.

"Faren, forgive yourself," she whispers, her intonation and accent without region or allegiance or history. Her voice careful and without offense, the sound of grieving. Her lips pursed in a confession of silence, like she hadn't earned the right to say certain words, or rather the word which stuck in her throat. An apology.

My tongue is no longer able to shape the words to forgive. I shift my weight and I see through her eyes. The poison I'd held onto. The cycle of screwing up relationships as if my goal was to ruin them all along. The constant disgust and anger and resentment and depression and blame collapsing me into a downward spiral of self-destruction.

Though I had forgotten most of Momma's stories and songs, the occasional melody flits through my mind. And a bad story bleeds out.

\#

There once was a young woman in Indianapolis. Life had thrown her more than her share of curves and she wanted to start over in a familiar place. She tried to make a home for herself in the community she once knew and felt safe in. One night a knock came from her front door. When she went to answer it, a man kicked it in and waved a knife toward her. His eyes were fixed and uncaring, caught up in the myal of heroin. He slapped her before she could process what was going on. Punching, kneeing, scratching, she fought as best she could, but the man was stronger and was soon on top of her. He choked her until she barely moved. She remembered the sounds of his grunting and panting, both distant and garbled, as she stared blankly at the open door. When he finished, he cursed at her as if he did her a favor by sparing her life. In the shadow of the doorway, exposed and vulnerable, her sanctuary violated. She wondered if she would ever know wholeness again.

But that was not the sum of her story.

\#

The wet heat of Indiana, accompanied by swarms of mosquitoes, makes the air too thick to breathe with ease. The noon day sun claws across the sky. The sunlight barely penetrates the thick foliage, but I walk the shadow-dappled ground like I am entering an unexplored world. The currents of the creek lap against the concrete barricade with the susurrus of a seashell to the ear whispering the secrets of home. The waters, a muddy green from the thick coat of algae, splash against the embankment. The languorous stream is all seaweed and a melody of shifting sands, with insect larvae under overturned stones trapped within chrysalis of pebbles. Too few fish swim about. From here, I see everything.

Places are sacred and have a history to be respected. The neighborhood. The house. Me.

My teeth are green as the algae bloom clotting the surface of the water.

Pass leads an expedition of four diesel-built brothers stalking through the trail behind him. Bound to one another as if they shared the same cell block. Pass doesn't bother to acknowledge either of us but goes straight to the water's edge. I recognize the look: we possess something he wants and are little more than means to an end.

"Can you see it?" Pass asks.

"Man, I don't … " One of the men looks about and shrugs.

"Right there. All of you reach in."

The drumbeat of *myal* fills my ears. The rhythm rises in my heart. A deep rhythm. It knits my spirit. I am. Whole. There's a splash, like a large rock falling into a deep pool.

The men, little more than cud-chewing oxen, wait for his next command. He snaps in their direction and one of them hands him some chains. Pass glares at him, but the man doesn't know what to do. Pass snatches the chains from him and begins to inspect an edge to fasten them to while the table remains in his sight. Eyes glazed over, he messes with the water. He's beyond the pleas of his own people or his own conscience, caught up in the throes of lust. The golden table ever just out of reach. He edges closer. His foot slips from under him. Off balance, he lands on his back, against the mud-slickened rise of the embankment. He slides into the canal. His eyes widen in panic.

My hand, long and veiny, flexing knife-sharp claws, slices through the water.

As the waters swirl and churn, Pass flaps his arms, thrashing about in the water, trapped in the undertow of its current. The clattering of tangled chains joins the rising chorus of his mens' terrified keening. Pass' head dips beneath the water as if something lashed around his foot and yanked him under the waves.

Pass submerges. His men freeze on the shore in panic. His flailing slows as the waters cover him. His lungs burn as the last of his air escapes them. The waters claim all who try to remove that which does not belong to them.

My eyes gleam red against the shadow of my face. My hair floats like drifting seaweed.

This is my canal.

In my mercy, I am there, wading into his pain. I wrap my arm around him, strong despite its complexion of a mottled corpse. With a swoosh, I propel us to the surface. I cast him to the shore where his people can care for him. They cart him off not daring to look back, much less meet my eyes.

#

I dip my hands in the cool water, letting the gentle current wash over them. An invisible umbilicus runs from me to my mother back to Jamaica through the drumbeat of my heart. The *duppies* of all who try to steal a piece of the community haunt the bridge, clearly seen as the noon day sun passes overhead. I protect the collection of stories that make up the neighborhood. Some with dark chapters. Some best left on the back of a shelf, no longer read and forgotten.

And I make room for a new story.

WHIMPER

NALO HOPKINSON

Da-da-de-dum the light burning within,
Because this cherry world is brighter than sin.

She ran and ran through the undark nightlit city, crashing past
parked cars and motorbikes, shoving between two raucous, dressed-to-
pussfoot women waiting in the line to get into Dutty Wine. They yelled
hey and wha de rass as she broke through them. Smell of orange blossom
shampoo and musk perfume from the two of them glazed the inside of her
nose. Screams from the Dutty Wine line as her leggobeast ploughed through
it, questing tirelessly for her. She sped away from the sound. The sea was so
close. Down that alley. She careened in that direction.

Her right footfront jammed up against something hard. Bright
pain blossomed in her toes. Probably a flagstone jooking up out of the
sidewalk. She couldn't take time to look down. She staggered in her purple
plimsolls. Right knee made a crunk sound, collapsed a little outwards. She
felt the dislocation but not the pain from it. Made shift to stay on her feet,
to runrunrun. Metallic quadruple thumps following behind her, repeated.
She had to reach to the sea wall, throw herself over the side. The air she
sucked in sandpapered her throat, debrided her lungs. Her heart in her chest
was a boiling kettle. Her open mouth the whistle. She pushed on down the
alleyway. Crumpled right knee now stabbing knives into her kneecap with
every stride.

Leggobeasts-them couldn't abide sea water. People said so. Don'
know which people, after nobody survived the touch of their leggobeast.
Every hour of day nor night nowadays, the harbour full up of desperate

bodies, only their heads showing as they bobbed on the oily water. Leggobeasts waited patiently at the water's edge until the person they were chasing gave up and swam back to them to be taken, or got too exhausted to swim and gave their lungs to the water. But she wouldn't. She wouldn't. If she could only reach before the leggobeast touched her.

She clattered through the alley, sobbing. Stumbled around a discarded mattress that reeked heavy of man piss. Sloshed through a reddish muddy liquid that smelled worse. Broken bottles crunched underfoot. And behind her, maybe only couple-three yards now, her personal leggobeast. Everybody had one. At least, is so people said. And when your time come, it going to get you, no matter what. Hers was an iron donkey. And tonight was her time. Her knee screamed with each step. But she moved. The clanking clatter sounded closer. Two yards? One? Her throat-hole was on fire. She broke out of the alleyway, hooves thumpity thump behind her, near enough to throw the shadow of an equine muzzle over her shoulder and onto the ground. Flat, dark sea in front of her, across the two-lane highway. Only things between her and the water: light traffic and the low metal restraining wall. Ranged out all along the narrow lip of soil between the sea wall and the sea; silhouettes of leggobeasts. Each one different.

No time. People had it to say that only the touch of your personal leggobeast would kill you; you were safe from all the others. She dodged cars, blowing panic and pain through her lips. Threw herself over the side of the restraining wall. Limped to the edge. Pushed between two of the shadows. One had deep, rough fur and rank breath. They breathed? The other felt like tree bark.

She let herself fall into the water. A floret of bubbles bloomed upwards around her as she plunged down. She stroked, pushing for the air above. She tried to kick, but her knee screamed at her. She broke the surface and kept swimming away from the shoreline as quickly as she could. She wasn't a good swimmer. The water might as well have been molasses.

"Ow!"

Her hand had smacked someone in the head.

"Sorry," she hissed through clenched teeth. "Beg pardon."

"Is all right," the other woman replied. "Just go easy. Plenty of we in here."

Treading water – though not with the bad leg – she looked around. Her sight had adjusted to the dark. Yes, heads bobbing everywhere, all of them staring back at their leggobeasts on the shore. She swiveled herself around in the water to face hers. "Why nobody swimming away?" she asked the woman beside her.

"Swimming to go where?"

She hadn't thought it through that far. "To a ship?" The harbour was strangely empty.

A man not too far off said, "Once you on the ship, you not in water any more. Your leggobeast will just materialize and take you." His voice was hoarse.

"How long you been in the water?" Sea salt was already making her lips pucker.

He replied, "I don't know. Maybe two days? I can't hold on a lot longer."

Voices called out from the darkness: one day; one hour; don't remember how long; so hungry. A man with bloodshot eyes said, "My own show up this afternoon. Been waiting for 'im. I throw two good bullets in 'im rass from my gun. The shots land, but the bullet holes close right over."

The woman she'd bumped into – who was now dog-paddling slow circles around her — asked, "Which one is yours?" She jutted her chin towards the shore line.

"The shiny one." Her leggobeast had taken its place in the line-up. It was perched, delicately as a hill-climbing goat, on the shallow ledge of land. It looked at her, she was sure of it. It stamped one foot. The air and water were so still, she could hear its bolts rattle.

The woman said, "Look my own yah-so. Three over from yours, to the right."

"The one that look like a tree?"

"A cashew tree, in fact. With a child's face embedded in the trunk."

Something touched her shoulder. She jerked away from it and yelled out before she saw what it was. A length of wooden plank, not yet waterlogged. She grabbed it, gratefully let it take some of her weight. She called out, "I find a piece of wood. Allyuh want to share?"

"Yes, please, lady, do!"

"And me!"

Pretty soon, five of the floaters were clinging to the length of branch, with the rest holding onto their ankles. Had been six of them, but one of them had disappeared as soon as he touched the wood. On the shore, the structure that had looked like a crumbling old shack had disappeared at the same time. She'd forgotten; that was a leggobeast, too.

Soon they had a third row of people clinging to the people clinging to the five. They all starfished out on the surface of the water. She said to the woman who'd first spoken to her, "How come the plank didn't disappear when the leggobeast took that guy?"

"Don't know. I really have to pee."

The water between her and the woman got warm for a few seconds, then cooled off again.

"Sorry."

"Don't fret."

They all floated in silence for awhile. From the horizon, a wash of blue was creeping up the sky. On the shore, her iron donkey reared. It thrust its muzzle to the sky, came down with a clank and a rattling of bolts.

"Yours talk to you?" the young woman asked.

"Only in my dreams."

"I used to dream about mine, too. That's how I knew it was coming."

She called out, more to make conversation than because she really wanted to know, "Allyuh not thirsty? And how you shit?"

"We do it right ya so, lady. The sea does carry it away."

The sea salt was burning her lips. She started to moisten them with her tongue. Thought of what she was floating in. Spat instead. She didn't have plenty to spit with; her mouth was nearly dry. "And how you eat?"

"We don't…"

"I see one boy. He get tired waiting for death. He swim right back up to his leggobeast. Grabbed its ankle. It took him."

She said, "You know what I wonder?"

Someone replied, "What?"

"How we so sure is a bad thing for our leggobeasts to fetch us away?"

"How you mean, how? Is obvious, nuh?"

"No, think; maybe they take us to something better than this. Well, of course better than this right here. But I mean, your lives before your leggobeast; what those were like?"

Thereafter came a litany of joys and woes: a good job; a dying husband; a call from a long lost friend; fifty dollars found between the couch cushions; poverty; prosperity; failed exams; cancer diagnoses. And the guy who admitted having just shot his best friend. The rest of them edged away from him, spoiling the symmetry of the starfish. He sobbed. They watched. Snot glistened on his upper lip. He wailed, "I so sorry, Robbie!" The sobs crested, then fell off. The man let go his hold on the person who was supporting him and floated, spinning in a slow circle. No-one moved to stop him. On the shore, a gelid lump, man-high, disappeared. So did the murderer's body. She couldn't see how he had died.

"See?" said the woman, her new friend in adversity. "That's how we know is a bad thing to let your leggobeast catch you. Even if they don't touch you, when you dead, they go, too. So they nuh must mean death?"

"And that's a bad thing?" The gonging pain in her knee was almost background noise, a spike being driven over and over again into her cold-numbed leg. One of the starfish arms was holding that ankle, but she barely noticed.

"So," said the young woman. "You didn't answer your own question."

She went silent. She didn't want to do this.

But the woman persisted. "What your life was like? Something to stay for, or to run from?"

She swallowed. "I running from the end of the world."

"Of course is the end. One of those things for every human on the planet. How running going to help?"

"I need to stop it. Cause is me who start it."

Murmurs from around and behind her. A voice said, "You? How you coulda do this?"

Someone else said, "Is not she. Is aliens."

Someone else ventured, "Messengers of God."

She said, "No. Is me. I dream them."

The youth across from her: "We all dream them. Is that make we know we number come up."

She replied, "I dream all of them. Every single one. Before this ever start. Dream them by the score. Dream armies of them. I still dreaming them. Six billion of them is a lot of dreaming."

No-one said anything. The sky had lightened to fore-day morning; enough for her to make out their stunned expressions. She pointed to the shore. "That one there? With all those foot-long teeth? I dream he last year. Looking exactly so. I dream the one that take away the Prime Minister last month." She pointed farther down the line. "That one that could be a little girl in her frilly princess dress, except she have too many legs? I dream she. The bruk-down house this plank come from? I dream it last night. Same time I dream my own."

Someone made a small, sad noise. "That duppy girl with the plenty foot is my one. You really send that thing after me? You send them after alla we?"

The creatures were starting to shuffle and shift about uneasily where they stood. Oh, god. She knew what was coming. "I didn't do it on purpose!" she yelled. "I tried to stop! But how you going to hold back your dreams?"

"I know a way," said a voice. A hand gripped the back of her neck and shoved her beneath the water. She stopped up her breath and struggled, but the hand was too strong. There was commotion all around her; legs kicking. Were they trying to help her, or to help drown her? She wished she could stop fighting, let herself die. Had been wishing it since this all started.

The implacable hand was still holding her down. Her lungs bellowed, airless. From underneath, the surface of the water was a refractive lens. It let her see all the leggobeasts in their long line at the edge of the sea. Spots floated in front of her eyes. She tried to stop struggling, but her body wouldn't give up. Her mind, though, was thinking quickquickquick. Do it quick. Because last night, her dreams had changed. The leggobeasts had changed. Even as she couldn't hold her breath any longer, opened her mouth and sucked killing brine into herself, she watched the leggobeasts.

Together, moving as one, they floated a few feet up into the air. As she twisted and drowned, she saw the leggobeasts, each flying towards their person. Her iron donkey was in the air above her, starting to descend towards her. She hadn't told the young woman, she remembered. Hadn't told her what the iron donkey said to her in her dre—

A CITY CALLED HEAVEN

DANIAN DARRELL JERRY

Sibyl started west on Beale Street toward the quarantine facility at President's Island. Thirty minutes late, she imagined Father Erskine pointing his quill, scolding her tardiness. She strummed her guitar and sang about her husband Lee finishing the sound box with black wood stain, making a strap from a leather belt. The predawn haze coated stone, pasted her collar to her chest. With hair parted and braided in two sweaty plaits, skin shining like boiled sugar, Sibyl's face revealed her restive spirit. She'd spent the night gambling, running an amateur showcase in a saloon on Beale and Hernando.

She passed an alley. When Sam leapt from the dark and roared, she pointed the guitar's head, raised her right hand. Chords designed for killing pained her fingers. Sam laughed, grabbed his stomach.

"I scared you, Mama Sibyl. You look like a clown." His shirt drooped off his shoulders. His tattered pants were tied around his waist. His bare feet were covered in dirt and ash. Too young for whiskers, he had amber cheeks and gray eyes that betrayed ancient mettle.

"Keep flirting with death, Sammy." She trekked up the cobbled street, mumbling, working a song she'd learned for her patients. "I heard a city called Heaven."

"Don't worry about me, Mama." Sam joined Sibyl. He reached in a Croker sack slung across his chest, produced a bowie knife. Light struck the tip and lit the blade's edge.

A bell rang, and two black horses pulled an open wagon toward Sam and Sibyl. A drayman with ebony skin sat in the box seat, tapped his toes on the floorboard. His gut sagged through a black frock and white shirt half tucked into wrinkled trousers. He wore a black bowler with a purple feather stuck in the headband.

"Bring out the dead." The man called, his voice a weathered horn, a hollowed bone. "Bring out the dead."

Padlocks and hinges answered the drayman like sirens. Beale Street opened its doors, and the bereaved pulled out lumps wrapped in blankets and rugs. Soiled and sweltering, dressed in the deathly stench like field folk, they glared at Sibyl. She passed the Munson's home. Tugging the bedding that swathed her husband Claude, Roda Munson stumbled. Sibyl grabbed the dead man's ankles and helped Roda drag him to the black wagon. The Munsons hated Sibyl.

Claude had called himself a guitar man, said he rode with his wife from Marked Tree, Arkansas. Running from flood water, he claimed. He had a good story but sang like a wet cat and played like pulling teeth without whiskey. When he auditioned at the showcase, the saloon patrons jeered. A mug flew and cracked his forehead. After that he kept an evil word for Sibyl. He called the showcase a sham, said the players paid to win.

"Humph," Roda Munson sneered. "The fever took your husband, but it skipped you and that damned guitar." Behind her the drayman secured the body with ties and hooks. "Claude had it right, you a haint, old bush lady. That's why you never caught it."

"Watch your mouth." Sam scowled, started for his gunny sack. Sibyl grabbed his wrist.

"Beale Street's angel rose before the sun to tend God's work." They called the drayman The Black Rider. His family named him Charles Laumon. He stepped between Sibyl and Munson, tipped his bowler.

"Your day's coming, bush lady." Roda smiled. "Tell Sibyl about her visitor."

Laumon wiped his brow with a handkerchief from his breast pocket. "After you left the saloon, a stranger came asking for you. He carried a guitar case."

186

"They call him Long John," Roda said, her eyes waning moonlight. "He came to take your guitar and cut your head."

"Mr. Black Rider, you're headed to the quarantine." Sibyl stepped around Roda and hopped onto the box seat. Lee had a nephew named Long John. The boy was ten or eleven, when Sibyl and Lee married and quit Greenville for Memphis.

Sam pouted beside Roda, as the wagon trundled between the dark facades and morning starlight that fell like quicksilver. A tomcat shrilled, and a bloodhound darted past the wagon. The horses snorted but kept their gait steady. Sibyl and Laumon rode with the corpses west on Beale and south on Riverside. They followed Harbor Avenue until it led them to President's Island and the quarantine set up by City Hospital. Sibyl shivered, as the giant wall tent spired the horizon. A mosquito buzzed at her earlobe but found her lavender distasteful. Wailing sounds escaped the quarantine and emptied into the Mississippi River. Laumon parked the wagon, grabbed Sibyl's wrist.

"Take care, angel." He stroked her palm with his thumb. "I can help you, put you in a circus. Let people hear that voice, see that face."

"I got a sideshow job, playing on Beale Street. They named you right, Mr. Black Rider." She jumped out of the box seat, walked up the hill. She hummed and thought about Lee. Sibyl saw his face discolored with fever, illumed with the sight of her.

At the top of the bluff, the stench churned her stomach, filled her lungs like pneumonia. A steamboat paddled upriver. She surveyed the riverbank and docks, spying Sam creeping across the deck of a wooden vessel covered in grit. Red letters on the paddle box spelled Look Out. Even from the top of the bluff, she could see the river in Sam's eyes. She imagined an old scavenger combing the Mississippi's bottom.

Sibyl shook her head, ducked through the flaps that covered the quarantine's back entrance, passed rows of bedridden patients bemoaning the boiling fever. Father Erskin perched at a wooden table. Sister Katherine stood beside the priest, calling the names of the patients who had died during the night. The priest crossed the autonyms from a ledger. When he saw Sibyl, he set his quill in the book's gutter.

"You're late. You delay the Father." Sister Katherine eyed Sibyl like a watchdog, her face grim in the shadows and sickening lamplight. Scar tissue dug a winding stream under her chin.

"The dead fill the streets this morning, more than usual." Sibyl admired the pearl rosary chained to Katherine's sleeve. Last spring before the fever, Lee had offered to build Sibyl a silver guitar, a lightning rod made to hurl thunderbolts.

"God sees your exploits, Sibyl." The priest added. "By day you work for the Lord, but at night you sing for Satan." He folded his hands over his lap.

"I am God's work, Father." She moved closer to the table and faced the priest.

"You play the devil's harp, but the Lord works in mysterious ways. He's chosen iniquity's agent to heal His children." Erskine sneered before his gloom lightened to apathy. "Follow Sister Katherine to your station." The priest returned to the names in his ledger.

Katherine led Sibyl to another table filled with clean towels, bedding, and clothing. Sibyl propped her guitar against the trestle and stacked piles of fresh laundry on a wheeled cart. Four buckets filled with water sat under the table. A bar of Sunlight lay at the bottom of each bucket. She lugged a pail to the cart's bottom tray, cut her eyes at the priest. He held the ledger at his hip, nodded to Sister Katherine. Leaving the quarantine, he flinched and smacked himself. He considered the bloody mosquito smashed in his palm and wiped his hand on his pants leg. The priest led the nun into the hall and left Sibyl to tend God's business.

She parked the cart beside the first bed, grabbed the bucket, a towel, and a set of fresh gowns. A middle-aged woman lay on her side atop the sheets, mouth gaping. Her arms dangled off the bed and she whimpered as if someone had thrown her voice into a canyon. Black scabs covered her skin. The scabs had cracked, and black blood seeped from the fissures. Streaks of black saliva crusted the corners of her mouth and flakes of black mucus coated her nostrils.

"Mamma Sibyl, will you sing for us?" The woman reached at nothingness, her black fingernails worn to nubs.

"Ms. Waters, I'll sing and play for you." Sybil brushed the hair around the woman's forehead. She groaned, smearing Sibyl's palm with inky sweat. Sibyl peeled the gown from the shriveled body. The scent exhausted her, settling behind her eyes. Removing the bedding, she tossed the soiled linen to the floor. At the end of her shift she'd wash her baskets of sheets down by the river. She'd wring them out where the water ran shallow and spread over polished stones.

"When I get well, we'll attend dinner at my house. We can have coffee and teacakes under my pecan tree." Ms. Waters coughed and wheezed. "You can knock on my front door."

Sibyl lathered the towel with Sunlight and soaped Ms. Waters from head to toe. Dabbing the open sores, she handled her patient like a newborn. She dressed the fevered woman in a fresh gown. Sibyl hummed, and the humming took shape. She sang of a balm in Gilead, a brilliant love to end all pain and bring happiness everlasting. She sang just above a whisper. Ms. Waters' eyes shone like frozen ponds.

"I heard a city called Heaven. I want to make Heaven my home. My love has gone to glory. My husband had to throw away his gin. He set sail on that old muddy river, and that's the last time I saw my man." Sibyl dropped the towel in the bucket and hauled the pail back to the cart. She crooned, wheeled her supplies to the next bed.

She cleaned and dressed five patients before the first corpse. The youthful girl had soaked the sheets black with blood and vomit, fashioning her covers into a funeral gown. Sibyl wrapped the sheets around the yellow cadaver. Later, Charles Laumon would carry the dead to his wagons. With the day's work squeezing her shoulders and the dead faces swimming between her temples, she piled the dirty laundry and wet towels on the cart. Pushing the load to a corner near the door, she heard the bell and The Black Rider's call. Laumon entered the wall tent through the open flaps.

"Sweet angel, that's too much work." He had a hard, gang drawl. His voice filled the infirmary. "Let my boys earn their pay."

"What did Long John look like?" She remembered a strong resemblance between the nephew and his uncle. They shared eyes shaped like raindrops, wide noses, and hair twisted into cones. She dreaded the possibility of hurting a face that would evoke Lee's scent or the salt taste of his skin.

"I don't know. He wore a big hat." Laumon raised his hand like he wanted to touch Sibyl, but he whistled. Five roustabouts uniformed in dark pants and sack coats fanned out through the quarantine. They wore wrinkled caps pulled over their eyes and heavy gloves. Heads lowered to task, they carried the bodies to the drays. Out of fifty patients, Sibyl had found twenty-seven corpses. The roustabouts toiled and heaved, their backs hunched with the dead weight.

In her mind, she saw the corpses stuffed in the black wagons and dumped at the public gravesite in Elmwood Cemetery. Lee had been hurled into a ditch filled with jumbled limbs, faces twisted with death throes and delirium. Always despising anonymity, Sibyl had carved Lee's name into the bark of a Holly tree planted near the burial ground.

With the corpses removed, Laumon bid Sibyl farewell. He grabbed her hand, raised it to his mouth, but she pulled away, breaking his grip. Katherine appeared in the doorway and told Laumon that the priest was waiting to pay the undertaker.

"Ha! Time to settle my portion of the Lord's work." Laumon clapped his hands and followed Katherine to Father Erskine's private tent. Before leaving he winked at Sibyl.

Laumon's voice faded beyond the walls of cotton canvas, drifted through the muggy afternoon. Sibyl grabbed her guitar from the trestle table, dragged a chair from an empty bedside to the middle of the tent. Rubbing their palms, the patients bounced and watched. She sat, strummed the guitar, and adjusted the tuners. Shade billowed across the ceiling. A current charged the quarantine like a thundercloud. The voltage surged between her fingers and the strings, quilled her forearms. Sibyl let loose another guitar lick, and

Ms. Waters, the lady of the fever, stumbled to the room's center and sat down crossed-legged. The other patients followed Ms. Waters, gathering on the floor.

"It's my turn to pray. The Bible says King David worshipped with dance and music." Sibyl's fingers flitted over the guitar strings. She rocked, closed her eyes and saw the face that she wanted to remember, her husband's face smiling in the front row of the saloon.

"Good news, I see chariots coming. Take us home, Lord, back to your throne on high." She played her black guitar, imagined a clear night festooned with iridescent clouds, stars spinning like marbles. A fleet of chariots barreled toward her. Lee led the charge. His brow was furrowed, and sun-fire lit his eyes. Horses formed from stars galloped under the reins.

"Coming, Lord, to carry me home," Ms. Waters sang. She pointed at the ceiling, and her eyes bulged. Her voice rang like a snapped piano string.

"I'm gonna see my husband one morning. Good news, the chariots are coming." Sibyl rocked and tapped her feet. She imagined stepping into the chariot, sliding her arms around Lee's waist.

"Coming, Lord, to carry me home," Sister Katherine sang. She stood behind Sibyl and chuckled, her voice a genteel first soprano.

Father Erskine and Laumon returned and stood by the open flaps. They did not sing, only stared. Laumon leered, his mouth stretched wide. The priest had a blank expression, all his stony indignation wiped away. His mouth was a taut thread, but his eyes shone as if some raw memory stirred his heart.

The women and the patients sang. Their voices flew, threatened to burst the quarantine. They danced like tumbleweeds, and their limbs sagged like dissolving gelatin. Sister Katherine clapped. Tears ran down her cheeks and neck. She folded her hands, put her thumbs to her lips. Laumon danced his shirt right out of his trousers, stretched his arms and praised God. The priest watched Sibyl with arms folded. His threadbare mouth stretched, and its corners curled like ribbons. After the song, the patients carried the fever back to their beds. Ms. Waters sat on her haunches, waved for help. Sibyl lifted her by the armpits and walked her to the bed. The former Central

Gardens mistress sang like a drunk. With her hands wrapped in the sheets, Ms. Waters covered her mouth and giggled.

That night Sibyl returned to the saloon on Beale and Hernando. She sat in a wooden chair on a wooden stage and tapped a rhythm with her heel. Once the crowd caught the beat, she started playing her guitar. Reeking of sadness and sour mash, the river folk whooped and beat the tables. Roustabouts, clean shaven men with thick hands, shook dice, threw coins at the bartender, or grabbed gypsy girls. A farmer split a watchful gaze between the woman on his lap and Roda Munson, who sipped whiskey at the bar. Before she could drink half, the bartender filled her glass. Bragging about his new hooch, he called it lightning water. A tall, slender man stood next to Roda and stared at Sibyl. He wore a bandana tied around his neck, pointed boots, and a yellow Stetson. His hand rested on the crown of a guitar with a red oak finish, light coursing the strings, scaling the frets.

Charles Laumon sat close to the stage and mimed as Sibyl sang. He threw his arms like a man chopping wood or tossing cotton bales on a paddle steamer. "I'll be so glad when the sun goes down. I made your living 'fore I was free. I'm in a world of trouble, down on my knees." Sibyl swung the field tune. Folks locked arms and stomped. The tall man grabbed his guitar, finished his whiskey. He sauntered to the middle of the gritty floor. Under the failing light Sibyl faced a younger version of Lee.

"Auntie, how's my uncle?" He raised the guitar to his torso. "It's me, little Long John, all grown up. He joined the rhythm, caught the groove a note below Sibyl. The crowd danced in a semicircle.

"The fever took Lee. He caught it on the riverboat, throwing bales." Sibyl quit the rhythm, let the guitar rest in her lap. She studied the man's build, the slender fingers, and the muscles in his neck.

"You brought my uncle up that cursed river. You took my friend." He stomped and hummed. The boards cracked under his bootheel. He stomped once then twice, once then twice. He drew the dark from the rafters, the floorboards, and the circling Beale Streeters. "Long John, the highwayman. I come for your guitar. Long John the highwayman. I come for your soul. Lee followed you to his casket. He should've kept his ass at home." Long John worked the oak wood sound box. His fingers darted over the frets. The strings glinted like tears.

The people hollered, yammered at the dark above their heads. Even Laumon strutted around his table, flapped his arms like chicken wings. Roda Munson danced on Long John's back, wrapped her arm around his waist. He pointed his guitar at Sibyl. The Beale Streeters threw money at Long John. He grinned and sweated beneath the Stetson's shadow. His guitar swept the saloon like an angry river. Roda sneered, rubbed Long John's chest. He grabbed her wrist and spun her into a table.

"What you got, Auntie?" He spoke like he tasted bile.

Around Sibyl glasses and lit cigarettes flared like lightning bugs. She pointed the guitar's head, brushed the strings with her fingers. Of all the Long Johns, fate had sent Lee's doppelganger. She wanted to say that Lee had planned their flight to Memphis. He bootlegged and gambled. He collected the pennies when she sang in the field. When he died, he held her hand and promised her power. He promised to live in her music. She considered Long John, and beneath her breath, begged forgiveness. She saw the hole that cratered his heart and decided to fill the hole with her own misery.

"The poor pilgrim, they call me sorrow. You left me in this world alone." She invoked Lee and the hordes disembodied by the fever. "I lost all hope for tomorrow, but I heard a city called Heaven. I want to make Heaven my home. Sometimes I fall, Lord. Sometimes you drive me to the bone, but I heard a city called Heaven. I want to make Heaven my home. Lee, handle your nephew."

Heads bowed. Eyes closed. Tears dripped. Hands reached for Sibyl. She coaxed her guitar and blessed the swaddled dead that rode with Laumon. She blessed Ms. Waters and the quarantine folk dancing to their graves. She blessed the bereaved who spat and cried. She forced Long John to drink the fever, taste the black blood. After the song, the crowd sloshed back to their places in the saloon. Someone grabbed Sibyl's sleeve. Others shook her hands. A couple of the river folk snickered behind Long John. He stared at

Sibyl. His chest rose and fell. She started toward the highwayman, but he grabbed his guitar case and blew through the door. After the saloon closed, Sibyl stepped outside, found Sister Katherine and Laumon waiting on the corner. Katherine folded her fingers, rushed the songstress.

"The fever has taken Father Erskin." Her eyes reddened, her voice trembled, the words scuffled with one another. "The headaches and the chills started some hours ago. He wants to see you. He wants you to sing for him."

"Put Father Erskine with my other patients. I'll sing tomorrow, but I refuse to play in his chambers." Sibyl picked a brooding medley as she started across Beale Street.

Long John stepped out of an alley that ran beside the saloon. He raised a single-action revolver, aimed the Colt at Sibyl. When he smiled, blood dripped from his mouth. Something nudged him in the side. He clenched his teeth and reached for his midsection. Sam had stabbed Long John in the stomach. Sibyl grabbed her nephew's wrist, forced the gun into the air. The gun fired, and Katherine screamed. Laumon ducked and covered his ears. Sam cut Long John's throat. Sibyl grabbed the boy, pried the knife from his fingers, and forced him to the cobblestones.

"That's my nephew. That's Lee's nephew." She cried, shook his arms.

"Get off me. I didn't know." Sam wiggled free, darted toward the gun lying beside Long John. "Mine," he laughed, spun the pistol's cylinder. Sibyl growled, thrummed her sound box, and sparks popped Sam's backside. He shrieked and grabbed his rear end. "Why'd you burn me, Mama?" Spittle hung from a lonely bucktooth.

"I better see you at Father Erskine's door, soon as day breaks." Sister Katherine considered Sibyl, Long John, and Sam. The scar under the nun's chin glistened like a snail. She rubbed her pearl rosary and scurried down Hernando.

"Precarious," Laumon looked around Beale Street. "I can make it go away, but what can you do for me?" He rolled his tongue behind his lip.

"I buried my husband in Elmwood." Sibyl knelt, grabbed her nephew's shoulders. She held his face to her stomach, stroked his hair, beady and thick as Lee's. She wondered if the circus hired widows and orphans.

"I'm throwing Long John in the river."

She pictured the highwayman, glaring eyes and frozen arms descending into the murk. She felt his soul cross the gangplank, board that black paddle steamer. She visioned Lee gifting Long John with the lightning rod, heard his music bejewel the wind. As the river vessel paddled to open sea, a thunderbolt cleaved the nightscape. Long John's body lay sprawled across her thighs, moonlight suffusing his guitar. The strings played by themselves, adding melody as she sang.

"I'll trade every possession I own. I heard a city called Heaven."

NUMBERS

RION AMILCAR SCOTT

1.

Out in the middle of the Cross River there is an island. It appears during storms or when the river's flooding or even on clear summer days. And sometimes it rises out of the water and floats in the air. The ground turns to diamond and you can hear the women laughing—I call them women, but they are not women. So many names for them: Kazzies. Shaunties. Water-women. The Woes. I like that last name myself. The poet Roland Hudson came up with that one in the throes of madness. Dedicated his final volume, *The Firewater of Love*, to:

> Gertrude, Water-Woman, my Woe, who
> caused all the woe . . . even though, my dear,
> you are not real, I cannot accept that and will
> never stop believing in your existence and
> beautiful rise from the river into my arms.

Drowned himself in the Cross River swimming after Gertrude, and there's something beautiful in that. Dredge the depths of the Cross River and how many bones of the heartsick will you find? So many poisoned by illusion. Don't tell me there's no island and no women rising naked from the depths, shifting forms to tantalize and then to crush. I've seen their island and I've seen them and gangsters love too; gangsters are allowed love, aren't we? Sometimes there's a fog and I know the island's coming and I snap out of sleep all slicked with sweat and filled with the urge to swim out there to catch a water-woman and bring her back to my bed. If you pour sugar on their tails they can't shift shapes on you and they have to show their true selves and obey you completely. If I had to do it all over again I'd dust her in a whole five-pound bag and spend eternity licking the crystals from her nipples. And Amber, a man lost in delirium. Poor, poor Amber.

2.

Last year, 1918, ended bad for me and Amber, and to think it began with so much promise. My mother got me a job driving Amber around town in February and I expected to be collecting numbers slips for him by May. But then Amber Hawkins fell in love with Joyce Little and became something like a lovesick pit bull puppy. So Joyce's brother Josephus got the moneymaking position I had my eye on, and I was stuck being yelled at from the backseat as I swerved about the road.

Amber was a killer, as was everybody I worked with. They were all, Amber included, minions of Mr. Washington, subjects of the Washington Family—I was now, as well, though I hadn't yet killed anyone. I tried to forget that my new job rendered me a criminal, but sometimes it made me nervous, especially when I drove. My job, I told myself, as a member of Amber's crew was to help make the operation as efficient as possible so we could make as much money as possible. If we earned more for Mr. Washington than other crews, then Amber rises and with him, I rise too. At least that was my theory.

I hoped Joyce would turn Amber into something akin to a decent human being. Most married people I knew became boring soon as they put on the ring; they lost some of their humor and spontaneity, but I had to admit they grew a little more humanity.

September 15, 1918: that was supposed to be the day. He booked the Civic Center for the wedding, displacing a couple who had reserved the place months before, but it was Amber Hawkins, nothing anyone could do. He ordered up nearly a hundred pastries. So many roses arrived on the eve of the wedding that I joked a garden somewhere had suffered a sudden baldness. Hundreds of people swarmed the Civic Center that Sunday. Everything was to begin at noon. Those of us who worked under Mr. Washington, and even people who worked for Mr. Johnson and Mr. Jackson, put aside our differences to show up for Amber. Joyce's family sat in the front. Mostly, I remember her cute little sister and the short socks resting against her tan skin. Her tall skinny father sat stoically holding the little girl's hand. Joyce's jellyrolled mother wiped at her wet eyes every few minutes.

And then nothing.

No word from Joyce. Amber made us get all dolled up and festive-like for his big humiliation.

Josephus, Amber's best man, stood near the altar next to Philemon and Frank and Tommy wearing a twisted guilty smile. The guys in the wedding party all sported big, ugly purple flowers pinned to their lapels. The way Josephus kept running his fingers over his flower's discolored and crumpled petals. He was an arrogant fucking shitstain, but I hated seeing him squirm.

At about five in the evening it was clear all was lost. Amber's father ambled to the front where bride and groom should have been standing. He was flanked by his assistant, Todd, ever at his side, and a huge simian-looking white man who glowered down at us. For the first time, Elder Mr. Hawkins, the ruthless killer and Mr. Washington's right hand, looked as frail and as wispy as the old man he was. There were rumors that his lifestyle—the women he kept around town—had left him so syphilitic that his once-sharp mind had rotted and his body was beginning to twist and fail too. I didn't believe or engage in the talk. He'd been nothing but good to me.

Thank you for coming, people of Cross River, Elder Mr. Hawkins said to the wedding crowd. You have been more than generous to my family and all connected with us. I'm sorry, but there will be no celebration today. Again, I thank you for spending your time with us.

We all slowly dispersed that night, and the next day Amber was back to work, mumbling the day's numbers from the backseat. Never mentioned

Joyce or showed any signs of sorrow or pain.

Amber waited a month. He waited two more. Then he had Joyce's whole family killed.

A single bullet to each of their foreheads and their bodies dumped in the Cross River. It was deep in December, near Christmas, and thin white sheets of ice skimmed along the river's face.

Three days after their disappearance, the family came bubbling to the surface, just as Amber wanted. The coldhearted bastard didn't spare even the ten-year-old girl. Amber's own best man paid the ultimate price for his sister's desertion.

With Josephus dead, I expected a promotion, but Amber gave that to Doc Travis Griffin's son. I let it pass without complaint; at least Amber hadn't tasked me with taking the lives of four innocent people. Frank and Tommy did the hit, I'd heard, and when I saw them I watched their muddy boots and thanked the Lord I didn't have to walk in them. But who am I kidding, though? I stood among the killers and the dirt was all over me just as it was all over them. I would have done the job with sadness and emptiness; with revulsion and cold rage toward Amber, but still I'd have done it.

Loretta, my love at the time, and I used to stand at river's edge and watch the sky reflecting on the water. Did it through all types of weather, but a pleasant March day was definitely a reason to be out. Felt I was safe from the river when I was with her, like it wouldn't dare open up and devour me whole.

What if you die? she asked, Amber had missed a payment to Mr. Washington and this sort of financial mismanagement was becoming a habit. His carelessness put all of us who worked for him in danger. What if they kill me? she asked, and I was unsure how to answer.

I didn't look up from the river. Amber's falling apart, I said.

And he should fall apart, she replied. Baby, this is not your problem. He made this happen.   Brought it all down on himself. So you gotta fall on his sword? My cousin, he in St. Louis, we could go up there. I could work for him and you could find a job—

Shining white people's shoes again? The type of job I got is the only way a Negro can live decently. At least Negroes who came up poor like us anyway.

On her face I could see the passing hellfire that she—an angry god—was condemning me to for all my mistakes. I suppose I have to take some credit or some blame, as it were, for how things happened. I've blamed Loretta for eventually leaving me, and I've blamed Miss Susan—it was her *Little Book of Love Numbers* that got all those thoughts of water-women cranking through my head. I've blamed Mr. Washington for his harshness, and even the whole society of water-women and their wicked nature. But really, if I had left the whole business behind like Loretta wanted, how could things have been any worse? Truth was, I couldn't leave Amber, the one who was destined to sit on the throne. If only he could overcome something as simple as heartbreak. His face sweating constantly now. His limbs shaking. This damn compassion. This damn empathy.

A breeze passed over Loretta and me. It was filled with heat and something that made me feel like a lover, like I could take Loretta into the river and after we finished she'd trust my word forever. Loretta kicked at the water with her bare feet.

Still cold, she said.

St. Louis, huh? I said, pitching a rock. Can't put your feet into the Cross River in St. Louis.

It's fine, she replied. I'll put my feet in the Mississippi.

The Mississippi ain't the Cross River, though. Look at that. No ugly parts. Ripple upon ripple of boundless beauty.

When'd you become a poet?

Girl, you know Elder Mr. Hawkins called me a poet when me and Amber met with him. He say that 'cause I like to daydream. I'm not Roland Hudson. I never rubbed two words together and made them rhyme, but he right, you know. I wonder how he know I'm a poet at making love, though.

We're talking about our future and you want to make jokes? Even if Amber gets himself together and you do move up in the organization, you want to end up a dirty old mobster like his father?

She was right, but I could never give Loretta her due. Instead I said what had been on my mind in the last several months:

I ain't never been nothing and nobody never expected nothing from me at all. Not you. Not even my mother. You all think I'm not that smart, and that's okay. I'm the underdog. I stick with Amber I could be up there in the organization in the number two spot like Elder Mr. Hawkins. Shit, I could be the next Mr. Washington if Amber don't make it. Don't doubt me. You could be the Washington Family First Lady. How about that, Loretta?

If that's what matters to you, then—

In my memories, Loretta turns to white dust midsentence and blows away, leaving behind the sweet scent of gardenias in bloom. And that's how she left me. Or maybe she just walked out after an argument. I can't figure it. My mind is so damaged I can't tell memories from hallucinations; daydreams from nightmares.

3.

Mr. Washington was so furious over the Little Family killing that he carved up our territory and threatened to give over our remaining operations to Philemon if we couldn't pay a $5,000 fine and restitution to the Littles. On top of the fines, Mr. Washington stripped us of half our territory and reassigned much of Amber's personnel. And still we were responsible for kicking the same amount to Mr. Washington every week.

Elder Mr. Hawkins delivered the news calmly and sternly in January—the very top of 1919—at the funeral for Frank and Tommy, Amber's best shooters.

Who the fuck am I supposed to pay restitution to? Amber asked, in a loud whisper. Funeral-goers glanced back at us and then averted their eyes. The Little Family is dead! And Mr. Washington didn't have to kill Frank and Tommy—

I canceled Frank and Tommy, Elder Mr. Hawkins said, so coldly that I felt grains of his frost sprinkle against my cheek as he spoke. I laid their bodies out by the river myself. They were stupid enough to follow your order to cancel Joyce's peoples, they had to— Trust me Amber, it was best for you that they go.

The debt became a millstone dragging Amber's operations to the bottom of the Cross River. I wondered why Mr. Washington didn't just put a bullet in him. Would have been more merciful than this slow usurious homicide.

Amber sent a fleet of prostitutes into the juke joints and commissioned truck hijackings, but it was never enough. With each day he looked less and less like the heir to the throne. When all seemed lost, Carmen shot into our lives, a little brown-skinned bolt from a cannon. Woke us up when we didn't even know we were sleeping. I was never clear on where he found her. It seemed as if she had always been there on his arm.

Carmen was a pretty number. From a certain angle her head appeared perfectly round. Her hair—shiny, black, and smooth—stopped at the nape of her long neck. She stayed draped in a green dress. Said it was the color of spring. And the spring of Carmen indeed felt like a rebirth.

Three sets of ledger books sat before me one April afternoon—Amber asked me to make the numbers work, but there was no making sense of these numbers. Carmen's green dress had been on my mind for several hours. I daydreamed, and when I got tired of that I leafed through *Miss Susan's Little Book of Love Numbers*. When I got to the chapter titled "Can a Woman Make a Man Lose His Mind?" I was damn sure for a few minutes that Loretta and Joyce were water-women. They made you fall so deep you never wanted to ever gasp for air again and then they disappeared, leaving your mind buzzing with madness until the end of your days, and that's if you're lucky. Loretta and Joyce hid their gills well. I thought of the creased skin beneath Loretta's breasts. Where was Carmen hiding her gills? They could shift shapes, you know. Maybe Carmen was Joyce returned. No.

Amber walked into the office holding tight to Carmen's hand. Her sweet smell deranged every thought I had of the water-women, until the images slid from my brain into my throat and felt like the smoothest ice cream.

You got time to be reading that witchcraft? he asked, nodding toward my *Miss Susan* book. Amber moved as if he had no control over his body and fell into the chair across from me, breathing heavy. What my numbers looking like?

I couldn't immediately answer him. I noticed Carmen's slant smile. Amber too had grinned when he walked through the door, but talk of business had twisted his lips into a grimace.

I'm not sure how we're gonna make Mr. Washington's payments again this month, I said.

With the reduced territory there were fewer businesses to intimidate, fewer lottery customers, and fewer workers to bring in revenue.

Carmen rested her soft hands on the back of Amber's neck.

You need to get yourself a woman, Amber said.

I'm sorry I can't get these numbers to make sense, I replied. I'll keep try—

I'm talking about what's really important in this life, and you stuck on business. I don't remember you being this stiff. Didn't my father call you a poet or something?

Amber was telling me about Loretta, Carmen said. You been out with anyone since then?

I shook my head.

Amber's a good guy, Carmen continued. He asked about my friends for you. I got a whole army of nice girls. You don't like one, the next one will be better. They all could use a guy like you.

See what I'm talking about? Amber said. This is a firecracker of a woman. What you think of my woman?

I looked up at the sweep of her hair resting on her cheeks. The black, breathing lines beneath her eyes.

She hides her gills well, I said.

Amber and Carmen laughed. I'm glad they took it in the spirit of a joke. Sometimes it was hard to tell what was going to make Amber lose it.

You know there's no such thing as water-women, right? Carmen asked with her slant-smile lingering and hanging over me.

Loretta wasn't no water-woman, Amber said. She just ain't like your ass no more. Same thing with Joyce. We got to live with that. It takes a special woman to be with guys in this life. Loretta and Joyce wasn't special enough, but my baby Carmen—he grasped her by the waist and pulled her tight—my baby Carmen ain't going nowhere.

Mean-fucking-while, I said, Philemon is the toast of the family.

Outrageous! Amber slapped the desk. What would happen if I walked up to him and shot him in his face right in front of Mr. Washington?

You know something? Carmen said, looking to the ceiling, her voice all distant and spinning with childlike innocence. There hasn't been a good firebombing since your dad ran the streets, has there?

In a different world, Carmen could have run this organization, I'm sure. I feared her and I wanted to devour her. Our action against Philemon was to be nothing serious; just a prank like streaming lines of toilet paper through his trees. We didn't mean for it to happen, but Philemon's house burned. Perhaps I daydreamed too intensely about Carmen's green dress and put too much gasoline into the Molotov cocktails. No one was hurt, but Amber yelled at the old-faced teenagers we hired to do the job: What was in that shit, sunfire?

He never gave them the second $10 he promised, but they kept their mouths shut, and everyone assumed the Johnson Family did it as retaliation for Philemon moving into their Northside strongholds.

Mr. Washington took Philemon's advice and ordered all guns turned on the Johnson Family in a sort of unbalanced warfare. When they largely retreated, most of our crew leaders were left with bigger territories, except for us. Somehow our territory shrank and we found ourselves scrounging for every dollar we could come across.

Amber shrugged it all off and I still have this vision of him with his feet up on a table in the office holding a copy of the *Days* or the *Times*, staring at the air above the ledger books as if the numbers were twirling before him. He nodded. He grimace-smiled, saying, Carmen got this all figured out. Every damn piece to the puzzle. Every piece.

4.

Shortly after I began working for Amber, before he became translucent to me—the way Josephus appears in my dreams—my mother sent me to see Miss Susan. She had seen Miss Susan before she married my father (and probably before she started seeing Elder Mr. Hawkins behind my father's back) and said everyone should see her when they think they're in deep with a lover. I hadn't even been paid yet and was still living off shoeshining bread, so my mother gave me money for that old witch. Miss Susan told me to go into the Wildlands and bring her three roots. My mother went down to the market and bought three roots and ground them into the dirt so they looked fresh from the earth. She said: That witch crazy if she think I'm sending my only boy into that old spooknigger forest.

Miss Susan stared at me. She fingered my naps. Squeezed my face and then turned my roots in her hand. I had heard rumors that she made you drop your pants and stared right into the eye of your penis. I silently prayed she would let me keep my pants on, and thankfully she did, but, God, the power of this woman! She looked nothing like the grinning old crone they had pictured on her books. Miss Susan looked smooth-skinned and serious. I would have done anything she asked just because of the forcefulness of her voice. So, I said, is Loretta the one?

She looked up from my roots with her glowing gold eyes and said, You're in danger.

You know who I work for, I said. You not telling me nothing I don't know.

That's not why you're in danger. It's your heart. If you know what's good for you, you're gonna stay the hell away from that river.

I left with a bunch of her books and walked straight to the river to sit and read. And that's when I heard them calling me. A wispy sound rustled in my ears and I felt drunk, pleasant drunk without the anger or the bitter taste on my tongue or the burn of liquor corroding my insides as it passed through.

The world looked wavy, but I saw it—that diamond island rising from the Cross River like a ghost ship out the fog.

And those water-women dove from land and swam to me. They rose out of the waves, brown and nude, their skin shining with the life-giving waters.

Numbers-boy, the water-woman in the front said. Hey, numbers-boy. You got a number for me?

All those women turned into one. She reached for me and caressed my face. You're beautiful, she said. Anyone ever tell you you're beautiful?

She grabbed my hand and placed it on her naked hip.

Don't be afraid, she said. When I looked into her eyes, we lived a whole life, from awkward first steps together to deep commitment. I could never look at another.

Loretta, a voice called from the island.

Your name is Loretta? I asked. Like my Loretta?

No, she said. I'm better than your Loretta.

Without another word, she turned and dived back into the river. Perhaps she didn't have all of me. Some of me was back with my Loretta, because I realized this was a trap. This was exactly how Miss Susan described water-woman seduction in her books. So many lovers, like the poet Roland Hudson, dived to their ends after these deadly tricksters. I took a step toward the water. And then I stopped. Self-preservation kicked in and I remembered they weren't even women, or even human.

The island descended from midair through a thick fog, sinking slowly into the black water. And even though it nearly caused my death, the feeling I had there by the Cross River was the greatest feeling any man could ever experience. I cried hot tears that night waiting for the water-woman's return.

I knew nothing in life would ever feel like staring into her brown eyes, touching the warmth of the flesh at her hip. Nothing. I decided I would love Loretta harder, but I wasn't enough, or maybe it was that part of me became a burning beacon at the river, calling out to that water-woman. Whatever the reason, Loretta left in the spring. With her gone from my life, I figured I would live as powerfully as I could. I would chase women, try to experience bliss in all things, but no experience I ever had could fill my soul

like the feeling I had with that water-woman by the Cross River, but if I ever
returned to the river and that island decided to rise up, I knew I would die.

Not a bad way to go, huh? Drowning in a water-woman's light.

5.

Carmen disappeared, not by train, but by wind. To hear Amber tell
it, they had spent the afternoon downtown on the way to purchase a ring
when she walked out ahead of him. She smiled, not the slant-smile, but a
broad true one, and then she stretched out her arms like a bird preparing
for flight. Oh, Amber, were her last words before the soft brown of her flesh
turned into a fragrant white powder. When the breeze came, scattering pieces
of Carmen throughout the town, Amber grabbed clumps and tried to put her
back together, but the grains of Carmen slipped between his fingers, leaving
traces of her in the creases of his hands, embedded between the threads of his
clothes and curled always in the coils of his hair.

It's like my dream, I said the night of her disappearance. The
numbers, which usually twirled in the air, stopped to watch Amber with pity.

Water-women, I said. A plague of them.

I need to smoke, he said, walking to the door. Come and get me in ten
minutes so we can finish the ledger. Business first, right? I'll be okay by then.

It only took two minutes to figure out that he was going out into the
pitch of the night to find Carmen by the river. He had left the car, so I figured
he was walking briskly south toward the bridge. Their voices would soon be
screaming through his head, crowding his lonely thoughts.

Turns out there couldn't have been a worse time for Carmen to blow
in the wind. I took two steps into the street and felt a hand grab my arm: It was
Fathead Leroy, a guy who took numbers for Amber over on the Southside.

Man, he said. I got rolled for my number slips. I don't know that shit
by heart like Amber.

Who got you? Somebody with the Jacksons?

Naw, look, you know Todd who work for Elder Mr. Hawkins? Him and a guy I never seen before. A white guy. I think he from Port Yooga. They looking for you and they looking for Amber. Told me to tell you not to burn nothing you can't pay for. Cracker punched me and threw my betting slips into the river. I don't got the standing to do nothing against someone as high up as Todd. You and Amber gotta get this shit right for us out on the streets.

I looked over Leroy's shoulder. It started to play as a setup. Not too far in the distance I saw Todd with a big white man who stomped toward us like a gorilla. How could I leave the office without my piece? Love-blind Amber probably hadn't spent two thoughts on packing. I dipped my head and turned from Leroy before breaking into a jog. Perhaps they ran behind me, but I wasn't willing to spare a glance. The shadows of the Wildlands called. When I entered them, the dark grew heavy, and I swore as I dashed through the stream that pieces of the black flaked off and covered me. I came out into a clearing and could see the gleam of the moon casting down on the earth. This was a circuitous route to get to the bridge, but it would keep me alive long enough to find Amber. I imagined him wading in water, waiting for Carmen to beckon him beneath the choppy surface.

The closer I got to the river, the louder the buzzing vibrated in my head. I felt as if something kept lifting me into the air with every step. It was as if I were walking along a beautiful tone shooting from the deep. My skin grew warm, suddenly flush with blood. Part of my mind called me to turn around to save myself. Who would I be if I bowed to the gods of self-preservation when Amber was in danger? But Amber could already be a bloated corpse, the beasts of the river tearing at his dead limbs. What a liar I am. This death march felt good, that was the truth. That was now the only reason I plowed deeper into the forest. It felt just like floating on my back beneath the sun when the river rocked with a loping rhythm. All that remained was for me to dip my head under.

While I indulged this daydream as one of the last I'd ever have, I came out of a long blink and before me stood Amber with his ankles steeped in the river.

That's when the whispers began. Images of Loretta. My Loretta. Then the water-woman Loretta.

I wanted to call out to Amber, but what if I missed my Loretta speaking to me?

A burst. A loud popping, like fireworks. I looked to the cloudy black of the sky, now hiding the stars and obscuring the moon. Another pop, or rather this time it was a bang, closer to me now.

Amber didn't move. Didn't react at all. He just stared down at the river, trying to see the whole world in the water.

Another shot burst toward us, this time from a different angle, and there was Todd on a hill looking down upon us.

Amber, I called. Amber! Run!

The whispering in my head grew louder. I saw the white man approach, an albino gorilla burning with murderous intent. There was nowhere we could run; Todd and the White Gorilla were tactical geniuses, cutting off our paths of flight.

It was often Mr. Washington's habit to give members of the family he killed lavish homegoing ceremonies, full of food and celebration. I imagined the twin homegoing Amber and I would receive.

My skin warmed and I figured I'd shut off my mind and give in to the creeping pleasures of the beckoning Woes.

Just as I decided my time lay at an end, the water parted and up in the sky rose that diamond island, the land of the water-women. Scores of them—brown and nude and river-slicked—floated down to us. Two of them caressed Amber. I locked eyes with a Woe and she whispered my name. Tall and skinny, with a sharp, gaunt face. She bounce-walked and after a few steps her movements nearly resembled floating. The Woe put her arm around me, softly touching my chest. With my eyes, I searched her naked body for gills, but soon I gave in and began softly kissing her neck and kneading her soft wet flesh, growing more aggressive with the increasing intensity of her breaths and her moans. Together they sounded like a new language.

There was that pop again. And another pop, itself a language I no longer cared to understand. I placed my tongue gently in my water-woman's mouth. We were melting into one being. Pop. She jerked and shuddered and I felt a hot wetness. I gasped. My heart felt as if it had shifted and now beat in the center of my body. My lover went limp in my arms, her head flopping to the side, her skin turning cold and scaly and silvery and blue beneath the crack of moonlight that spilled from behind the cloud cover.

I looked at the blood and chunks of flesh that covered my skin and my clothes. Some of the water-women ran and dove back into the river. I scanned the water's edge for Amber. He held a water-woman in his arms and another stood behind him rubbing his back. The one in front took hold of his hand and led him deeper into the water.

I ducked, expecting a flurry of bullets to buzz by like mosquitoes. Todd and the White Gorilla stalked toward me. I crouched to the ground with my hands covering my head.

What happened next, in my state, I never could have guessed.

Todd and the White Gorilla stepped over me, mumbling apologies. They stumbled toward the river and its bounty of naked women.

As grateful as I was for their mesmerism, it also saddened me. That was to be my fate, my thoughtless death march to a land under the water.

I rose to my feet and ran to Amber. He screamed and cried as I snatched at him and held him down. I knew it was just a matter of endurance. When the island sank back into the depths of the river, he'd regain a certain sanity. His water-women didn't fight—that's not how they did things. They blew kisses and walked out into the river until their heads were fully submerged.

As for Todd and the White Gorilla, water-women gazed into their eyes, laughing playful laughs and twisting their naked hips. It was a beautiful invitation to a drowning and they accepted, holding tight as they walked to the bottom of the river.

For Amber, the sinking of the island was the worst part; he twisted, thrashed, and cursed. But when it was over, when that island was again tucked beneath gentle currents, Amber grew calm and docile. He lay on his back atop the wet soil with his hands on his face.

Take me home, he said. I need to go home.

I looked off into the distance at the glowing town and realized that Amber and I would never again be allowed there. He moved his hands from his face and it was as blank and innocent as a newborn's. His voice sounded simple and soft. Part of him was now submerged somewhere within his depths and would never surface again. He was my responsibility now and I had no idea where we would go.

SPIRITS DON'T CROSS OVER WATER 'TIL THEY DO

JAMEY HATLEY

Rabbit Grace had been on his second tour of Vietnam long enough to start getting mail. There were letters from his mother that he answered as quickly as he could, brimming with false cheer. Some from his sisters that he answered as if he were talking to all of them at once. It was Rabbit's turn to sort through the "Dear Soldier" letters and get his first choice. Amber Hawkins was going on and on as he always did. Hawkins looked like his name. He was tall and brown and solid like he was lit from within with gold. Hawkins was one of those guys with a thick neck but keen features that looked like he had been carved with a chisel. He was telling a story about some long-dead uncle of his who had been a big gangster back in the day. A numbers runner whose downfall was a Woe.

"A hoe? Every nigga's downfall is hoes," said one of the new recruits, baby-faced Davis from Arkansas.

"Not a hoe. A Woe. You Bamas don't know shit. You don't have Woes?" said Hawkins.

"The fuck is a Woe?" Davis asked and a groan rose up from the mess hall.

"Please, please don't get him started," said Rabbit. "Please! Here, take a letter from one of these nice ladies from Chicago."

Hawkins's story went that where he was from, every so often an island rose from the middle of the river full of naked women who sang you to your death or granted your every wish. Water Women he sometimes called them. Or mostly: Woes.

"Man shut up that noise," the other soldiers would tease.

"I was named after my uncle. If I make it out of here, I'm gonna do what my namesake didn't," said Hawkins and counted his goals off on his fingers. "One. Keep all of my money. Two. Catch me a Water Woman. Three. Keep her. Four. Stay alive."

"Nigga, is you crazy? Who wants a woman like that?"

"You can catch them though. I told you that," said Hawkins.

"Plenty of crazy broads out here that don't need catching, Blood."

Rabbit chuckled to himself; it was something that Two used to say to him. *Why would I want anybody don't want me of my own free will?*

"Look here, unless that bitch come with a pot of gold, she can keep her ass in that water."

"All I need is this," Hawkins said and shook the sugar packets from his tray at them. Hawkins was crazy for sugar. Always hoarding it. Drank his coffee like syrup.

"Just dust their tails with sugar and they'll do whatever you say. I'm gonna be one of the only niggas to get me one of those Woes and live to tell it. Just wait and see."

"You mean to tell me you dust their asses with sugar? What kinda freak shit is that?"

Rabbit laughed along with the rest of the unit, but the Woes stayed on his mind.

Why would I want anybody don't want me of their own free will?

Free?

Free.

There wasn't a real letter from home, so Rabbit stretched out going through the "Dear Soldier" letters. He knew better than to hope to get a note from Two, even a cussing out in her lovely handwriting. He had decisively and on purpose ruined any chance of this. That was the point. Two's package hadn't traveled across the water from Memphis to get to him. She left it in the treehouse loft that he had built with his own hands. There, sheltered in the arms of an ancient magnolia, under a canopy of too, too hardy wisteria, they had talked each towards a kind of wholeness. Or tried to.

He had been preparing to leave for his second tour when he found the black calico bundle in his pack. He kept the packet intact for as long as he could, squeezing it and shaking it gently to try to intuit its contents. When he finally untied the red string that held it together, he found a small St. Michael locket inside. It was resting on a thin sheet of pink writing paper. *In case I miss you, Two* was written in the center of the page with the date. He had told her about St. Michael when they were in the perch in the sky. She had seen the medal on one of his photographs and asked him about it. Lots of the Bloods on his first tour had worn St. Michael for protection, Catholic or not. St. Michael was the patron saint of warriors.

"That's what you are. A warrior," she said. "Don't feel much like one," he had replied. "There's a knowing deeper than this moment," she said. He had believed her then, but that was before Two's baby nephew flew to heaven on the very day the neighbors of Wayfarer Homes in Memphis, Tennessee decided to celebrate the infant twins. He now knows that the baby made the third death, Otis Redding and Martin King preceding him.

Instead of a portrait, the locket held a pinky colored salve smelling of earth and pungent oil. This is what Two did. She specialized in potions, concoctions, charms, and the like, whereas her sister specialized in dreams. Rabbit had been warned about the bewitching sisters. It was why he refused her coffee that first day. That insult almost cost him the time he spent with her in that tiny blossom covered world they made together in The Gap. Even folk who claimed they didn't believe in that old timey hoodoo voodoo mess worried about their personal concerns being mishandled. When he faltered with the cup, she knew exactly why.

Why would I want anybody don't want me of their own free will?

He knew without asking what it was in that salve, tinting it pink. Blood. King's blood. He had been doing odd jobs at the Lorraine when his shell shock would let him. After the shot rang out and they carried King away in the ambulance, he helped clean the blood from the hotel balcony. Helped the preachers gather some of it up. Two had been at the hospital on the other end. Her sister was having the twins as the ambulance with King came rolling in. She had wandered into the hallway where he was. They had both been called to try to save something of this man. Even after his killing she was trying to restore some wholeness to King, and in turn they, to each other.

Even before Two's nephew died, Rabbit was starting to see the seams of his world unraveling. What little work he did at the Lorraine wasn't a life. He was a grown man. No car, living between his childhood bedroom and a treehouse. After Otis and The Bar-Kays died in the plane crash and King being murdered in his hometown on his watch, getting on at STAX as a songwriter seemed more and more improbable. Once the baby died, none of that seemed possible. Trouble comes in threes, and Memphis seemed intent on taking out anybody with a dream. Even a little three month old baby. Rabbit ceased to be able to imagine a Memphis that could be his home.

When he found the medal, he had already filed his papers and his date to depart had been set. It was done. Two probably could have sold that concoction for lots of money elsewhere, and maybe she did, but she had also saved some of this power for him. This attempt at wholeness. Once he understood that she knew before he did both that he was returning and that he probably wouldn't face her before he left, he got a sudden flash of shame.

In case I miss you, Two.

Two wasn't tentative. He knew that from the first time he asked if she wanted to walk in The Gap with him. She had waited until she knew her own mind before answering. That *"In case I miss you"* was a grace. She was stepping in again. With the medal around his neck he remembered how her own sister slapped her in the face after the baby died because she needed somewhere for her grief to land. He can feel the slap on his own face now, far too late. He thinks he started leaving then. Left a little more in his spirit when he signed the papers to reenlist. By the time he found the black packet sprinkled with tiny bright flowers, he was mostly already gone. His body, the least of him, was all that was left. No wonder he couldn't figure out a way to tell her goodbye. He couldn't risk the broken helplessness that he felt around her. She was holding too much. The scale had been tipped too far.

Rabbit wore the medal back out of the World and into The Jungle, the tiny globe nestled among his dog tags. After a few weeks in the country, in the deep black of a moonless night, Rabbit felt something like a hot ember drop on his chest. By the time he got the medal off there was a miniature world-sized burn where it had rested. The next day Rabbit sent St. Michael back across the water in an envelope addressed to Two in care of her brother-in-law. He kept the quilting square and the tiny slip of paper. *In case I miss you, Two.*

That same week Rabbit had his first death with him running point. Baby-faced Davis from Arkansas. He had light eyes and a gap-toothed smile. Rabbit didn't have the medal. Two didn't either. St. Michael would not have made it back to Memphis by then, but Rabbit could still feel a disc of heat on his chest where it would have hung beneath his uniform. Right before Davis died, Rabbit had caught sight of a flash of rainbow-colored light hovering right beyond the tree-line. And the night had been filled with the sudden creamy sharp smell of wisteria. He ran, signaling for the rest of his unit to follow. The rainbow light was running point. He was following it. Everybody made it but Davis. He hadn't lost a single soul until he took the charm from around his neck and sent it back. Rabbit couldn't shake the feeling that the light was somehow Two. She was stepping in.

"I'd know you anyhow you come," he'd told her once in their leafy perch. "Just your feet, your hands, a flower, or a fire. Anyhow you come. I'd know you." He'd held her hand over his heart and she kissed his fingers. It was her. A bit of Two-shaped rainbow lightning threading him again through the eye of a needle. He had left her without a word and sent her gift return to sender. Rabbit took Davis's Polaroid from the pile and drew a black line through his name, wrapped it along with Two's note in the piece of calico.

When to his own surprise, Rabbit made it through his second tour alive, he thought that he would make a home elsewhere. He was new, so his home should be, too. Rabbit thought this was one of his big mistakes on his First Return—he didn't understand that he was new. On that First Return he had been drawn home like a planet to its sun. Rabbit was determined to make his own orbit this time, to shine his own light instead of just reflecting it. He tried Chicago and NYC and DC. The buildings so straight and razor sharp cast shadows on him in the street. The icy whip of seasons kept him searching for a nip of something for his nerves. The clipped sound of proper talk from black folk didn't fool him. He could hear the *ArkansasMississippiAlabamaTennesseeGeorgia* no matter how they tried to corral the country of their tongues.

He wandered from soldier to soldier and then from sister to sister until he wore thin, but not completely transparent, the goodwill of his hosts. Rabbit became fluent in the language of scraped bowls and lingering glances at the dinner table to get out ahead of the invitation to exit. He stayed dressed in concealed weaponry, his fist ever-ready to strike, and he kept a running inventory of everything in reaching distance that could be used to maim or harm. There seemed nothing to restrain him in those Northern cities, free from the constant gaze of his neighbors in Wayfarer Homes or some commanding officer. He could feel his wildness acutely, like a pet snake ready to unfurl from its basket. He was holed up in some SRO, unsure of what to do next when he thought of Hawkins.

Hawkins lived somewhere called Cross River, Maryland. Rabbit hadn't thought of it before, but once he ran out of the cities that he had heard of only from envelopes from his father, he decided to take his friend up on his offer to try out life in Cross River. Cross River. It was an auspicious name. Spirits don't cross over water. He had heard that saying his entire life. He wasn't so sure. Hadn't he returned across the water to Memphis the first time as mostly haint? This time he was traveling with a stack of Polaroid ghosts wrapped in Two's black calico.

As far as he could tell, Hawkins had done what he said (at least the first part of the list). He made it out of the Jungle alive and was working a mostly straight job driving for a car service.

"So, what about the Woe?" Rabbit asked.

"Come home with me and see," said Hawkins with a chuckle. "You wanna go by the river now or later?"

"Doesn't matter to me."

"Blood? You scared?" Hawkins threw back his head laughing, his nose slicing the air like a cleaver.

"I ain't scared. Did two tours. Ran point the whole time. Ain't dead, yet."

Hawkins looked at his watch. "Shit. Coral'll kill me though. She's home cooking half the seafood in Maryland. You like crab?"

"I'll eat whatever she cooking."

"We can settle this Louisiana v. Maryland crab argument I was always having with Toussaint. Whatever happened to him?"

"I didn't ever make it to Louisiana," Rabbit said. He and Two had talked about going there. She wanted to visit a woman The Mississippi Sisters told her about in Algiers. You had to take a ferry to get to her house across the river. But that was Before.

"And Toussaint—" Hawkins started. Rabbit shook his head. Rabbit showed Hawkins the photograph he had taken of Toussaint, his name marked through in black.

"Awww, man. That was a good Blood."

Rabbit's stomach twisted. He had been living hard before calling Hawkins. Too much whiskey and food worse than C-rations. He thought of Toussaint from New Orleans, one of the ghosts traveling with him now who always said in his thick accent, "Look, you wants to drink, you gots to eat. In New Orleans, man we drink. We eat. Jambalaya, stewed okra, barbeque shrimps, stuffed mirliton, gumbo, red beans. You drink. You eat. You pass a good time. You make some love. Go to church. Confess it all. Become new."

"Look. You ain't gonna wanna no other crab after Coral's. Warning you now, some of her friends will probably 'stop by," Hawkins said.

"Water-Women, too?"

"Some yes, some no," said Hawkins with a wink.

"All I need is sugar, right?" Rabbit was trying to keep his spirits up, but his head was starting to throb.

"Right, Blood. You got it."

They drove on past the Cross River, but didn't stop. Rabbit tried to shake the notion of the river pulling on him, causing his foul mood, but he couldn't fight bad thoughts and weariness at the same time. Or maybe he could. He was new, he reminded himself.

When they pulled up to Hawkins's home, he was glad that he had spent almost the last of his cash on a pack of Polaroid film. He hated showing up empty-handed. When he sent the medal back to Two, he kept trying to write her a note or find some trinket to include, but everything looked silly and false. St. Michael looked too lonesome by himself in the envelope, and he couldn't figure out any words that made sense. Each time he started a note, he just ended up writing and writing and writing her name again and again on a slip of tablet paper, but he would ball it up and throw each successive one away. At the very last second Rabbit took one of his mirror portraits and put it in the envelope with the medal. He tried to remember which one it was, but couldn't conjure his own face anymore.

Hawkins's wife Coral looked like Rabbit had imagined her, light-skinned with hazel eyes full of mischief. They entered through a lush garden in the back of the house, right into the kitchen. The buttery, salty, spicy smell of seafood greeted him before they even hit the door. Hawkins would feed him well. He would rest. A rush of relief fell over him.

"Nice to meet you Mrs. Hawkins," Rabbit said. Mrs. Hawkins shot a look at her husband.

"Coral is just fine. No need to be formal. I feel like I already know you. Amber and all his stories. You're a bit of the reason that I married this one."

"Me?" Rabbit asked and raised an eyebrow.

"You. Go look in foyer on the key table."

Hawkins was busying himself getting glasses for their whiskey.

"Go on. You'll know it when you see it."

Hawkins pointed and Rabbit made his way to the front of the house with its impossibly shiny floors. There was a tiny table with two bowls on it. One for his keys and one for hers he guessed. On the mirror was a portrait of Hawkins that he had taken. Rabbit knew exactly when he took it, right after

Davis died. There was something somber in Hawkins's look and a little tender, too.

When he entered the kitchen, he handed the portrait to Hawkins.

"Same handsome devil, right?"

"Amber, would you please get some newspaper to cover these tables?"

"At your service," Amber said with a flourish.

"That one is yours," she said nodding to a whiskey on the table.

"How did that picture help?" Rabbit was thankful for the familiar burn of the whiskey in his throat. His head was still throbbing and with Hawkins out of the room, Coral still seemed light but more intense.

"I put that picture at the front door, because when Amber sent it, I could see something beyond all of his sugar talk and silliness. He uses all that big talk to cover up. Your picture let me know that there was something else there. You helped me see that. I was about to push him off on one of my friends! So when he gets ahead of himself, I tell him to go look at that picture to remind himself of who I married."

She turned to the stove and dipped a spoon into a pot to taste it. She did a little shimmy and shook some seasoning into the pot.

"Almost perfect."

"I'm excited," Rabbit said.

"Look. That man will talk you to death. Get you a nap before dinner. Your room is fixed up. First one on the right. Bathroom with towels and everything across the hall. I'll keep your friend busy until dinner is ready," Coral said.

"Thank you so much. I appreciate it."

"You mighty quiet, but I guess anybody is next to my husband," Coral said.

"Just tired," Rabbit told her which was the honest truth.

"Amber been spooking you with that Woe business?"

"Ma'am?" Rabbit drank the rest of the whiskey and she poured him another.

"Coral. Just Coral. And Rabbit, there's no such thing as a Water-

Woman. Woe. It's just a tale. Relax. Make yourself at home."

"Thanks," Rabbit said.

"Plus. Plenty of sugar in the pantry. Just in case," she said with a wink.

Rabbit stood under Amber's shower and then stopped the tub for a bath. What a luxury. He couldn't remember his last tub bath. When he came to himself he was waking up in Amber's guestroom.

"Get up, Sleeping Beauty! Come get some crab before these people eat them all." Rabbit dressed and followed Hawkins into the kitchen. The hi-fi was playing. In the garden, the picnic table was covered in newspaper and piled with steamed crabs, shrimp, corn, and other covered pots. On the kitchen table were cakes, pies, and such. The women had arrived as promised. They were all in brightly colored dresses, flitting about the kitchen like birds. Amber introduced them to Rabbit, but their names didn't stick in his head. They weren't all related but looked vaguely like Coral to Rabbit, but he wasn't sure if it was a trick of his fatigue or a trick of these Water-Women. He tried to remember the rules that Hawkins had laid out. Could a Water-Woman get you away from the river? Would they look like a fantasy or a real woman? When did you dust them with sugar? Where did you look for their gills?

Why would I want anybody don't want me of my own free will?

Free.

Free?

There was another whiskey in Rabbit's hand and a bounty of salty, delicious food that wasn't like a feast his mother would have made for him. Even if it didn't taste like home, it tasted of kinship and care. He ate and let the women teach him how to crack his crabs with the wooden mallets and dig out the flesh with the skinny knives that were designed just for that task.

"Grace, you're from Memphis, right?" said an older man graying at the temples named Jasper. He was broad through the shoulders and fit. Former military, too from the looks of him .

"All day long and twice on Tuesday," Rabbit said.

"Put the man on some music of his homeland, Amber! I got cousins in Memphis," said Jasper.

"Just about everybody does," Rabbit said and smiled at one of Coral's sistercousinfriends—Ruby, Pearl, Opal. He couldn't keep them straight. She was stealing glances at him, browner than the rest. Quieter, too. Rabbit nodded hello to her and she blushed into her aqua sundress.

"Memphis. Hmmm, were you there when they killed King?"

"Man, that still ain't set right by me. Got to be a set up with the Feds."

"Ain't no way."

"You was there right, Grace. After your first tour," Hawkins asked.

"I was there. I had just got back," Rabbit said. It wasn't exactly true. Rabbit had gotten back in time for Christmas and the killing didn't happen until that April, but those months had all slid together. He had just gotten back to himself, collecting himself with Two in The Gap.

Suddenly, the night was filled with a voice so familiar that Rabbit looked at the kitchen door waiting for Otis to walk through it. To join the party and toss him the keys to his Cadillac like on that one perfect day Rabbit drove him around Memphis. But like the other ghosts he carried, only their likenesses were left behind in this world. Rabbit looked down at the knife on the table, considered what damage one of the crab mallets might be able to do. He made note that his switchblade was still in his pocket and some guitar pics he still carried out of habit even though his guitar had been stolen months before.

Otis sang on.

The rest of the party seemed to float away as Rabbit was many places at once. Driving Redding's Cadillac. Back in that firefight where they lost Davis. Watching his cousins sing at the WDIA talent show. In the courtyard of the Lorraine when the shot went off that murdered King. Scraping up the blood from the patio. The scar on his chest flared with a sudden heat as Rabbit tried to still the swirl of worlds around him.

"Blood. Hey Blood." Rabbit stared but the face was all faces. It wouldn't stop shifting. Davis. Toussaint. Evans. Harris. Finally, Hawkins's face emerged.

"Grace. Grace. You want more crab? As hard as you're gripping that knife looks like it. Ruby will crack some for you. Won't you, Ruby?"

"Sure. Let me fix you another plate. We still got dessert. Cake? Pie?" Ruby said. And there was something so tender in it that broke through Otis Redding's voice and the words swirling. Rabbit's vision cleared then. He returned to himself and saw that he had the crab knife up at his throat near the scar. Rabbit dropped the knife and it clattered to the table. He plopped back down into his chair, newly aware that he had been standing. Ruby sat next to him and stared, cracking crab again. The women looked nervous and the men wary, but the party picked back up and settled into an unsteady rhythm.

Rabbit was feeling himself again. As the party was winding down, Rabbit set up a chair in the garden, taking photos. He took lots with his 110 since the film was cheaper and carefully rationed the Polaroids.

"Why don't we get some air? Get to the river. You can play this."

Rabbit stared. It was a guitar. This confused him. He had bought a guitar at a pawn shop when he first was discharged, but it had been stolen several cities back.

"Your letters, Blood. You told me how yours got stolen." Otis was still singing in the background. Hawkins held the instrument toward him and Rabbit considered that this is how it felt to the folk behind him when he ran point. Hawkins was stepping in. Like he had. Like Two.

Let's take it to the water and see if this thing is just decoration. I don't know shit about guitars."

Rabbit rubbed the scar at his neck with his thumb, a raised coin of his own flesh. He took the guitar in his hands and strummed a bit.

"Let's see this river, mane," Rabbit said.

"Don't be gone too long, Amb," Coral said.

"We're just gonna stretch our legs. Get some air. Be back before you miss me," Amber said.

"Impossible," said Coral. She leaned up and kissed his sharp cheekbone, and Rabbit felt a flush of heat in his belly. He snapped a picture of them. He envied Hawkins and Coral's easy open teasing and the life that he had built so quickly. This is what the Life After the Military booklet promised.

"I promised to introduce him to some Water-Women. He's met you, so there's one. But you're already accounted for."

"Amb!" said Coral and shoved her husband towards the door.

"They call this the Hail Mary Bridge," Ruby said. She and her sister Pearl had come along to the river. Coral had begged off to look after her mother, who everyone called Mother Beryl. The Hail Mary Bridge. Maybe it was time for some wild, new luck.

"The river is high," said Pearl.

"It's hungry," said Hawkins.

"Let's go closer," said Rabbit. They descended the stone steps down to the shore. Rabbit felt a thrum building that he couldn't tell if it was inside of him or out.

"You gonna play that thing or what?" Hawkins pointed to the guitar.

"Negro, you think I can't play it?"

"Well, you *know* I can't play it, so I want to hear it."

"So how did you end up with this thing?"

"Won it. Dice," Hawkins said. "I know you can sing, but I've never heard you play."

"What you know about my singing?"

"Grace, don't you know you're always singing?"

"So I've heard," Rabbit said. "You a heathen, but even you should know this one."

This little light of mine, I'm gonna let it shine
This little light of mine, I'm gonna let it shine
This little light of mine
I'm gonna let it shine
Let it shine, shine, shine
Let it shine!

Hawkins lifted his baritone and the women joined in. A singing family. Like his cousins, The Amazing Graces.

All up in my house, I'm gonna let it shine
All up in my house, I'm gonna let it shine
All up in my house, I'm gonna let it shine
Let it shine, shine, shine
Let it shine!

Rabbit joined his voice with theirs and felt himself rise, rise, rise. Their voices joined together in communion seemed enough to make the island (if there was one) rise out of the water. He had missed singing with others. Not since that summer over with his cousins, The Amazing Graces, had he sung regularly with other people. Singing made that light he was chasing burn. How could he have forgotten the power of his own voice? Even when he felt his stutter try to catch, his voice was his. He owned it, the guitar vibrating against him as he played. All the vibration becoming sound seemed to be tuning him, grounding this new Rabbit into now. Just as they ended the song, a flash of lightning spilled from the sky, the crack of thunder chasing it from the heavens. A sudden steamy rain started and they scurried towards the bridge.

Rabbit felt that it must be true. That Cross River was raining some new luck down on him. As his friends climbed the steps, he watched Hawkins's hand linger at Ruby's back as they climbed the steps. Watched her lean against Hawkins as they climbed. The quick shower lasted less than a minute, leaving behind a furious steam. Even the moon had come from beneath the clouds. Rabbit offered Pearl his hand to climb the stairs to the bridge.

"I hope you stay awhile," Pearl said.

Rabbit pulled the rag out of his back pocket to wipe down his new guitar. Pearl passed Hawkins and Ruby in the doorway and up the stairs to the apartment they shared. The light was perfect, and Rabbit was framing the shot in his head since he had left his cameras behind.

Hawkins trotted towards him and the men walked back towards his house, smoking in silence.

"So—" Rabbit said.

"All of 'em got Water-Women in 'em. I know you don't believe me."

Rabbit shrugged. He had been reviewing how Ruby was the one who followed all of Hawkins's instructions, while Hawkins followed Coral's commands. Two types of Woes.

"It's a good place, Cross River," Hawkins said.

"Seems like it," Rabbit said.

"You should try it. Stay awhile. Think about it, Blood."

"I will."

Rabbit took another shower when he got in and found that Coral had washed and folded his clothes. Rabbit tried to get to sleep on those crisp sheets. The bed seemed too soft, so he tried the floor. Coral had put one of the half-finished pints of whiskey on the dresser, he guessed to keep it from Hawkins. He drank some of it. He was restless and wanted to play the guitar. Even though Mama Beryl just lived in the house a few steps down, Hawkins told him that she was probably asleep up in the good guest room. He didn't want to disturb her. He went to the bathroom and got his camera. He snapped a few shots of himself in this Cross River mirror. He was trying to see himself at home in this place, in any place.

All of these row houses in Hawkins's neighborhood had been family homes. He wondered how many generations had turned that glass doorknob, looked into this gold-framed mirror. So different from the houses in Wayfarer Homes that had been theirs for only one generation. Uncle Jasper told Rabbit that Cross River had been the site of the only successful slave revolt in the entire U. S. of A. Rabbit had thought then, at the beginning of the whiskey and crabs covered in Old Bay like sand, that this was another sign that Cross River was the place that he could be new. Among these freedom people. Instead, just a few moments later, Memphis came right to him where he was with Otis Redding singing on the hi-fi.

Was it then he started leaving or before?

He didn't have much to pack. Rabbit was out into the Cross River night before he knew it, headed for the river. He left the Polaroids of the Hawkins family on the dresser where the whiskey had been.

He descended the steps from the Hail Mary Bridge and settled on the shore, as close to the water as he could. Although he had tuned the guitar when he got it, with the quick humid thunderstorm it had fallen suddenly out of tune. Rabbit played on and filled the night with his own voice, just to hear it.

I'm going home on the morning train
I'm going home on the morning train
I'm going home
I'm going home
I'm going home on the morning train
That evening train might be too late

Rabbit sat and played and waited for the Water-Women's island to rise. He could feel something tugging, tugging at him from the depths. Willing and ready, he waited for a Not-Two Two, a Not-Ruby Ruby, or a Not-Pearl Pearl to rise, wet and bare-breasted from the island so he could join his voice with theirs and sing himself to a home in the depths of Cross River. He waited for the Polaroid ghosts he carried to emerge from the depths of the forest for him. He waited for the spinning black diamond of an island to rise and gather him up, to claim him, but knew that it would not come for him.

He had already chosen.

He would make a Second Return.

AGAINST THE VENOM TIDE

HENRY SZABRANSKI

At first Osami drifted alone in the cold and the dark, the ache in her chest unbearable, the weight of the seawater above crushing the air from her lungs. But what terrified her most was the dim light far below. Growing brighter. Growing closer.

Because this was a memory as well as a dream.

The dark erupted into life. Countless glowing tentacles squirming out of the murky depths, tapered ribbons studded with suckers and venomous spines. No matter how much she struggled and kicked against them she knew there was no escape from the many-fingered hands of Ueldu. They slithered and rasped against her skin, pulled her down towards the hungry maw that waited below.

This was when she usually woke. Struggled upright. Dizzy and gasping for breath.

Her skin drenched with salt water.

#

Half-starved, dressed only in rags, the young woman pressed her scarred face against the glass wall of the temple, struggling to peer inside.

Osami watched from a distance, crouched below one of the huge bellows forcing air into and out of the temple. She was supposed to be checking the wheezy bellows for cracks and wear, but the cloth she used to polish the creaking apparatus lay abandoned near an amphora full of fish-oil. Instead of concentrating on her work, Osami's attention was fixed upon the disfigured woman. It was years since she had seen another storm survivor. Galipo had said they had all been driven away: sold into slavery, forced off the islands, or simply starved or gone mad—but there she was, her storm-sister, reflected and distorted by the great salt-rimed sphere of the temple alongside the setting sun and the distant wheeling gulls.

For what seemed an age, Osami could not bring herself to approach the woman, afraid she was some wishful apparition who would simply melt into the gathering sea-mist. But Osami's feet had a determination of their own. She found herself striding across the matted reed floor of the temple plaza, reaching out to touch the woman's shoulder. "Excuse me…"

The woman whirled, fast and feral.

Osami stumbled back as a knife blade thrust towards her. "I'm — I'm not going to hurt you! Look." Without thinking, she pulled open the collar of her grease-stained tunic to reveal the scars around her throat.

The woman's eyes widened. Aquamarine and dark-lashed. Osami's attention wavered between them and the blade pointed towards her. She said, "My name is Osami."

The woman took a step back. Hesitated. "Leesha."

Osami pointed at the circular scars along Leesha's thin arm, the ones that had first drawn her attention. "How did you get such marks?"

Leesha pushed back her braided hair from her face, tucking it under a rag tied round her head. A splay of bright red tentacles embroidered the dark cloth. "I was touched. By the hands of Ueldu."

"Then you are blessed."

"Oh yes. I am blessed." She grimaced. "I feel Ueldu's love every second of every day."

As Leesha spoke, Osami noticed her blue-black stained gums for the first time and her heart sank. A venom addict. For some time, judging by the darkness of the shade. "The temple — the priests." Osami struggled to keep the disappointment from her voice. "Maybe they can help you."

Leesha's expression was withering. "They'd sooner sacrifice me to Ueldu than look at me."

As if to vindicate her, the late-evening chimes to prayer rang out from the spires surrounding the temple. Osami gave a guilty start. She should have finished cleaning the bellows she had been assigned today, but she hadn't even begun. Now it was too late. Galipo would be furious when he found out.

A line of crimson-robed priests shuffled across the square towards the temple's oblique entrance. Osami automatically bowed her head as they passed, the way she had been taught. She didn't expect any acknowledgement — she was unrecognizable in her greasy robes, and her spilled fish-oil stink discouraged attention — but she looked up when the line stopped moving.

The lead priest stared at her, a frown on his leathery face. His right eye sagged, its socket riven by some old wound. Osami clutched her tunic tight, realizing her open collar still exposed her scars. She could almost hear Galipo's voice reproaching her: "Don't ever show your wounds. Don't ever reveal your past."

She flinched and drew back as the scarred priest stepped forward, but a colleague grabbed his shoulder and murmured urgently into his ear, pointing towards the temple's entrance. The priest grimaced. With a sharp parting glance, he resumed his progress towards the heavily guarded tunnel's hatch. The others shuffled after him.

Osami turned back towards Leesha, but her ragged storm-sister was gone. Taking advantage of her momentary distraction, the woman had fled back into the rat's nest of streets from which she had emerged.

Osami's shoulders sagged, the only other survivor she had seen in years. Apart from herself, perhaps the only one remaining in the whole of Saltris. Did she remember the storm? The hands of Ueldu? Did the same dreams haunt her?

So many questions now with no chance of an answer.

#

Sunset had long since faded by the time Osami stumbled back home. The circular scars covering her body itched and burned, an unfading reminder of the storm and the dwellers it stirred from the deep. Her brief excursion into the temple district's outer streets to try and find Leesha had been frustrated by the growing darkness and terrifying glimpses of open water.

The High Khresmon's private quarters were humble: a tight-woven reed hut, domed-roofed in imitation of the temple under whose shadow it nestled. Galipo stood waiting for her, leaning in the hut's doorway, tendrils of greasy whale-fat smoke drifting from the lantern he held aloft. In his other hand he clutched a shell-encrusted goblet half-full of wine. A knot of fear tightened in Osami's belly. She had hoped he would be asleep by now.

"You asked for responsibility, so I gave it to you." The strength of Galipo's voice belied his age. "Now you throw it back in my face?"

Osami hung her head. A guard or supervisor must have complained about her abandoning the bellows. Probably the hard-faced priest who had stopped on his way to the temple, the clawed-eye one who had stared at her as if she were bilge-waste. She knew she owed the High Khresmon, knew she should be grateful for all he had done for her, but all she could think of was Leesha and her dark-lashed, aquamarine eyes. She only hoped Galipo didn't know the reason she had been distracted from her job. He wouldn't understand. Not until after he had calmed down some. Probably not even then.

"The bellows need maintaining." Wine slopped from Galipo's goblet, spattering the reed floor. "D'you mean to choke all the priests on their own stale air? Or the bellows to spring a leak and sink the entire city?"

Osami knew better than to argue. Galipo's temper was up and fresh drink lay in his belly. "Of course not," she muttered. She had a sudden image of the airtight couplings between the giant bellows and the vent holes drilled into the temple breaking loose, air and then water spuming out in great jets, the whole vast structure listing and then sinking, taking much of Saltris with it. A great crystal blow to Ueldu's upturned face as He slumbered below.

"Oh, Osami." Galipo's expression suddenly softened. He stumbled inside the hut, holding the door open for her. After a pause, she followed.

"The currents are unpredictable these days. People are hungry. They're sick of living on boiled barnacle stalks and gilly crabs; they're looking for someone to blame." Galipo leveled a trembling finger at her as he sat upon his cushioned, throne-like chair. "You especially should be careful."

Osami made no attempt to hide her exasperation. "It's not my fault the catch is poor."

He waved her words away. "You've heard the protesters, Sami. On every island. We've strayed too far from the old ways. It's not enough to feed Ueldu the city dregs, the slop and the night earth and the rotting carcasses of the dead. It's not enough for the people to lose themselves using the venom from His cast-off spines." Galipo slumped lower in his chair, his chin buried in his chest. "It's not enough."

She had heard the rumors, too. Even around the temple and the wealthier inner districts, whispers of bloody rituals, of a desperate priesthood struggling to appease Ueldu's insatiable appetites. But it was all nonsense, bitter rumors. Or for some, wishful thinking. That the priests had the power to change matters, regardless of the means.

The High Khresmon suddenly launched himself upright, caught her in a bear-hug. They both staggered across the hut's rich serpent-patterned rugs, she half-supporting his weight. "Don't worry, Sami," he slurred. "This tide'll soon pass. Ueldu will smile up at us once more."

She endured his grip, thankful at least for his change of mood, and guided him back to his seat, covering his thin legs with a blanket. In this humble hut of his, in the shadow of the temple but not part of it, he eschewed the servants his role entitled him to. He kept only her.

Later, as he often did, he became even more garrulous with drink. He reminisced about glories past, before the storm, when Saltris had ruled the waves, floated amongst plentiful shoals of fish, the gleaming jewel of the seas. He spoke of his hopes for Osami, how she was like a daughter to him, a precious catch turned up in the wake of the storm, her beauty shining through the devastation. She nestled beside him in his cocoon of blankets, the way he liked, and she asked him, "Did you ever see Ueldu Himself? Beneath the altar pool?"

As always, Galipo paled, reached for more wine, changed the subject. "Be a good girl, Sami. Rub my sore old bones. That's it. Like that. Snuggle close, the way you used to."

Somehow the opportunity to mention Leesha never arose.

#

Below her, the face of Ueldu slowly rotated, hideous and divine. A thousand glowing arms twisting and dividing like the rays of a submarine sun. They grasped Osami ever tighter, drew her ever closer; all fear gone, dissolved by sweet poison. Her flesh was torn by the venom-tipped spines jutting from the tentacles that gripped her. Only deadening calm and a vague sense of loss remaining.

It was going to be all right. Soon she would be together with her mother and father, her sisters and her brothers. They were down there, waiting. They had been ever since the day of the storm.

No need to be afraid.

She was going home.

#

The next morning she loaded an old knapsack with a handful of hard-boiled cormorant eggs, a fold of flatbread and a skin of watered wine. Who knew how long her search would take? Galipo remained snoring on his ornately carved driftwood bed, oblivious, his dreg-stained goblet clutched to his chest as if it were some precious relic.

Osami tried to suppress her growing nervousness as she emerged into the mist-ridden dawn. She stood no chance of finding Leesha unless she ventured from her familiar haunts around the temple. Her scars itched and burned at the very thought. She would need to cross wide swathes of open water, and the prospect terrified her. Normally she did her best to keep away from the canals and the inconstant gaps between the islands, staying close to the great crystal temple at the heart of Saltris. It was where the reed island was thickest and most stable; where the ocean's undulation could hardly be felt.

She had been barely four summers old when the wrath winds blew and swept the island on which she lived beneath the sea. Memories of her scoured-away family were more wish than reality now, but the all too vivid images of the storm's aftermath remained: the floating maze of smashed timber and woven reeds that once made up her home; panic-stricken livestock floundering amongst the bodies that slowly tumbled in the water like sodden bags of grain. Worst of all, concealed below the water's dark surface, the waiting hands of Ueldu, their razor-sharp teeth and writhing tentacles ready to drag down anyone who strayed into their path.

Osami had been luckier than most. Picked out of the wreckage at random by Galipo and provided food, shelter, a chance of a new life. Thanks to his intervention, she had avoided the worst of the prejudice and mistreatment the other survivors suffered. For surely the outer islanders had brought this upon themselves? Committed some dreadful sin to stir up Ueldu wrath? Now the storm and their fate had faded from memory, it was a subject to be avoided. Just a bad dream. But she could never forget. For days after Galipo rescued her, as the priest struggled to nurse her back to gray life, she had lain feverish and full of strange dreams.

And like memories of the storm, those dark visions lingered still.

#

The morning sky shone like fresh-boiled shellfish as Osami passed through the central plaza. Ueldu's temple glistened beneath the rising sun. The dread pearl of Saltris, the buoyant core around which the city's countless islands orbited. The hollow sphere's true origins were lost amongst the layers of myth and history grown round it, varied as the laminar veins of cratered limpets and salt crackling that etched its uneven surface. Some said the great crystal bubble had erupted full-formed out of the fires that raged deep beneath the waves; others that it was dislodged from the jaws of a monstrous clam by even larger beasts lumbering across their seabed arena. Galipo insisted Ueldu Himself had welded seawater together to forge his godkin a vast hollow cathedral, a gift so that they might better worship Him. Osami was pretty sure no one knew — or could ever know — the actual truth.

She steeled herself before crossing the first rickety looking pontoon bridge that led out towards the islands she had not visited since she was a child, when she was Galipo's freshly rescued new attendant. She swallowed hard and forced herself to stumble forward with eyes half-shut, refusing to look down or to acknowledge the increasing queasiness in her stomach. If she continued on, as she planned, the islands would become smaller and less rigid, eventually nothing more than haphazard rafts loosely tied to the central mass. She consoled herself that at least she could not get lost, not for long. The temple's globe and ring of spires were visible from every point in a city of low-rise huts. Most were made of dried seaweed and reeds, the most expensive daubed and domed so that they could withstand the winter winds and not act as sails to disturb the complex configuration of the archipelago.

Osami fought a mounting sense of hopelessness as well as fear. What chance was there of finding any single soul amongst these teeming islands after all? She had no idea which district Leesha called home or whether she called any place home. She thought only that Leesha might still linger somewhere near the temple, for she had seemed drawn by it. But once beyond the plaza surrounding the temple, the temple district itself was a warren. Crammed with bustling fish stalls and apothecaries and suppliers serving the priesthood's needs, the district held all types of business that a large metropolis of any kind, floating or otherwise, required. Beyond the markets lay a ring of islands housing the temple's functionaries and lower order priesthood, the craftspeople and bureaucrats that made their living near the center. This was the farthest Osami had ever ventured; she knew little of what lay beyond the perimeter canal, only that Galipo held the outer areas in little regard. "The border islands swarm with venom-addled fools," he warned her. "Most hardly know whether its day or night, and care less."

A flag slapping in the breeze caught her eye. Red tentacles vibrating across black cloth. The dilapidated drinking den to which it belonged was no more than a shack leaning near the edge of the last island before the true outer zone began. *The Red Kraken*, a hand-painted sign read. Osami supposed the material for the den's sigil had belonged once to some entirely different and more upmarket establishment. But was it only coincidence that Leesha's hair scarf had been of a similar design?

A brawl's worth of disgruntled-looking fishermen clustered outside the *Kraken*, staggering and obviously drunk. Or worse. A faint bitter tang in the air. Despite the looks the men gave her, Osami approached closer. They lost interest when she began to rummage around in the mounds of garbage behind the shed. Just another starveling, searching for whatever she could find.

But soon Osami's heart jumped. Her instinct had been right. There: a form lying slumped against the woven kelp rear wall of the *Kraken*. Leesha, crumpled, her mouth slack, her aquamarine eyes rolled back to better regard her venom dreams.

Osami's surprise and relief were swiftly replaced by anger and disappointment. Leesha's head lolled in response to Osami calling her name. A thin loop of tar-dark spit escaped her lips. A handful of discarded venom spines littered the ground nearby, crunching apart beneath Osami's feet.

Osami cursed. Of course she had known this could happen. That she would discover Leesha collapsed in a drugged stupor. Hadn't she, in fact, relied on it? How else had she planned to ever find her? Still, she was shocked. Where was the vital young woman she had glimpsed yesterday?

Osami heaved Leesha up until she leaned against her shoulder. She was surprisingly light, her skin all parchment, her bones like tinder beneath her waste-soaked rags. Osami checked to see if anyone was looking, but the *Kraken*'s clientele were too busy arguing amongst themselves to take any notice of another pair of ragtag drunkards staggering away from the shore.

#

"Do you...do you remember the storm?"

A stirring in the shadows. Osami woke from a doze, bleary eyed. She had been more tired than she realized. "Hmm, what?"

Deep aquamarine eyes stared up at her. "It's why I take the venom. So I can forget."

"It's your business. What you do. Why you do it." Osami rubbed her face with the heel of her hand and stared around the place she found herself in. An abandoned warehouse near the temple district, an old fish market unable to sustain enough traffic during the current famine to remain open. Only rats, seagulls, and a pair of survivors of the storm who had literally stumbled inside called it home now.

"Don't pretend you don't judge me."

"I can't judge you. I hardly know you."

Leesha made a dismissive noise.

"Anyway, I don't believe you. About taking the venom to forget."

Leesha dry-swallowed, looked away, changed the subject. "I dream of them every night."

"Of what?"

"The hands. His hands."

Osami did not reply, did not mention her own dreams.

"They say once you've been touched by Ueldu you belong to him forever."

Osami said, "We all of us in Saltris belong to him." Something Galipo had once told her.

Leesha shook her head. "He wants more than us to just belong to Him." She wriggled up onto her elbows. Osami could feel the heat emanating from her sweat-slicked face. "He wants us down there." She stared down at the reed floor. Beyond it. Beneath it. "He wants us down there with Him."

Leesha was shivering. Instinctively, Osami reached out to hold her. She expected to be rebuffed, pushed back, but instead Leesha clung tight. Her thin fingers gripped Osami almost painfully. She could smell the bitter venom aftertaste on Leesha's breath and shuddered at the memories it evoked. The urge to scratch her old wounds was almost irresistible.

For a long time they clung wordlessly to each other as the streets and canals outside the old warehouse hazed golden beneath the nooning sun.

Eventually Leesha stirred in Osami's arms. "You said you didn't believe me."

"Hmm?"

"That I take the venom to forget."

Osami hesitated. But with her storm-sister, why not the truth? "You don't take it to forget." Her voice firmed with conviction. "You take it to remember."

She shivered herself now.

The sun climbed and then the sun set. Together Osami and Leesha lay in the cool darkness, and took turns running their fingertips over each others' scars.

#

"It's late. Where have you been?" Galipo stood waiting inside the hut entrance, his shaved head gleaming like a fallen moon in the lantern light.

"I'm not a prisoner am I?"

Osami expected him to fall into a rage at her impertinence — which surprised even her and which she regretted even as she spoke — but the old priest was silent, his face a mask. He swung the door open and waited until she eventually ventured inside.

"You're smiling," he said, when her back was to him. An accusation.

Osami assumed a frowning expression and turned to confront him. "It was such a beautiful day. Clear blue sky once the mist was gone. You've always told me I should appreciate the second chance Ueldu gave me. Well, that's what I did."

"The city can be dangerous." Galipo appraised her with unblinking eyes. "It's full of hungry, desperate people. Thieves and venom addicts."

"Not my fault."

"Maybe true. But your problem if they ever discover you once escaped Ueldu's hands. They'll make sure you're returned to Him. Only I can keep you safe."

Osami's stomach clenched. She felt suddenly dizzy. "I don't feel well. I have to lie down." She stumbled away, to her own little corner of the hut.

A little later, when Galipo called for her, she stayed prone on her blanket, pretending to be asleep. He clomped into her room and pulled drunkenly at her arm, but she rolled over so her back was turned to him. Muttering and cursing to himself she heard his goblet being tossed against the wall. She lay still, mouth dry and heart hammering against the hide that covered the bamboo ribs of the floor. She concentrated on appearing inert, senseless, uninteresting. An object not a person. Eventually she heard Galipo's muttering subside, the sound of wine being poured into the retrieved goblet. A little later, snoring.

Beneath her the ocean slowly roiled, as if Saltris rested upon the chest of some sleeping leviathan. In stages, she began to relax, allowing herself to be infected by the giant's slumber. And hoping her dreams that night would be aquamarine not golden.

#

"We can leave Saltris. Leave Ueldu and His rotten hands behind."

Osami stared at Leesha, considering her words. Saltris was the only world Osami had ever known. Not even Saltris, really, but mostly just the temple district. She tried to control a shudder. If she were to ever leave the city, she knew she would have to cross vast swathes of open water.

"We could go to the Ustormengi archipelago." Leesha was oblivious to Osami's discomfort. In the few days she had known her, Osami had never seen her so full of enthusiasm. So alive. "Stay on one of its islands. One that doesn't float, but is anchored to bedrock. Or we could head north, to the mainland."

Osami rolled onto her back. The ruined warehouse's roof rattled above their heads as a pair of seagulls fought over some scrap. The unassuming building had become Leesha's home, as much as any place in the city was her home. "I move about a lot," she had said. "Never stay in one place too long. It's not safe." But wherever Leesha was, that's where Osami wanted to be. She didn't care about the old fish stink or their rough shelter composed of overturned trestle tables. The rats scuttling in the corners. She hadn't returned to Galipo's quarters or to her job cleaning the temple's bellows for over two days now. She hardly thought of her old life. The future, the unknown horizon, that's what filled her thoughts. Sometimes she wondered if she was caught in a dream. A new one. One she did not want to wake from.

"...We could see mountains, rivers, forests." Leesha was still in full flow. "We could start afresh, where no one knows or cares about the storm or Ueldu's hunger. Somewhere where nobody knows anything about us at all."

Perhaps that's where the other survivors had gone, Osami thought. Not driven mad or killed or starved, but living new lives in places Osami had never heard or imagined of.

Leesha rolled tight next to her. Dark braids caressed Osami's breast. "Will you come with me?"

"Yes," she found herself saying. She grasped Leesha's warm fingers. "Yes, I will go with you."

#

She no longer needed to breathe.

Poisoned blood pulsed thickly through her veins, richer and sweeter than any festival brandywine.

There was no pain as the spikes rasped against her skin, flayed it into ever finer slivers. There was no discomfort as her body dissolved; more flesh shed each time Ueldu's hands coiled around her, pulled her deeper, deeper, deeper.

Down into the tightening gyre.

#

"Look at her: it's obvious she's been touched. I knew it the first time I saw her."

It was the priest from the procession, the one with the clawed-out eye. He glared not at Osami, but at Leesha as she stirred in their shared tangle of blankets.

Osami tried to wake from the nightmare, rouse herself out of the cacophony of snarling dogs and screeching gulls. There was too much light, streaming in from huge and growing punctures in the side of the building.

Temple guards, armed with tridents and encased in chitinous armor, were pulling Leesha away. Her legs cycled, kicking out, kicking Osami, as she was lifted up.

With growing shock Osami realized this was real. She was awake.

"No!" she shouted. "Leave her alone. She's my friend!"

Galipo was there. At the back, stooping so that his High Khresmon's hat would fit under the jagged border of the ripped out opening. He stared at Osami with dead eyes. "Friend?" he called. "You have no friends. Only me."

Osami's robes tore as she struggled, exposing her scars.

The clawed-eye priest who held her leered, revealing a gap-toothed grin. "You may have got away from Ueldu once," he hissed, leaning down until his nose touched hers. "But He wants you back now."

And that's when Osami saw his blackened gums. Smelled his breath, hot and bitter. And knew there was no hope of escape.

#

Priests clustered around the edge of the altar pool like a ring of crimson-robed barnacles. They stared down into the water, their backs hunched as they tried to gain a better view of the depths below. This was their window into their underwater heaven. This was the only place they could glimpse the true face of Ueldu.

Leesha's sucker-marked body lay half in the water, trussed to a wooden pole spanning the width of the circular pool. Torches set in polished sconces focused their light into the water, but even their flickering beams were unable to penetrate far.

Osami searched around for some means of escape, but the curved walls of the temple rose unbroken around her. A vague light source shimmered through the mineral-veined glass, but so dilute that Osami could not tell whether it was the full day sun or the midnight moon. All these years she had been the High Khresmon's protégé, this was her first time inside. Only the most senior priests, the most exalted dignitaries were allowed to enter the temple. The entrance to the underwater tunnel that snaked under the city and emerged beside the altar pool was locked and barred. The tunnel, the altar pool, and a half-dozen brass-ringed vents where the bellows forced air in and out of the globe were the only openings in the whole of the great crystal sphere. The air was thick and humid, rancid with the stink of brine and stale venom, water shimmering and dripping from the gray-green walls. Hidden from all but the most privileged eyes, severed tentacles hung on racks, dried and hardened, bristling with dark gleaming spines.

Galipo stood at the edge of the altar pool. He motioned at Leesha. "Cut her." One of the priests, face obscured by a deep cowl, stabbed out with a trident. Osami flinched as if the blow had been against her own flesh. Leesha screamed. Blood welled from the shallow wound.

Galipo leaned over the water and pronounced, "It won't be long."

Osami glanced over her shoulder. The clawed-eye priest had been standing behind her, but now he shuffled forward to get a better look at the pool, an eager look on his ruined face, the discarded venom spines that littered the sloping glass floor crackling beneath his feet. She could see no other guards, none of the armored brutes who guarded the city-side entrance to the tunnel. Perhaps they were not considered high enough status to attend this arcane ritual. Perhaps there was no need of them: she was just a weak woman, after all, and the only escape was no escape at all. Her hands or feet were not even bound. Perhaps Galipo intended to be her savior for the second time. Perhaps he intended her to return to him after this. Leesha only a brief delusion. A bad dream.

The priests gathered closer to the edge.

Osami stood and ran towards the pool. The hunched priests did not even turn. She pushed and they fell into the water with a heavy splash. Clawed-eye first. Then another one, two, three. Old men, once the water stripped the cowls from their horror-stricken faces. They floundered in the water in their heavy robes, spluttering and struggling to grasp the smooth glass edge.

Galipo wheeled towards her. His face a mask of incomprehension. "What are you doing?"

Osami did not hesitate as she pushed him into the water alongside the others. "You'll make as good a sacrifice as any of us."

Clawed hands tried to grasp at her, a whirl of crimson, as at last the others began to react. But she was young and strong and full of anger, and they were old and weak and still not entirely believing what was happening.

Osami ran from the edge of the pool, shaking off her attackers. They did not pursue her. Already some of the bedraggled priests were crawling out of the water, spluttering, coughing. The remaining priests leaned in to help them out. They knew Osami had nowhere to run.

The drilled air vents were set high on the upward curving wall. Osami had to stand on her tip-toes to reach the first one and yank hard on the lever protruding from its large brass collar. For a moment she feared it was stuck, that she truly was too weak to move it, but she jumped and dangled her entire weight on the long handle. It wrenched down, and immediately air began to hiss out, under pressure of the huge weight of the temple. The way the bellows usually worked, the collars were only ever opened in carefully choreographed fashion to allow air to be forced in and sucked out. But no one was standing by to work the huge bellows now.

Osami did not wait. She ran to the next vent, pulled it open too. Behind her she could hear the water begin to gurgle up out of the pool like a storm-driven tide.

Priests began to scream. Suddenly tentacles flashed glistening in the torchlight. The hands of Ueldu, reaching up from the depths, summoned by blood and commotion.

Osami pulled open a third vent. Wind billowed through the temple, stirred her hair so that it streamed towards the opening. Outside the temple she heard creakings and shiftings and crackings as unfamiliar weight settled upon structures never designed to support it.

"Osami!"

Leesha's voice cut through her bloody-minded purpose. It was enough. She had done enough. She hoped it was enough.

Osami waded through the surging water towards the wooden frame to which Leesha was tied. It was already almost submerged. Priests waded past Osami, intent only on the vents, closing them. The temple shifted, water sloshed and they stumbled and fell, terror in their eyes.

"You're safe, you're safe," Osami repeated as she struggled to untie the drenched knots that bound her storm-sister's hands. Leesha said nothing. Her eyes were closed. She breathed rapidly.

"What have you done?" Galipo rose out of the water, his soaked crimson robe sagging from his body like flayed skin. "You've doomed us all, you stupid girl!"

"The temple rose from the sea." Osami burned with decades old rage as she brushed away his claw-like hands. "It's time for it to return."

A thin grey limb twined around Galipo, pulled him into the water. Surging foam closed over his mouth and drowned any reply.

#

Osami held Leesha tight as the water swirled around them. Above, the great globe of the temple listed and groaned; the escaping air filled with loud pops and snaps, with the priests' desperate shouts and screams.

In the depths below dark shapes twisted, glimpsed before the last torchlight sputtered out.

"Don't worry," Osami gasped. "We'll be all right."

Vaguely seen through the murk, an eager bulk rising. A leathery limb suddenly curled around Osami's foot. She felt a sharp sting. A tug downwards.

Familiar black ice roared through her veins. She was four years old again.

Her grip on Leesha grew weak. It seemed like only yesterday she had felt that delicious darkness. Been swept away by it.

For a moment Leesha's body almost tumbled away to join the slow rain of wreckage upon Ueldu's upturned face. Like everything eventually, swallowed by the ocean. Only Osami would be left, drifting alone in the cold and the dark, the air dwindling in her lungs.

Waiting for the dream to end.

...We could see mountains, rivers, forests. We could start afresh...

With a great spasm she began to kick her legs. Fueled by desperation, determination, burning acid in her veins. A chink of light above, a tear in the floor of Saltris where the temple had pulled away, huge bubbles of air churning through it.

She powered through the undertow, Leesha still gripped in her arms. Away from the dark. Together. Alive. Up, up, up.

Against the venom tide.

THE HALF-DROWNED CASTLE

LYNDSAY E. GILBERT

Some fathers sell their daughters to the beast. Villages sacrifice virgins to bloody thirsty dragons and power-hungry gods. But I have no father and I am no virgin, so when the Lord of the Half-Drowned Castle comes looking for a bride, I wait alone. Fathers whisk daughters inside and barricade the doors. Maidens utter pagan vows in haste and hide betwixt sheets tangled in secret lovers' legs and arms.

I huddle in the doorway of a church, back pressed to the solid wooden doors. My knuckles are bloodied from knocking for shelter, my ragged gown soaked through with rain. It sticks to my skin, its hem heavy with mud. My feet burn, cut to shreds through sole-less boots, but soon I will feel nothing in this cold.

I alone see him coming. No curtain twitches. No nosy biddy peeks between cracked blinds. No child peers, trembling through squinted eyes to fulfil a wicked dare. He walks tall through the play-dead town as if he thinks the game is hide and seek. As if the people are here just for him, hearts pounding, praying they will win.

He carries a lantern. Dusky light plays on the pallor of his skin, its faint tinge of blue makes me colder still. He detects my tiny shiver and his eyes meet mine, his gaze searing the distance. He walks faster, his boots splash the muddy water. I look away, there is nothing I can give him; my knowledge of the town is new. I was lured by his towering castle, by the fruits of the sea, flakes of salted fish clinging to discarded bones, rotting behind taverns and houses.

But this town has nothing to spare, not even a kick to the ribs, a sneer, a lip curled in disgust. Today fear flew like little birds from nest to nest twittering.

He is coming.

The Lord of the Half Drowned Castle.

He is coming for another wife.

His footsteps stop and light falls on the tips of my boots. I draw my feet back into the shadow of the archway. He smells of wood smoke and when the wind gusts in my face, this time it leaves a crust of salt on my lips. I lick them and dare to look up. I see my own hunger reflected in the stillness of his eyes and the way his cheekbones are like cliffs, gaunt cheeks sunken under them as if worn down by the sea.

He kneels on the steps of the church so that I am looking down at the crown of his head. There is seaweed, glinting green in the blue-black of his hair. "I am lonely and in need of a wife," he says. The wind rages and the shutters of every window in town clatter like an army thundering on a thousand horses but his soft voice carries clear to my freezing ears.

I want warm boots on my feet, his cloak around my body, salt in my veins. I stand and stagger down to him through the gale. The rain pelts me like tiny stones as he gathers me in his arms and carries me to the edge of the town. The castle is carved into the cliff but the sea has risen so that now, like the tip of an iceberg, only the highest turrets reach up from the waves, piercing the clouds and freeing moonbeams that set the dark stone glittering.

The sea is not satiated. She roars, crashing against the towers over and over. She wants more of it. All of it. We climb higher and higher, and cross the rope bridge. It sways and groans in the wind and I clutch him tight until we reach a newly wrought set of silver doors.

They open silently from within, not a creak or whine to add to the night's mad song. We need no vows, pagan or priestly. The Lord of the Half-Drowned Castle carries me across the threshold and I become his Lady.

#

Marriage is a transaction, a giving and a taking. It is dangerous, like birth, death, we move between worlds, stand a moment on the border where we are nothing and yet everything we truly will become.

I traversed these borders daily as a beggar, stuck on the threshold of humanity. I hung in doorways seeking shelter, forever trying to dip my toes into the world of plenty. Now here I am, carried as something precious into a new life. He takes me to a winding stair and sets me down before it. It goes up to a high tower or down into the sunken depths. Water laps at the hem of my already soaked gown.

This castle is between worlds too, and as I take my first step upward, I wonder if I will walk into another dimension when I finally reach the top. He comes after, his shadow chasing mine between the flickering candles on the wall. I can sense his hunger again, promising to devour me if I stop too long.

He prods me when we reach the next floor and I leave the staircase and step onto a marble floor, a landing with many doors. All of them are closed save one. Steam rolls out and curls like a crooked finger, calling me to it. I walk inside the dimly lit room where a claw-footed bath waits full of fragrant water.

He reaches out and undresses me, shedding my rags until I am naked. I cross my arms over my breasts and step into the water, sinking down into the heat. It is delicious. I close my eyes and lie back until my whole body is submerged.

When I look up, he is no longer there, and I lift my head, looking behind in time to see a woman in a black dress enter the bathroom. I cannot see her face. It stays in shadow even as she comes closer. She unbuttons her sleeves and rolls them up as if preparing for some momentous task.

Without any introduction she soaps my back, neck, and hair, working it into a thick lather before dunking me under. I splutter and struggle up, only to have a bucket full of steaming water poured over my head. She scrubs me all over, prying my arms away from my chest.

Then she is wielding a razor and I stop resisting her. I hold still as she scrapes it over my legs. Tutting at my coarse hair which dares to be darker than the people of this land.

I want to ask what her name is. What my husband's name is. But I'm scared to interrupt her concentration. When I am smooth as silk she drops the razor and whips out a towel. I step out of the bath and she wraps it around me. When I turn to thank her, she is gone.

I walk into the hall. There is another door open just across from the bathroom, and it is bright and welcoming. A draft of air passes through me like a ghost. I dart across the corridor, eager to get into the light.

The door slams behind me and I spin to face it with a shriek. I try the handle but it rattles against the lock. "Hello?" I rap my knuckles on the hard wood.

"Yes, my lady?" a voice whispers in my ear. I turn again, but the shadow woman is standing by a tall dressing screen on the other side of a grand four poster bed where light cannot touch her.

I walk to her, past the heat of a roaring fire in an ornate hearth which makes my skin tingle with pleasure. I conjure in my mind every winter spent shivering and fevered and alone in doorways and alleyways, hiding from the bite of the wind and the touch of the frost king always reaching out for me. I am Lady of this castle now.

A creepy maid is not going to conquer me.

She pulls a nightgown over my head. The feel of the clean, soft fabric against my skin makes my eyes prickle with tears. It has been so long since I have been warm and dry. The maid ushers me to sit at the dressing table. I watch her closely in the mirror as she begins the mammoth task of detangling my long, thick hair. No flicker of light ever catches her face or glints in her eyes. It is as if she doesn't have a face at all. Just a pit of darkness framed with hair.

My scalp aches as she drags a fine-tooth comb along it, but I don't protest. I won't look weak. I will be a strong mistress, a respected one.

When she is finally done she has amassed a great deal of my hair clumped between the teeth of the comb, ripped from my head. She goes to the fire and casts it in; it crackles and burns.

"Leave us," says my husband, surprising both of us. His entry was stealthy indeed. The shadow maid bobs a curtsey and slips from the room.

"Does your bedroom please you?" he asks. He remains standing by the door, hands clasped behind his back.

I get to my feet, suddenly vulnerable in my thin cotton shift. "Very much," I answer, and I mean it. "I fear I will pinch myself and wake to find this all a fever dream dragging me on to the afterlife."

His smile is ravenous and he crosses the space between us. "Then I must ensure you know it is real," he says, pulling me toward the huge bed.

I have said I am no maiden and yet my cheeks burn as he lays me down, and I tremble as his salty kisses brush my lips, skim along my collar bone. He pulls at my shift exposing my shoulder and gently bites.

My body hums like a plucked string and plays in perfect harmony with his.

#

I wake to light searing through my eyelids from the low hung winter sun. I do not know where I am for a few disoriented seconds. A wave crashes against the window pane and rattles the frame. Then again and once more before my mind recalls how I came to be here in this grand, four-poster bed. I am alone now but there is a note on the pillow beside me and a large set of iron keys.

Wife,

Here are the keys to my half drowned castle. Explore at your leisure. I have been called away on business but will return to you soon. All is at your disposal but my study. It is forbidden. It is a dangerous room, close to succumbing to the watery depths below.

Your husband

I lift the keys and marvel at how heavy they are. They represent my freedom and authority as a lady now. And yet they feel like cold shackles, binding me to a single place and to a man whose name I do not know.

Goosebumps rise over my body at the thought of him, and I writhe under the sheets and feel a dart of disappointment pierce my chest that he is gone.

#

Is it possible that I yearn so fiercely for a stranger? I hunger not only for his presence but for knowledge of him. Why he lives in a half drowned castle. Why his servants are shadows, and where he learned to please a woman so? I weigh the keys in my hand and feel the possibilities of each one. My whole life I have been on the outside, knocking on doors that would not open, to places I was not good enough to go.

I rise from the bed to find a deep red gown already hangs by the changing screen, and lurking in the corner of the room where the murky light cannot touch her, is my shadow maid.

"Good morning," I greet her. She dips a tiny curtsey but does not speak. I step behind the screen and suddenly her cold hands are pulling a corset over my head, then lacing me into a red bodice and layered skirts. A thick golden chain is secured at my waist and I realise it is not only decorative but useful. I attach the keys to it and their weight tugs at my hips.

"Will there be breakfast?" I ask and then berate myself for the pathetic question which should have been a demand. *I will take my breakfast in the drawing room.* Something authoritative like that. Only I have no idea what a drawing room is.

I step out from behind the screen and now my maid is back in her dark corner in the blink of an eye. She points at the door and it opens onto the hall by itself.

I conjure up courage enough to walk with purpose and when I am outside the bedroom door there are no windows where light can get through.

My maid appears at my side and leads me up flights of winding stairs and through labyrinthine corridors. I lose count of the many closed doors we pass and instead find myself entranced by the portraits on the walls. They date back five hundred years. Every lord and lady, every noble child that ever lived in this castle is beautifully rendered and immortalised.

There is not a single wall that does not feature at least a few. There are pictures of the same lord as a child, as a young adult, with his wife, and in his elder years. I wonder about the rest of the castle now under the sea, think about how many portraits are lost forever.

Eventually my maid stops outside a door and opens it, ushering me inside. The smell hits me, and I pause at the sight of the table, a small banquet just for me. A jug of orange juice and one of apple. A plate of eggs still hot under a silver dish. Toasted bread and a whole stick of soft yellow butter.

I forget being ladylike or authoritative. It has been days since I last ate, a stale confectionary with mouldy cream that tasted vile. Now I eat my fill, not bothering with the shining knives and forks. I use my fingers and shovel the food into my mouth.

Only when my belly is warm and sated do I stop and hear the whispering laughter.

No manners.
A street girl.
Not a lady.
Disgusting.
He was desperate...

I stand up and spin around, there are shadow maids all along the walls. They fall silent. I wonder once again if I am really here, really the lady of this magic castle. If this is not some dream conjured by my frozen body as I drift into my final sleep on the streets. I am too scared to pinch myself. I don't want to wake.

Instead I leave the dining room and slam the door behind me. I play with the heavy set of keys, press the tip of my finger against one until it slices into the skin. Then I taste the blood and tell myself that I really am here. I really am a lady. Then I set about exploring.

The week passes in a haze of empty chambers, vast libraries and delicious food. But day by day the sea grows angrier. Wind howls through the highest towers of the castle, and in the depths the water creeps upward until it laps against the stairs to the next floor, as if licking it to get a taste of what might be. Waves crash against the castle, and I feel at night that soon the walls will crumble and we will dissolve into the sea, never to draw breath again.

The idea terrifies and enthralls me. I jangle the keys at my hip, dipping my velvet slippers into the water from the bottom of the stairs. My husband's study is on this floor. He forbade me to enter it for fear of my safety, but surely there are things inside, treasures and documents that should be saved.

I step off the bottom stair and wade ankle deep toward the left-hand corridor. Whispers raise the fine hair on the back on my neck.

She's going to disobey him.

And so soon.

Foolish girl.

We should stop her.

We can't stop her.

He wasted his time with this one.

I slosh angrily onward to drown the maids out. I haven't disobeyed him. I don't even know which door leads to his study. Yet.

Water makes the hem of my gown heavy, and I walk closer to the wall for support. The candles are still lit though they flicker and dance in the draught that freezes my skin.

Then a portrait catches my eye. A young boy with sunken cheeks and a single string of seaweed hanging in his hair. There are more portraits, telling the tale of a sullen youth growing to a man, and with the passing years his features grow sharper, his hair further strewn with seaweed. And then come the women, the first an otherworldly being with a fey face and a sad faraway gaze. Then more and more portraits each a different woman, wife after wife and yet my husband no longer grows older, only his eyes grow darker, more intense.

What has happened to all these women? I reach the end of the corridor and glance behind to see if any of the shadow maids have followed. I am alone. Before me is a single ebony door. I find the key that opens it easily. It is the one already stained with my blood. The study within is sparsely furnished but papers float in the water, whatever words once inked on them long washed away. But the truth is I have no desire to save my husband's artefacts. I aim only to unravel his secrets.

I find only another question. There is a second doorway behind the hardwood desk to the left. A flooded stairwell leading down. But most curious of all are the chains bolted to the stone walls on either side of the door. There are a multitude sunk on the stairs, snaking down into a watery abyss.

I pull on one of the chains. Something pulls back. I scream, the chain slipping from my hand and splashing back under the water. My curiosity flees and I rush back into the hall, my wet hands struggle to get the key back in the lock and turn it.

#

He takes me to his bed as soon as he returns. For a time I force my mind to quieten, allow my body to enjoy the sensation of a touch that is not meant to frighten or hurt me like the blows and kicks I have become so used to over the years. After, it is the delirious tiredness and the security of my body flush against his, my head resting on his chest, that makes questions about his portraits run from my lips.

"This castle is cursed," he says, his baritone vibrates through me. "I am cursed. I owe a debt to the sea, and until I figure out how to pay it I will not grow older, will not die. The sea will claim the entire castle eventually and me with it. Those portraits...my wives, my companions through these long years. I have outlived them all."

I see in my mind's eye the flooded stairwell, the twisting chains, but something stays my lips. I could be a portrait on that wall, belong here and live my life in comfort until I die.

"Can I help you repay the debt?" I ask. "I could travel with you where you go, be of aid somehow."

"Knowing you are here at the castle, watching over the rising of the water is all the help I need. Soon we will be free of it, I just need a little longer. I need your patience...and obedience."

I feel the weight in his pause. He knows I have been in his study, seen the chains. He turns so his face hovers over mine and looks into my eyes, but instead of accusation I see the light of wicked amusement glowing in the green of his irises, as if he is enjoying the fear he must see in my face. "My name is Lukas by the way."

"Aura," I say, and laugh nervously as he kisses my hand.

"It is a pleasure to meet you, Aura."

#

Lukas leaves once more, and as the months pass my stomach swells with child. The waters rise another level, submerging the mysterious study, but further mystery comes in its place. Seaweed grows from my scalp and tangles in my thick, black tresses.

#

Lukas shows me the gills on the back of his shoulder blades. "See, I have them too. It's our baby that is changing you." His voice softens when he mentions the baby, his hand running over my swollen belly possessively.

I lie propped on my elbows, unsatisfied, with a thousand questions swimming on my tongue. "But why this connection to the sea? And where do you go when you leave for so long? And what are the maids that wait on me?"

His body grows taut and still. "All will be explained soon and all will be as it should, too, Aura. Remember I asked only for obedience, your loyalty to carry me through."

I hold my tongue. The cold fire in his eyes counsels me to bury my questions deep. If not for my own sake then for the babe's. I have nothing without him. What could I give a child if I cannot feed and clothe myself, keep a roof over my head and a fire in the hearth?

I lower my head to the pillow and force myself to relax. He studies me close for a moment, then his lips form a languid, satisfied smile.

Come morning, he is gone again.

#

By the ninth moon of my pregnancy, I am no longer quite human. A sheen of fine, iridescent scales shimmer on my large belly and with them come gills, first on my stomach and then on either side of my neck. My fingers explore them curiously, and instead of horror I feel only hunger, a desire to understand.

The rising waters whisper louder than my shadow maids now. What have I become? And what lies under my husband's study at the ends of those heavy chains?

#

I dress in a light shift, ripping it so the gills on my belly are exposed. The water is half way up the grand staircase now, and as I sink into its chilling embrace I marvel at the way my lungs draw air through the gills without my conscious thought. My body acclimatises to the cold and I dive deeper until I reach the corridor to my husband's study. Portraits float around me, faces melted or washed to pale ghosts.

I realise I can see; the salt does not sting my eyes and everything glows with effervescent light. The ebony door moves slow through the water, and I struggle to pull it open. The study is now a graveyard of books and eerie floating furniture. I swim to the stairwell and use the bolted-on banister to aid my descent, the chains still lay heavy on the stairs but I see a few moving by the force of whatever is attached on the other end.

I reach my destination, an underwater prison, but one without bars, merely broken windows that lead out into the ocean. Women. Women like me are chained like animals, and like me they have seaweed hair and gills on their bodies. Some on their faces, others on their stomachs and shoulders and breasts. One woman stares at me with horror-wide eyes. Coral grows on her face and covers her mouth like a smothering hand. Most of them are skin and bone, hungry wraiths that watch me with greedy eyes. One with teeth like needles smiles. "Welcome, sweet one. Come closer so I may answer your questions. Your many, many questions."

"Leave her be, Eliza. Can't you see she is one of us?" another snaps, one with deep, sad eyes and legs merged together in the semblance of a tail. Her thighs glitter with purple scales like bruises.

"What—" I begin, but stop when someone appears at the broken window closest to me. A mermaid swims from the ocean into the room and circles me. Her webbed hand reaches out to touch my belly, and I snap from my trance to slap it away.

She grins, her mouth overfull with rows of pointed teeth. "This child is the one," she says. "He finally did it. Mistress will be pleased." She stares at my stomach, eyes alight with joy. The other women watch me now with hate-hardened expressions, no longer curious.

"She will be like all the rest of us," Eliza hisses. "Her babe will die, and she will join us here. There's nothing to make her different."

"No," the mermaid croons. "This child will belong, simply because its mother does not. Your own babes were poisoned by your desires to return to human beings; you were not able to let go."

She runs her hands through my floating hair, and chills erupt through my body.

"This is the debt to the sea he talked about. A child...my child?"

"Yes, Lukas stole a daughter of the sea, and kept her here as his wife until she pined away for her home and died." Eliza hauls her chains to come closer to me. "Since then he's been trying to produce a replacement. She was a princess, daughter of a great Sea Goddess, heir to a kingdom. But all us wives have failed so far."

The purple scaled wife speaks gently to me, "It is a lot to take in, but he is a monster. Our babes were not suited to land or water and died. He has trapped us down here since, starved us. We have been forced to eat the bodies of wives he killed for finding out before they were impregnated. Their spirits are the castle maids now, bound to serve while he hunts down prey to feed his own growing hunger. Eliza," she appeals. "If this babe is the one, we may all be freed." She looks to the mermaid. "Is that not so?"

"The castle will be freed. Who knows if that includes you sorry lot." The mermaid keeps her eyes on me, as though I am a great prize.

"I'm going to speak to him, confront him," I say, swimming back to the staircase. "My child is payment to no one."

A chorus of laugher greets my announcement, then my stomach clenches and I double over in pain. The babe is coming. The shock has woken her. I grasp the banister and start to half swim, half climb. When I reach the study I know she is coming now. A cloud of blood and white fluid trails out from under my shift. The baby slithers into my hands, wriggling and writhing as though trying to escape her fate. She slips and I watch with a mixture of horror and wonder as she swims from me using a beautiful, silver mermaid's tail.

My baby swims right into the arms of her father. I freeze at the shock of seeing him, of reconciling his beautiful, mysterious face with that of a man that actually preys on human flesh, imprisons women he turns into monsters at the bottom of his drowning castle. I curse myself for choosing warmth and food and luxury. For ignoring my own questing inner voice. For giving myself to this beast.

"I did it!" Lukas cries, as the baby squirms in his grip. "It's over."

"Give her back," I say, grasping hold of the umbilical cord, but he is already slicing it with a dagger. He swims past me as though I don't exist and dives down the stairwell. I follow on his heels though blood clouds around me, still coming from under my shift where I know I must be torn.

The wound stings and cramps rend my abdomen as I kick hard to keep moving downward.

My daughter is already in the arms of the mermaid when I reach the prison. I fumble with the keys to the castle and find one that looks old and rusted. I swim from wife to wife releasing them from their chains. Eliza snaps at me with her sharp teeth and laughs when I recoil.

"The debt is paid," our husband is saying. "Release my castle and make me mortal again."

"Wait!" I call. "Let me stay with my child. Let me raise her in service of your Goddess. I pledge my loyalty, my entire being."

"Be silent, woman!" Lukas snarls. "This transaction has nothing to do with you now." The disgust on his face is familiar to me, I am still a meaningless beggar girl to him. I was his last resort in a tale filled with dead babes and mutilated ladies.

"Let it be undone," the mermaid says, fixing her fey gaze on me.

The seaweed in Lukas's hair falls out and floats away from him. Then the gills on his back seal over, leaving smooth skin in their place. The water level at the stairs begins to lower slowly, and Lukas swims eagerly toward his freedom. Eliza grabs his ankle and he spins in horror to see all his wives gliding toward him. They are not free of his curse. Seaweed and gills and coral and misery remain shackled to them.

Eliza holds him as he kicks and writhes unable to breathe any longer. The others dive toward him, and I see nothing more but the cloud of his blood and bits of his flesh floating in it. I taste iron in the water and my stomach rumbles. I run my tongue across my aching teeth, sure that they are sharper than before.

"A pledge of loyalty and service is no small thing," the mermaid says, unconcerned with the horror of Lukas's demise. "What boon do you ask in return?"

"Make me Lady of this castle. Let it drown in this ocean and I will raise a princess worthy to be a sea goddess when the time comes."

The mermaid hands my baby back to me and bows. "When the time comes, you must be willing to give her up to her duties."

I clutch my beautiful daughter to my breast and bow in return. The waters start to rise again.

#

I belong now in a world where I no longer beg for scraps at any man's table. I belong with my daughter in my arms and my sisters at my side. We are the wives of the Drowned Castle and I am its Lady.

The castle is mine.

FOLLOW DEATH

STORY BOYLE

I should have been asleep— I had to rise early the next morning to
see Mother off before she went to trade in the city. Once every season, she
traveled to Cardenstae to sell pelts and pearls and bone carvings, all the finer
things we made or found by the sea. It fell to me as the oldest to load the
carts, to herd my brothers and sisters through their tasks. While Father was
gone trapping and she was away, I was the one who ran the household.

Instead, I watched the sea. Under summer's late sun, I picked up
pieces of smooth-worn hole-speckled shells to weave into grass braids—
charms to hang from my mother's cart, to keep her safe from bandits. It was
something my grandmother taught me. She promised to teach me to weave
hexes, too, but she died many years past. My mother had no talent for it, and
my sisters were too young, which left me a lone little half-witch on the shore.
Even so, my sisters begged to learn even that. So I promised to teach them. It
kept them quiet while I practiced charms I barely knew.

When the sun's glow was almost gone from the sky, I saw a figure in
the surf. I peered at it for a while, until it struck me who she was: the Wind
Flower Child. When your name leaves *her* lips, you follow— out of your skin,
across the sea, to the Shadow Vales. I didn't look away, even though she stared
back, unblinking, walking over the waves. Her wet black hair hung like ropes of
seaweed over bone.

I had seen her only once before, when she came to whisper my
grandmother's name, no more than four years gone. Grandmother had been
ill that winter, her chest rattling at every breath like a pouch full of knuckle

bones. On the night she died, after Father gathered us around the table for dinner, I watched the Child slip in through the door. Grandmother rested in her bed tucked into the wall, her eyes closed, almost asleep.

"Kevyeh," the Child called, "come have dinner with me tonight, instead," and my grandmother rose from her bed. I followed them out to watch, down to the cove where Little River met the sea. I followed them until they walked out over the water and could follow them no more.

When I spoke of it, my mother said I had the sight and wouldn't let me keep vigil over the body, or place dried flowers in the wrapping. Mother's smile drew into a tight dark line, and she didn't speak much to me until long after we gave the bone-ash to the sea. So my grandmother went to the Shadow Vales without my voice to guide her, though my sisters were allowed to sing, and my brothers to carry her to the burning grounds.

Even years later, when I asked her why it was that if I could see the Child, I couldn't sing the death, my mother wouldn't say. She looked down at her hands, and said instead, "I was very good at weaving. I thought that would be enough, somehow. To make the charms, to make the magic come. Or maybe to make her proud of something I could do. But there is something else to it. There was something she couldn't tell me. I do not know how I could hand a daughter of mine something I couldn't myself know or see."

I didn't ask again.

This time, I would keep quiet. If I couldn't sing the death, why tell them what I'd seen?

But she whispered "Keskeh." My name.

I turned the other way, toward the moon rising over our house. They'd be asleep now, ready to load the carts in the morning. I wanted to go back up the dunes, past the beach grass, and crawl into the safety of the bed I shared with my sisters, but the Child's call settled in the corners of my heart.

#

When dawn came, a thick mist rolled in with the tide. I sat on the shore and let the surf catch at my legs. Time paused to keep me company; the angle of the light never changed.

I wondered if I'd missed my mother's leaving. She must have met the caravan at the crossroad by now, and my father and brothers come trundling back. I would have chores. There was a soup stock to make.

I twisted my dress hem until I finally gave in and climbed the hill. But the mist grew thick as eider down in my lungs. In the haze, I lost the light from our one horn window.

The dunes here had no sand spurs, but my feet found them anyway. When my hem snagged in unfamiliar brambles, I fell, and like a bird in a net, the more I struggled, the harder it was to rise.

Forcing the panic from my fingers, I worked my dress free of the thorns one by one, but even once I stood, I couldn't see the slope before me. The wall of white clenched a fist in my chest, and crying, I crouched down, afraid to truly sit for the briars.

"It's not fair!" I cried, but the fog swallowed my voice. "Who will sing me over? How am I supposed to find my way? Mother won't let them raise their voices for me... because I have the sight. Because I'm not the child she wanted. Because she's already gone to Cardenstae. Because... because..." The tears burned streaks down my face, until I couldn't speak anymore from the weight of them in my throat.

A body can only cry so long. When I could breathe again, I stood and brushed the grit from my knees. It wasn't any easier to pick my way back— the brush was just as thick and sharp. I only found the shore by following the pull of my legs down the dunes.

The brume had not lifted, the light had not changed, the fishing boats had neither left nor returned, though the tide had gone out. I squinted at the horizon to make them appear, and realized there were no gulls, either.

My grandmother had calmly followed her down to the inlet and out over the waves. It was my turn. I took a deep breath, closed my eyes, and went west. And so I splashed through the surf, wading out up to my waist until I gave up and trudged back, shivering.

"So how am I supposed to follow you, little girl?" I asked the water. "What am I supposed to do? Swim all the way? Steal a skiff?"

We kept our boat high above the tide mark, and I thought of taking it out after the Child. But what ordinary ship could follow her? And how could I reach it at the top of the dune? I twisted beach grass between my fingers, absently threading on holey shells, a makeshift charm. A charm for what? Guidance? Guidance, then.

Maybe I could build a craft like a charm. Maybe I could gather dreams and wishes like the worn charm stones and weave a skiff. It was the only idea I had left, so with my grass braid in hand, I went in search of charm-stuff along the beach.

Dreams, it seemed, lingered where the crabs lived, exposed only at low tide. Some were broken, sharp-edged like pot shards. Some were the dreams I still hoped for, gleaming like mother-of-pearl. Physical things, all of them, and there for the taking.

I gathered what I could find and tried to piece them together. Even when I wove them like charms onto grass braids, they wouldn't hold a form, any form. I tried for hours, but they wriggled like eels, came unthreaded, kept stubborn gaps no matter how much grass I used to stitch them.

"Why won't you stay!" I threw a fish bone out to the waves. "This is supposed to work! It *had* worked up until now!" I picked up a piece of broken dream and remembered what it was. Wanting to be my grandmother's apprentice. Wanting to be a shore witch. It was suddenly very heavy in my hand.

"My own dreams aren't supposed to abandon me." But I had already abandoned them. I let it drop on the sand.

"I promise no more of you will break!" Weren't the dreams of a dead girl as good as broken?

A silence crept up. It was no use speaking when I didn't mean it. What could I say to them that mattered?

But I could remember them. I could think about them all the way to the Shadow Vales. I took a breath and said, "I promise I won't forget you."

And now as I worked, they obeyed, sealed together with a promise thick as pitch. I wove, and the hull hardened, took a shape I didn't even intend.

Time came unstoppered as I worked. The light grew golden, the light leaned low, and then the light caught fire before slipping away. I labored late into the night, weaving sails of memories, braiding ropes of prayers to Mother Ocean.

By the second morning, it was done and the mist lifted. That was the first I saw it whole, gauzy sail, and charms clattering hollowly against the mast. The grass braids that ran its length were as solid as wooden planks.

The wind by my ear whispered, "Name her," so I spoke it aloud: "Dream."

The breakers at my back whispered, "Hurry," so I climbed aboard Dream just as a great swell broke across beach and defied all I'd learned about the currents of the ocean. Like a toy boat from an overturned wash tub, we were carried out to sea.

#

Through the endless daylight hours, Dream and I had seen two tall rocks on the horizon. I don't know how long it took to reach them. I sang every song I knew, and then sang them all again. I told and retold every tale. I told Dream of my grandmother. Dream listened, so I kept speaking.

"She promised to teach me to weave hexes," I told Dream.

Dream was quiet.

"She promised that before I turned seventeen, she would teach me how to take kelp, fish bones, and crab claws and weave them into hexes. She said there were more ingredients, like in charms, they were the ones you pulled from yourself. But she died before I turned seventeen."

Dream did not answer.

"Dream, I died before I turned seventeen."

I stopped talking after that. Day faded at last, and we approached the stones by the light of a waxing moon.

A gargoyle leaned over the passage, covered with barnacles and dripping sea spray from his lips. He stopped us with a word I didn't understand.

"I watch the seas beyond and all those who enter by this Gate. Those who pass this way may not return to brighter waters. Keskeh, is this the path you seek?" he said.

"How do you know my name?" It was a stupid question, and he didn't answer it. I hesitated, then answered his. "I don't have a choice," I said, and the firmness of my voice surprised me.

"We all have choices, though you are not wrong. Neither are you right, though it matters little here. What I have to ask should be known to you. Are you ready for my test?"

"I am." I was not.

"What follows every cart, yet breaks time's axle? What humbles warlord and newborn, but sleeps in the shadow of the dandelion seed?"

I didn't want to say the answer, though it was an old riddle, taught to babes in the cradle. As if saying it were admitting it. I could say it to Dream. Dream was a skiff. But I couldn't say it to the gargoyle.

"Did my grandmother come this way?" I asked instead.

"I cannot tell you, child."

"But you said you watch all who pass this way, and she passed four years ago! You must have seen her. She had a sharp nose, and wide cheek bones, and dark eyes, and there was still black in her hair, though most of it was gray. You had to have seen her!"

"Child, yes, I see all who come this way, but I cannot speak of it. I cannot tell you that she entered here, nor can I tell you that she did not. Peace."

"She promised," I said as much to Dream as to the gargoyle or the empty ocean.

The gargoyle said nothing, though his eyes changed.

"It's death," I finally answered, staring at the water.

"Some promises can't be kept," said the gargoyle, and I looked up at him before the ship moved on. I am not certain what I saw in his eyes as we passed.

#

Dawn would not come. The waxing moon hung unmoved in the sky. I slumped low to Dream's deck, facing back, toward the home I would never see again. It was under this dark that we reached the next gate.

It was a ring of stones that barely peeked above the waves. Three mermaids lounged on one of the rocks— a youth hard and pale as frost, a warm black-skinned matron with a kind smile, and a crone whose every brown wrinkle read like the lines of a book.

"Greetings," called the youngest.

"Greetings," I murmured back.

"Tell me, child, why have you come this way?" asked the matron.

"I was called by the Wind Flower Child."

"Ah, death herself came for you. And so it is," the elder said solemnly.

"You have a test, so I may pass?"

"I know of none," the youngest said, "but come, sit. We have food and drink."

She held out a conch filled with a golden liquid, and the middle one offered me oysters. The eldest held out steamed kelp in a clam's shell. I climbed from Dream's deck onto the nearest stone. I hadn't realize how hungry I was until I put the conch to my lips— I ate all they gave me.

After the meal, the merfolk began to sing. It was not a tune I knew, yet the song was familiar. I listened for a while, and then raised my voice, too. Our blended voices were an acceptable offering to the stars, I think.

When we finished, I folded my hands on my lap and shut my eyes.

I woke stiff, the moon still high. The mermaids were gone except for the youngest, who sat combing her hair, a mirror held high in her other hand.

I saw myself reflected in the glass, along with half her face. Her eye caught mine in its surface, and I saw half a smile form, as she separated her tangles. I didn't move, but lay damp on the stone watching her fingers work her tresses.

When she finished, she turned, her smile full, and asked, "Would you like for me to comb *your* hair?"

"Yes," I answered, though I wasn't sure I really wanted her to.

She dove into the water and resurfaced next to me.

"Turn around," she directed, and I did.

I felt her fingers dart through the clumped knots I'd have had to cut or tear out myself to remove.

"Oh!" she cried, all breathy sweetness. "How many months has it been since you've set a comb to your hair? It's all dried mats, with spurs and grass!"

"I don't know," I replied. "A while ago. Early in the day, before I was called."

"That must have been ages," she said.

Despite her remark, I relaxed as she worked, drifting into a trance. No one had ever touched my hair so lightly. I was a little disappointed when she was done.

"What will you give me, for combing your hair?" she asked.

My stomach sank. "I don't have anything with me."

"Oh, surely you have something. You have stories. You have memories."

"I do, I suppose. I could tell you about some of my life."

"Do! I thirst for memories. Tell me about the first time you did something. Those ones are always so tender and sweet."

I held back. "What do you do with the memories you're given?"

"Eat them of course. They are delicious. One can't live by conch and kelp alone. Besides, if the Child has called you, what use do you have for them?" she laughed.

A chill spread over me.

"What might I give you instead?"

"You could answer me a question."

"Ask."

She held up the mirror, her arm around my shoulder, so I could see us both in the glass. "What do you see?" she asked, smiling like a cat smiles.

"I see myself," I answered immediately, then amended, "And... a youthful mermaid with milky skin. I see... Dream, my ship."

"You've seen only the surface. You'll have to give me a memory," she shook her head. "But your hair is almost as lovely as mine, now."

I trembled, then began, "I remember... once, when I was small, my mother saw me trying to catch fish, the little silver pin fish you can cook in a pan or use as bait, with a hoop net in the shallows. I had been trying for hours, and I couldn't catch any. I held still, let them come close, and then dipped the net to sweep them up, but they always scattered.

"I think my mother had been watching for a time, because when she called out to me, I was startled. I remember she laughed. She often laughed. This time, it made me angry.

"She waded out to where I stood, and took my hand holding the net. 'There, like this,' she said, and set the hoop in the water. We held still together until the fish came back. Then, very slowly, she turned the net, let me feel the way she did it, and encircled three at once. Only once they were in the net did she flick it upward, and they were all held suspended, shining and flopping in the sunlight.

"I never thanked her for that. I was embarrassed and pulled away, and later I was too angry to tell her."

"Mmmm, that memory is bitter-sweet," said the mermaid, licking her lips.

"What memory?" I asked.

The other two mer-women swam up, carrying more oysters and kelp. One held aloft a dry bundle of grass and some pieces of driftwood, keeping them from the water. They hauled out, and with a lens from a spyglass, they lit the bundle.

"How far did you swim to find the grass?" I asked.

"All night," said the matron.

"A few minutes," replied the eldest.

The dried grasses caught, and the women tended the fire until they could add sea-damp things without fear, though the smoke was thick and dark. They roasted the kelp, and portioned some out to me. I ate silently, afraid to ask anything that might exact a price.

Finally, the matron spoke, "Why do you linger here, when you have been called?"

I stared at the rock.

"If you can't answer that, answer this: what do you see when you look at me?" she asked.

"I see...," I paused, picking my words with care. "I see a mer-woman, with hair like my mother's. No! I... I see my mother. Like a reflection." And it was true, I did.

"Tsk. Better, but there's more. And you've tarried too long."

"How can I leave when my ship won't?"

None of them answered, and I slept again in the mild night with no breeze.

When I woke, the three mer-women sat on one of the far stones. The matron and the elder played a game, while the maiden looked on. A long shallow tray sat between them, strung with threads; to the side, another tray— they took turns rolling a pair of dice into it.

"A Hinge," said the matron before she rolled, and the dice clattered in the tray to come up six and one. The youngest handed her two lengths of thread, which the matron strung across the board between them.

"Damn," said the elder, taking dice in hand. "I call Twin Flowers."

"Risky," said the matron. "Roll."

The elder tossed. The dice bounced and clattered in the tray until both faces rested on five.

"Ha ha!" cried the old one, and snapped five threads.

"How long have you been here?" I asked.

"Us?" asked the matron. "Not long. We've been playing just a few minutes."

"Oh child, we've been playing this game for days," said the elder.

"No," I said, "I meant, here. On these rocks. All told."

All three of them looked up at me, then. Their eyes were so intent I let my gaze fall to my toes.

"This is the last time we will ask," said the eldest. "What do you see when you look at us?"

I lifted my head and looked.

And I saw who they were now, Fates. I saw myself, my mother Kityeh, and my grandmother Kevyeh, the three of us tangled tightly in threads stronger than iron. I saw these strings stretching away, crossing the game board at odd angles, twisting, then running parallel. I could almost read what these webs meant...

A hand gripped my chin and turned my face— the eldest mermaid was before me. Her touch was a shock. Those old clear eyes searched mine, pierced deep enough that I felt myself falling forward into them, or the sky, or the sea.

"Yes," she said. "That answer is a correct one," and released me.

I didn't let myself cry again, even though I felt the tide of it in my throat.

The matron nestled their game board into the rolling box, and handed it to the maiden, who was first to turn and dive. The eldest followed. The matron moved to go, but paused.

"You can have it back, if you like. It might be useful. There are many fish in these waters, and it was a valuable trick your mother taught you," she said. Then she, too, dove.

I watched their three wakes become one, then disappear.

#

Daylight came again, but the sun did not dry me. It was not yet noon when the sea grew shallow, though the sun was high. Out on the horizon, I saw a shape like a person.

Stiffly, I rose to better make it out. Bone white skin, dark hair like a dress. She didn't look back at me, but I sat back down and stared at Dream's charm-woven deck. When I caught up to her, I would have to ask, and she would be as silent as the gargoyle. I stayed low, pretending not to see or feel anything.

I ignored the feel of Dream's hull dragging bottom over sandbars, until one caught her like the waiting arms of sirens. Still, there was no shore in sight.

We sat an hour, maybe four, under an unmoving sky. The tops of my ears became hot, my arms blistered, and my eyes grew sore from the dazzle on the water. With no wind, the air I breathed thickened like steam from a stew just ladled from the pot.

It was too much—I stood and leaned over the side. Next to the sandbar, fish schooled and light played through the water. It was an invitation; I accepted.

After a satisfying splash, the fish darted away in ripples. I squatted so that the sea swallowed me up to my neck, savoring the difference. Then I waded a few feet from Dream, just to test how deep it really was.

A crack from the boat caught me short. Dream groaned again as I turned to see why. Wading back, the noises ceased, but I could see some of her charm-braids had frayed and pulled loose. Tracing them with my fingers, I could see they weren't as rigid as they had been on the other shore.

The sun battered from above, and the ship's shadow was the only haven. The Wind Flower Child dwindled in the distance, but Dream could go no further.

Knowing that did not make it easier.

"I'm sorry," I whispered to my ship, then started after the Child. Behind me, Dream creaked a warning.

I paused, looking down, but not back. "I promised. I won't forget." Dream was silent, but I remembered what the gargoyle said.

I sloshed forward through the shoal, and heard the splash of the sea accepting the tattered pieces of my Dream.

The Child led me through the shallows, no land in sight, and no place to pause. Salt clung to my lips. The water became no deeper, and no waves disturbed its stillness. Night fell, and nothing changed.

#

The gray before dawn brought me to the Shadow Vales. It was strange to feel the sea shrink back and lap at my calf. It was here that The Wind Flower Child stopped and faced me.

At first, in the soft light, I could see only the Child and my own hands and feet, but as it grew brighter, I saw that the sea we had left did not match the shore where we'd arrived. Here, it dropped off quickly with little shelf, and the tide was lively with crabs and birds. To my left, a creek wound down to an inlet, feeding it with sweet water. Just up a rise from the beach, beyond the dune grasses, I saw a tendril of smoke uncurling toward the sky.

I looked at her, the land around me. "These are not the Shadow Vales."

The Child was silent.

"My grandmother...?" my throat constricted.

The Child shook her head.

"I came all this way, and there is no reunion, no peace? I came all this way to die, and I'm alone?"

"You are not dead," she replied. "But dead is the girl I called to me on a distant beach, who built a ship of her memories and dreams. That girl was not a witch."

"Am I a witch, now? I can't weave a hex or set a bone."

"Being a witch is none of those things."

"What is a witch, then? If not those things, I don't know. I passed the gates you set. My grandmother is gone, I can say it now. I don't pretend to understand what passed between her and my mother, but I see how it tangled among us. And my dreams, as I knew them, are gone. I only feel empty, now."

"Empty is a priceless treasure."

"A treasure?" I looked back the way we had come, the miles that hadn't been, the loss I'd knew was coming but did not come. Would come tomorrow. Would come in fifty years. When I turned to the Child to ask what she meant, she was gone.

This was the beach where I'd begun, the river I'd known all my life. But they were not the same. It was not the fall of light, nor the angle of my view. It was nothing I could place.

After I smeared the tears from my cheeks, I walked up to the house in the dawn light, and saw my mother readying her cart— my brothers and sisters scattered about, the youngest with her fingers in her mouth.

"I was worried," my mother said as I approached.

"I'm sorry. Let me help load the cart." Numbly, I hefted the bundles of otter skin, while my brothers and sisters carried the strings of pearls and packages of shell charms and dried seaweed. My father hitched the mules.

Then my mother kissed my brothers and sisters goodbye. She embraced my father, and then paused, looking at me.

"Take care, while I'm gone," she said.

I nodded. "Mother?"

She stopped. My tongue froze. But she smiled before she left, the cart jostling down the road to meet the caravan to Cardenstae, my father and brothers in tow.

Then, "Put the soup kettle on," I told Kalyeh, the eldest of my younger sisters.

She ran off.

The youngest, Meyeh, pulled the fingers from her mouth and asked, "Why are you all sun blistered?"

"Because I spent too long in the sun," I replied. She stood and stared before she scurried after Kalyeh, and I walked down to the shore.

I sat on the sand facing the ocean, no longer certain of east or west. I let the tide catch at my legs, and puzzled on what the Child said until noon ascended, until the sun sank, until the full moon rose, and the fishermen came in.

Kiri, the second youngest of my sisters, came to sit next to me. I hadn't heard her come down the dune.

"Will you show me tonight? How to see my husband in a bowl of water? You promised! You promised that as soon as you knew how, you would, and I can see it. You know something new," she said in a flurry.

I let the silence settle before I answered. She looked much younger than she was.

"I don't know," I replied, but I did; I could see it. She hadn't the talent. I looked down at my hands. They were my grandmother's small brown hands, not at all like my mother's big calloused ones.

"Please?" she begged.

It's not my mother's hands, but her pride I have, instead. My mouth, though, is truly my own. "I can't show you that, Kiri. But I can show you how to weave lace from sea grasses."

"It's not the same."

And all those years between my mother and my grandmother untangled before me, spooled out like a tow line between my sister and myself. I did not want that bitterness to sit in the corners of rooms we both sat in. I did not want to break both our backs carrying around impossible promises like stones.

"No," I agreed. "It isn't. But you said it yourself, I know something now. It's one of the things you have to learn, but are sad when you do. I don't want you to be hurt reaching for something you can't hold in your hand."

"I could try anyway."

"You could try."

She could not read the surface of the water in the bowl. But I could read her quick manner, the little smile as she concentrated.

Maybe that was being a witch, then.

LILIES AND CLAWS

KATE HEARTFIELD

Bruges, 1302

Supper was salt herring again, skinny and bony. Margriet grabbed her herring by the tail and dangled it over Nicholas's plate, the fish-skin rippling silver in the light of one candle. Her brother frowned and pushed her little headless fish away. He probably thought himself too big to play floppy-swords, now that he was fourteen, now that there were French soldiers in the streets with real swords at their belts.

Margriet shrugged, lifting the fish to her mouth with a roar before devouring it.

Nobody laughed. They were all so grumpy these days. Mother frowned, Katharina rolled her eyes, and Father did not react at all, gazing wearily at the candle.

"Is there any bread tonight, Mother?" Katharina asked.

Mother shook her head. "I'm sorry, darling. Perhaps this summer the harvest will be better."

"It won't matter how good the harvest is," muttered Nicholas. "Flanders could become as rich as Cockaigne, with fat pigs running everywhere, ready for roasting. It wouldn't matter to us because we'd have no coin to buy any of it. The damned French King will tax every morsel that passes through the gates of Bruges."

Margriet's stomach growled at the mention of roast meat.

"Hush," Mother said. "Nicholas, you must not say such things, especially not outside the house. Your Father must be seen as neutral in all this. A boatman needs customers; he needs trade. He cannot make enemies of the other guildsmen or the wealthy families. He must be neither Claw nor Lily, for the time being, until things are settled."

"The Bible says a man cannot serve two masters," said Nicholas.

"No, he cannot," Mother said sharply. "But he may serve none, if he's careful. In times like these, if a man chooses a side, he has already lost."

"I wonder why lilies and why claws," Katharina said.

"I know," said Margriet, swallowing her fish. "It's because the French King wears a lily on his shield and the Count of Flanders has a lion on his."

"I know, of course," Katharina spat. "What I mean is, I wonder why the King and the Count chose those symbols in the first place."

"Oh." Margriet didn't know the answer to that.

"You're such a show-off," Katharina said.

"It is a little unseemly, Margriet, this habit of yours," Mother said. "You need not be so hasty to show the world every time you think you know the answer to a question."

Margriet's eyes stung.

"That's why you don't have any friends," Katharina said.

"I'd rather have no friends than no brains," Margriet shot back.

"Girls, girls," Mother said, sighing.

Father gazed at Mother's face. It was a beautiful, disappointed face, like the image of the Madonna in the Church of Our Lady.

"Children, be peaceful, for heaven's sake," he said. "You're only restless because you have nothing to tire you out, now that the Crane is shut down. I am sure it will start up again soon. You won't be cooped up much longer."

Margriet ate the last of her herring, licking her salty, fishy fingers. She hoped the Bruges Crane would be out of order for a while yet. She took her turn once a week like the other boatmen's children, but she hated walking in the wheel that powered the Crane, walking and getting nowhere. Still, the

Crane helped Father and the other boatmen load their wares.

She preferred the days Father took her as a helper in his boat. She would float along, dipping her fingers in the soft green water of the canals. She collected bits of wood and feathers from the surface. Each day she chose one of her treasures to ride along in the pocket tied beneath her apron. She was good at finding, good at watching. That was how she had spotted the giant serpent that lived in the canals.

No one else knew it was there, for the creature was invisible. But Margriet was clever and could read its rippling traces on the surface of the water. She tossed a twig onto what she guessed was its back and found that the twig disappeared too.

Maneuvering the boat through a clump of weeds, her father only scolded when she tried to show him. "Don't pester me while I work. The Minnewater monster is nothing more than a story, no more real than Reynard the Fox or Ysingrim the Wolf."

Margriet didn't talk about the serpent with anyone after that, but she watched for it. Often, she spotted it near the Minnewater, the widest part of the canal near the southern wall where Father moored his boat.

Nicholas was complaining again.

"I would rather fight than walk in a Crane like a beast."

"Well, that's too bad," Mother said. "If there is any fighting you must stay out of it. When the killing is over, we'll make our peace with the victor. I will not lose another child to this war. I have asked God to spare my children and I believe he will if I keep them out of it."

"You won't lose me, mother, don't worry. I'm a good fighter. I'll be a good soldier."

"Will you now?" Mother asked, her voice high and strange. "And in whose army? Perhaps you have not noticed that the Count is a prisoner in Paris? And the men of Bruges who fought for their city are exiled, wandering out there somewhere, or dead? Perhaps you'd rather be a Lily, and fight for the French King?"

Mother clapped her hand over her own mouth, but Margriet couldn't tell if she was trying to stop herself from crying or from talking.

"If I met the French King, I'd show him a thing or two," said Margriet, because things were awful.

"Oh ho, is that so?" Nicholas asked, smiling. "You, an eleven-year-old girl?"

Margriet nodded, continuing to talk to keep him smiling. "I'd trick him. I'd sneak up on him in his sleep and cut his head off like a chicken's."

"Show-off," Katharina mouthed.

Her mother made another of her noises but dropped her hands.

"Really, Margriet. Such a thing for a girl to say."

Nicholas was not smiling any more. He and Father looked at each other across the table, then looked away.

Margriet chewed her lip and vowed to say nothing more until morning. She wondered if anyone would notice.

#

Before bed, Mother took the distaffs and wool out of the basket. Katharina and Margriet used short distaffs but Mother's was tall as a broom-handle. The speed of her spinning was the subject of stories and rumours as far away as Ghent, Father said.

Margriet did not have her mother's talent. The wool bunched at the top of the distaff and tugged, and her spindle banged between her knees.

"I can't see what I'm doing with only one candle," she complained.

She remembered too late, her vow of silence.

"We don't need to see to spin," Mother said.

"Maybe you don't, Mother, but I do."

"Oh, I swear, I'll have to file the edges of your tongue one of these days. Pull that yarn off and start fresh. It's about to snap anyway."

Margriet tugged the wool apart. She stuffed a long line of bunched, ugly yarn deep into her pocket, to join the feather.

Father and Nicholas came upstairs. Father's face was grave; he held a lantern.

"Bedtime?" Mother asked.

Father said, "You get the girls into bed. Nicholas and I are going to check on the boat."

"Now? It's past Compline."

"Yes, and we'll have to have the boat ready by cockcrow for whatever use the French might require, else it will look as if we're staying home on purpose. With all these soldiers tramping through town I shouldn't wonder if someone's put a hole through it or done some other mischief."

Mother pursed her lips. "Must you take Nicholas?"

"I might need his help. I'm not taking him far. Just to the Minnewater."

She said nothing and bowed her head.

After Father left, Mother made no sign to get the children into bed. She kept spinning so the girls did too.

"I'll tell you a story, shall I?" Mother said.

"Reynard," Margriet said.

"You always want Reynard," Katharina argued.

"You chose yesterday. I want Reynard."

"All right. Katharina, don't argue with your sister. Where shall I start, Margriet?"

"From the beginning."

Katharina sighed heavily.

"It was Whitsuntide," Mother began, "and the trees were all dressed in green, when King Nobel the Lion decided he would have a great feast. He summoned to his court one of every kind of animal to speak for their kin. They would spread word throughout the land, of the King's generosity..."

#

Father and Nicholas had still not returned when Mother stopped, saying as she always did that Reynard had got in quite enough trouble for one day and would get in more tomorrow. She kissed them goodnight and knelt to pray by the big bed near the staircase. Katharina and Margriet cuddled under the covers. Spring had come to the days but not yet to the nights.

The girls' bed was near the outer wall where the house jutted over the street. As if it were right beneath them, they heard men laughing and shouting in French. A woman screamed.

Katharina sniffed. "I'm frightened, Margriet."

Margriet put her arm around her.

#

Margriet woke to the sound of something clattering against the shutters. She eased herself out of bed and walked to the window, her skin all gooseflesh. She opened the shutter a crack.

A group of women stood below. She recognized one as the wife of the baker who sold the twisted bread. Margriet liked the bread but not the baker. He once told her that she was destined to be a shrew and a scold.

The baker's wife, in any case, did not seem timid. She called up in a hoarse whisper, "Our exiles are back in the city. The Claws are rising! Tell your men that if they go toward the Belfry they're sure to meet up with the others. Tell them to bring knives and axes. We'll be rid of these French pigs by dawn."

Margriet nodded and turned to see if anyone had heard. The open window let in a little moonlight. Her mother still knelt by her bed, but her head and arm rested on it. She had fallen asleep praying. Nicholas's bed was empty. He had shared that bed with his brother Jan, before Jan went off to fight against the French. Jan died on the field.

Father and Nicholas were still out there. They must be warned. They must get out of the streets, away from the fighting. They might not have heard about it yet, since the Minnewater was at the edge of the city, far from the Belfry in the city centre. But the fighting would come this way eventually, for the castle the French were building was also in the south.

Margriet slipped on her cloak and shoes. She tiptoed past her mother's bed and down the stairs.

#

The half-moon lit the cobbles on Casteelstrate and the ripples on the Minnewater at the end of it. Though Margriet heard shouts and noises, her own street was deserted. Please God, she prayed. Please let me reach them in time and bring them home before the fighting comes.

Where Casteelstrate met Assebrouckstrate, under the sign of a cobbler's shop, a swarm of men shoved and punched a wiry, redheaded man.

"Wait, stop," cried one of the bullies. "Let's give this young fellow a fair trial."

Margriet pressed herself into a recess between two houses. How to get past them? It would take forever to go around by other streets.

The mob of angry men pushed their victim to the ground.

"Say the words in proper Flemish! Say, 'scilt ende vrient.' Shield and friend!"

"Say it, traitor, say it now!"

The poor fellow only sobbed and stammered.

"He can't say it."

"He can't say it because he's French. He's one of them,"

"I'm not, no," the trembling Frenchman stammered in heavily accented Flemish.

"Come on, come on, speak up. You'll have to say it sooner or later." The ringleader repeated the words in French. "Tost ou tard, ce que vouldras, tost ou tard." The bullies laughed. Their torches threw shadows on the buildings. The redhead murmured something Margriet could not hear.

A raised club cast a long shadow on the torchlit house. The Frenchman screamed as it fell with a thud. Margriet put her hand to her mouth. The man groaned in pain. She ought to go home, to comfort Mother and Katharina, who must surely have woken by now. But Father and Nicholas were out there somewhere, and although they could pronounce "scilt ende vrient" properly, like anyone born and bred in Bruges, they had not chosen sides. They worked with the Lilies—had been seen carting their goods and bowing their heads to them. Mother always urged the two to stay neutral, to work with anyone.

"Scilt ende vrient!" the Frenchman burbled. But he had neither shield nor friend. The c and the v were wrong; it was all wrong.

Margriet could not see him anymore, for the shouting bullies surrounded him. The attackers wheeled and staggered from the sheer force of their own kicks and blows. Finally, they stumbled down the street, shouting in some wordless tongue.

Margriet left her hiding spot and ran. It was a relief to match the pace of her legs to the pace of her heart. Her feet slipped in a patch of something wet—offal or night waste—but she righted herself and kept running. Panting, she raced to the water's edge.

The Minnewater, where the Bruges canals opened into a wide expanse, lapped quietly in the moonlight as if all were well with the world. Its sour smell was as familiar as her sister's breath, her mother's bosom.

There was no one at the water's edge.

And Father's boat was gone.

Margriet walked the length of the mooring wall, inspecting each boat. Things looked different at night; perhaps she was simply not recognizing it. No, the boat was gone. And her father and brother with it.

Margriet turned in a circle, peering down streets and alleys that lead to the centre of the city. Father and Nicholas were out there. She was a clever girl. She would find a way to get them safely home. In the morning this nightmare would be over, and one side or the other would be in command of the city. She would accompany Father in the boat as always, trailing her fingers through sunlit water.

She bit her thumbnail, staring into the water. The moonlight bounced off swirling ripples at a strange, impossible angle. The canal serpent! Nicholas and Father were bound to be near a canal. Perhaps the serpent could help her find them. It would be faster than paddling! Besides, if a twig became invisible upon its back, what else might become so?

Margriet knelt on the stone wall, gripping the slimy edge, watching the swirling waters. In the rippling movement of the swells, she could see the outline of the creature quite clearly. It was long, huge; as broad as a horse. It could carry three people on its back!

Margriet asked God to bless her enterprise and untied a good long rope from the closest boat. Her fingers grew cold and she struggled with the wet knot. Next, she pulled the balled-up yarn from her pocket, doubled it and used it to retie the boat. It would not hold, not this disgraceful yarn she had spun, but she had to make some effort. She was a boatman's daughter. It was one thing to borrow a rope and another to let a boat drift away.

Now, what sort of knot did one use to catch a canal serpent? She needed an inescapable knot, one that would bind the serpent to her will. She tied an overhand loop, leaving plenty of room. Her hands shook, and her knees were cold from kneeling on the stone.

She pulled the white feather from her pocket and tossed it into the water. It twirled in the air and landed. As it hit the water it vanished, neither sinking nor even getting wet. Margriet drew a silent breath. The pattern of ripples had not changed. Her feather had not startled the water-monster.

The first time Margriet threw the rope, her aim was off. The loop slapped quietly on the surface and vanished. It must have hit the creature's back!

"God's blood." She pulled the rope back, but the creature had begun thrashing, splashing water in a way that made Margriet suspect it had reared its head. This was a chance. She threw again, and this time the loop at the end of the rope vanished. Margriet gripped the taut, quivering rope that seemed to simply end in thin air. She braced her feet as the invisible thing reared, yanking her toward the water.

"You *could* pull me in," she gasped, "but then you'd have this rope around your neck and no one to take it off! I take it you don't have fingers? I'm a boatman's daughter. That knot won't work itself loose, especially not wet. It will just get tighter and tighter until one day the long end will catch on a nail or an anchor and then —"

"I know what you want," the creature said in a voice like oil.

She was taken aback. "What?"

"There are only two things any human has ever wanted of me."

"Well, I want to know if you've seen my father and my brother."

"Just like all the others, I see. One of the things humans want is to ask me tedious questions."

"My father is tall, and my brother has blond curls. They might have taken a boat —"

"I pay no attention to the comings and goings of humans."

"Then will you take me to —"

"And there it is. The second thing humans always want. No. I will not let you ride on my back."

Shouting came from the streets behind her, a great inhuman roar. Margriet twisted about, half expecting to confront a dragon. Instead she saw orange flames staining the sky. The city was on fire. Where would Mother and Katharina go? Where were Father and Nicholas?

"You must pay attention!" she cried, tears thickening her voice. "The city is burning!"

The serpent's laugh was a wet sound, like the coughing fits that had taken Grandmother before she died.

"I can wait while your city burns. It has burned before and I survived, cozy in my cold home. Those ugly new walls will crumble to the ground and I will remain. Long ago I lost interest in carrying humans from place to place, or in listening to their boring questions."

Margriet heard the false note, recognized it from hearing her own voice, her own protestations when the children would not play with her or share their jokes as they walked upon the Crane.

"I bet I could ask you a question that would not bore you."

"Ha! Not likely."

"If I do, you must take me wherever I want to go."

There was a pause. Then: "If you could ask me a single interesting question, I would gladly carry you one time, even if you do smell of sheep's wool."

In the distance, the cacophony grew. Mother would be beside herself!

"I need you to carry two others as well."

"Oh ho ho. No question is worth that."

"I bet I could ask you three questions, each more interesting than the last."

"That is unlikely indeed. If you could do such a thing, I would carry you and two others."

"But I might need more than one trip. What if I could ask you seven?"

"If you could ask me seven interesting questions, girl, I would carry you and two others, any time you asked, for the rest of your days."

"It's a bargain."

"Ha! We'll see. Remove the rope then and ask."

"Remove the rope? But how do I know you'll keep your word? I might ask you a question and you could lie and pretend to yawn and say you found it boring."

"I am a Nix and you are a child, and there are no two creatures anywhere on this Earth who hold a bargain so sacred," said the serpent.

"A Nix?"

"And I do not yawn, in any case."

"How do I know? I don't even know what you look like. Do you have to be invisible? It would be easier to get the rope off if I could see you."

The air above the water shimmered and the Nix showed itself. It was bigger than she'd expected, more like a wingless, limbless dragon than a snake. Its skin was the green and brown of slime and sticks, with a thickly ribbed trunk and a large head. Gleaming golden fangs lined its long flat jaw. The creature swam close. In the night air, its breath, now visible, seeped like smoke out of great nostrils and curled around the shining fangs.

Margriet braced herself against a bollard so she could stretch her arms out over the water. With both hands she scrabbled at the knot. It had jammed, and she had no knife. She should have tied a bowline! The creature's thick green skin lapped over the rope. She tried not to look at the face, at the great bloodshot eyes. Her fingers were cut and bleeding by the time she pulled the knot loose. Bits of rope fibre floated on the water. A thin red line encircled the creature's neck.

The Nix nodded its great head, enjoying freedom. "All right," it said. "You have injured and insulted me. Ask your question."

"I am sorry," Margriet said, and she was. She wished she had considered just talking to the serpent, instead of roping it. It must be lonely in the water, and humans always asking you for things. People were frequently boring, too; the Nix was right about that. Margriet tried to think of interesting things like feathers, bones, and skeins of string. She pictured mother spinning her distaff and telling stories.

"Why did Reynard the Fox stay away from King Nobel's court?" She said.

The Nix blinked, an oil-paper eyelid sliding over its eye. "That's your question?"

Margriet shivered from her wet knees to her ratty hair.

"That's the first question," she said in a small, defiant voice.

"You have before you a creature of long experience and this is what you want to know? Not whether the sun is the centre of the universe, or whether a thing has thingness of itself or only in symbolic reference to a posited ideal, or the number of people who will be saved on the last day, or whether the Holy Ghost proceeds from the Father and the Son or just the Father? I have answers to all of those questions. I don't know the answer to yours."

"Well, I do," said Margriet. "You see, Reynard knew all the other animals would be there, and they all had some reason to complain about him to the King. Chanticleer the Cock came in with the dead body of his daughter on a wagon, claiming Reynard murdered her. The king sent the bear, Bruyn, to fetch Reynard the Fox. But how did Reynard outwit the bear?"

"I don't know."

"Well, I do. Reynard knew Bruyn was a glutton. So, Reynard said he was unable to come to court because he was too full of honey to move. 'That is the food I value above all others,' said Bruyn. He promised that if Reynard would show him where he found the honeycombs, he would argue on behalf of Reynard at court. Reynard agreed and led him to a split oak, persuading the bear to thrust his head inside. When the bear was good and stuck, Reynard hid. The villagers came and beat the bear badly. Now if a great bear couldn't bring a little fox to court, what animal would the King send next?"

"I can't say, but I should think a clever one."

Three questions, Margriet thought. She'd earned a ride on the beast's back for herself, Father, and Nicholas, too. She might need to get off the Nix to find them, however, and then she would need to get back on again.

"Well, you're right. Next, King Nobel sent the cleverest of his courtiers, Tybeert the Cat. Reynard mentioned that a priest's house nearby was overrun with fat mice that no one could catch. Tybeert thought he was clever enough to catch one, but Reynard scoffed at him. Tybeert marched off to show his skills and walked right into a snare. Now, if a strong bear and a clever cat couldn't do it, who could?"

"Well, this Reynard can talk his way out of anything," said the Nix. "What you need is a senseless fool who can't be swayed from his task."

The din of the waking city grew louder. A baby cried close by. Margriet would not be alone at the water's edge much longer. She needed help this instant, and the creature was just gawking at her, enjoying a good tale. She kept her desperation in her belly, out of her voice.

"You're right! The bravest of all the animals was Grimbeert the Badger. He was Reynard's nephew, which I don't think makes sense, because the nephews of a fox are foxes too. Anyway, Grimbeert appealed to Reynard's honour, telling him that if he kept resisting the king's summons, Reynard's wife and children would be punished. What do you think Reynard did then?"

"I imagine he played some trick, but I can't think what."

"Well, I know. Reynard said Grimbeert had shown him the error of his ways. He went to court and showed humility before the king. He said he wanted to die right away. He said the people he had wronged should have the honour of building his gallows. So, the king sent Ysingrim the Wolf and Reynard's other enemies to build the gallows. While they were waiting, Reynard told the king he had one more sin to confess. What story do you think he told?"

"How should I know?"

"He said he had listened and done nothing when Bruyn, Ysingrim and Tybeert plotted to kill the King and use their wealth to buy the loyalty of all the noble animals. At the last moment, Reynard said, he got up enough courage to foil their plans by stealing their money and burying it under a tree. In that way he had saved the king's life and got himself some treasure for his old age. Of course, he would never see that old age now, he whined. So, the King pardoned Reynard and set off after the treasure. And where did Reynard go?"

"With the King, I assume."

"No, he went to the Holy Land. That's seven questions."

"What?"

"That's seven questions. I've been counting on my fingers. Will you take me?"

"But was the treasure there?"

"Of course not. Now I'm going to get onto your back and you're going to take me to the Belfry."

The Nix made a strange sucking, clicking sound. It took Margriet a moment to realize this was the sound of a Nix chuckling. "You have amused me, girl," it said as it slid along the wall next to her. "Do you know any other tales?"

"I will come and see you tomorrow and tell you every tale I know," Margriet said. "Tonight, I need to find my family."

Margriet used the bollard for balance and stepped onto the Nix's back as if she were getting into her father's boat. Her foot slid, and she grabbed the bollard with both arms to keep from falling in, scraping her knee.

"At some point you're going to get wet," the Nix said. "I'm not a barge. Just get on, or we'll be here all night."

Margriet snorted. She kicked her shoes off and dropped her cloak over the bollard. They might stay dry, if no one stole them. She dropped one leg into the cold water, grabbed the serpent's neck and pushed away from the wall. The Nix swam fast with a sideways wiggle. Margriet held tight. Soon, she was wet through and freezing.

Behind the walls of the Beguinage, the Matins bells were ringing. Did the Sisters know what was happening outside their walls? How could they not? A wide, cobbled street opened onto the water's edge. A crowd of people pushed and shouted. They screamed "Scilt ende vrient!" in tones either mocking and belligerent, or pleading and halting, depending on the accent.

Margriet held tight to the Nix and ducked her head. Her braids were heavy with water. "Can they see me?" she whispered.

"Of course not. Do you think I would be so foolish? They can't see you, but they can hear you."

"Nobody will hear my voice in all that tumult," Margriet said.

It seemed everyone in Bruges had some reason to scream; even the dogs were barking. As the two traveled deeper into the city, the prim bells of the Beguinage got fainter, replaced by an irregular, angry clanging. Someone was up in the Belfry, pulling with more fury than skill.

To the left, the dark walls of Saint John's hospital grew straight up out of the canal, throwing moonshadow on the other side. There, boats were tied up against a little mooring place.

First Margriet spotted her father's boat among the other small craft, and then she saw her father. He was one man in a crowd, yelling and shoving.

"Stop here, please," Margriet whispered.

The Nix grew still, snorting like a nervous mule. Despite his protestations, he didn't like all this fire and shouting, either.

Now she had to get Father's attention. What would happen if she ran into the crowd? Would the angry people hurt her or even capture her?

"Do you see your folks?" the Nix murmured.

"Yes, Father and my brother Nicholas are there. Father is the one holding the broken oar."

"Scilt ende vrient!" Father screamed. His face, lit by torchlight, was the face of a stranger.

A small, bald man knelt before him. "Ie ne peulx ..." he sobbed, gasping out French phrases. "Ie ne parle ..."

I can't ... I don't speak ....

A knife flashed in Nicholas's hand. The man clutched his belly and screamed in no language at all. Nicholas looked to Father. Father's oar crashed down on the man's head.

"These are your people?" the Nix asked, its voice very quiet.

Margriet wept. She did not know what to do. She ought to bring Father home. She had wanted to protect him, to stop him from getting hurt, to stop him from choosing sides. She did not like the look on Father's face.

"I don't understand. They must have walked here looking for the boat, and when they got here, the other men made them fight."

"It must be so."

"Or they're pretending to be with the Claws now because they have to, you see. Like Reynard. The way to outwit your enemies is to make them think you're a friend."

"And are the Claws your family's enemy, then?"

"No," said Margriet, confused, watching as Father and Nicholas dragged the man to the edge of the canal.

She remembered the way Father and Nicholas had glanced at each other over the supper table, then looked away. Both had avoided mother's gaze.

Mother must be sick with worry. How could Father and Nicholas have betrayed her so?

"Take me away from here," she said.

The Nix turned. Margriet clutched his neck, weeping. She should have stayed with Mother and Katharina. Perhaps she could have helped them. Perhaps she still could. She had the Nix, and permission for two more riders. She heard a splash behind them, and cold water lapped over her. She did not want to look back. She buried her face into the Nix's wet skin, letting her fingers trail in the soft water.

In the moonlight, the waves rippling on the water looked like stars streaking across a black sky. She could not see the colour of the water. She fished up a weed. It was red with blood. With a cry she dropped it back in the water. Three bodies floated by—men in hose and cotes. Their bashed faces turned to the stars. The Nix made a noise and swam around them.

Margriet held on. She must get to Mother. She was almost there, almost back at the Minnewater.

It was not yet dawn but the sky was light in the east, and fires lit the city rooftops like the torches of giants. In the short time since the bells of Matins, when Margriet had left home, the streets had utterly changed. The cobblestones shone with blood or with the orange light of fires. People milled about in panic or leaned from windows shouting to one another.

On the rooftops women knelt, their skirts tucked around their knees. Whooping like boys throwing stones at squirrels, they threw rocks and bricks and roof tiles down onto the fleeing Frenchmen. A half-dozen women and girls knelt on the roof of the Cock tavern. Among them were Mother and Katharina. They had stones in their hands, too. Mother was wielding her distaff just as Father had used his oar.

"Stop here, please," Margriet said again.

"More of your people?"

"Yes," Margriet said, keeping herself from crying. "I don't need you anymore."

The Nix did not move. "I can swim beyond these city walls, you know. They don't hold me. The canals and rivers go on for days."

"Swim closer to the wall, please."

"I can take you with me. Overnight, or until this red, human rage passes. It always passes. I could drop you somewhere else if you like. Some other town."

Margriet looked up at the faces of her sister and mother. Mother didn't appear angry, like Father. She looked more than ever like the Madonna, triumphant and sad. But up on the roof, she raised her distaff like a weapon. She handed a brick to Katharina and Katharina threw it down. It landed at the heels of a man fleeing a crowd of attackers armed with axes.

"I don't understand," Margriet whispered.

"There is nothing to understand. It is not worth your while to try."

"But Mother said... No, this isn't what Mother said to do. Nobody tells me anything. I could understand, if they would explain."

"There is nothing to understand," the Nix said. "Humans are a riddle with no answer. Believe me. I've been here since before the first of you came—brutal and boring, then as now."

"Then why do you stay?" Margriet cried. "Why don't you just go away forever? Flee to the deepest, farthest water you can find."

"This is my home," the Nix growled. "I was here first."

Margriet drew a wet sleeve across her runny nose. She wanted to vomit, to let all the anger boil out of her. She wanted to run to Mother and bang on her with small fists like she did when she was little. Mother would hold her close and explain everything. Surely, Mother would be wondering where Margriet went. She had asked God not to let her lose another child. Perhaps that was why she was fighting and not hiding; perhaps it was all Margriet's fault.

No, it was the Lilies' fault. They were the enemy. Father had never looked like that, so angry and frightened, before they came. They had forced him to pick a side, and Mother too. Margriet would never forgive them. She hated the Lilies!

"Bruges is *our* home." Margriet shouted.

Mother had been right of course to make the Lilies believe that their family was loyal to them. But that was before. Now the ruse was up. Now was the time to fight. Margriet understood now. Everything was simple, as hard and sharp as rocks.

The Nix was still, floating at the edge of the canal.

Margriet grabbed the stone wall and scrambled off the serpent's back.

"You are visible to them now, don't forget," the Nix hissed.

She bent and pried a loose cobble out of the street with cold wet fingers. She tried to imagine hurling this stone at someone's head, tried to keep the anger in her belly hot. Her throat hurt from not crying, and from all the unanswered questions.

"Do you think we will win?" she asked, teeth chattering. "Do you think the Claws will win?"

"What a boring question," the Nix said.

Margriet trembled, the gritty stone heavy in her hand. She glanced toward the water and the serpent's voice but saw only a distorted reflection of fires and fading stars.

THE WEAVER'S TALE

CECILIA QUIRK

Nobody knew where Ruskim had travelled in his months away, or where he had found his foreign wife. She followed him into the village, a black cloak drawn over her shoulders, her uncovered hair black too. Not brown-black like the villagers' but blue-black and gleaming. So thick, straight, and long was her hair, the cloak seemed part of her. In none of the nearby countries did married women wear shining black cloaks. Brides arrived bejeweled. Married couples pranced on horses, scattering coins as they came.

Because we'd heard of Ruskim's coming, we gathered along the village main street, expecting a celebration. The fishermen pulled their boats in early. I set aside my weaving. Ruskim walked with his eyes straight ahead, supporting his wife with a hand against her black-clad back, another at her elbow.

There was no fanfare. Only the even, matched tread of the newlyweds, and the rustle of the bride's long cloak against the sun-hardened road. I watched them come from the door of my family's shop, next to Old Jaid's daybed where he lounged away his days. The couple was somber, not blissful as newlyweds usually seem.

"Ruskim's wife is... strange," I murmured.

"She must be a fool to boot." Old Jaid shifted his pipe from one corner of his puckered mouth to the other. "No woman with wits about her would marry that lump."

But Ruskim's foreign wife walked with her chin raised, her eyes watchful. Villagers froze as she met their open stares. When she peered at me it was as if I'd been drowning. As if her hands had raised me from the water, as if her lips had pushed air into my lungs. I found I'd stepped towards her, mouth open, to watch her pass. My basket, somehow, had fallen to the ground.

Where had she come from? Were all women from her land so enchanting? I stared even after she disappeared into Ruskim's house.

Old Jaid lowered his pipe to his knee, rasping, "She's no foreigner. She's a sea wife."

How could I disagree? Those words shivered and hummed through the village. Everyone had heard the tales of seals in the great river, who shed their skins and basked in the light of the full moon. We also told tales of men, tall and graceful, who lured lonely girls to ruin, and tales of women who could be trapped if one captured their seal skin while they walked on land. These seal women made lovely, obedient wives for their husbands it was said, but always returned to the water.

Could Ruskim's bride have been so fey? Those were only stories, after all. But I knew Ruskim well. He was the type of man such stories spoke of: Well looking and arrogant, eschewing the advances of local women. He had tried to court me, not for my appearance, but because he believed I understood him. Perhaps that was true. I knew how his heart beat. I knew he liked the look of a wife over the fact of having one.

I married the weaver, in the end.

"No wedding feast?" Old Jaid scoffed. He sank back onto his daybed, shaking his head. "That's an ill-fated marriage."

"A wedding feast didn't save my husband," I said.

Before he could respond I picked up my basket and returned to the shop. I sat at my loom and took up the pattern where I'd left off. I was making a Wool fabric with vertical stripes of green, blue, yellow and red. It would be lined in brown silk and made into jackets for women who had borne children. Widows, childless widows like me, could never wear such bright stuff. But I could make it, charge three saçe a metre for it, and keep a roof over my head. In the tug and clack of my loom I imagined the tides of the great river. I remembered her eyes, grey-brown like the water.

Tales of sea-wives ended badly. The wives yearned for return to the water, for their families left behind. Years after their skins had been stolen away, the wives uncovered them, donned them, and abandoned their land-dwelling husbands. Magical beings are not bound by human rules of loyalty, and I wondered as I wove, why should they be? Yet their husbands, having captured and kept them, expected them to remain. Ruskim was arrogant enough to believe he was different, and perhaps he had discovered a way to avoid that fate. A good wife need not be a happy one.

#

My husband's family kept an orchard on the hills above the village. Summer had nudged its way through the country, and the first apricots were beginning to redden. In years past I would have joined the unmarried girls, singing as they climbed the narrow hillside paths, throwing nets over the trees to keep out hungry birds. Later, I came up with my husband to pluck fruit, to lie in the grass beneath the sweet-smelling trees. In one another's arms we would watch the passage of clouds, then make our way home laughing, hair and clothing mussed.

This season, I did not mean to miss the pleasures of the harvest. I went to the trees alone and memories came in like the tide, drawn by the scent of apricots. Sour.

The girls had thrown the nets over our trees. There was no need for me to be there. I walked amongst the gnarled boughs, running my fingers over the threads of the nets that perhaps my husband had made. I could not sense him in the thread. I told myself I had not expected to.

I came upon another, standing in the grove alone. Ruskim's bride, no longer cloaked in black but in the soft red of a newlywed. Whether she had noticed me or not, I could not tell. Her gaze rested on the horizon, and I followed it. I saw the distant, purple river, snaking across our grey and misted land.

"I'm sorry," she said. She stared at her feet, her hands pinched by her sides.

"You want your home," I said. "There's no need to apologize. I hope I didn't startle you."

"My husband says I must not look," she said. "This is my home now."

"Your husband." I snorted a little.

"I love him," she said.

I wanted it to be true.

She turned away from the view, peering instead at the trees. "I suppose things here are beautiful. The green. The warm."

She touched a leaf, running her long finger over its serrated edge.

"I'm Osran," I said. I hoped she had a name. None of the tales mentioned names. Perhaps the seals had no use for them at home. "Osran the weaver."

"I don't know what a weaver is," she said, with an apologetic smile. She had a soft and husky voice. She spoke with eyes downcast.

"Let me show you one day," I said.

She let go the leaf. "I am Ruskim's wife."

"I saw. You don't have any other name?"

"Should I have?"

"If I'm honest, I would prefer that."

She contemplated my words, finding an apricot to caress through the thread of the net. "Humans call out names on the shore. They walk along the beaches and cup their hands around their mouths, and they shout. I think it's for the lost."

"For the lost," I agreed, my throat aching. Tears came fast and unexpected.

For the lost. Had I been one of those people? I couldn't remember, in the haze of hours and weeks following my husband's death. Had I shouted for him over the water? Had I tried to see him? A drowned man is a tiny thing.

"Then I will be Esmeni," she said. "So many people have come to the river searching for Esmeni. Like my family must be searching for me."

Esmeni, a common name. I thought of ghosts on the wind over the river, hearing their names called. "Harjad! Harjad! Esmeni!" I imagined them, crying back, "Which one? Which one of us do you want?

Should I ever have children, they will have uncommon names, so if they should drown they will know I'm calling them and no one else. They will come back. Their spirits will find peace on the land, as my husband's spirit never could.

I called my husband's name after I was rescued from the river and he was not. Then again as part of his funeral. That one syllable wore my throat ragged.

Esmeni rubbed the small apricot between thumb and forefinger.

"Are you allowed to eat them yet?"

"You can try one. Sometimes people take the green ones for pickling, or to flavour alcohol." I approached her. My shoulder, my fingers brushed hers as I reached under the net. I plucked a fruit, green and blushing red where it had glimpsed the sun. I passed it to her and she popped it into her mouth. She wrinkled her nose as the tart, dry flavour struck. But she chewed it.

"Remember to spit out the stone," I said.

She deposited it, tiny and green, in her palm.

"You could plant it. Maybe here, or in the garden at Ruskim's house. In three or four years it will give you fruit."

"Three or four years?" Esmeni said. "Please by the moon don't let me be here for that long."

I said nothing.

"Oh," she said. She licked her front teeth, grimacing, perhaps smarting still from the sour apricot. "I mean, because my husband has plans to move away from this town."

"Ruskim always was one for plans," I said.

She sighed, and peered once again at the horizon, at the river turning grey as the afternoon deepened. The sun beat hot over our backs. My neck prickled, and I unwound my headscarf, draped it over my head and shoulders to cover my flesh.

"Ruskim has your skin," I said.

"My father warned me against such men," Esmeni said. "But I thought I was wiser than my sisters who were trapped. There aren't so many of them. They return in the end. I will, too."

"I will help you," I said.

To my surprise she threw her arms around me. Her human flesh smelled lightly of salt. It had been a long time since I had been held in the arms of another. I did not want her to let me go. We relaxed against one another, her head on my shoulder, her breath on my neck.

We walked down the hillside track with hands joined. I knew it could not last. That she must leave. But I had tried in marriage for eternal happiness, and that had failed. I would take this fleeting bliss.

#

Esmeni took to visiting me at my work while Ruskim was at his. She had no children, no family in the village, and her own tasks could be managed or moved. She brought spices to grind, bread to knead and let rise, thread to ply, hand-sewing and any number of other things. Whatever magic she possessed, it made her a skilled worker, and she rarely ceased, springing from one task to another. My father was the same, making busy to keep his mind away from sadness.

She sat beside me while I wove. Sometimes we spoke, and other times all that passed between us were glances, touches. In the afternoons we sat or stood outside my shop, sipping tea with guests, or else we walked about the village paying visits to neighbors. I had stopped going on such visits after my husband's death. I could not bear the hand-squeezing, the soft smiles.

My husband and I had understood one another. He had been my best friend. I knew, of course, that another man might come to know me in the same way. He might accept a marriage knowing I would never wish to share his bed. I could not attend on every man the villagers mentioned in hope. For them, it did not do for a woman to live on her own.

By Esmeni's side I re-learned the gossip of the village, the factions that had formed in my grief-driven seclusion, the petty wars and pettier victories.

I laughed once more, a strange sensation. As I walked, as I cooked, as I wove, I began again to hum, to sing. The greyness that had lowered itself over my life lifted.

Esmeni always returned home before dark. I missed her at night.

On the holy days, I visited her and Ruskim, my weaving set aside. I sipped tea. Esmeni and I made certain to appear no more than friends and I tried with gentle questions to pry open Ruskim's hiding place. Though he must have heard the rumours circulating in his stead, he didn't know that I'd learned of Esmeni's origin.

"Your wife isn't wearing any of your mother's jewelry," I said over tea at his kitchen table. "Have you tucked it away somewhere? Are you frightened she's going to take the finery and run away?"

"What does she need jewelry for?" Ruskim grunted. "Maybe if there was something in this place worth dressing up for, she would wear it. Once we move to town, she'll wear fine silks and jewels every day."

I tapped my fingers on my cup, then reached out to pat his hand. "Oh, Ruskim, you're too cruel. I was trying to be so diplomatic."

"Hm?"

"Your mother had such lovely earrings. I was thinking of having some like hers made for myself." I tugged at my ear, where I wore simple silver loops. "But it's been such a long time since I saw them, I've forgotten the closer details. Could you show me? I'd only need see them for a few moments."

"Is business going that well?" Ruskim asked. "Even with you by yourself now?"

"Yes, I'm planning to hire an apprentice soon too."

He frowned, though I was telling the truth. Until Esmeni arrived, I had very little to distract me from work; since Esmeni arrived I had reacquainted myself with my customers. I had orders backed up for weeks and months. One apprentice might not suffice.

"Or an assistant. If you could spare your wife for a short time, maybe two or three days a week? Only until there are children. I can get a credit from the money-lender tomorrow, pay her two saçe a week."

He looked over his shoulder to Esmeni, who was busy cleaning rice over a bucket by the fireplace, and every so often refilling the tea kettle with hot water from a pot that rested on coals near her leg.

"The earrings are in the box on the mantelpiece," Ruskim said. He nodded toward Esmeni.

Esmeni stood to fetch them. I hoped my face was as blank as hers. When she passed him the earrings I noticed her fingers trembled. She stooped back over her rice. Ruskim furrowed his brow, turning the earrings over on the table.

"So that's what this visit is about?" he said. "Do you think I'm stupid?"

"Ruskim," I said. "Your wife might love you, but I know you will never love her, not the way a wife should be loved."

"You can talk."

"Ruskim. It's wrong to keep her here, away from her kin. Don't you see that? I know you Ruskim. You're not a wicked man. I won't flatter you. You're many other things, but you've never been wicked. Why would you keep her here? She belongs in her home. Give her back her skin so she can return there."

He clenched his jaw, the earrings tight in his fist. His chair scraped against the floor, the table quaking.

"I think you had better go," he said.

"Ruskim," I tried once more.

"Leave my home."

He spoke softly, with poison. I tried to catch Esmeni's eye as I backed away from him, out the door. I wanted my love for her to be stronger than my fear of him, but in those seconds, it failed.

Breathless, I hurried home. I wept as I wove for the first time in many months. My bed was so cold, so empty, it ached.

#

Beating waves woke me. No, the beating of hands against my door. I shook away memories. The struggling boat, the rescue.

My neighbours must have heard me screaming. I pulled on a shawl and hurried downstairs to the door calling, "Atiya, Atiya, I'm fine!"

Atiya was not there. Esmeni crouched on the doorstep, her shoulders shaking. She covered her face. I knelt before her, prizing some tattered thing from her hands—seal skin, hacked and burnt. I gasped, and let it fall.

"What has he done?" I cried.

"He's killed me!" she whispered. Her face and hands were smeared with ash. There was a catch in her throat. "He's killed me! I can never return!"

"No, no!" I held her. "No, it's a trick. Just a trick, I'm sure."

I tried to recall the stories of sea wives. In none of them had a husband ever destroyed his bride's skin. I could not know if such a thing would kill Esmeni. I kissed her forehead and scooped the skin from the ground. I bundled her inside and locked the door in case Ruskim followed. Barely inside the door, she collapsed at my feet again.

"No, no!" A panicked sound escaped me. I stooped beside her, dreading to see her die. She folded into herself and howled. Her sleek hair, like a stream of dark water, seemed to soak into the boards beneath her.

I could not make her stand. She cried to herself, moaned and shrieked. I covered her with a blanket. For a long while I rested her head in my lap and stroked her hair while she hissed and wept. I shed tears too. I rocked her and sang low songs, hymns of leave-taking, of grieving.

As the dawn light edged into the windows I tried once again to coax Esmeni upstairs to my bed, to try and make her sleep. But she would not. I leaned into her ear, brushing her silky hair aside.

"I promised I would help you," I murmured.

I let her lay there. I sat on a stool beside my loom. By lamp and fragile daylight, I examined the remnants of the skin Ruskim had destroyed.

It stank from the fire. Like Esmeni's human flesh, it smelled of hair, burning oil, and salt. When I stretched it out it frayed, threatening to break apart. I leaned close. Wondered could I draw new fibers through warp and weft, delicately woven to seem smooth, seamless.

A new skin could be made if one had the right materials.

I sagged back against my chair. But what materials could those be? Perhaps I needed the stuff of magic to make magic.

I did not open my front window as usual. Fighting sleep, I sat thinking, checking over my loom, the pawls, beams, and wheel. I'd left a piece of patterned wool unfinished. Well, what is wool but the hair of a sheep?

"Esmeni," I said. "I know what I must do."

She did not reply for a long time. Finally muttering, "No, no. No, no." Her voice seemed broken. Yet slowly, she understood. I watched as she pulled herself out of despair. She sat up, knees beneath her chin, arms wrapped around them. In the flat morning light her eyes were liquid black.

"I know what I must do," I told her again. She listened.

#

Ruskim had made an error. In the sea wife tales, the wives were trapped in human form because they could not don their seal skins. What bound them to their husbands, though, was the hope of recovering those hidden skins. Esmeni's seal skin had been destroyed. She could not return to her home, but she no longer had a reason to remain with Ruskim.

Instead, she built her landbound life with me. She learned my trade. She shared my bed.

Ruskim tried to claim her back. He knocked on my door, shouted through the windows. The village was against him. They did not know what had truly occurred. It was enough that Esmeni fled him. Old Jaid and his sons kept watch over us. They lingered around Old Jaid's daybed, and when Ruskim came they forced him away. After weeks of this treatment, Ruskim was worn down. He left the village, cursing us, vowing never to return.

With Esmeni's assistance my business thrived, and as the years passed I brought on three apprentices, then more assistants. We constructed a second shop, with twenty weavers there and another five in my house. We sold our fabrics in nearby villages, my own work the most sought after. Esmeni's was a close second. Lacking children, we took in stray cats from about the village. Our days were filled with work, with laughter. In the evenings, resting on the comfortable, warm bed, I brushed Esmeni's long, black hair. With another brush, she brushed mine. We began and ended our nights this way.

Each morning I took from the brush loose strands of hair. I knitted them together. My only desire was that the cloak should never be finished. That Esmeni might live forever with me, my own sea wife. Yet, when I watched her alone amongst the apricot trees, or sitting with her hands in cold water, soaking 'til the skin wrinkled; when I heard her call out in her sleep, using the language of her own kind, I could not bear it. She must be free, and I must do without her.

I wove, each day advancing a little further. With each new thread the fabric lengthened. Whether the magic of her kind survived in those fibers, I could not know. Esmeni might have told me, but she refused to look until it was done. Like me, perhaps she did not want to know. She waited with hope, and I with fear.

#

I knew the cloak was finished when the consistency of the fabric changed before my eyes. The threads had knitted themselves together, closer than I could have woven them, perfect and black.

Esmeni slept. I did not wake her. My hands itched to tear the fabric, to tuck it away between the floorboards where Esmeni could never find it. I could not give it to her. I could not lose another to the great river. I would not. I cursed her for wishing, still, after this long time, to abandon the happiness we'd found. Why must she continue to yearn for her family, the water, a life that could not be the same, now? Why, I wondered, should she be able to go back, when I was caught in a forward current? I'd spent a decade laboring for her. She should choose to stay. She should choose me.

I walked between my loom and my bedchamber, up and down the stairs. Her sleeping face, smiling, ever youthful, spelled betrayal.

I left the house. The streets were empty and cold, with winter pushing the winds down the mountains. The air tasted of snows to come. Head uncovered, I marched up the stark hillside to the apricot trees. I shivered, seeking a view of the great river. It was too dark, too distant to make out. The wind froze my tears in place. I waited until dawn, so I could curse the river. May it turn to poison and all its creatures die. May its banks become glass.

Cold crept over me as I waited. I was shaken from my drowsiness by Esmeni's shouting.

"What are you doing?" she cried, shaking me by the shoulders. "Osran, what are you doing?"

She threw a cloak around me.

"I needed to see the river," I said. "So I always know where you are."

She touched her forehead to mine and kissed me softly. "My Osran" she said, her breath warm, her arms tight about me. I realized then what she wore—the cloak-the skin I'd made for her. She had not yet taken her true shape.

"My Osran," she said again, and drew away from me, holding my hands. I'd never seen her face with such a smile, eyes sparkling like sunlit water. "See what I've made for you."

She had wrapped me in a snug cloak that kept the wind out. Black and dense, it was a skin like hers.

"You gathered my hair, I gathered yours," she said. "Sometimes I switched them. I wove as you wove, both of us with threads of magic and love."

My breath caught. My heart filled.

"You don't have to come with me," she said. "You helped me to freedom. I won't make you my prisoner."

Guilt and doubt roiled in me. I had never thought to make so much of my life, to have such wealth, such respect in the village. I was a weaver, after all, and what weaving could be done in the river?

I let go of Esmeni's hands and peered down at the village. Dawn had arrived with its streaks of lilac and orange. I loved the low rolling hills, the cloth of the land crisscrossed with bare winter farmland. Smoke, scented by baking bread, rose from the chimneys of the waking village. No smoke came from my house, empty now, with an empty bed.

Esmeni touched my shoulder. "You don't have to choose now. Let me take you there. Let me show you."

I nodded.

We walked hand in hand through the barren, bitter country, all the long way to the great river. Mist curled over the water's surface. Waves lapped the gray-pebbled riverside, splashing black rocks that jutted from the sand.

As we neared, those rocks approached us. I realized they were seals, Esmeni's people shuffling towards us on their bellies. They shed their skins and rose to meet us. First, only three or four approached, but soon dozens rose from the water. They were tall people with dark hair and smiling faces, arms spread in welcome.

Esmeni ran to them, embracing each in turn. She wept, running her fingers over their faces, clinging to one then another. I waited. I might still lose her to the river. One particular couple held her longest, resting their heads on her shoulders.

"My parents," she said, looking back at me. "They're so thankful for what you've done for me. I wanted them to meet you, my own wife."

She beckoned, and I followed her to the water's edge. The tide pushed against my boots. "Will you come?" she said.

"I..."

"Let me show you," she said.

Her parents held her as she entered the river. The three of them shrank into their coats, vanishing into the dark waters. My breath caught as I waited for Esmeni to resurface. What if the coat failed? What if she drowned, and I lost another to the river?

Then her head, a seal's head, splashed to the surface. I recognized her by the liquid eyes. She could no longer speak, but I knew what she meant.

I pulled my coat tightly around me, bracing myself against the river's cold. The water rose around my ankles as I followed Esmeni into the depths. She floated calmly beside me. I reached for her, and the magic cloak did not fall away. No longer had I arms to hold her with.

"My Osran," she said without human words.

"My Esmeni," I said. She had chosen me, and I chose her.

ALL OF US ARE SHE

JASMINE WADE

"You ready?" Nana would say at the beginning of any tale. "Get ready." If the story was long or scary or important, she'd repeat the ritual.

"You ready?"

"Get ready."

Nana took a deep breath. "They tried to break Her. The Master of the plantation would come 'round, searching for a woman to make him some strong, resilient slaves. He beat and sold her mother on the same day he decided he wanted her. She knew without anyone telling her that her mother did not survive the trip to the Louisiana sugar cane fields. Maybe it was the separation that harmed them both. Maybe it was one last beating or the march from the Atlantic Coast to the Gulf. She didn't know what killed her mother, but she knew without a doubt that she was dead. When he grabbed Her arm, she collapsed into a coma. They thought he had killed Her. If it wasn't for the old woman with the seeing eye in the shack next door, they would have buried her alive. She woke up two days later, like nothing happened. The master, intrigued, thought he would have her anyway. Every time he touched her, she fell into that coma. That didn't stop him though. But try as he might, he couldn't get her pregnant. After a while, he left her alone, declaring to the overseer that she was damaged goods. And don't you know what happened next?"

I did.

"A year after the last time that man, if we can call him that, touched her, she showed up pregnant. Her belly button poked out. Her torso was a warm, golden brown, a few shades lighter than the rest of her."

#

That's the story my grandmother would tell me whenever I asked why I didn't have a father or a grandfather like other kids. For a long time, I believed it—that we came from a line of women who could reproduce on their own. We all had the same wide noses and dark reddish-brown skin. Our eyes were brown with flecks of green. If you lined up baby pictures of me, Mom, and Nana, you wouldn't be able to tell us apart. There was no evidence of a male influence as far as I could see. But then, 7th grade Health class and 9th grade Biology class told me it wasn't so. English class, on the other hand, prompted me to believe Nana's story was myth, like gods and goddesses of old. Like that other story Nana tells about the slaves who got to the shores of the American colonies and said, "Nope! This is not for us." And they jumped into the Atlantic and swam back. Though, sometimes when Nana tells it, she says they flew.

I was okay with the myth being the answer to my questions until I encountered Joey McLemore. Joey had small craters all over his pale face like the cellulite that has since grown on the backs of my thighs. But somehow with a mix of pranking prowess and serious football skills, he rose toward the top of the popularity pool. Nobody would kiss him, but he was allowed to sit at the popular table and go to all the parties. I was not in that group. I was the scholarship kid at a fancy private school where everyone had a second house in nearby Myrtle Beach and another house in Aspen.

Joey came up to me at lunch, the most vulnerable time of day for high school introverts. He said something I didn't hear because I had my headphones in. I pulled them out just in time to hear him say, "—and that's why you have no daddy."

I cocked my head to one side, immediately picturing the Woman from Nana's story with her long kinky hair and golden belly. She was my Blessed Mother.

"Your mom's a professor, right? Over at USC? One of those raging feminists. I bet she scared your dad away."

Two boys at Joey's table behind him shouted "ooooo."

"No, no, wait. Even better, you're probably a turkey baster baby. You know how those feminists do." He said feminist the way Nana said motherfucker when the cashier wouldn't take her coupons.

I put my headphones back in, picked up my lunch tray, and practically marched to the library without a word. As I sat on the 2nd floor of the library in the section on medieval literature, I couldn't shake the image of Mom inseminating herself with a kitchen tool. His words rolled around in my brain like seeds; they found a spot to bury themselves and took root.

#

"Chile, don't you know She was the talk of the plantation, in the fields and in the Big House. Everyone thought the baby was a boy because her belly hung low. No one knew who the father was. Some tried to claim paternity, but their stories didn't pass muster for the groups of old women who made it their mission to figure it out. The master made it clear he didn't care who the father was—that baby was his.

"One night, that ole master told Her he was going to take Her child. And he was gonna sell her."

"'I own you,' he said," I said, interrupting.

"Who's telling this story, me or you?" Her mouth pulled into a tight, harsh line but her eyes were still full of the love I'd come to rely on.

"You are. I'm sorry." I motioned for her to continue.

#

"I own you, he said. She didn't say a word. But that night, She wrapped Her long dark hair in a black cloth, dressed in a thin black cotton dress that reached Her shins, and left the plantation in the dead of night.

It didn't take long for Her to hear the dogs coming after Her. She kept to the darkest parts of the forest surrounding the plantation. She ran east, not north. Soon She heard the dogs moving north, hoping to cut Her off. They'd never find Her. She waded through every creek and stream She saw. She ran until She reached the coast and didn't stop. She waded into the water, letting it press Her dress to Her body. Its coolness sent a shiver up Her spine. The waves lapped at Her, pushing against Her gently, like a dog welcoming Her home. When the water was up to Her chest, She reached out Her arms, knowing She'd never swum before. She'd really never left the plantation before; it was where She was brought as a baby. But instinct took over and the baby helped Her stay afloat. She began to kick. She pulled Her arms back and forth like She'd been swimming her whole life. She couldn't tell this, but Her belly was glowing, showing Her exactly where She needed to go. She swam for two days and two nights."

"That's why we can swim so well."

Nana paused at my interruption. Her silence screamed the question: do you want me to tell this story?

"I'm sorry. I won't do it again." I promised this every time.

#

My mother called at 2:37am one Tuesday morning. It was an especially humid summer in Philadelphia, where I was working as a first-year associate for a second-tier law firm. I loved it—the hustle and bustle, the smell of a freshly printed brief, the feel of old law books, the technical and peculiar nature of the law. It was my intellectual home. But that morning, my other home beckoned. I rolled over, the sheets sticking to my sweaty legs, and answered the phone with a muffled, "Hello?"

"Come home." My mother spoke softly, something she never did. All my life, until that point, her voice was one volume: booming. I jumped out of bed sensing the urgency that was absent from her voice.

I rushed out of the apartment with my scarf still tied around my head and a hastily packed bag banging against my thigh. I drove as fast as I could—keeping in mind the danger of Driving While Black. Usually on this drive, I would take Highway 13 along the coast, slow down, and roll down the windows to take in a bit of the ocean air. But not this time. I stayed on 95 until I got to my childhood home.

I paused at the dark wooden stairs of the porch that encircled my brown two-story house with bright purple shutters. It looked smaller than it was in my memory. The sun beat down on my bare shoulders. Sweat pooled under my breasts. I wondered if either Mom or Nana would say something about my not wearing a bra. I hadn't been home in months; I'd just been too busy with work and life.

I knew my mother was dead as soon as I stepped into the house. The living room, her favorite room, was cluttered with chopped up magazines for collage projects, books covering the ottoman and parts of the floor, the old record player and its accompanying wall of records. This space that had been so full of her my whole childhood was inexplicably empty. A brain bleed took her, stole her from me, like a common thief. Her presence, the very thing that made her...her...was gone.

#

Nana nodded once. "When she reached the island, She thought She had found the Gullah people—that's what we call them now. But She didn't. She found her own people. Some sense, maybe it was the baby, led Her there."

Nana leaned back in her chair, satisfied with the ending. The woman of the story was the first of our ancestors to arrive to an island where women could give birth in peace.

#

Grief latched on to me immediately like a red-eyed monster with deep fangs that caused an ache in my chest. I couldn't shake it. I couldn't leave the house with purple shutters. I moved into my childhood bedroom and slept underneath posters of boy bands whose songs I couldn't remember. My eyesight went blurry the day after the funeral. I went to five different eye doctors, insisting I needed glasses. Each one declared my eyesight was perfect. The last doctor threw out the term "psychosomatic," and I stormed out. I read dozens of articles about the five stages of grief. With each one, I wondered why paralysis wasn't its own stage. I didn't have denial. I knew she was dead. I just wasn't sure how to move, breathe, or exist without my mom.

After a week, Nana forced me out of bed to help her pack up the decades of stuff Mom had accumulated. Paralysis was replaced by a perpetual empty feeling, as if someone had scooped out all my insides. I was left mobile but numb. I reached with my mind and gently touched the hollow spaces the grief monster created, like craters formed by a sudden and devastating crash. I was pulling boxes out from under mom's bed when I came across one tattered hat box with floral print.

I called for Nana. "What's this?" I asked.

She shrugged. "Open it and see."

I hesitated, somehow knowing it was private. Mom wouldn't want me to look. I pushed the hat box aside and continued pulling out boxes of clothes, mostly her winter sweaters from the years when she taught in Massachusetts. I tried to focus on folding the sweaters, sorting them into piles to donate and keep. But I kept looking back at the hat box. After about an hour, I gave in. I opened it slowly, as if something living inside would jump out and bite. Instead, I found dozens of thin notebooks. I reached to the bottom of the round box and grabbed one.

It began, *No foreplay with this one. He lifted my skirt first thing.*

With a half-squeal, half-groan, I slammed the journal shut. My mother never brought men around the house. So, I had never imagined her as someone who had sex.

Once I got over my initial shock, I went back to the journals. I laid on my mother's bed, on my left side as I imagined she might have done when recording her sexcapades. Each tiny book was filled with sordid details about each man's tongue, powerful arms, tree trunk thighs, and other naughty bits. At first, I blushed and groaned like I was 12 and watching my parents kiss. Then, I giggled and rolled on the bed laughing at the disastrous moments, the sex injuries, as if Mom and I were girlfriends. In all my rolling around on the bed, my shirt slipped up, and I noticed a slight discoloration on the side of my abdomen, like a patch of lighter skin. I dismissed it.

I took the hat box to my room when I realized it could be used for a different purpose. I stacked up the notebooks from about 9 and 10 months before I was born. There were about six. She had been busy. Maybe, just maybe, these notebooks would lead me to my father.

"What are you doing in there?" Nana called.

"Nothing!" I called back.

She swung the door open and it hit the wall with a bang. "Since when do we lie to each other?"

I hesitated. I didn't want another lecture about how we reproduce without men. And I was sure Mom wouldn't want her mother seeing the journals. "I'm just going through some of mom's things."

She stared at the journal in my hand. "I see." She turned and closed the door behind her.

I hadn't missed her red eyes or the fact that she hunched over more. The grief monster had her, too.

I scoured notebook after notebook in the months around my conception. Mom was fucking like she was running from something. I knew this kind of fucking—the kind that wasn't even about physical pleasure and definitely not about building relationships. It was about slapping a small band aid over a gaping, oozing wound. Each night was a different guy. She didn't use names and unlike other notebooks, she barely described what they looked like. Just as I was about to give up, I saw a mention of Mom's belly.

My stomach is getting lighter. Golden brown—just like Ma's old stories. Am I ready for this?

I lifted my own shirt. The discoloration had spread. It reminded me of a moon bear's markings. Soon I would be dark with a huge splotch of light across my middle. It was either panic or keep reading. I lowered my shirt, tugging on it to make sure it fully covered my belly. I knew it meant something, but I chose to ignore it. I chose to keep reading.

I miss her. I know it's only been a week since we put her in the ground. I say "we" like I'm part of the family. She was just a mentor. But no, she was more than that, wasn't she? She was a second mother.

I had no idea who Mom was talking about. But reading about her grief felt like a sharp bite in my neck, like something was trying to take away a piece of me. My stomach began to burn. I cried out. Nana was there in a flash.

"I'm fine. I'm fine. I just need some Tums."

"Let me see your belly." She reached for my shirt but I pulled away.

"What? Why? No."

"Let me," she said softly.

I lifted my shirt just slightly. Nana clasped her hands together. "Oh, Tasha!" She exclaimed, her mouth the shape of a perfect O.

Neither of us said anything for a while.

"We'll turn your mother's room into the nursery."

"What?" I whispered.

"I bet we can get you a job teaching at the university. Your mother was loved and respected there. It's a good job, flexible."

"What?" I said a little louder.

"You know, we might still have your crib in the basement. That'll save some money." She smiled.

"Are you saying I'm—?" I practically screamed at her.

"Pregnant? Yes. Haven't you been paying attention?"

"No. Yes. I mean..." I groaned. "You told me that story like it was a fairy tale, like Cinderella."

"I told you that story like it was our history. *They* told you it was a fairy tale, and you believed them."

I stood and faced her. I was a good head taller than her. She wore a purple housecoat and slippers. Her hair was still wrapped and in curlers.

"I can't be pregnant. I haven't had sex in—"

Nana turned and walked out.

"You're walking away from me?" I called after her.

"Yes, so long as you insist on saying stupid things to me."

"No." I refused to accept what she was saying. I was a normal 26-year-old black woman. I worked too hard, drank too much coffee, didn't sleep enough, and liked a little brandy before bed. I read health magazines even though I hated to work out and the beauty tips were always for white women. My mother had just died, and I was sad. I was *normal*.

I followed Nana down the hall. "Tell me the truth. This is some hereditary skin condition, right? I just need to go to a dermatologist."

She didn't say a word.

I began to panic. My voice rose in volume and octaves. "It's like a vitamin deficiency. Or dehydration from all the crying. It's some absolutely normal thing with a name and a cure. Tell me that. Please."

We had reached the top of the stairs. She whirled around, her face twisted with frustration. She reached for the top of the banister, missed, and fell all the way down the stairs.

#

When I sat down with Ernest of Ernest Johnson's Funeral Home for the second time that month, I thought for some reason that planning a second funeral would somehow be easier than the first. I was so wrong. The weight of grief doubled as I put my grandmother in the ground. The monster became a part of me, working its way under my skin. I'd heard stories from Nana and from Mom about people jumping in the casket or in the grave, as if that would somehow keep the dead person close. I understood the impulse at Nana's funeral. I was unrooted, a red balloon floating in one place as the rest of the world whirled around me. The choir sang, Nana's poker buddies gave a collective eulogy, the casket remained open the whole time. At least, I think that was what happened. I say "I think" because I planned it that way, but I couldn't tell you for sure that was how it went down.

When Mom found out she was pregnant with me, she switched to a new journal. She started keeping track of what she ate. In the upper right corner of each entry, she wrote a number and "inches"—3 inches, 4.25 inches, 7.75 inches. It took watching my own belly for me to know she was tracking the progression of the golden color across her torso.

Mama says it's time to go. I keep telling her we can go after my qualifying exams. I've tried to explain time and time again that no, I can't postpone them and yes, this is very important. Pregnancy on its own is not reason enough to uproot my whole life. Still, Mama insists the earlier we go, the better. I'm putting my foot down though. No, I've never been pregnant before. Sure, she knows better than me on this one thing. But it's my life.

The gold on my skin continued to spread across my belly. Three months after I buried the most important women in my life, my belly began to grow. After another month, I took pregnancy test after pregnancy test, thinking they all had to be wrong. I finally decided to go to the gynecologist.

My gynecologist was a petite Filipina woman who always folded her hands when she talked. "What brings you in today?"

"I keep taking pregnancy tests that say I'm pregnant. But I can't be pregnant."

"And why do you think you cannot be pregnant?'

I paused. Suddenly unsure whether this was a safe space. "I'm not sexually active."

She politely asked for a urine sample and directed me to the bathroom.

Twenty minutes later, she came back in. "Our tests do indicate that you are indeed pregnant," she said slowly. She took a breath and handed me a slip of paper. "Are you safe at home? These are some organizations that can help if you're not."

I mumbled a thank you, grabbed my bag and rushed out.

After that, my mother's journals became my refuge.

Mama packed a bag and says she knows a guy who knows a guy who has a boat. I keep telling her I'm not ready to leave. Mama says the size of my belly says otherwise I look like I'm having twins. The little one likes to kick at night. Lord, I hope she's not nocturnal.

For all Mama's insistence on leaving as soon as possible, she is refusing to answer my questions. Our conversations go like this.

"What is it like?"

"It's unlike anything you've ever experienced."

"Of course. It's childbirth. I saw the video at school. I know what happens."

"No, you don't. We aren't like them."

That was Mama's mantra once I found out I was pregnant. "We aren't like them." I realized as she kept saying it, I felt that statement everywhere I went. At the university where I was the only person of color in my department, when I went to Martha's Vineyard with my white ex-boyfriend's family, heck even walking up and down the streets of Boston with people staring, clearly wondering where I was going and why I was there. Now, I have just another reason to feel separate.

I struggled to come to terms with the child I was carrying. I stayed up until dawn every night going back and forth between reading mommy blogs and medical sites about hysterical pregnancies. The doctor said I was about five months along. I knew I should have been nesting, preparing for the "little one's" arrival (as my mother would probably say). I did none of that. I told myself, out loud, every day that it was a hysterical pregnancy.

I couldn't bring myself to respond to the emails my bosses kept sending about when I would return, reminders that I only had five days of bereavement in my contract.

All the mommy blogs agreed on one point: motherhood was all consuming. It was for me, too. But instead of being consumed with excitement or anticipation, it was as if I had taken a paralytic. During the day, I left my bed only to pee, which it seemed I needed to do every five minutes, and eat, which I also needed to do every five minutes. At night, I devoured the blogs.

I wondered about the trip Mom kept talking about in her journals.

Nana wanted her to go somewhere. Somewhere that involved a boat. I'd never known my mother to like water even though it always seemed like we lived near it—near a river in Massachusetts and near the coast in South Carolina.

One night, I fell asleep with the journal I'd read a dozen times in my arms and dreamt of my mother on a speedy boat, speeding off to bring me into the world.

"Tasha, Tasha baby, wake up," Mom called to me. I stirred in my sleep and my eyes flashed open. The entire room was covered in an orange haze. Mom stood just out of reach. Little streams of blood dripped from her nose.

"I'm dreaming?" I asked.

"I don't have much time. Tasha, you have to go to the island now."

"The island's not real." I had heard of people being visited in dreams by loved ones after death. I wanted to ask Mom all the things I didn't get to ask. "I love you," I said. "I didn't get to say that in time. I love you so much. I wish you could help me with this."

I swung my legs over the side of the bed and reached for her. She took several steps back. "I love you too, baby. And I'm sorry I can't be there to help you through this. But even if I was here, I wouldn't be able to help you. You have to go to the island. They are the only ones who can help."

"The island's not real. It's just a story."

"I had to go by boat because I waited too long. I was too pregnant to swim."

"That's why we're such good swimmers," Mom and I said together, repeating the line from Nana's story.

"Where is she?" I asked, looking around for my grandmother.

"She wished she could come, but only one of us could make it through. You have to go."

"How do I pack a bag if I don't take a boat? Wait, are you telling me I'm supposed to swim to some island? Are you for real? What is supposed to happen at this island? How do I even know I'm at the right island? Do you know how many islands are off the coast?"

Mom looked over her shoulder. I peeked too but didn't see anything but my white and pink childhood dresser.

"I have to go now," she said.

"Already?" I said in a whiny voice I hadn't used since adolescence. A sharp ache punctured my chest. I grabbed at my shirt and tried to fight back tears. I wanted to look strong in front of her so she wouldn't worry when she left.

"Oh, baby." She reached out for me, but as I reached for her, she quickly pulled her hand back. Her hands were the same shade of brown on the top but translucent on the side of her palms. I knew then she couldn't touch me.

"I'll be fine. I'll be fine." My voice broke on the second fine. Mom faded away as the sobs erupted from the pain in my chest.

I laid on my left side and stared at the spot where Mom disappeared. I waited, as the sun rose, for her to come back. Her visit, and the ugly cry after, changed me. Something had been unlocked. I imagined it was in my chest, where the pain was. But I knew it wasn't physical. I felt more connected to my mother than I ever felt when she was alive. I kept thinking: some ancient thing has been awakened. The thought came to me over and over, as if someone were whispering it in my ear to make it mine.

And then, I felt it. It was light at first, almost like the butterflies you feel when a cute guy looks your way. Then, it was stronger and stronger, until I realized it was an undeniable kick.

I sat up straight. The baby was real. I said it aloud in the empty house just to be sure. "The baby is real."

It took another hour for the paralysis to wear off. My mind was a flurry of mommy blog knowledge—onesies, nipple cream, cribs, running strollers, pacifiers, diaper genies. But I realized I wouldn't need any of that. Not yet at least. I stood before my closet trying to figure out what one wears to swim to an unknown island. Everything in my closet was too small except my tangerine orange bathing suit cover up. It was essentially a thin piece of fabric that covered me in a way that was no longer sexy. But it would have to do.

During the drive to the beach, I turned back three times before I decided to go all the way and park. I said a mental goodbye to my Prius and stomped toward the water. I had to stomp. Each step had to be forward and determined or I would chicken out. "The story is real," I whispered. "The baby is real," I said a little louder in case it could hear me. I stomped right into the water.

Swimming was a lot like dancing. My arms reached and pulled, like I was tangoing with a partner. My legs thrusted to a beat. My hips twisted, moving my body through the water, against all resistance. It was a dance. The water was my partner; the baby, swinging back and forth, was the metronome. I heard the whistle of the lifeguard on the beach, warning that I had gone too far. I kept going. He whistled again. I twisted my hips harder, feeling the heft of my belly. The ocean's temperature turned a new flavor of cold, a cold that felt a little like death. That's when the baby began fluttering. I kept swimming. At first I thought it was my imagination, but no, the baby fluttered to a beat. Kick, kick, flutter. Kick, kick, flutter. As soon as she—I knew then that we are all she's—started her own dance, a fog rolled in. I popped up my head every third breath to see where I was going, but I couldn't see a thing. The fog was thick and tasted like the nastiest cotton candy. My rational mind was screaming for me to turn around, to head back to shore, to scream for the lifeguard. But I kept going. A force bigger than me, older than me, older than Her even, was calling to me, to us.

The fog was so thick I couldn't tell for how many days I swam. It felt like forever. And the whole time the baby kicked to her own beat. The fog began to lift just as I felt sand under my feet again. I tried to see if it was a sand bank, just floating in the middle of the ocean. But as I kept walking, I felt more sand between my toes. I was on land. I paused when I saw a figure standing on the shore. It waved for me to come in.

A million questions spurred a panic in my mind. My fingers twitched. Was this the right island? Was this even an island at all or was I still in South Carolina? What did this person want with me?

"Tasha! Come here!" The person called.

I broke into a run toward her, but my legs gave out. My body finally succumbed to the massive undertaking I'd put it through. I let my body sink into the sand. My legs throbbed; my arms burned. My baby was quiet, like she was tired, too.

The island was not filled with palm trees and waterfalls like I imagined. A forest of pine trees was just a few hundred feet from me, signaling the edge of the beach. They were the tallest pine trees I'd ever seen. Their branches reached up and out like they were reaching flirtatiously for the sky. A mountain rose from the center of the island. Its peak was white and grey with a mix of snow and fog. I didn't see houses or any people other than the woman in front of me.

She came to me. "You're okay. Let me see you." She had thin but muscular limbs. Her face showed both the brightness of youth and the wisdom of age. I had no idea how old she was. We had the same eyes and nose.

The fog disappeared in an instant, and the sun shined down on us directly, as if she was controlling them both. She wore a thin black dress that went down to the middle of her shins. It looked old and had been mended several times. I knew without her saying that it was the dress from the story.

"I wear it to greet people. So you know me." She answered my unspoken question. "You're not scared," she said. I couldn't tell if it was a question or a statement.

"I feel ... like ... I'm home."

"You are, in a way. The others are coming."

"Others?"

"Oh, yes, you'll give birth soon. Well, not too soon. But the others will set you up so you're comfortable for what lies ahead."

"Is it terrible?"

She took my hand. "Yes. But sometimes things that cause us terror are also magical."

I raised an eyebrow and tried to think of a single thing that was both terrible and magical.

She laughed. "You doubt me. Oftentimes the things we fear the most are what will bring us the most joy, the most beauty." She glanced at my belly. "She brought you here, you know."

"That's how it works?" I thought back to the rhythmic flutters.

"Ah, here come the others. Tonight, you will feast and then you'll sleep the best sleep you've had in ages. We will take care of you here."

She stood and waved to a group that was too far out for me to see clearly. I rubbed my eyes hoping the island would come into focus. But everything was still blurry, perhaps even more blurry than when I initially stomped into the water.

She cocked her head to one side. "It is grief. It will pass."

I nodded as she walked a couple steps toward the group.

I grabbed both sides of my belly in an attempt to hold it, to take it all in, and I felt a warmth that was almost too hot to touch.

I whispered, "Babygirl, I am going to have a story for you. You ready?

"Get ready."

THE STONE

NAILA MOREIRA

It was unusual. Down the length of the beach, surf-tumbled pebbles littered the sand, but this one was different from all others. Large as a walnut, pure black, and riddled with spears of silvery mineral like a checkerboard, the stone lay partly embedded in a boulder by the shoreline, as though it had drilled its own depression in the rock.

The boy picked up the wonderful stone. The sphere lay heavy in his palm, darker than his own hue. It was hot, burning his skin – like a chunk of meteor from outer space, the boy thought. That's what it was, he decided: a fallen star. *Uma estrela cadente.*

The boy had walked a long time, trying to forget.

Now, he remembered walking here with his father months ago. His father had found a seagull feather. "A beautiful shaft of nature," he said, spinning it between his fingers. "Let's leave the feather here for others that may need it."

The boy clutched the stone, hot and brilliant in his hand. He frowned, closed his fist around it. This cooled star, fallen from the sky, must have been sent to him who needed it. The stone could take care of him now that his father wouldn't.

He stuffed it in his pocket. The stone burned against his thigh. Feeling a wave of satisfaction, he sensed he'd been chosen. The ocean crooned its rhythmic sounds.

Each week the boy's mother took him to cello lessons.

He had begun to play several months ago. Now, the curve of the instrument felt warmer, more familiar. The boy drowned his thoughts in its supple wood. He bent the bow against the strings and swam on a tide of music. The cello breathed like the sea. The stone, the little meteor, lay always in his pocket when he played, and shone above the waters of his soul in a blazing streak.

Sometimes, he took his cello onto the sand and played to the open sea.

The boy grew. His playing became known for its passion and grief. He was in demand, a soloist. He began to travel. From the small village of his upbringing he went to the country's great cities. He went to Rio, São Paulo, then to London, Paris, Vienna. He played with the greatest orchestras of the world. He kept the stone nestled in his suitcase. When the hour came to play, he tucked it in the deep pocket of his tuxedo. The stone was his guardian, the shooting star of his career.

He journeyed to Lisbon. Arriving a day earlier than the concert, he went out in the evening for the festivities of the Feast of St. Anthony. Along the streets in the darkness, vendors had set up grills to sell sardines on a chunk of bread, or little pots of fluffy, freshly sprouted basil. Hundreds of people walked to the top of the hill and the castle, laughing and talking.

In tradition, young revelers were expected to sing from below to the homeowners who leaned, laughing and listening, from windows and balconies of graceful, stucco row houses. This year, though, few young people bothered. An occasional small cluster of singers paused in the buffeting throng, but their voices were drowned by drunken shouting. Amid the increasingly rowdy horde, the cellist, disillusioned, turned away. He headed back down the narrow streets of the Alfama. So many people jammed the street, pouring downhill, that he feared he would be crushed. Gasping, he finally escaped into a side alley and slipped away back to his hotel on the Avenida da Liberdade. At every street corner he was stopped by a dealer trying to sell him a joint.

The next morning, to get out of the choked city, the young man rented a car and drove to a long, quiet sandy beach. He walked for hours, breathing in the clean salt air. At last, at one of several clusters of jutting rocks, he paused and sat down, slipping a hand into his pocket. The stone was there.

Perhaps influenced by the night before, he felt a surge of displeasure – in himself, in his life. How silly and superstitious he was, carrying this stone everywhere he went. The world was not one of magic; it was a world of smelly, tangled human beings and their desires and goals. Not the stone, but his own ambition, had brought him to the stage and the city, far from the peaceful rural hamlet of his childhood.

He took it out, gave it a purposefully careless glance. Then he set it on the sand, and before he could think again, walked with brisk strides back down the beach toward his car.

Two children distracted him from his thoughts, running by him laughing and pointing. *"Baleia!"* they cried to one another, voices ringing. *Whales.* Near the entrance to the beach a modest crowd had gathered. The famous whales of Portugal had come close to shore, and he joined the people to watch their shapes roll and slip through the water, silver black, breaking the waves.

That night he arrived at the concert hall stiff and formal in his expensive tuxedo. He found he did not know what to do with his hands.

From the first things went wrong. He caught his foot on the music stand of the concertmaster and spilled his music onto the stage. In the glare of the lights the audience seemed closer than ever. The people of Lisbon coughed and shifted in their seats. He missed a note. Never mind. Then he missed another. He tried to chase away distraction and enter the music as he'd always done, but the door into the ocean of silken sound was shut.

At intermission he sat alone in a side room rubbing his temples. Seldom had he played so badly. This orchestra, he feared, would never ask him back. The ache of absence in his pocket deepened.

With a sigh he rose and walked back up the hall. The conductor, hurrying the other direction, paused to greet him. "Tough night," he said.

"Indeed."

"Oh," said the conductor, "have a look at what I found today!" He dug in his breast pocket. "Beautiful, isn't it?"

The cellist's heart stopped in his chest. At first his voice did not come.

"Where ... where did you get this?"

"I went out for a stroll in the afternoon on the beach near my home," he said. "I often do. Lovely, hm?" He dropped the round object into the young man's hand.

In his palm, under the fluorescent lights, the stone glowed and shone and flashed and burned as it had always done. His stone. The only one. The young man turned it, gently, gingerly, hungrily.

"Yes," he said. He swallowed, and with difficulty held it out again, trying not to show his emotion. "A brilliant piece."

"Oh, I won't keep it," said the conductor airily. "If you like it, it's yours. Perhaps it will bring you luck." He chuckled and went up the stairs.

As though to compensate for his terrible first effort, after intermission the cellist played as he had never done. His bow had wings. It soared, plunged into the depths, and returned. In his pocket the silver spears of the stone seemed to ring in answer like strings.

Before his flight the next morning, he asked the taxi to drive out to the long beach again. Leaving the driver to wait, he hefted his cello down to the strand line. No gleaming whales broke the water. He settled on a boulder and played a thanks to the rhythmic surf. On the way back, stuck in traffic, he heard the final strains of last night's concert on the radio. "Like none other," the announcer said. "They say he coaxes the wildness of Brazil from the wood of his cello."

For many years he seldom let the stone stray far from his pocket. He grew older, and older, middle-aged; he married and became a father. As he grew, the world around him seemed to change still more. Rio, where he now made his home, became larger and more crowded and smellier. Car fumes hung in the roads.

He went home to visit the village of his boyhood where his mother still lived. It was not a small hamlet anymore. His mother's house was still there. But on both sides, skyscrapers had sprung up like mushrooms. The stucco walls of the house cowered, shadowed beneath hard steel and blank windows. All along the coast, the little villages had transformed into hulking metropolises.

Even so he sometimes took his cello to play by the shore, in his hometown, or in the tourist towns, even in Rio. People stopped to listen to him.

He did it less now that he had a family and a burgeoning career to worry about. More and more, too, whenever he found time to carry his cello to the ocean, he never seemed to catch good weather. Indeed the weather seemed worse each time, and the crowds grew smaller.

He found that the longer he stayed away from the shore, though, the cooler the stone seemed in his pocket.

So he played in brisk breezes that blew sand into his eyes. He played in a misting rain.

He played when lightning flickered angrily on the horizon. He played the year the sea turned blood red in a red tide and swimming was forbidden.

He played in Santa Catarina the year of Brazil's first hurricane. The wind tore at his cello. Later, under a sky still blue-black and unsettled, he read the newspapers. *The storm has destroyed 1500 homes and left 3 people dead*, he read, *and 11 provinces remain without electricity.*

He reached to caress the stone's warm curve. Beyond, he could hear the angry surf gnawing at the sand.

He grew older, and elderly at last. He played a concert in Rio: his last, he announced. His son was grown now, a successful businessman. His wife was dead. His mother, too, had gone. But it was time to go home once more.

He arrived in the bustling tourist city of his home. He found it difficult, now, to drive in the city, and twice took a wrong turn. Never before would he have done that. The construction project in the town center, he thought, had confused him.

Eventually, he managed to arrive at his favorite restaurant by the sea. He settled down for dinner. Since his boyhood this restaurant, at least, had been here.

He ordered his usual.

"I'm sorry, but we can't offer a tuna steak today, Sir," the waitress told him.

He frowned. "Why is that?"

"The price of tuna has risen," said the waitress. "Overfishing, I understand. We've removed it from the menu."

The boy, now a man, pondered her words. He ordered a different dish. After dinner, in the gathering dusk, he walked beside the waves.

Thick clouds hung above him. At the horizon the last of the sun's light still pierced through, and a reddish glow stained the sky's edge. It painted the tops of the swells.

For a long time he stood beside the water. In his pocket his guardian star still lay. Even after all these years it still felt alive, warmer than rock. He took it out and observed its round shape. Its silver spears glimmered in the blue evening.

His stone had taken care of him all these years, carried him, made a success of him. Its glitter was embedded in his heart, burning at the core of his art. Now at last he was old. He didn't need it now. His son had made his own way in the world; he also had no need of the stone. He looked up and down the beach for any young boy who might be passing by. He could give the stone away. But the beach was empty.

Beside him, the sea murmured and choked and struggled against the sand. He turned the stone in his palm. And for one heavy moment he felt the guilt of his gift.

He reached his arm back, flinging the stone over the sea. It rose in a high arc, caught a last scintillation of light from beyond the thick clouds at the horizon, and fell.

All night the sound of waves played, a cello against his sleep.

HAGFISH

RYLEE EDGAR

The girl in the back booth was definitely staring at him. It had taken a while for Ronnie to be sure. She would turn away whenever he looked, but he could feel her eyes tickling his back when he didn't. He was almost certain she was watching him.

He swallowed another shot, chasing it with beer before the taste could take hold, and hissed as chaos threatened to erupt from his stomach. He was already floating on two others from moments ago when he was trying to decide if she was looking at him or not, and this third would determine if he was going to do anything about it. But as he stood there, his guts burning with well tequila, and the beer doing nothing to cool it off, he began to find reasons to hesitate.

He checked his reflection in the glass behind the bar and watched his own face fall. His round cheeks were pink from liquor. Sweat sparkled on his temples beneath the brim of his trucker hat. His beard could have used a trim a week ago. Other than that, still business as usual—still too tall, still too fat, still ugly old Ronnie Buckley. Brick Wall Buckley, Ugly Buckley, the kind of guy that folks compulsively called Bubba.

It was unlikely that anyone was looking at him.

He wondered if it was even worth finding out if a girl like that was into hulk hicks. Better to leave things as they were, he told himself, and spend the evening seeking out a game he actually understood. He let his gaze drift along the mirror to check the line for the pinball machine, and that's when he saw it. She *was* watching him, her eyes pinned to his back like a cat as she sipped her drink, flickering up and down his body. Her gaze finally met his in the mirror and rested there, smiling as she gently tongued her stirring straw.

A rush of hot blood shot up his back and he got to his feet, his body having made the decision for him.

He took his chaser beer, nearly empty now but useful as a prop, and sauntered to her table, not expecting the slight buckle in his legs. He swayed, thankfully only once, and continued his path. That tequila wasn't messing around. He hoped it would be as loose on his nerves. She was looking at her phone as he approached, but when he stopped at the table her eyes suddenly lifted, striking him cold.

"Hi," he said.

"Hello," she replied. Her eyes were dark, like black coffee. They warmed with her smile.

"I noticed you were staring," he said.

"Was I?" she said. She was cute from a distance, absolutely devastating up close: full cheeks to match her round eyes, delicate nose, lips unlike any he'd ever seen—a thick rosy pout gleaming with gloss. He could see himself in those lips, and he struggled to not let his mind wander at what they could do.

"I didn't mean to stare," she said shyly. She looked down, still smiling. "I thought I knew you from somewhere. Guess I got carried away..."

"Well, my name's Ronnie, so now you know me," he said, smiling back. He felt he was doing well, despite the slush in his words. He tightened his lip and pressed forward. "And anyway, I noticed you before I noticed the staring."

"Oh, really?" she said, her smile curling into a curious grin. She lowered her chin and looked up at him, her gaze sending a chill up his thighs. Briefly, they moved to something just over his shoulder, and glided back to him, smooth as melted chocolate. "Well, I saw *you* first."

"Hey!"

The voice jabbed like a dart in Ronnie's back. A scrawny guy with a beanie and a hard scowl came up to the table, his knotty fingers balled around two bottles of beer at his sides.

"How's it going, *man*?" he said. His tone was not friendly. His left ear gleamed with hoop earrings all the way down the lobe. Ronnie could see the guy was puffing himself up already, which was something of a relief—maybe he was intimidated—but it also meant trouble. The guy was smaller but ropey, obviously a frequent fighter, and guys like that had the potential to go wild even on someone as big as Brick Wall Buckley. Ronnie considered all of this as he tried to craft a response, only for the girl to beat him to it.

"Tobey, this is Ronnie. He was just introducing himself," she said evenly. Her voice seemed to put the guy at ease, but only a little. He held his glare on Ronnie as she continued, "I thought I knew him from somewhere and he caught me staring."

After a moment, Tobey finally relaxed and broke his gaze, taking a swig from his beer. He reached into the booth and tugged at her arm, pulling her to her feet. He shoved the other bottle into her hand.

"Come on, let's dance," he said.

She obeyed, slipping out of the booth after Tobey. They passed Ronnie without another word and headed towards the back, where the dancefloor trembled behind metal doors.

He watched her walk away, and everything in him screamed after her. He felt a cold sweat breaking over his skin, the unbearable heat of humiliation flooding his nerves. It had been nothing, he knew that—he hadn't even asked her name. But something sparked in him within those few exchanged words, a tremendous need that was swiftly turning to a deep throbbing ache. He couldn't just let her walk away.

But what could he do? Working up the nerve to talk to her had gotten him nothing except shitfaced. It was pointless from the jump, he reasoned, and figured the only thing to do now was have another drink and check in with the pinball machine. He nearly looked away just as she turned and looked back at him, coffee eyes watching just over her bare shoulder, a look with language to it. A look that said to him, *come find me.*

So he followed her.

The dancefloor was a thunderstorm of heat and lights, bodies writhing against one another in an angry humid cloud. He felt like he was swimming through flesh, a thousand wriggling limbs sliding against him.

When he finally spotted her, she was dancing with her back to the scumbag Tobey, her chest glistening with sweat. Her hips switched with expert rhythm as she rocked with the beat, the lights painting her skin black and red.

She was already looking at him, black orbs against neon skin. Relief came over him, and something like adoration, warm and overwhelming. Her eyes stayed pinned on him as she spun around to whisper in Tobey's ear, and in an instant, Ronnie lost her in the crowd again. He could feel his heart swelling, what felt like the beginnings of a panic attack pinching at his chest.

But then, like a vision she appeared out of the crowd, drink in one hand and the other in running through her sweat-curled hair, her eyes shut as she swayed with the music. He watched her move towards him, dancing in orbit around him. She would draw close enough to kiss and then twirl out of reach again, flicking in and out of sight under the strobe. Until finally, so smooth he almost didn't notice it, she slid into his arms and began to dance with him. The smell of her filled his senses as her ass filled the space between them.

They moved together against the beat. He lost track of the moments, only tried to catch more of her scent, gather more of her heat. She didn't open her eyes, throwing her head back and letting her hair flicker along his face. She seemed not to notice him, lost to the music, yet her body wound against him with deliberate intention. His own body responded with an eagerness he feared may spill over at any moment. He didn't know the first thing about her, not even her name, but he needed her, deeply, desperately. He needed this feeling to never go away.

And then, she spun away from him and vanished, like she had never been there at all. He was empty and alone on the dancefloor again. And just as suddenly, the tequila crashed down upon him in a terrible wave as his stomach spun in panic. His vision winked in and out as he went staggering towards the bathrooms.

Ronnie stumbled into the corridor, slamming into the wall to stop himself. The dancefloor continued to thud behind him, but the air was cooler here, still and nearly silent with the ringing in his ears. The world was settling again. The stillness of the single fluorescent bulb in the narrow hall soothed his pounding head, and the rumbling in his stomach began to relax. As his sight fell back into focus, he could see a silhouette leaning in the hallway, waiting below the sign for the ladies room. It was her—by now he had her etched in his mind, the fall of her hair down her back, the slope of her skirt, the cocky strut of her legs. Even in the sharp relief of the dark hallway, she gave distinct curves to the charcoal walls.

He didn't think, only surged forward on pure momentum. In an instant, he was against her, his hands on her hips and grinding her into the wall. He could hear her laughing into his ear even as the pulse of the club shuddered all around them.

"You like to tease, huh?" he whispered, and he was sure he heard her moan in response, a sound of pleasure.

"Ronnie..." she squealed, giggling, squirming against him.

"You think you can do all that and just walk away?" he said. He heard himself in a slurring growl, almost inhuman, and somewhere in the haze, it frightened him. "I want you."

He pulled away to look at her face again, needed to see her beauty again even in the shadows. But something was off. Her eyes were different, cold black beads burning into him. His heart dropped as a smile began to creep along her lips, and embarrassment flooded him like ice water. He had misunderstood, he had been fooled. This enchanted encounter with a beautiful stranger would end in another rejection. He felt sick as the laughter in her smile looked suddenly, horribly familiar, the shadows of a hundred other girls passing over the creases of her lips.

And something else lay there too, darker, something he couldn't name, something hidden behind her teeth. For an instant, the lightbulb above flickered and sharpened the curves of her face into vile points, her eyes pockets of pitch.

But then the bathroom door burst open and two girls rushed by them, giggling. The new light blew the shadows away from her face and she was lovely and soft again, radiant with sweetness. Gently, she put a hand to his cheek. Her fingers were cold.

"You want to keep me warm tonight?" she whispered, and his thoughts melted away.

The bathroom door slammed shut again and as the hallway fell back into darkness, they plunged into one another. He drove his leg into her groin and kissed her neck, breathing her in again, floral sweat filling his senses. She clutched him to her with surprising strength, the jagged edges of her fingernails biting into his back and sending shockwaves down his spine. He was hard despite the tequila, and he wondered briefly if he would fuck her right here in this hallway, only inches away from being up her skirt.

A punch in his ear sent his vision sparkling. The next two hits came in flashes of bright color—featuring that skinny scumbag's face—before everything went black. He came to moments later, lying on the grimy floor of the hallway, a collection of shoes with worried voices gathering around him. A few guys helped him to his feet, and someone asked if he needed a cab home. He didn't answer, just began walking, dazed, surging with booze and delayed adrenaline. Suddenly he was outside, alone in the cold night.

His legs moved with staggering purpose towards the woods, like a collapsing ship on a set course for home base. Humiliation washed over him in fresh, hot waves. He figured it was that Tobey that decked him, and it killed him he hadn't even gotten a chance to take a swing at the guy. He imagined it must have been a sight for anyone that caught it, a big denim walrus getting KO'd by a meth-head's suckerpunch. It would have been devastating if he wasn't still drunk. For now, the loudest voices in his mind cried out to go home.

The bar wasn't far from his place. His usual route was to cut through the scattered forest lining the roads to the river, then over the old concrete bridge and a quick walk up the hill to his apartment complex. But it always felt longer in the dark, especially on the way home, away from all the potentials of the night. This night in particular, as the cold began to piece his sobriety back together little by little and memories came crumbling in. He tried not to focus on them, or the cramps of regret in his gut. He just needed to get home.

The crunch of gravel behind him made him jolt. He whipped around, waiting for another punch. But there was no one, only the empty road under the hissing streetlight. He shivered, watching over his shoulder as he dove into the cover of the trees.

The dark gets darker in the woods.

The light on his phone was little help, barely illuminating what was directly in front of him. He ran into branches when he watched the ground for holes, and tripped into holes when he tried to watch the trees. His head ached, and his cottony mouth tasted of sour tequila. He longed for home and bed and a long drink from the faucet. And her, he still wanted her. Despite the pain in his ear and his gut, still he ached more for another whiff of her earthy sweetness.

Sticks snapped in the distance to his right, and he froze, waiting. Probably a possum, he thought, till he heard the rush of thrashing leaves, the thud of feet pounding on soft ground and the sudden silence that followed. His blood ran cold. Someone was out here with him.

He opened his mouth to call out, but his voice died in his throat as the sounds began again, closer now, rising towards him in a wave of snapping twigs.

"Who's there!" he screamed, finally.

Barely beyond the reach of his light, he saw something speed through the brush and tear past him. His eyes followed the sounds, and as the trees thinned out up ahead he could see the wink of bare flesh in the moonlight. A naked woman was running through the woods, hair streaming out wildly behind her. In the echo of settling leaves, he could swear he heard giggling. And in a flash, the vision was gone.

"Shit! Shit..." Ronnie gasped, his heart clattering away like a panicked bird.

His head spun and he groped for a tree to steady himself. He had really had too much to drink tonight. Approaching strange women, getting into fights, seeing babes in the woods...he couldn't remember a dollar shot night going so poorly. The ache in his gut was throbbing like a rotten tooth, spreading through his limbs and pinching his forehead behind his eyes. He needed to get home, for this night to just end. He heaved forward, swallowed back his whirling stomach, and kept walking, searching for the sound of the river.

Finally, after what seemed like hours, the whisper of running water came from somewhere up ahead. Groaning in relief, Ronnie picked up speed, watching his step through the softening ground. The trees finally broke and the river came sparkling into view, cooling the air around it with rushing mist. The cement bridge stood silently further up ahead, a single streetlamp burning white light like a false moon on the inky water. Only a few hundred more steps to home, but first, he desperately needed a drink.

Ronnie charged towards the bank, his boots skidding slightly as the mud turned to smooth wet rocks, and collapsed at the water's edge. He plunged his face into the cold, sucking in long gulps of icy relief. He splashed more behind his neck and through his hair before finally coming up for air, his cheeks tingling. He crouched there a moment, catching his breath and slurping down more handfuls of fresh water. Soon enough, the sound of the current soothed his head. He could breathe again, that ache in his bones at last beginning subside. He watched the river move by for a while, stretched out before him like a black silk curtain.

Then he heard splashing.

It was coming from somewhere between where he stood and the bridge upriver, where the tree line carved deeper into the water. The sound was beyond the babble of water rushing over the rocks, something lighter, trailing against the great black vein's current. Something alive was out here with him.

He wondered if he should investigate, though a thousand reasons flew through his head for leaving it alone. But as he froze in indecision, half-squatted with his knees in the mud, his questions were answered when a girl swam into view.

In the light from the bridge he could see her silhouette, her hair slicked to her scalp and wet beads clinging to her shoulders. She stood just barely hip-deep in the water, her arms held out for balance with the delicate poise of a dancer. Even from this distance, he could hear her voice trill with pleasure from the feel of the water. She twirled around and dipped below the surface, appearing again as just a head and the wake of her arms as she took backstroked deeper into the river. Ronnie's stomach flipped when he noticed the swell of her naked breasts gleaming just above the water. She turned her back to him again and continued to stroke effortlessly against the current, her head bobbing slowly in his direction. Carefully, he rose to his feet, but a rock slipped under his weight and he stumbled into the water with a sloppy splash.

He caught himself and looked out at the water again, only to see the head was already looking at him. His face flushed and, not knowing what else to do, raised his hands in greeting.

"Hey there!" he called, waving. The girl's face was a mask of shadows, but he could feel her eyes boring right through him. He felt like a guilty idiot. He smiled, hoping she could see it. "Sorry! I was just...resting here. I wasn't...I didn't mean to, uh, scare you!"

She didn't reply, just held her stare and her shadows.

At last, so slowly he barely noticed it happening, she moved closer towards him, the black curves of her body rising smoothly out of the shallows as if formed out of the river itself. She stood like a dark Venus in the waves, water lapping her thighs not ten feet from where he stood, her hand reaching out to him.

"Ronnie," she said, and his hair stood on end. It was her, that silky voice already as sweet and familiar to him as a song.

"You're here!" he said. His head spun in confusion and joy. "What are you doing here?"

"Swimming," she said. She waved her hand, beckoning him. "Come."

His hands moved on their own as he bent to unlace his boots. He couldn't tear his eyes away from the slope of her hips, the light from the bridge betraying just a slip of pale shoulder, a matted wave of black hair. His shirt came off with ease but he fumbled with his belt. She turned away from him again and he froze—briefly wondering if the invitation had been revoked—but then, catching sight of her firm, full ass just before it disappeared into blackness reignited his haste. He kicked free of his jeans and staggered into the water, barely managing to keep his balance on the algae-slicked rocks. Sticks and god knew what else pricked his bare feet as he sloshed deeper into the water, but all he saw was her, diving below again up ahead of him, her buttocks like a fleshy white peach winking into the black.

But something made him stop short. He was in up to his waist now and though the water tasted clean before, now didn't feel right on his skin... it was thin, slick. Even in the dimness, he could see what looked like oil spots shimmering on the surface, spreading in a faint trail through the water.

"Hey, uh," he called out. She paused and stroked towards him, her smooth black head appearing like a seal charging at him. "This looks like runoff or something. Maybe we shouldn't be out here..."

She appeared closer now than before, the water just covering her breasts, and finally he could see her face. She was even more beautiful in the moonlight. He swallowed hard, his heart pounding. For a moment he wondered if he was dreaming, if maybe he knocked his head on one too many branches and was actually out cold somewhere in the woods. He blinked hard, flexing his fingers in the water to be sure he was really here. All the while he watched her, waiting for her to disappear, hoping she didn't.

"What happened to that other guy?"

"Tobey?" She scoffed. "He's not really my type. Too skinny."

He blushed at that and was thankful she couldn't see it.

"I'm so happy to see you again," she said.

"Really? Why?"

She smiled.

"I had to make it up to you."

"What?"

"It's like you said. I can't do all that and just walk away."

He felt his blood surge, despite the cold.

"Well," he gulped. "What..."

He trailed off as he met her eyes. She was watching him carefully, wet curls falling over her eyes, pillowy lips slightly open, and it was enough to ignite the ache in his chest with fresh agony. He didn't care about dreaming, or runoff, or anything else. Her closeness, the promise of her warmth in this freezing void was too much to bear. She smiled, barely a twitch, and he took that for an answer.

In one move, he met her embrace and they were entangled, her body slipping easily around his, weightless and writhing. His senses tumbled together with the sound of rushing water, of thirsty breathing, of her voice, light and yearning, whispering in his ear.

"Oh Ronnie..." she gasped. "More, give me more..."

Ronnie obliged, grinding against her eagerly. Her skin was impossibly soft in the dark water, wriggling free of his hands no matter how tightly he held her. Her touch shocked his nerves, sending tingles running up his spine down to his toes. He pressed his kiss deep into her lips, trembling from the cushion of them against his own. He was hard despite the cold around them, feeding from her sweet soft mouth. He twisted his legs around hers and arched into the crease of her thigh, probing for heat. Her skin was so warm, and for only the briefest flash did he feel the hint of the slick inside, even warmer. He burned for it, but he steeled himself to hold back, not to ruin this, not yet.

Ronnie cried out suddenly as his back pressed up against something hard and cold. His eyes sprang open, sure he would wake up from this wet dream on the cold dry ground, only trees around him. But he was still here, naked in the river and pinned between a girl and a concrete wall. They had been swept downstream, and he was now clinging to the foundation of the bridge above, the force of the water holding him there against the slick stone and mud slimed with algae. They were on the center beam, the bridge's arched shadow cloaked them in even deeper darkness, winking out the street lamp's glare above. The echo inside turned the river's steady pulse to a hollow roar.

Ronnie clung tighter to the wall and managed to pull himself up enough to lean against the lip of the base, which was more mud than concrete now. He could feel an unsettling squish under his feet, felt it creeping into private crevices. He wanted to get back on the bank. The water was moving too fast, the air suddenly, terribly cold. He looked at her, but before he could speak, she was climbing up to reach his mouth. The softness of her lips was dizzying. Metallic desire filled his mouth, and he struggled to swallow it.

"Listen," he gasped, trying to break away. "We should...we can go somewhere else. I have a place nearby...we can—"

"Ronnie..." she moaned in his ear. "Please."

She kissed him again and his thoughts dissolved.

She continued to peck his face with her soft mouth, sending shivers through his skull. He mumbled something else half-heartedly, but the cold was fading, and the sound of water filled his ears again. Ronnie felt pins and needles crawling through his limbs. Her mouth moved down his neck to his chest, moving to his groin. His nerves followed her touch, feeling heavier.

She took him in her mouth, slowly at first then deeper, and even for the cold rush all around them, he was suddenly lost in the heat of her. For a few moments of Ronnie Buckley's very bad night, there was no cold, no noise, nothing but the sweetness of her lips wrapped tenderly around him.

He came quickly and violently, his hips jerking with electric orgasm. He descended back to the world again in shuddering fragments. Dimly, he could already feel embarrassment setting in, but he let himself stay lost in her warmth for just a little longer.

But then, it was too much, much too much. She was sucking him harder now and every nerve was screaming and he screamed along with them. He tried to move away but his limbs wouldn't budge. They felt heavy, the pins and needles now turned to cement. He shrieked, struggling to buck his hips out of her mouth, but she seemed to take it as encouragement and sucked even harder. He wasn't even hard anymore, and his limpness slid easily down her throat. He howled in agony.

"Pleasepleasepleaseplease!" he cried. "Stop! STOP!"

With all his might, he swung his leaden arms around her neck and clutched her head, struggling to pull free. She wrapped her arms around his thighs and buried her face into crotch. Ronnie twisted his fingers into her hair and pulled. He could feel his deadened nerves twitching uselessly as his grip slipped through her oily hair. He tried again, grabbed the roots of her hair and twisted, and finally with a sharp yank and a sickening wet POP he was free. He pulled her face up to his, panting with effort and at least slight relief.

"What the hell's the matter with y—"

He looked down, and choked on his words. There was no sound for what he saw. It just didn't make sense. His groin was torn open, black blood oozing over his thighs, pooling in his belly button, running down to join the river's stream.

But that couldn't be right. That's what it looked like but it couldn't be real. He blinked furiously, trying to see properly, sure it was just a trick of the light. It had to be. Why else couldn't he feel it? *I am dreaming...*he thought, *you don't feel pain in your dreams...*

Ronnie's gaze drifted across the bank, and he saw someone lying face up on the rocks, half in shadow under the bridge. The man was naked with both arms spread above his head. His face was frozen in a scream, the street lamp painting his skin ash white. Ronnie could just see the gleam of silver hoops shining in his ear.

She began to writhe in his numbed hands. She looked up at him just as the clouds passed away from the moon, her face glowing and lovely. In his head, he could hear her voice *"I saw you first."*

The clouds passed over again and as the light faded, his mind spun out completely. Her mouth was wide, shrieking, and something squirmed beneath her skin. Then, her face broke apart. Her jaw opened like a flower, unfolding over her chest into a gaping maw of rosy muscle flanked with lips made of teeth, layers upon layers of slimy grey gums and sharp ivory points, a long fat tongue of pink barbs spilling out.

He blinked, unbelieving, sputtering uselessly. The mouth struggled against his hands, shrieking, spraying slime in his gaping face. As he sat there trying to understand, she lunged out of his grip and latched onto him again. Blood and flesh pulled easily into hungry, grinding teeth, sucked down in juicy slurps. Ronnie watched her eat from somewhere far away.

He didn't feel a thing as her thorny tongue shot into his ruined groin, ripping through his intestines like an arrow. As she dug into the rich juices of his liver, his vision began to blur and any thoughts he had left swiftly faded. He stayed awake just long enough to hear the dull crack of his pelvis breaking. He watched his legs twitch uselessly as she pried him apart. Then Ronnie Buckley sank away into soft black mud.

The mouth ducked her head into the ragged wound, using her elbows to stretch it wider, and continued her meal, slower now that the struggle was over. She sucked on sweet innards and clawed through the steaming dome of the ribcage, cracking bones along her way. When she had finally eaten her fill, she dragged him down, off the mud slope and deep into the murk below.

It was quiet down there, soft with algae and safely away from the pull of the river. She pushed him down and crawled back inside, curled up in the hollow of his chest, and they sank together to settle at the bottom. She coiled around herself, contended. This one was so much roomier than the other. She fell asleep inside the man once known as Ugly Buckley, safe against the darkness around them.

The streetlamp overhead winked out, and the river rushed by with indifference, a great thick vein of black blood.

THE SEA DEVIL

SUSANA MORRIS

The ad for the apartment said it had a claw-foot tub. Besides that there was little else to recommend it. For one, calling it an apartment was generous. The place was one oddly shaped living room and bedroom in one, buttressed by a kitchenette and a bathroom. Plus, it was a fourth-floor walk-up in a building sandwiched between two taller buildings. The grimy window offered views of more grimy windows and soot-covered brick. Even for this city, the neighborhood was loud and smelly, teaming with people hawking wares on street corners. Screaming voices bubbled up from the guts of Chinese food restaurants and pizzerias or out tenement windows.

But that stuff really didn't matter. I just wanted to make sure that the tub was big enough, deep enough, for me to stretch out. I'm barely five feet—but if the tub, or any container really, is deep enough, I can make the change happen.

I viewed the dusty claw-foot tub, sinking into it fully clothed. The dust left a thin layer of muck on my jeans, but I wasn't concerned. I signed a short-term lease - the kind that can be renewed week by week. I did notice that, even after years of practice, my signature was a childish doodle, graceless as a right-handed person writing with their left.

The super stood there stupidly, gripping the wad of cash I'd paid. With large yellow teeth, his smile was a snarl. It was hard to tell if he was happier about the money or the prospect of a new female tenant who lived alone. His rheumy eyes roved all over my body, drinking in my blue-black skin, stopping momentarily at my unbound breasts which were visible beneath my t-shirt. The landbound fool even offered to come on by and check on me, see if I needed anything. I told him I did not, in fact, need anything from him. His wolfish grin only grew brighter. A pity for him. I smiled back, keeping my teeth retracted.

I moved in that very day. Didn't have much furniture, so the move went swiftly. I could eat standing up and sit on the floor when tired. And when the moon replaced the sun in the sky, I could sleep in the tub. And I did.

#

I was standing in my tiny kitchen, eating the remnants of a seaweed salad I'd ordered from the Japanese restaurant down the street, when I heard a knock at the door. I'd been in the city for almost a month resting, thinking, but no one save the old bucktoothed landlord knew I lived in the apartment. I knew it wasn't him. I'd spied him from the window walking into the bodega across the street, probably to buy more cigarettes and cheap beer. He had all the predictable excesses.

I went to the door and looked through the peephole. Akira stared back me. Even through the lens blurred with dirt I could see her annoyance.

"Open up, Gem. I know you in there."

I cracked opened the door. "How you find me?"

Akira scoffed and pushed past me into the empty living room. "As if I don't know you better than I know myself. As if your own heart beating isn't as loud in my ears as my own." She kissed her teeth. "I'm not like these landbound people dem."

True, but she had lived here a long time. Her voice was a mix of city grit and island twang.

Akira looked around grimacing.

"And what the hell is this? She stretched her long, graceful arms wide. "This...is a dump. You know you can stay with me."

I sighed. Stay with her and that landbound dud of a husband she chose? No thank you.

"This is why I didn't come to you first. You like a cyclone, kicking up waves wherever you go. Goddess knows I need to clear my head and figure out what's what."

Akira narrowed her eyes. "You didn't talk to me because you knew I'd try to bring you to your senses, gal. That's what."

"Maybe that too," I grinned.

"Put away all dem teeth, you shark," Akira said, trying to shield her own small smile. Impulsively, she wrapped her arms around me, squeezing me into a tight embrace. Her hair smelled like hibiscus and saltwater.

I let go first, the scent of her made me feel slightly giddy. "Come sit down. You can try to convince me now that you're here."

Akira looked around again. "Sit where?"

I had very few clothes, but I produced a large scarf and placed it on the ground.

"Sorry I haven't gotten around to cleaning yet. I've been busy." I gave her a wry smile.

"Busy with what?"

"Figuring out my next steps."

Akira looked ready to object. I asked if she wanted aqua vitae. Her face brightened like a child being offered a treat.

I went to the kitchen and opened my fridge. It was empty save for a large plastic jug of clear liquid, a precise mixture of water, salt, and lime juice. I poured out two cups and returned to the living room.

Akira grasped her cup with two hands and gulped the mixture without stopping. I smiled in pleasure. I knew she could not drink much of this among the landbounds. They wouldn't understand her need for brackish water. I got up and refilled her cup.

She drank more slowly this time, savoring the tartness. "You always did know how to make aqua vitae." She flashed me a full smile, revealing even white teeth with a gap in the middle.

Her compliment made me feel shy. "Our elixir always tastes better when somebody else mix it."

She put the cup down. "Gem, what you doing here?"

I forced myself to meet her eyes. "You know why I'm here. I couldn't...I can't let him get away with what he did."

She sighed and put my cold, clammy hands in hers. "He already paying for it. Lia and the baby both gone. He just a sad, dry up thing now." She squeezed my hands. "He no die easy."

I pulled my hands from hers. "As if I care he drinking himself to death! He only have himself to blame."

Akira shook her head, her dark eyes brimming with pity.

I frowned. She could keep her pity. "You have spent too much time with these people dem. This man kill our sister and you want me to leave vengeance to the gods!"

Akira drew back from me. "You spit out their names like bitter bile." Her voice was low and tight with anger. "Remember what the gods have done for you and for me."

"You think me forget? Is the gods dem who need to remember."

#

These days my dreams are all the same. I'm in an indigo sea gliding, my sister Lia's hand in mine. Her hair floats around her head like a halo. We stay like this for hours, laughing together over private jokes, chasing each other in the water, snuggling each other close. Then I close my eyes, savoring both the weightlessness and the solid feeling of her holding me. Then I feel a tug. I open my eyes to see my sister slip out of my hand. She turns and swims away from me, always away. No matter how I call for her she doesn't answer. She doesn't swim back.

But last night was different. Akira left stiff and resentful but with my promise to visit her and the children soon. I sat in the tub all day, sipping aqua vitae, my tail slapping water over the edge. My nerves were jangled. I felt angry and chastened, but desire also throbbed in my gut like a stomachache. I wanted nothing more than to be out of this place, away from Akira and the confusion she always left in her wake, away from the pulsing need to find that blasted man and squeeze the life from him. Exhausted, I fell into spells of fretful sleep.

This night my dream is an old nightmare. I'm a little girl holding my mother's hand. We're walking to market. When we get there she bends to kiss my forehead and tells me that, if I am good, I can get a treat on the way back. When I look into her ebony face, it is missing, blurred by the centuries between us. But her voice is still the same after all these years, husky and sweet as palm wine.

When we walk into the market, mother and I go into a large tent. Suddenly I am taller, my mother's height. Just outside the tent I see someone I recognize: a young man, the goat herder's boy. He is smiling at me. I am smiling back. I hear my mother calling to me from a far corner. I turn away, still smiling. Mother says, "Look at these bolts of kente cloth. Aren't they lovely?" I nod. I am not thinking about the lovely bolts of cloth that will become a wedding outfit. I'm still thinking about the boy, the one I am not betrothed to. I am still smiling.

Loud noises erupt outside the tent. Slavers waving guns rush in, knocking over tables of jewelry and fine cloth. Mother tries to grab me, but the hulking brute gets to me first. He pins my arms behind my back. I am kicking and screaming. My mother drops to her knees pleading first, then fighting. Swinging her arms, kicking, biting until finally another slaver hits her with the butt of his musket. She crumples without making a sound. I stare at the blood pouring from her temple until my mind goes black.

When I wake up, there is more water on the floor than in the tub. The skin on my new brown legs is grey and ashy under the glare of the bathroom's dim bulb. I turn the faucet on again.

#

I tried to stay awake, but the rain pounding the windows of the crawling city bus was lulling me to sleep. I didn't want to fall asleep and miss my stop. Akira's directions were simple enough. I had to take two trains and then a long bus ride to get to her place. You can stay the night, she'd said. My husband, he will drive you back the next day. I tried not to make a face when she said that, but I failed. I see you skinning up your face, gal. As if you've never been with a landbound man. I said nothing.

What could I say? There have been many men, of course. Although I still dream about him, I never did get to taste the goat herder's lips. But I did get to taste many others. And I even have children and grandchildren. But I am not like Akira or Lia; I have never forgotten who I was and who they were too. We are no longer the same.

I never saw my mother again after the slavers stormed the market. They chained me and dozens of others together and we marched to the sea. Then there was the ship and more chains and more strangers. After the woman shackled next to me died in her sleep, the slavers threw her body out like she was yesterday's fish. Akira took her place. We huddled together, whispering in Twi. We tried to reassure each other that all of this was just a terrible nightmare.

I remember being grateful for the pounding rain when they allowed us above board. I could wash away some of the stench and stiffness instead of sitting in my own and other's filth, chained to my fellow captives, for days. It didn't matter, not really, that the crew wanted Akira and I to dance, to shake our breasts and buttocks for them—and do more.

I danced. Not to please the bearded red-faced men who stank of desperation and sweat and piss, but to thank the gods that I was actually alive and had not been banished to a circle of hell. When I was down in the hole it was hard not to think that they had not forsaken me. Dancing in the rain was a benediction, though every droplet felt like a needle on my bare skin.

Akira came up with the idea to leave the ship. The crew was demanding we come on deck more frequently. She said it was either us or them. We had to make a way.

Everything changed when we jumped into the ocean for the first time. Lia and the others were there to grab us. Not being able to breathe did not scare me.

Lia's face made me unafraid even though I was drowning, and she was pulling me deeper, even though she and the others who had grabbed Akira had no legs, but glimmering, iridescent tails. I wanted to ask where they got them, and could I get one too? I never wanted to go back to another ship. I longed to stay in the sea with the women who would become my sisters - and be free. And so, I did.

I jerked to my senses just in time to make my stop, and stumbled from the bus, disoriented, breathless.

#

"How you even find that place, Gem?" Akira asked.

We were sitting on her small back patio. The sun was a bright orange orb in the sky. The air smelled sweet and humid. "Seriously?"

I poked at the salad she set before me, spearing a tomato harvested from her own garden. I popped it in my mouth and bit down. The juices exploded on my tongue. I thought of Akira on her hands and knees working the earth. The vision was strange but appealing.

I decided to answer the question that she did not ask.

"I needed somewhere to stay. And, yes, I knew I could stay with you, but I wanted somewhere uncomfortable. Somewhere where I could think about what I wanted to do. What I had to do. You understand?"

Akira said nothing. She just stared at me with those doleful brown eyes and, for a moment, I was completely undone. She could've asked me anything, even to stop my plan for vengeance, and I would've said yes. Then she blinked, and the moment was gone.

She said, "I understand, I think."

Martin, Akira's husband, came in. He smiled at me shyly, but his face was a celebration when he looked at Akira. She grinned back, and it was like I had disappeared into the floor. I cleared my throat.

Martin tore his eyes away from Akira to gaze at me. "You ladies ok out here?"

I inclined my head. Akira flashed another radiant smile that Martin was all too ready to bask in. "Just fine, baby. Thank you."

An explosion of shrieks burst from the back door of the house. Akira's smallest children were a giggling pack of chubby arms and legs. They bounded towards us. Two ran for their mother, while the baby made her way to me. She stared at me, arms akimbo. "Up!" she said in her raspy toddler voice. I could not help but laugh. How long since I'd held a baby? I hadn't seen my youngest grandchild in years. He might have grandchildren of his own by now.

I kissed her cheek and she nuzzled my neck. "Bradley said you can swim like our mama. Is that for true?"

Bradley, her six-year-old older brother, tried to shush her but the news was already out.

"So, you been telling my secrets, Mr. Bradley?" I winked at him.

"Bradley, you mustn't chat so much. This is private family business!" Martin said, alarm ringing in his voice.

The young boy hung his head. "Sorry, Auntie Gem."

"Is ok, baby love. But your daddy is right," I gave Martin a small smile. He looked surprised. "There are certain things about our family others won't understand. And that means you'll always have to protect your mother. You hear me?"

Bradley nodded, solemn as if taking a vow. "I promise."

The baby tugged on my ear to pull me closer. "Will you show me your tail?" she whispered.

#

The guest bedroom was an old converted attic. From the small circle of window, I spied a sliver of water gleaming in the moonlight. I wondered how cold the water would be this time of night.

"Ok, love. You have fresh sheets and towels." Akira said patting the bed. "And here are your clothes, freshly washed," she looked at me pointedly.

After dinner she informed me that I'd done a poor job of rinsing out the clothes myself, and that I stunk like a hog. This only made me laugh. But

I handed over the only clothes I had: a t-shirt, a pair of jeans, and a scarf. She told me to shower—scrub some of the city off and gave me a nightgown.

"Thank you, sister." I crossed the room and gathered my oldest friend in my arms. "Thank you."

We stood there a few moments. She broke the embrace. "Do it," she said, her eyes glittering with tears. "Do it for our sister."

I nodded, too overwhelmed to speak.

"I will," I said when my voice returned.

"That's right, my little shark," Akira said, smiling through the tears.

She left the room and I sat on the edge of the bed, collecting my thoughts. Randall, Lia's husband, lived about a mile from here. I would walk. I stripped off Akira's nightgown—I wouldn't need it where I was going. I made my way down the stairs.

The summer night air was sultry against my bare skin, and the walk was pleasant. I smelled the nearby water, an inlet buttressed by a dirty patch of beach. The streets were empty, save the occasional stray cat out for a night's prowl. No one bothered me. If any nosey neighbors looked down through a bedroom window and spied a naked woman, dark as jet, making her way through the streets, they'd think their eyes had deceived them. By the time they looked again I'd be gone.

I turned down a dark side street and found the small cottage Randall had shared with Lia. His mother lived with him now, Akira told me. He was too sick to live alone.

I heard him before I saw him. He had some sort of cough, alternately hacking and wheezing, so loud I could hear him from the street. I made my way to the back yard. My enemy sat in a lawn chair, gripping a bottle of white rum. He took a long swig and coughed again.

He was smaller than I remembered, like a shrunken doll. In my memory, he stood tall and proud, shining next to Lia, his arm wrapped protectively around her shoulder. Grinning about how he caught himself a real-life Arawak girl. Lia must've told him some semblance of the truth about her past. He probably felt like a big man, having this pretty, penny-colored girl with straight black hair beside him. She looked young enough to be in secondary school, but she was older than his great-grandmother. This fool never understood how precious Lia was. Else he wouldn't have taken her from me like he did.

Then again, maybe I misremembered his size? I'd only met him properly once before, last year. For a while, he was just one of the many landbound men that would hang around Lia and me when we came ashore on the island. She would take him to the shallow waters by my small lean-to and get her fill of pleasure from him. Then one day she said she was getting married and going with him to the mainland. Months later, Akira sent word that Lia and her unborn baby were dead by her husband's hand.

"Randall," I called out.

His head snapped up at the sound of his name. He wore a t-shirt and boxer shorts. The skin on his arms and legs gleamed with sweat. His bleary eyes focused slowly. He leered at me greedily, drinking in my full breasts and hips.

"Well hello, darling. You look like a dream come true."

I smiled, baring my sharp, pointed teeth.

"No, no, no, no, no!" He let out a strangled gasp, frantically shaking his head.

I fought to master myself. I wanted to unhinge my jaw and snap him up right then. "Patience, Gem," I whispered, "Patience. Hey, you had to know I was coming for you, Randall! Your time has come."

Randall tried to stand but could only stagger and stumble. He tumbled back into the chair, fumbling with his bottle of rum. A wet spot spread across his crotch.

"I didn't mean to do it, I only wanted her to listen. To stop going out at night," he whined. "She had another man!"

"Stop telling stories, Randall. Lia only had eyes for you. She left everything for you. Even me."

"Then why she no stop going out, then? Why she no stay at home like a good, proper wife?" Fat tears streamed down Randall's face. "I give her everything. Everything," he sobbed.

"You couldn't give her everything. You are not the sea."

In a flash, Randall's face contorted with pure rage. He stood, pushing over the lawn chair. "My mother did warn me about you sea-devil women. But did I listen? No. And look at the heap of crosses I have! Look at my crosses!" He hiccupped and swayed. "Well, that bitch got she sea now, don't she?" He giggled, stumbling toward me.

A light flashed upstairs. A woman, Randall's mother, pulled apart curtains and stared down. I wanted to tell Randall that he was weak and pitiful and that whatever crosses he had, he had a right to bear each and every one. I wanted to tell Randall that he had no right to put his workworn hands around my sister's neck and squeeze until she collapsed. I wanted to tell Randall he was a bastard for killing his own baby. I wanted to tell Randall that it would hurt me for the rest of my days to know that, once done with Lia, he dumped her body in the sea like she was an old rotten fish. But I didn't say any of those things. I simply smiled again, showing him the rows of razor sharp teeth I usually kept hidden. Randall froze. There would be no running and certainly no more talking. I pulled him close and though he wriggled in my arms like a fish out of water, it didn't matter. My teeth sank into the skin of his neck. He tasted sour like dried sweat. But the blood and marrow below was sweet sweet like mango in high season. My jaws snapped shut and Randall fell back, convulsing and blubbering. His voice box dangled from my lips.

Randall's mother rushed out of the house, screaming. By the time she reached her dying child, I'd be down the street, headed for the sea. She'd tell her neighbors and anyone else who listened that a devil came in the night and killed her only son. And she'd be right!

Down by the sea the moonlight danced on the water. The waves in the distance sounded like Lia's laughter. I swam towards home.

CALL THE WATER

adrienne maree brown

"you, fix it! mami-o, call water, come, please fix it."

sinti wished she could fix everything for maria. the world was full of problems even water could not heal. she felt small, and young, even on this side of menopause.

maria was the oldest woman on vinewood, maybe the oldest woman in southwest detroit. her street was residential, but there were also a million little hustles happening on front porches, in back yards, on the corner. she knew every dream and failure. she had outlived everyone she had ever loved and most of those she hated. now she stood with an empty jar in her tilted tiny kitchen, every inch of her brown surface folded, pleated by life, eyes sharp and pleading.

maria was part of the fabric that had held every child in this neighborhood, had watched each one come home from the hospital, go on a first bundled stroller ride, catch their first school bus, bring home their first dates, lose their parents to age or the million cancers. maria knew how to break fevers, calm colds, bring sleep, and give warnings even teenagers would heed. maria had been steadier than sinti's own distant grandmother. the old woman knew there was magic in the child, magic in the woman.

sinti could still feel her grandmother at her back in the bathroom, drooping ancient hands cupped around sinti's small ones, as sinti had played with the water caught in the sink. she hadn't known she was doing magic, not then. she'd simply swirled her fingers, inches above the surface of water that had a slight soapy sheen to it, and the water had danced up towards her hands, tornados upside down trying to touch her. her grandmother hadn't spoken words, hadn't said sinti was special, or not special. that had come later.

now maria wanted sinti to call the water, too parched for doubt. the water woman decided to try, even though she'd never intentionally done her water work around anyone that wasn't her grandmother. it still seemed like a private act, a hallucination or a prayer or witchcraft, but she felt possibility alive in her. she stepped past maria, to the dry, useless sink.

it had been seven years since water flowed freely in this house. seven years of citizens punished for political incompetence. of bottled rations and dry nights, of maria getting used to the dusty sour smell of her own body.

sinti leaned down close to the faucet until her own warm, aged cheek went soft against its cold metallic bend. she made a wet sound that no one had ever taught her, a hushing behind her pursed 'o' lips, a sound like water flowing over a cliff far away. she brought her hand up slow, moving water lightward from a buried spring, moving through earth and salt. she slipped her left fingertips gently against the knob marked cold, following a shadow of feeling. she didn't turn it, she caressed it, letting her fingers move over the grooves, tracing the distinction between clear plastic and the silver heart of the knob, feeling that it could move, would move, once there was something to turn for.

she pulled, up and somehow out from within, pulled with her own longing, and maria's longing, and the city's longing.

and waited.
and pulled.
and waited.

and then, between breaths, the rumbling was felt more than heard. she could feel that what was in the earth was coming up, was glad to be called on.

everything in maria's kitchen was old and mismatched, backwards, mislabeled. sinti looked at the deep sink under the pale flowered curtains that might have been yellow once, at the chunky faucet, it's singular pearly knob that had a big H on it for hot water, even though only cold ever came out. sinti twisted the knob open in case maria was watching. because then, of its own will, water was thundering through the faucet. sinti moved her own mouth to it, opening, licking and then letting the freezing water fill her cheeks, swallowing as fast as she could until she couldn't take anymore. she stepped back, wiping her mouth and nodding so maria knew it was good, drinkable.

maria's mouth was a pleated oh, and she smoothed her thinning white hair back, half smug, half awed. she stepped over and put her jar under the faucet to fill. she opened a low cabinet full of empty wine bottles, mason jars, pitchers. maria pulled them out and stacked them on the counter.

sinti wanted to tell maria that there was going to be water now, that it was plentiful down in the earth. but the normal hesitation came...would this work? would it work if she wasn't around? would people be excited for her gift or burn her alive? was it illegal? the questions that kept her magic small, closed in around her. she didn't know enough about her own power to make such a commitment, so she helped maria fill every container in the house. they moved as one body through the railroad of rooms overcrowded with furniture that had been replaced but never really removed, side stepping archives of the street newsletter maria'd produced for years, a sweet gossip rag that no one read, fresh or dated. in each room there were empty containers, in each room they left water.

"let me check now," sinti said, reaching to turn off the knob. she wanted to know if the flow would be available now whenever maria wanted it. but maria grabbed her wrist.

"wait," maria said. "'others are thirsty. can we let it run?"

"it will flow now." sinti felt her feet get more solid on the ground, tipped her chin up. "don't waste it."

she found certainty in her voice that had no roots in her gut. hopefully this spell didn't rely on certainty.

she turned the knob. together the women watched the flow slow until it was mere droplets pooling at the edge of the metal, and then, finally, until it stopped.

maria looked at her, face an arched mystery. sinti felt the weight of maria's eyes on her as she turned the knob the other way, opening.
the water came out strong. they both exhaled.

she tested the knob a few times, closing, opening, closing. then she stepped back to make room for maria to try it.

it worked. it worked each time.

maria smiled at the water, then turned to smile at the water woman already slipping out the door.

she looked back and put a finger to her lips.

maria just smiled, committing herself to no secret keeping.

#

the city of detroit had sent the notice to everyone: no more private water access in homes.

that was the language the city officials used, perverting the meaning of everything.

the socialists had spent the last decade succeeding in local campaigns against privatization, in favor of public ownership of everything that was a basic human right—water, yes, and fertile land, air, health.

but the mayor had been one year into his term and emboldened by federal austerity measures to address the debt to china. he was regressive and so was the money he rode in on. water was the thing they could control that everyone would pay for.

the socialists had spent the two months between the posting and the actual water shut off trying to figure out new campaign language that explained the economics of this latest water grab.

sinti kept her distance, then and now—she agreed with them in theory but bristled with introversion at anything that required showing up to meetings and rehashing arguments she'd landed in herself when she was half this age.

she didn't need teach-ins or presentations to know that there would still be private water access in certain homes, certain neighborhoods. the enclaves with the waste-gates built up around them: boston-edison had water. indian village had water. most of midtown and downtown had water.

you had to go through extensive financial screening to determine if you were the kind of person who would be willing to pay the exorbitant fee for water flowing into your home. if you weren't, you got denied housing or evicted.

but if you made it through the gauntlet of credit checks and bank account reports, then you were awarded the kind of home where, when you arrived and turned on the faucet, it worked.

the underused pipes were sourcing from dwindling lakes further north. everything was drying up so much faster than anyone had expected. the water that came out of the working faucets needed to be filtered at least three times. the water elites created a system that involved a filter on the faucet itself, boiling the water that came out, and then pouring it into a filtered pitcher.

pouring, processing, and storing water was a weekly activity for the extremely wealthy. while there was no way to justify the limited access, it gave her some small respite to know that water wasn't an easy thing, even for them.

#

sinti never had that problem. her water never stopped, it came to her as Detroit water always had, cold and clean on the tongue.

she'd ignored the emergency-red all-cap notices in her mail, and then the signs posted on the front door of her small house. she lived in a two floor stand alone victorian, nestled and resistant between two newish apartment buildings on the gentrified east side.

her father had left her the house, paid in full. other than her life, this was the most meaningful gift she'd ever received from him. her father had painted the porch 'tokyo tangerine' and 'flamingo fuchsia' to please her mother. he gave her a hibiscus house when he couldn't give her the fidelity she craved. the rest of the structure was a sallow brown.

sinti composted organic waste into rich soil. the city fined residents for any overt form of rain catchment, but she cultivated rain-fed crops and fruit trees in the backyard overlooked by neighbors in the apartment buildings, who tried to be nice, to swallow suspicion. they failed. she was strange, always had been. but she smiled at them when she remembered to.

two blocks south got her to the water's edge, where she could walk the mile along the river to her boat most of the year. three blocks directly away from the water got her to the bus line.
before the water shutoffs, people loved to go on her boat excursions, to feel the rhythm of water underneath them, to see the parts of the city that still had access to electricity explode into color at sunset.

that was before the mysterious wave, before the crisis all the time everywhere. now no one trusted the water.

but she got by.

the city wanted to make sure everyone knew the exact date when private water access was ending, for them to feel their power. but sinti had felt something else, like the water knew her and would find a way to her.

a decade earlier she had watched water change the face of the city with impossible waves that rose up from the river and swallowed many of the colonizers. then the water moved as if by its own direction, now the water's absence was changing the city again.

#

the day of water shutoffs had come and gone, and at first she'd thought they had failed to shut hers off, that they hadn't reached her little block yet. but then sinti began to notice the sort of signs that never get printed on paper, the indicators that her running water was a very rare exception: people with homes began to look like the homeless, those lifelong detroiters who had been pushed out of every part of the city, slowly, over years—dirty, dusty, ashy. everyone smelled like a body gone sour, even when they tried to cloak it with perfumes and deodorants.

on fridays when recycling was picked up, a new pale blue bin was added just for water containers. they rolled out a new fine for selling water that wasn't bottled by the city, said it was for the safety of the citizens, that only they could guarantee quality water. then they introduced another fine for mixing water jugs in with the rest of the recyclable containers—the city had to gather the containers back to distribute their precious overpriced water.

her neighbors were regularly seen carrying jugs of water home from the nearest gas station. the stations now distributed water that cost more than gas. you could bring your own containers, jugs, bottles, or buy it prepackaged in plastic that was getting recycled over and over.

she'd quickly realized that if she didn't fit in, she would become a target. she'd kept personal cleaning to a minimum, let the dust build up on her face, the black soot settle under her fingernails. she'd cut her short hair even closer when she couldn't handle the dirt in it.

at least once a week she made sure she was seen with a jug. she let her eccentricity see to the rest

#

but maria told.

of course she did. just her closest friends, but every closest friend has other closest friends. secrets are just a matter of proximity and connection.
the water woman couldn't explain what had happened, that she had called up a deeper water, an abundant water, a freshwater sea under the earth. maria

couldn't either, she just told people that, like any problem, it could be fixed.

who was she to deny anyone water? once a day they would show up on her sorrel-colored porch, sometimes familiar, then, more often, strangers who had heard of her from someone else who had heard: she knew a way to make the water run, clean and free.

each time, her task was easier, the water came faster. she perfected her method. sinti would get under the sink, letting her soft belly and raised knees fill the cabinet door so people couldn't see what she was doing. she took to carrying a wrench hooked in the belt of her coveralls. she hoped people would think she knew some way to turn the wrench and change the source of all life.

that would be easier to explain than what was happening.

#

when the administrator came to the door, he wore a strange uniform, his beige pant legs gathered into a white boot scuffed with tar. the outfit was bright and militant, as if he was running undercover ops at the taj mahal. he stepped into her house. she didn't point out to him that there were no shoes allowed inside.

"ma'am. name's maxwell. yours?"

she blinked at him.

"ok. fine. ok, i am going to cut straight to the point here. it's implausible, but - you running a black market for water?"

she felt her body chill a bit. she expected a fine for turning on what the city wanted off. at the turn of the century she had done a direct action to turn on heat in her cousin's building when the city shut it off; she and a friend had gotten caught and set on payment plans for disobedience. the judge had seemed personally offended that she, a black girl, would take anything so freely.

maxwell had the same perplexed, hurt look on his face. how dare she?

"excuse me?"

"have you been stealing water, ma'am?"

"no. i have not." this felt true. how could anyone steal water? maxwell the administrator was blond, his hair long and a bit greasy. perhaps he also had rationed water.

"well we've been watching you. we know you're doing something." he paused to swallow a burp, his bland eyes looking all over her house as if she was hiding a magic water machine in plain sight. "my bad, indigestion. anyway, lying won't help you now. just come clean and i will work to get you reduced charges."

she stood up and moved towards her front window.

across the street was maria's dilapidated building, boards in some of the windows where people had left to look for water. the old woman stood wiry and attentive with a small group of gray friends on the sidewalk. that ancient woman felt things, knew things. had probably stood there watching her father slip their lives from sweetness to suffering.

now maria started, as if she felt the attention. when maria looked up, spotting sinti standing there, she got other people's attention. the water woman recognized them as neighbors whom she had helped. maria punched a fist her way.

maria was so small. the group was so small.
the administrator was small.
so was she.

the city was small really, on this planet, itself small in the universe. only the water was vast.

but so many cities had no water left. so many people were gone to thirst. even detroit, once the forever freshwater city, was drawing on resources that would be gone in another decade.

the species was not going to make it far on politics, even on science.
"tell me what you're doing. tell me what source of water you've found." the administrator did that move where he stepped in front of her, to dominate her line of sight. he had a concave air about him, collapsed and indignant in the tight space between her and the window.

she looked up at him briefly, and then over him, through him, to maria and her neighbors.
why was she being so stingy with her magic?
why was she keeping this good water from anyone?

"i'll show you." she pivoted away from him. she was going to go in the kitchen, but then as she took a step, she realized she didn't need to. she turned and stepped around the useless man. she walked out onto her porch, where she could see maria, where she knew maria could see her.

she closed her eyes and spread her hands until her palms were wide, opened to the earth.

she called the water. she pulled.
the peak of the mountain was the core of the earth, the spring was running

down, cascading up, pouring down the mountain, ascending to the world.
she could see it in the darkness behind her eyelids, blinding cold blue water
pouring up through black dirt, spreading like fingers.

she let her eyes flicker open, and saw maria mimicking her, all the grey hairs
across the street, mimicking her, hands open to the earth, shuddering together.
"ma'am!"

her body began to shake like waves, like there was a turbulent sea storm
inside of her.
"ma'am that's not necessary. none of this hoodoo is helping your case here."
she felt the water as close as blood in her veins, rushing in every direction,
too fast to comprehend. her body could feel the landscape of the city, flowing
under southwest so powerfully it went further, water mains under michigan
avenue as it regressed from modern pavement to cobblestone and back
again, flowing into gentrified corktown, up the cass corridor to the north
end, spread far west, far east, beyond the paltry public transportation, under
the streets that no longer had lights, where the popo never answered the 911
calls, where the fire department was only ever in time to douse the ashes, the
parts of the city that myopic government had tried again and again to shed
or deny. she flowed towards every place there was a heartbeat, into water
fountains, bursting up fountains in hart plaza, bell isle, clark park. the water
was clean, it was cold, and it was flowing through detroit now, raging up and
into pipes. she heard screams of surprise and joy begin to echo across the city
landscape. she opened, and opened, feeling pleasure in this undoing of her
solitary self.

she was the blue in the dark.

she was the water

that called

THE ANCESTOR ABIODUN TELLS ME ABOUT THE TIME SHE FORGOT OSUN

Excerpt from *The Ariran's Last Life: A Memory Work*

MARIA OSUNBIMPE HAMILTON ABEGUNDE

Osunbimpe Abegunde. To forget your primary *orisa* is like walking with your head in your hands, beating it with a rock, twisting the eyes back so that they cannot look at you in pity or see anything. Those were the days I wandered in the woods by myself, talking to the river that flowed past my small house. Other women feared me. Whenever I came close to one of their men he lost his head and found the river, never to return. At night, I could hear voices of men calling me to release them from the devil in the water, the one with the hot yellow tail, gossamer hair, small breasts, and talons.

Where did I exist at this time in my history of many lives lived over centuries? In a small clearing where a house and garden once sat. The house was built against the trees. The trees that did not support her guarded her. Only the children came. Sometimes their mothers would walk as far as the row of trees and release their hands so they could run to me. Tia, they would call, and I would come out with breads and biscuits. Their mothers would run quickly if they caught my eye. Before the sun set, they would return and call for their children from behind the trees.

In one of my many lives, I forgot Osun, but she did not forget me. She controlled my desire by giving me others. Desire is that touch in your belly, your feet, in the back of your heart that whispers possibilities. What I desired most was a child. Even knowing that she would be sold. Or worse. I desired a child. Someone who would know what I knew. Someone who could comfort my loneliness, remind me that I would not be forgotten. Someone I could teach what my mother had taught me, initiate into the secret ways of the Memory Keeper. I thought that this was how I would fulfill my destiny.

When I gave up Osun my desires became dreams. The difference you wonder? Desires are tangible. You can touch desire, see it, breathe it, allow it to lick the small folds of skin under your arms, behind your knees. The places where memories hide in the dark to surprise you when you bend and lift. Dreams? These are the things you hide, can never touch. I began to dream my desires.

It is a penance this. Deny the self what she desires most and turn one's own self into illusion. Discover that and tell yourself that all these beautiful children who call you tia are illusions. Your desire cannot be fulfilled and so you begin to kill it. It is a good thing that Osun rules me or the children would have gone the way of the men. I would not have been able to live long with their crying every day and night from the river flowing by the house, sometimes spitting rocks into my window, overflowing into my garden as if she wanted me to remember that she knew what I had done.

I tried to kill Osun by denying my desire. The children stopped coming then. My breads and cakes would crumble in their hands. Worms would writhe from the flour and enter my skin. My desire turned against me the more I believed that Osun had tricked me by showing me what I could not have. I did not understand that she was giving me comfort. Giving me another path to transform myself. It was not her fault that I could not have children. That I could be reborn again and again through others but no one could be reborn through me.

Did my father know this when the *ebo,* the sacrifice, of my life was made? That there would be no one to prove that he and I had existed? Who traces back to me? No one. I trace back to myself. No mothers will mourn for me the way my mother did that day, her back towards me, tearing her clothes.

Osun was not part of that bargain so she could not stop it. All she could do was make it better. I know now that Ye-Ye was a good mother to me, keeping me folded in her love.

374

I missed the children so badly that one day I ventured past the trees to see them. No one would look at me but one little girl. She was unafraid of my wildness, the way my hair wound down my back, how the cloths I covered myself with were strips because not even the man of the plantation would buy me clothes. I made do with what I had, what I could negotiate with others at market.

But this little girl, she would come to me and I would tell her stories and she listened. She stayed with me until she was taken some place else. Afterwards, I was alone for a long time. I didn't even know if people still lived at the plantation house.

Dreaming. And what did I dream? That one day I will return to the place you call Africa. Perhaps the dream is for you. Or is it your dream?

One day, I will return with this body to Senegal, Benin, and every other place from where I was stolen.

I will know what to do when I get there.

It won't be as mundane as falling to my knees to kiss Earth. Or entering the castles and keening until all the village weeps with me and sends the priest out to get me.

No, it won't be as expected as carrying a small pot with earth from the cells where I was once held. After I have emptied the bones of those who asked to be returned. No.

I will know what to do when I return with the visions that have plagued me for centuries, but especially these last years.

My husband will return with me. The one I loved so long ago so deeply that he was sold away.

Our children will bury me, but not before the wind rises up in me and walks me to the bottom of the ocean, and I have answered each of my family in their first tongues. These are the children, like you, Osunbimpe who have answered the call to carry me in your Spirits, to take memories that are not your own into your cells and weave them into blood and sinews until you cannot tell what belongs to me, to you.

You will not fold my bones in woven cotton from the araba. You will not call Eleda, Mama Iyami before I have returned leading my family back to the small houses that once housed them. Oh how I have missed them and the thought of touching them, smelling the air on their whitened, smooth bones makes me ask that this life be hastened.

Are you not yet ready Osunbimpe to take up my burden of memory? Are you not ready to make this journey back with me? I am so tired, child. So tired of waiting no where, listening to your questions. Dreaming you dreams. Watching you – how do you say? "Process" what you already have and know. All you need to do is say yes to me and open the other spaces in yourself that you shield from my entry. Is that so hard to ask—just for once that even you would let your interminable reasoning be overtaken by your desire to know all, to step into the burning bush?

But, I know it is not the time for Olokun to rise, for the Iyami to churn the Atlantic with their fingers, hot with the branding irons that once touched our skins.

Oh, yes, I will sing as you have never heard anyone sing before. First you will think it is the sand rubbing together, then you will think it the water separating, rearing back. You might even think it is the wind in the leaves picking about palm and coconut, regrowing dende. But no, it will be me. Wave cresting, foaming, meeting shore. Watch my feet form from sea weed and gaze at how perfectly my toes are formed from my tail. Me and each piece of sand behind me shaking our tails until they are feet, singing ourselves into being until we are tornado.

There is no place to hide. There will be no place to hide. After we speak – and this will take years to do – bury me then. Wrap my body in white damask silk. Build a monument at the base of the castle where nothing has ever grown. Bury me there. Mark that headstone with my name so all will know that I returned to fulfill my destiny and to return Destiny to the Truth.

Each year, my children will water the baobabs that grow from my soul.

Do you know how Osun saved me?

The woman was unafraid to walk past the trees. She walked past the trees with a basket of fruit and stood at my door. *I am needing your help*, she said. *I dream of you at night and hear you singing under my pillow. The women say you know how to make salve to heal all wounds. I am needing you to heal my wound here.* She took her hand and placed it between her legs. *And here.* Then on her breasts. All the time I am looking at her from the window. *I am needing you. African. Can't be nothing else. Out here in the middle of nothing.* She looked around then through the window to find me. When I did not answer, she said. *William said to tell you I be the one you looking for but not how you imagine it.*

I was afraid to move then. And she refused to move. We remained like that for what seemed a long time, long enough for the sun to change direction. Me, standing against the wall listening to her breathing. She sitting on my stoop, her basket of fruit between her feet. She picked up a pear and began eating it.

What does it mean to love a woman at Osun's river? What does it mean to be saved by a woman you don't even know, have no cause to remember?

It means learning to love yourself in places you did not know you had. In cells long singed close, cut in half. It means finding a way to love even when you don't want to.

I opened the door slowly and watched her finish the pear and wipe the juice on her skirt hem.

I don't bite, she said. *Though hear tell it, you eat up everything.*

She turned to face me as I closed the door. I can't say that she was beautiful, just barely pretty. Pecan-colored, with short dark brown hair that had a little white at the temple. Her mouth was like a plumb and as she licked the juice off her lips the cracked bits dissolved as they soaked in her saliva. She had one oddly roving blue eye. Yes, one eye only. Where the other eye should have been there was instead a sewn down flap that used to be her eyelid. Without thinking, I moved to touch the crescent-shaped scar that still revealed where a needle had entered and exited the skin on the upper part of her right cheek bone. She stepped back and slapped my hand away.

I don't need no healing there. That my one good eye.

I looked at her for a moment then laughed. It took a moment to hear that she was laughing as well.

No one ever laugh before when I say that. We gonna be alright you and me. She picked up the basket, pushed me aside with her elbow and walked into the house.

For a moment, I stood outside, listening to the echo of that laughter coming out of the river, bouncing off the trees. I had not laughed in so long, not even to myself, that it felt strange this sound that had end. It seemed that the earth had absorbed it and refused to let it go. Just wanted to hold on to it so she could play it back in the middle of the night when we were all sleeping.

I needed to tell her nothing. When I walked in, she had set the fruit in the table's center and had taken the flour, eggs, and salt and placed them on the table.

The children say you used to make good bread. Days when they hungry they talk about you.

Are they hungry often?

Only when the Madam get mad. These days she seem to be mad a lot.

So, you have come to make bread for the children because no one will come here. I sat down and watched her sift the flour into a large clay bowl.

Yes. But I come because I am needing you to heal me.

She removed her hands from the flour, stepped back, and lifted up her skirts, gray on top of white both under a brown apron. *I am needing you to heal me. The women said you know how.*

She stood in front of me, her head looking over me, waiting. She was accustomed to being inspected.

Put down your skirts, I told her and returned outside to breathe.

The scent of her. Old sweaty boots soaked in camphor, drying in salt and dying leaves. Her skirts were perfumed to contain it.

On the ship, I had awakened to the *oyinbos* blowing smoke in my face. Inside me. I do not remember what happened after the first or second one rolled off my body. I only remember blood being wiped on my breasts and burning inside me. Not from the hot candles they would place inside me later. No, the burning from them entering and entering. For me, so small at that time, it was like the branches of trees covered with thorns each time one heaved up, back, out, in. They did not wash these men. Who would want me after this one? But there was another. Sweat rolling down his body on top of me into my mouth as I began screaming.

This was before they had cut out my tongue and cut it again in half in front of me. I think now that as horrible a sound my own voice was – the moans and screams seemingly endless even as I rested. As horrible as the sound was, it was the sound of my own voice, above the waves beating the ship. Above their laughter, muffled under their hands and lips.

They had laughed. When I tried to close my eyes, one stood over my head, dug his fingers into my eyelids and held my eyes open. Then another placed his *okó* on top of my head, the tip into my eyes, then shoved it into my mouth.

This memory rose and fell in me like the waves when we traveled. I could not contain it and so I ran from the porch to the nearest tree and touched it, threw myself against it, until the nausea subsided. But not the tingling and burning of hot wax dripping down my skin while the flame scorched me. Between my legs, deep inside me. I wanted to pee. Needed to pee to get it all out what had been rubbed and burned into my cells. So much of it that not even *abikus* wanted to be born through me. That is the ultimate sadness of my life. Not even spirits born to die want to come through me.

I clung to the tree and placed my feet on the rocks I had placed around it. This was the place I made *ebo*. A big old araba. Cotton. I stepped inside the circle and held the tree tired. It was fitting that I be inside it now. This life I was *ebo*. Had been sacrificed without asking permission and blessing to be used as such. Even a goat had more privilege than I.

The door swung open. *It don't do no good to always remember, you know. I'm good at forgetting. You should learn how.* And she returned inside.

Lana. That's what they had named her at birth. *My mama was like you. Old. African. Her mama, too. Not me. Born here. Live with mama till she die. And when she die. Well, when she die she come to me and tell me*

things I shouldn't know. Some days, her mama come as well. It's like I got
all them and me in my head, my whole body.

We are sitting at the river shelling peas from my little garden.
Thirteen days now and no one has come looking for her. The river remains
quiet except for brief moments of spitting out rocks. I cannot look at her
without thinking of the woman who was with me in the castles those first few
months. It is a better image than the men. A better feeling.

When mama die, I was washing clothes in the yard. But, it's as
if I could hear her calling me, then pulling me to her. I put down the pail
and start walking towards the house. The big man who watch us work, he
yell: Get back over there. *But I can't. I feel this hand pushing on my chest,*
my head, and I hear my mama's voice inside my head telling me how to
use rootworm to kill what the white people eat. So much stuff in my head
so loud that I don't hear the horse even after it kick me down and the man
is beating me. When I fall my skirts fall up. The first place he can touch is
inside my legs. He don't stop, and I stop breathing. But only for a moment.
My mama and grandmamma say it gonna be all right. Ugly, but all right.

When I wake up, my mama dead. Aunt Shel is washing me while
Delia and Mar holding me down. The man, the one who bought me, like to
smell me and touch me up, he beat him like he beat me. White people can't
get as good as they give. He die and they bury him out in the woods. Didn't
have no family.

Her eyes do not stop counting peas. Her fingers do not stop
separating the rotting from the still fresh. There are no tears in the blue. I
wonder if the sewed lid contains them. There is no more story for today. That
is how we go. She tells me a story and I listen. At the river. The river wants it
all. I listen. Today I tell her:

I will show you that you are not alone.

We shell the remaining peas as if it is all we have to do. And, when we
are done, we help each other up. We gather our bowls in our hands and walk
back to the house in silence.

A woman saved me once. From dying alone and remembering things

I needed to forget. It is different with women. The loving. At least with this woman it was different. In the house, we put the bowls on the table. Standing where she had stood the first day she came to me, I lifted my skirts, blue on top of green, white apron. She came towards me and pushed them back down. Untied the apron, folded it in half and carefully placed it on the chair. She untied my skirts, removed the big white blouse I always wore. Then I did the same for her, untying, folding, placing. Breathing.

I was very young, I say, younger than you are now. I did not know what it would mean in my life, how it would mark me forever. How I would cry at night for even the ones who die to come. Just so I would know a life-giving pain. I did not know I would desire children so deeply that eventually I would devour them with my sadness.

We stood looking at the other as one looks at her reflection in water for the first time. Men do not look at you the same way, without desire or malice. She walked behind me and ran her fingers along the deep scars on my shoulders.

It is how and why I was born into the world.

My grandmamma had some just like that on your shoulder. My mama too. She say that if you the first to remember, that's how they get the memory into you.

We stand like this, too, for a long time. She behind me, breathing onto my shoulder. Me, waiting. Or perhaps she is waiting. And when I think this she turns me around.

Where do I look? The eye that is blue or the one that is missing.

They say a witch cursed me before I was born. When the man on the horse beat me, he beat every place he hate, every place the man who say he own me love.

I keep looking into that one blue eye as if I will find the river flowing into the ocean, the ocean carrying the ship that carried me. That somehow, somehow, time will move backward, and I will step off that ship, walk into the compound and hear my father say: *Forgive us. We did not know.* And I will be small again instead of this woman scarred and marked with no children to tell my stories.

She has had children. The stretches on her belly tell me so. But the mark of the knife. A difficult birth.

All gone, Lana says. *Don't know who or where they are.*

I rest on her belly. To go below it is to know what I don't want to know but feel. That is where the tip of the whip stripped the hair from her body. No more will grow to cover the four-inch scar that begins there and winds itself midway down her lips, also scarred inside and out. A smooth mound that looks full of pus but is hard when I touch it.

She does not move.

Does it hurt?

Only when I dream at night. Or think of my mama dying.

I place my right palm over this wound, and she opens her legs a little. So much heat escaping. It is not possible for a body to go on living with so much heat leaving it.

You see. I knew you would know what to do.

I leave her standing and go out into the yard. No one will come to visit so my nakedness will not startle or shame. Under the house there are pails and I find one that can carry enough water for a washing.

The river is silent, as if she knows what I am about to ask and do. And she refuses me this moment by saying nothing, not even spitting a rock. *It is not for me I say into the water. It is for the one you sent me.* Still, I know this means nothing. To do the work, I must make my own peace with the river, the sea, the scars born in both. I have not entered water easily since I fell into it, outside the castle, when I was forced to get into the boat that would take us to the ships. I have cursed all waters since then, damning them for not rising up and saving us.

I sit at the edge of the water. Does it matter what Osun will claim from me when all has already been sacrificed? I enter, right foot first, and walk until I am shoulder deep— who knew this little river ran so. I walk until I can no longer feel the bottom, until I am forced to hold my breath as my head disappears.

At the bottom of the river you expect to find sand, shoals, creatures, and the dead. But you don't expect to find yourself or the river. What the river wants from you is everything. Everything you never wanted revealed. That is what the river does, hold Her mirror to you. She offers it to you whole, only, you see shards. The current does not push the shards together. The sand does not smooth edges down. You must grab the pieces of the mirror, cut yourself deep, and bleed for a long time. Until you nearly bleed out. That is how it goes.

What did I find at the bottom of the river?

What did She say to me?

Wash myself clean. Of all the bits of rope that had never been removed from my wrists. Wash myself clean. Of all the metal fired into me, in wounds that had never been salted clean. The first one at the entrance to the sea, when I pushed so hard into the iron that the *oyinbo* had struggled to remove it from me. And when they did free it, parts of the iron remained in my skin, in my bone. That is why the women had to work so hard to heal me. The long nights shackled in the castle and the woman who screamed.

What did She say to me?

Wash myself clean. Of the wood that splintered into my neck each time they unlocked it. Wash myself clean of the lock and the key, so rusted by sea and salt, they had to be broken with a rock. What is it like to have your head locked in a wooden vise that leaves you only enough space to inhale half a breath before choking you? It is the smallness of a mother's birth canal, jagged and rotting, around her child's head and throat as she exits and enters the world.

Always these people wanted you to remember that they—and only they—

controlled your life and death. But how can you remember what you have never known, what you have never experienced before? They did not control my life or death. That was Olodumare. The Mothers. Me. The river that flows into the sea. They wanted us to remember that we were their creations with no past and a future tethered to their pasts and presents. But they were wrong.

Osunbimpe, I walked into the river, walked down into Her. Who knew she was so deep, and who knew that I could breathe so effortlessly beneath her skirts? The sand and rocks dug into the soles of my feet and the warmth that was on the very top of the water was not to be found in her center, under the ripples. Neither were the men who had never returned to their families. There were no bones, no cloths, no fish even. Only silence.

I came up for air and found that I was still alone. The sun was all about me and there were birds. But, the woman had not exited the house. She could be sleeping or waiting. I had not said where I would go. I had left hurriedly, intent on getting to the river.

I inhaled deeply and submerged myself again. There, in front of me, towards the back, where the roots of another big araba descended, was a large rock and what appeared to be a cave. A woman, or what I thought was a woman sat there, a pale yellow gossamer veil floating around her hair and shoulders. Her feet touched the sand, but a heavily scaled tale wrapped the rest of her body. Her eyes were the color of carnelian, and her hair black with white at the temples. Her skin was the color of black coral.

"Not what you expected, Abiodun?" she asked me then began laughing so hard that the vibration lifted me above the water and I emerged gasping for air. After a few minutes of breathing deeply, I inhaled, and entered again.

"Not what you expected." And she rose from the rock and walked with the tail behind her, sometimes folding over her legs so at one moment it appeared that she was walking, and at another she appeared as if she were being lifted and propelled. Another as if she were swimming with the small fish around her. As she moved, the roots of the tree clung to her.

I opened my mouth to respond and she put up her right hand and said. "Do not speak. Look. See. My hands."

In the center of her right hand there was a labyrinth intricately drawn with yellow roses at the entrances. In her left, there was a large spiral carved into the palm as if it had been mistaken for stone. In the center of both were small mirrors, and there were small mirrors on the tip of her fingers.

I gazed in the mirror of both hands and saw nothing. Not even my reflection.

"This is what you will become if you do not wash yourself clean, Abiodun. How you do this is for you to determine, but you must do so before you can move on."

She began laughing again and I was pushed to the surface. I found myself floating on my back. I came to my feet and walked to the edge where I had left the pail. I walked back to the center with it and dipped as deeply as I could, placed the bucket on my head, balanced between my hands and got out of the water. Wash myself clean.

Basil and rosemary together will purify and wash away and protect one from evil spirits. I gathered these from my garden. Roses. Roses and the fruit they bear will heal the skin of scars before they form. Heal a woman's rotting or burning womb and the growths that surface there. I added it all together in the water, rubbing them until they became a small pulp of leaves and stems and roots.

It was not true that I saw nothing. I saw nothing in the mirrors, but I saw much when I looked only at the labyrinth's path.

When I returned to Lana, I was holding the pail. The river had said to wash myself clean in whatever manner I wanted. She did not say that someone else could not wash me. That is what mirrors do, no, reflect you to yourself and others? I brought the pail to Lana, then took another from beneath the house and returned to the river. Then another. I did this until I had placed ten pails on the back porch where I kept the big tub for washing clothes. It was not like my father had built for my mother. No, this was a big wooden wash tub, with the skinny slats jutting up. It was big enough to curl comfortably for twenty minutes before my legs and back cramped. I gathered more herbs and leaves and when all was ready, I turned to Lana who was already standing before me in one of the old white towels I kept to cover the floor when bathing.

We do together. Last night, my mama dream to me and say that the women who wash you before you arrive here, they love you. Not like

*your own mama when she wash you, but they wash you to remember.
Not to forget. So what's the point. No, they wash you at the boats so you
remember. Today, we do together so we both forget some things. For a little
while. You ain't never forgetting nothing.*

I looked at this woman before me and undressed myself before her,
the trees. The river on the other side began laughing, and I felt the first pain
surfacing in my heart before my hands reached for the tin cup I used to pour
water over my head. Lana reached up and began unbraiding my hair. She
took down my plaits and let the loose hair settle on my body so that I was
costumed with my own locks. I gently rubbed the herbs in her hair, then
down her neck and shoulders in a sweeping motion. I took another handful
and continued down the front of her body, sweeping away every hand and
whip's tongue that had touched her. Swept it down to the earth where the
earth would take it and transform it. I turned her around and did the same to
her back, her buttocks, the backs of her knees, her feet and heels. She lifted
her arms up and held them out to allow me to do her sides. And then she
lifted her feet so I could clean beneath them. Then, she filled her hands with
herbs and turned to me.

It is not the same you know: being washed for purification and
being washed for love. The first is deliberate, a searching out of things to
be rooted out of you. The second is caressing and soothing of all the things
found, allowing them to fall or surface where they might. I could not tell the
difference with Lana. She washed my hair with such keen attention to every
strand as if she were pulling out my hair, and the next moment, it was as if
she were massaging every loose end back into the strand home. She brushed
my body with a force that stinged and then followed the stinging with her
breath blown through the leaves. She then poured water over my head in
small amounts as if she were afraid she would drown me.

You go into the tub first she said. And walked me over to the tub,
lifted my feet as I leaned on her shoulder. I sat. She poured more water
over me, then left suddenly. She returned with milk and honey. And poured
them into the water. I used to burn all over my body. As if the fire that had

been placed inside me struggled every minute to leave. I could feel the small pieces of metal hitting my lungs, touching my heart until I became so afraid of breathing, moving, dancing. When the milk and honey hit the water, I was cool. Cooler than I had ever been, even in the river much earlier.

In the river, you don't expect it to suddenly heat at the bottom where it is coolest, not where streams flow beneath and through rocks from other streams. It is supposed to be cool there. But in this river, the bottom began to boil as I entered deeper. No voices, no bodies, no missing men, or children. This does not mean that spirits are not there. What throws out the rocks when I walk by? What whispers as I pass by? Or who? In the river, you never expect to find the Mother of the river herself. Surely she has other places to be. There must be a source. Why would She be here in my river? Yes, I considered the river mine and after so long of living alone I did not know how to live without Her.

Osun would not allow me to abandon Her. True Love is like that, is it not? Lets you go, be free, but does not allow you go so far if leaving means you will die. At the bottom of the river, the water seemed to reflect me wherever I turned. The Mother of the river was there, Her mirrors reflecting nothing and everything of and to me. Her hands labyrinth and stone, river and reflection. What could I do but look into the water and cry. What did it matter that I could not separate my tears from the water around me? Except for the saltiness in my mouth, I had no way to know what was the river and me, and after a while there was no separation. The river is like that, too: All that I am is in Her, part of Her. She does not separate Her pain from my own.

"Abiodun," she had called, her gossamer flowing towards me like tentacles. "One day, you must come to me fully. You will know what it means to be whole. To be without fear. To be at peace. Do you not want that?"

That skin, so smooth and black like coral. Her arms reached out to me and from where she sat it seemed as if they stretched without her moving, but she was sitting next to me on the right side, holding me. In her left hand she held sand and before I could protest she knelt before me and began to scrub my feet.

"Do not worry about breath, Abiodun. Time. There is no time here. No air. That you need them here, this moment, is deception. Illusion. What you believe is what you know. But, I am what you need. There is only water and water is all you need now."

To be washed by Love is different than to be washed for love. To be washed by Love is to give permission to yourself to surrender to something you cannot name, do not understand. Yes, after so long—because by now I knew how long I had really lived—I wanted peace. For a moment, I allowed myself to surrender under her hands, the hot sand scrubbing the soles of my feet, then the palms of my hands. Then my back. In water, the touch of things is lighter, not as hard, and the pieces of rock in the sand, the shards of mirror in her hand did not scrape or make me bleed.

When I had been young, I would sometimes try to climb into the tub of my mother. She would pretend she did not see me, and when she discovered me she would feign surprise then pull me in by my shoulders. We would laugh so much that the aunties would humph and step out and ask, "What is all this noise, this hour of day? Do you have nothing better to do than waste water and light instead of working?"

One night, when the moon was half full, I spied my mother and father together in the tub, she washing his feet as if he were a baby, holding them in her hands, small circles at his ankle, separating his toes. That is to be washed for love. Between the toes as if there is nothing else to be washed on your body at that time. I knew this once. Before my tree was cut down and I was forced to bathe where one man could see me.

This was different. To be washed by Love does not imply gentleness. It does not mean it will not hurt. Had the river been sea I would have burned and scarred. But here, in the river, at the bottom, there was only warmth, the type that suicides discover when they have let themselves bleed into warm tubs.

Oh the things I wanted to forget but could not. Lana would not understand this for a long time. It was more than washing my skin and body. To forget meant unweaving the skin that covered my bones and untwining the nerves and sinews, dissecting the cells where the threads of memory had pulled tight. It was more than bathing in milk and honey.

It was first scraping away skin that had crusted, risen up where screaming had not escaped. It was removing centuries of dead away until only decades remained. Osun knew this. She was not there at the bottom of the river to unknot me, to unweave what had been given to me to hold, story, remember. She was there to help me forget what I believed hurt me most. Afterwards, under Lana's hands, I would remember what really pained me.

"Illusion," Osun had whispered. "The mirror reflects what you want to see. Distorts what you do not so that only you can un-imagine what wakes you at night." She said this as the waves washed by so I was uncertain if she spoke. It seemed her lips never moved but I heard her. What she said after this I do not remember. There was no laughter. I awoke on the dirt beneath the araba, my pail filled with water.

MISSISSIPPI MEDUSA

ELLE L. LITTLEFIELD

Part I: Groundwork

Reeva Lee Walker was a baby only the Lord could love, born with a veil and two sharp teeth like a cottonmouth snake. Scared every shitting breath out the young midwife, who shortly thereafter passed out and conked her head on the nightstand. Somehow this shaky girl had managed to breathe through the birth itself—granted with some struggle. Even as Shan Lee, the expectant, had sat up straight and practically pulled the babe down from her womb unassisted. But when the midwife, Sistuh Perryman, reached over to peel that film off her face—and a Baby Reeva Lee, stead of crying, stretched back like a cat exposing them teeth—then, the midwife gasped, reeled back, conked her head, and exhaled what came to be the last sane breath of her life.

Thank God this baby's aunt was there, but just a child herself—a smart little one they called Miss Poca. Poca had skipped her next best part of church—the spaghetti after—to make it to BJ's and see Sistuh Perryman catch the baby. The midwife was coaching her youngest girl, Patty, who Poca sat next to on the mourner's bench on Sundays. Tall, red, freckled girl Coreen called *touched*, known to be a real brain with facts and numbers. Patty was 'sposed to be setting up the birthing table, while Poca waited in the kitchen for old Sistuh to call. She had just determined to fix herself a snack, when she heard somebody crashing down a lamp and flew in to see. There she witnessed a tangle of bloodied sheets and young Patty splayed out, hugging a tall, brass lamp along the floor. The elder was making her way round the bed to see. Patty's face full of red, roller-set curls dripping blood over her eye. Poca, all but ten and having seen what she took for a body, got the mind to run tell it. She didn't wait for nobody's instructions.

The time to her house from BJ and Shan Lee's whatn't but three minutes driving and seven on feet. Five, if you ran. And Poca ran straight out the door, down the drive, and round the curve to get out to the road. A choir of frogs ratcheted up in waves as she passed through. Cicadas buzzed over her head watching. Trees leaned in. Buzzards called. All of them sent up their warning.

Miss Poca found her mama, Coreen, in her slip watering plants on the porch. And her old daddy leaned against his truck chewing tobacco. Just home from church. Bouncing and panting she told what she had seen. "Mama, Patty bust her head, and she ain't wakin up!" she hollered, bursting outta her skin. Her shiny eyes thrilled with fear and gangly, walnut legs moving in place.

"Oh Loord!" her mama stopped sweeping, started making the sign of the cross. "I knew sum'in was gone happen bad, today."

"Awww, shiit." Her daddy frowned, shook his head. He threw his hands and spit tobacco on the grass. "Nih, how the fuck dat happen, Poca?"

"Ion know, Daddy. I just heard somebody clangin and bangin—fallin down, so I ran up in there."

"And, what you see?"

"Daddy, some ah everythang. You 'ont wanna know." She raised her eyebrows.

"I knew they shoulda had dat damn baby at the hospital. I told Hayward dat dis morning," went Coreen.

Poca carried on. "Shan Lee had the baby on the bed, and Patty was on nuh flo' bleedin."

"*The baby*?" went Coreen. "Ween been gone a hour! See, I dreamed about a bad storm last night, so I knew sum'in bad was gone happen."

"Well," Poca said, they both looked fine to her. From what she could tell, the baby was nursing already.

In forming words to tell it, Poca saw Patty whatn't dead at all. Was probably wake by now. The thought hit her like an electric jolt.

"Well, run on back, Poca," her mama relieved her. "I see you got dem damn aints in ya paints. Imma thow my dress back on, an' we gone pull down the way and get Pastah."

Her daddy complained, "You thank he done made it, Co-reen, it's barely pass three".

"What I thank is, Hayward, we gone pull on down there and see." She swung open the door, let it slam at her back. Hayward took his cue, made his way to start the pickup, and Poca turned and flew back out the drive to her brother's.

BJ Walker was working his last of twelve weekends at the penal farm up the river in Shelby County. A kind sentence, the judge offered, being that he claimed he had a baby on the way. His was a luxury modular home planted with pearlbush and sweetspire, claiming his quarter of the two-acre property. A matte-grey trailer installed a week before the wedding, cattycorner to Shan Lee's six-room inheritance. *An altar house*, Coreen called it, the *Lee Family Museum*. But in her private mind, Poca called it the dead house. Next to the well made of bricks and surrounded by heavy stones. Where both Shan Lee's people, who passed inside a month of the ceremony, had been spread and sprinkled in remembrance of their living. A slab of covered concrete, between the dead house and BJ's, open on both ends, connected the two like a breezeway. The driveway curved like a machete up to the slab, splitting the land in two between the seen and unseen.

Poca ran a good time, but her heart outraced her. In a minute, she hit the machete driveway sticky and starving. Her dress stuck to her back, her breathing loud, as she slowed to walking. Flopping her feet hard on the gravel—disturbing the little tan, and orange, milky white, and brown stones held together by packed dust and man-made sand. She arched back and swung her nose up, threw her arms up across her face. She shut her eyes, steady walking, pulling long streams of air, letting the sun beam down through her eyelids. Thinking about the sweet lemon tea and cornbread muffins, the crispy drumettes she dipped in her salad dressing. The light dizzy of walking forward in motion with no sight gave the girl a sensation of drunkenness. She liked it. She walked on a piece, till the fear of tripping, falling, or meeting a wall took her pleasure. Playing like a soldier, she stopped, snapped her feet together, and stood straight, locking her knees. Then opened her eyes to see a glittering, powder blue sedan parked in the drive. License plates, Shelby County.

Poca thought to run, but her folks was gone now. Her feet was stuck, and besides, whoever it was went in the house. They whatn't in that brand new car glittering like the beach at Arkabutla. Feet still heavy, she stretched out her neck. Best to look close, but not get closer. Thick white fabric and blue eyelet lace lined the back window, flowers and beads. A line of painted shells edged the glass, set off by a bowl—a shining, brass bowl—with a teeny, baby watermelon dead center. *What in the Sip*? She laughed. *Wait till I tell BJ bout this one.* She glanced up at the trailer. Door was closed, so she side stepped the car to pass it by. Peeped in the backseat. Nothing to see but fruit spilling out of milk crates—goldenrods and more lil watermelons. Look like some pears, maybe. *Must be selling it*, Poca thought. Then clean out the blue, she heard the door snap a creak. Quick, she followed the sound. Searched the door to the trailer, but didn't see nothing. Set to fight, her pulse bumped in her ears. Then out her right eye, she caught the source. Pulling back the door to the old, dead house.

A high, white scarf, tucked and tied in a cone of patterns, formed in the mesh behind the screen door. Then the shoulders appeared and the base of a neck—tall, brown, slender, stately. Upright. The torso became the form of a woman. Emerged only dots at a time. Poca knew herself to be in full trance. The figure opened the door, and strutted out into the sun. The lady wore a soft-pleated dress in light denim. Pinched in the waist by a strip of dark fabric, buttoned down the front from the bosom to the knees. A small, square, canvas purse slanted cross the front of her body.

"Little. Miss. Poca," dragged the lady with the scarf.

"Dat's my name, don't wear it out." Poca sang slow. "You mus' be some ah Shan people?"

"Kinda," went the lady, "and some ah yo people." She reached out her hand for a shake. Poca kept hers right down at her sides.

"Sandra," smiled the lady looking her over. She reached in the purse and pulled out her keys. Whishing past her body, a train of smells—perfume, smoke, and sweet honey following.

Poca stepped back, "*My* people? From Memphis?"

"Why Memphis?" laughed the lady.

"Cause I read yuh tags."

"Oh, is that right?" She raised her eyebrow.

"Shelby County," went Poca pleased. "Dat's where my brother at. He at the penal farm."

"*Is?*" went Sandra, posted up listening.

"Yeh. He posed to come home tomorrow."

Sandra looked into the girl's face. "Whatchu made, gul, bout eleven by now?"

"Naw, not chet," shot Poca. "Won't be fuh another month."

Sandra grinned, taken with the girl. Opened the driver door and sat, slamming it closed. "Well, Miss Poca," she paused, "tags say de cah came from Memphis, not me. Can't believe everythang yuh read." She winked at the girl.

"I guess," Poca shrugged.

"And don't go tellin everythang you know—everythang you *see*. Save sum'in for yo'rself. Okay?"

Poca liked that thought. Smiled at the lady.

"Well okay then," Sandra rolled down the window, clangin bracelets on the glass. "Make sho you tell yo people I was heah." The lady laughed, started up her car. "Tell Hayward I said I'll be right back."

"*I will,*" Poca hollered, as the lady backed out the driveway.

Fore she made it inside, the Pastor was pulling up. His big, pearl Lincoln bobbing like a boat on the sea. Hayward's old pickup growling behind him. They pulled to the edge of the slab and stepped out. Pastor stood in his car door and peeled off his jacket. Hayward took a minute to clean the snuff from his jaw, stuff it in the wrinkled foil pouch and find his pocket. Poca ran to her mama as she stepped out the door.

"Why you ain't in dey house, lil gul? Couldn't wait to get ya' ass back down heah."

"Shoot, I ran like a bullet down heah," Poca whined.

"Un huh," mama grunted.

"For *reeeal*, I did. But they had a lady out heah when I walked up, Mama."

"A lady?" Coreen slowed but kept moving with the group.

"Yeh, mama, a lady in a shiny, blue car! Wit all type a decorations cross the back window."

"You had time to look all up in the lady winda?"

"Yeh, she wutn't in theah so I looked real good."

"So where was she, in the house?"

"Naw," Poca shook her head, "she was coming out the *other* house. The dead house, Mama." At that, the party stopped to look back at the girl.

"You talked to her?" Pastor said.

"Shole did," went the child.

"What she say her name? What she look like Poca?" her daddy rushed. The pastor had made the top step. He held the screen door open waiting for the answer.

"She *ain't* say." Poca took her new advice. "But she look like a ol' fortune teller to me, Daddy. And ack like she know you and Mama or sum'in."

Coreen raised her eyebrow. "Ack like *like how*? What she say?"

"Say tell yo people," Poca grinned. "—*Hayward*, she'll be right back." Coreen shook her head and glanced at her husband. He turned his head to ignore it.

Each one got through the doorway and stopped in the kitchen. Alarmed by the sound of Patty laughing or crying, one, in madness. Her hysterical shrieks echoing through the hall. They could hear Sistuh Perryman trying to soothe her, whispering loud, "Shhh, shhh, hush nah chile, hush."

Pastor and Hayward led the line. Poca went ahead of her mama, who held the young girl back by the zipper of her dress.

They found Sistuh Perryman still in the bedroom. Patty on the floor rocking back against the wall. A knot sat at her hairline, on the left side. She opened and closed her eyes in long blinks, looking over at Poca, then to Sistuh Perryman, then to Reeva Lee. The baby dangled in a swath of navy linen held by the hook of a hanging scale Sistuh Perryman had raised over the night stand. One at a time, each that entered found their place, backs pressed against the wall in disbelief.

Shan was sitting halfway up against the headboard ringing her hands. Her hair was wild, and her eyes drooping with fatigue—the yellow nightgown she wore wrinkled and bloody down the chest.

"You almos done, Sistuh," she asked the midwife repeatedly. "I'm ready for you to gih my baby back nah."

"Almos baby," the elder said, more to Reeva Lee than to Shan.

"Come on, she hongry, Sistuh Perr'man. I gotta feed her," she begged.

The Sistuh laid the baby down and pulled the hook from the linen, then swaddled her tight as she hummed a song. Then, she slid her finger under the baby's lip and rolled it across one side to the other. Opened her mouth up, turning Reeva Lee to face the parties on the wall. All pressed against it hard like a door they could run through. Nobody talking. Nobody breathing.

"See, she hongry," whimpered Shan, pressing her hair back in distress.

Sistuh Perryman beckoned for her bag from the floor. Poca grabbed it and handed it off. The elder nodded, reached in and brought up a dark red cloth. She bent it between her thumb and forefinger, wrapped them both twice around, then reached into Baby Reeva Lee's mouth. She gripped the right tooth in the crook of her forefinger, placed her thumb on top, and twisted down hard, pulling it straight out. Everybody gasped. The baby let out a squeal, started to cry for the first time. "I seent it," Patty shrieked, watching and sniggling in hysteria, grinning on the floor.

Sistuh reached for the left tooth, but the baby's mouth was twisted with tears. She tilted her down, cradling the baby in the bent of her elbow, grabbing at it again. The second tooth dropped in her palm like raindrop—a dot of pasty blood gathered at the root.

Patty slapped the wall, startling the group, "Y'all seen it!" she cackled. "He, he, he, y'all seen it, too."

Sistuh Perryman took her pinky and rubbed across baby's gums, surveying the injury. Satisfied, she turned to Shan and handed the crying baby back. She rattled the snake teeth in her palm like dice.

"Pastah," she turned to the line of them anchored to the wall.

"Yes ma'am."

"Take Patty on ova theah cross de hall." Then she changed her mind. "Naw—" went the woman waving her hand, "mattah fack, Hayward, you take huh on cross theah." She pointed to the bedroom across the hall. "I need tuh talk to Pastah heah a spell."

Poca's daddy raised her leg, pushing off the wall. "Will do," Sistuh Perryman said, reaching his hand out to Patty. Patty frowned and turned her face away. Folded her arms but Hayward grabbed her softly and stood her up. Coreen gripped his free arm, shuffling behind her husband as he dragged Patty stiff-legged out the door.

The whole time Poca kept watching Shan nursing Reeva Lee. The baby smacked and Shan Lee laid back near sleep, holding the sweet possession against her chest.

"Miss Poca!" The voice of Sistuh Perryman snatched her back to. She turned her eyes to the elder. "Care yuh lil self outside for some air," she told her glaring. "I b'lieve you seen enough for de day."

But the day was not done with Miss Poca yet.

Outside, a church of cicadas played call and response, and behind the trailer, Poca counted time in between. *One Miss Sippi. Two Miss Sippi.* The dead air let her catch her daddy's voice under the carport. "Alright damn, Coreen. I heard jah."

"*Don't damn me*, Hayward. Damn yo sister! She duh witch been out here doin that voodoo."

Three Miss Sippi. Pastor was there, too. Poca heard him sucking hulls out his teeth like he did anytime he had to listen. "Well—" he told them. "Sistuh Perr'man say to baptize her."

"Talmbout Patty or the baby?"

"The damn baby, Hayward," hissed Coreen.

"Yeh, no water ain't gone help Patty now," went Pastor. "But Sistuh say get dis baby washed today."

"*Today?!*" Coreen fanned. "Well, kin you baptize me, too? Cause I lef' my soul back innat room."

Pastor chuckled slow like stone skipping water. "Jus' hol' whatchu got," he told her. "Hol' whatchu got."

They heard bamming in the kitchen beside them, then voices. Patty still sniggling like a car trying to start, and the elder going "Hush, Patty Perryman, hush."

They slid they talk down to the edge of the slab. Pastor and couple agreed the best they could do, what had to be done, solely to keep they word to they elder, of course, was to baptize the baby. The question was where. Too far to the lake or baptismal pool in Thyatira. "Sides, the day damn near gone now." Hayward trailed as they took a natural pause. "And Sandy ain't no damn witch, neither, Coreen!"

"You-on know what she is," his wife cut him off.

"Okay, Co-reen, den I'ont know shit. Let *chu* tell it."

"Well den, gone. Let me tell it."

But the growl of spewing gravel cut the air. Poca popped out from behind the trailer, and Sandra's wheels bent the turn in. Gleaming like the beach at Arkabutla, Poca grinned. *Musta heard her name.*

Before Sandra braked, old Sistuh dotted the door. Her creased, yellow hand clinching Patty like a girl. "Hayward, Coreen," she eyed Pastor, too. "Bend y' legs on up heah," she said. "Take Patty back to the room in theah."

Poca watched Sandra like a dog had got in. This time *her people* wasn't wearing the scarf. It sat balled up in the dash of her car. Hair flung in every direction like branches. Thick, black dreadlocks, the size of fat pencils, spiraled in a swarm of gold-wrapped coils. Silver beaded strands draped down her forehead, swooped in five petals with a center tween the eye. Rings and cuffed bangles flashed in the sun. A blinding grapefruit low in the sky.

Sandra pranced up and slammed a washtub down. Winked a quick grin and shook her keys on her finger. "This it?" she turned to the elder.

"Naw," frowned the midwife, "but it's gone do."

Poca was instructed to help her Aunt Sandra, who had her line salt round the trailer, the dead house, and carport, too. *In a circle*, she told her. *Don't break the line.* Sandra went in one direction, Poca in the other. Then they met behind the concrete to march back through. Poca waited till they had reached Sandra's car to ask her question. "So what's all that stuff in de back uh yo windah?"

Sandra smirked, pointed to a sack taking up the front seat. Grabbed a baby melon out the back and a bowl. She blew the dust out, as Poca lifted the sack. "A prayer," she told her. "Nah come on, lil gul, 'foe Coreen get cha."

Sandra walked her over to the well by the road. Behind the brick structure, hid from the drive, she laid out flowers and placed white stones. Arranged shells hidden in the grass. Poca held the sack open wide while she worked. She cut small squares in the small watermelon. Then, used the switchblade to fill them again, stuffed them all good with oozy, raw honey. Watching the trailer with quickness, Sandra pumped the well till an old rusty pail rose from the bottom. In the clean, black water, she dipped her hands. Spit in her palms and rubbed them together. Then she knelt beside Poca, filled her hands with earth as she dug. She spoke in a hush. Recited words Poca couldn't translate, but repeated—per her auntie's welcome command.

Poca carried the bowl, and her auntie brought the pail. They filled the washtub and waited. By then, the sky over the carport had turned sherbet cream. Wisps of pink and orange melted west behind the sun, spread tangerine as the evening came. The smell of water lingered under the breezeway. Whatn't three minutes fore Hayward hit the door, with Coreen trailing his heels. Pastor held Patty's hand, leading her out, and the midwife was toting the baby. Reeva Lee was wrapped like a prize, still bound in the navy linen. The elder passed her over to Sandra. This caused Coreen to roll her eyes and breath loud, pinch Hayward hard on his arm. Pastor shooed them into a huddle together.

"People ah God," he started, "fam'ly, and love ones—will you welcome dis child into a life with Christ?"

All of them but Sandra mumbled "We will."

Pastor looked warmly on the baby face. "Today, in front dees witnesses, you receive de sign of the Cross." He dipped down his finger in the tub. Crossed a wet "T" between her eyes. "I baptize you in the name ah the Father," he dipped back down to the water. "And of the Son," Sandra squatted, leaned the baby toward him. "And of the Holy Ghost." He cupped his hands, letting water drip down her head. "Amen."

Reeva Lee started to squirm in her swaddle, twist up her face bout to cry. Silver streaks shined where the water had touched, as Pastor laid a palm over her eyes. In silence, he said a few words to the Lord his own. Then stood, beckoning the group to join hands. They linked around the washtub, form of a circle. All but Sandra in center, holding the baby by the tub.

"Every head is bowed, every eye is..." Pastor started. "Let us pray."

Poca bent her neck. She strained her eyes up to watch Sandra with the baby.

"Loid," Pastor prayed, "we know yo streinf and yo might. And Loid, we feel yo mighty hains upon us this ee'nin."

Sandra untucked the swaddle and started unwrapping, lowering Reeva Lee over the tub. Poca heard a frog groan.

"We know 'erry creature, Loid—what can walk up high or crawl down low on this earf," he said. She heard another frog close by.

"The birds crossin the heavens and the fish what breaves in the sea. We know is under yo command, Loid. *Made!*—to yo likin." She could feel the mosquitos eating her legs. Sandra had the baby undressed by now, turning her feet down into the pool.

"I seen it!" Patty giggled, finally catching eyes with Poca. She giggled so hard, she was bouncing the Pastor. Her roller-set curls shaking wild all over. Red hair hiding and revealing the knot settled right at her hairline. The sky over the circle had gone thick gray, rippled with streaks of purple and blue. Smelled like water and dirt in the air.

Pastor kept going, "So we come to you 'umbly, Loid. Under the darknin sky. To ask if any paht of dis chile be made in ya image, Loid—just keep huh in duh palm a yuh hain."

The water in the washtub rose with the baby. Sandra still held her up by the arms.

"Grab holt to her soul tonight. Make her grow in the *rrright* way, Loid."

Her feet started shining like silver in mud, like slick, dark clay on the side of the river. The slickness ran up her little legs, then her body, as Sandra let her slip, whole face in the tub.

"Let dis chile do yo lustrous biddin."

Poca raised her head, not hearing the prayer. Baby Reeva Lee lay full in the tub, her legs and chest rainbowing like scales. Feet barely kicking. Face turning slick just as fast as her arms. Patty shouted again. "I seen it." She laughed, bouncing the Pastor.

"Protect this heah chile' ah yurs and ours."

The baby's whole body pearled over, poreless. Dazzling. Iridescent black as she moved, throwing off a ray of colors. Her mouth fishing, open, closed, open, closed. Eyes shining up through the water.

"Bind the devil!" shouted Pastor. "Shine yo light in dark places."

Poca managed not to scream out loud.

"And let not yo *favor* be ever fah from us. Dis we ask, in yo son Jesus name—" he prayed. "Amen." He prayed, "Amen." He prayed, "Amen."

The prayer circle broke. The twelve hands dropped, and Poca raised her head to match the level of her eyes. Scanning the faces of her people, looking to see, forgetting Sandra, watching the baby. Her colors changing back fast as alcohol drying. Sandra scooped Reeva Lee out naked and held the baby, water be damned. Wetting her dress and splashing the tops of Pastor's shoes, but he didn't seem to notice. Every eye had turned toward a rumble rising from the well, a gurgling deep like drowning. The stones around the hole vibrating in wait. The well next to BJ's trailer, where upon the ground the ash of Shan Lee's people, who passed inside a month of the wedding ceremony, had been spread and sprinkled. Poured down the shaft to float out to the river. This done in remembrance of their living.

Poca watched Sandra, holding the baby to her chest. She was mumbling but Poca couldn't make out what she said. And just before it all exploded, just as Sandra finally squeezed her eyes shut and pressed Baby Reeva Lee to her breast to shield her face, Poca read the words on her lips. *Breathe, my baby, breathe. She who is the water cannot drown.*

And then, like a whale spout, the tunnel erupted. Baptized the land and all within the sound of the voice of the Lord. Sent the prayer circle shouting in every direction—hollering, fanning, waving, shielding they faces, searching for safety.

Shan Lee appeared in the doorway. Straight-faced and eyeing Sandra, holding Baby Reeva Lee. "What chall doin to mah baby? Give her back to her mama." And Sandra did.

Poca piled in the truck wet with Hayward and Coreen, watched her aunt back out the driveway to Memphis. *Two new Walkers,* she said out loud as Sandra turned on the paved road. Sistuh Perryman stayed with Shan and Reeva Lee, and Pastor drove Patty away never to be seen in her right head again. Coreen got it right when she said, *Patty woke up but she never did come to.*

BJ would be home in the morning. Hayward would pick him up and drive back to Mississippi. Nobody was sure what or when to tell him, or if to just keep it til' he made it to Shan. Poca had so much to say. But in the end, she couldn't find words to describe it, so really wasn't nothing even to be told. *Some shit had to be seen.*

GHOSTS

JAQUIRA DÍAZ

Three weeks before we pull the body from the river, I find Kofi waiting for me behind our camp. I spot him as I hike through the palms toward the outhouses. He's sitting under a mango tree and I assume he's waiting for me since villagers aren't allowed near the latrines, the command post, the sleeping quarters, or any of the DRASH tents.

The night before, as we unloaded supplies for the hospital corpsmen, Kofi introduced himself to Gunny Winchester, asked how much he had to pay for a night with me. Gunny explained that I wasn't for sale, and that there would be more women Marines coming, so he better get used to giving us the same respect he gave the men. I thought that was the end of it, but afterward I noticed him following me to the river, the armory, the motor pool. Everywhere I went, there was Kofi, watching me, a toothless smile on his face. I made a point to know his name, to say it as I passed him. *Kofi.* Know your enemy, Gunny always says. Know your enemy and know yourself. Kofi may not be a hostile, but he's a threat, and I'm stronger because I know this. I don't mention this to any of the guys. I know how some of them feel about women in combat, and although technically we're not in combat yet, I don't want to give them any leverage.

I stop to light a cigarette. It's before sunrise, and most of the platoon is still asleep, but the old guy doesn't worry me. He leans back against the tree, peels a ripe mango and takes a great bite off its flesh, the juice running down his forearm. He tosses aside pieces of the peel as he's done with them, swats at flies. I check the perimeter for the fire watch, but I have to pee so I'm not waiting for them to make their rounds. Besides, I can take care of myself.

I make it to the outhouse without another glance at Kofi, toss my cigarette butt before locking the door. Then, as I squat over the hole in the ground, I hear him outside, moaning. I can make out the shadow of his bare feet on the other side of the door, his toes curling as he pulls on the handle.

I tap on the door a few times with the sole of my Gore-Tex boot. He stops. For a moment, no sound comes from the other side, so I finish my business. Then he pulls on the handle again, harder this time, and I worry that the makeshift lock will come loose, that he'll catch me with my cammi trousers around my ankles. I know what will happen if he bursts through the door, so I don't waste any time. After I pull up my trousers, I take one step back, and with all my strength, kick the outhouse door. It flies open, lock breaking, then a crash I assume is wood against Kofi's skull. When I step out, he's flat on his back covering his nose and mouth with both hands. His flaccid penis hangs out of his shorts. He is still moaning.

I stare hard at him, pull the brim of my cover low to shade my eyes, cracking my knuckles and kicking stones out of my path as I pass him. On my way back to camp, I run into Corporal Ramos smoking a cigarette by the tree line. Ramos is small, shorter than most of the guys in our squad, but muscular, a devil dog tattoo on his forearm. He's a serious guy. We got pretty close during our tour in Iraq last year. A couple of weeks before we landed in Campo Verde, he told me his wife is expecting their first son. I congratulated him, but secretly I envied his happiness. Still do.

"You okay, Vega?" he asks, and right away I know he saw the whole thing. I'm glad he didn't step in like some of the other guys would.

"I'm cool," I say, turning into the trail.

Ahead, through the canopy of tropical palms and ceibas and bamboo, the sunlight is beginning to filter in.

#

When the first bombs dropped, half of Campo Verde was destroyed, most of the people injured or killed. The survivors were left with no homes, no crops, and no potable water. Our platoon was ordered here to assist with the relief effort, mostly water purification, but we arrived six days after the grunts and hospital corpsmen set up camp. They'd been operating and treating the injured but were running low on supplies. By the time we landed, most of the critically wounded had died of infection and dehydration. Out of almost three hundred villagers, forty-one remain. Seven of them are women.

The villagers are surprised to see a woman Marine. They watch me, but will not look away when I catch them like they do with the men. They look me up and down like I'm a strange thing, an apparition they don't recognize.

Out of our whole squad, only Ramos and I speak Spanish, so we spend most of the day translating for the hospital corpsmen. It isn't our job, but we've lost more than half our guys since the war started, so we do whatever needs to be done. I work with the women and children, and Ramos helps out with the men. The rest of our squad takes to the river with the water purification units.

I'm opening boxes in the field hospital when Lieutenant Harris, a fleet surgeon, rushes in. He carries one of the women in his arms. Two corpsmen follow, pulling on surgical gloves as he sets her on a bed.

"Corporal Vega," Lieutenant Harris calls over his shoulder, "get over here."

I push aside a half-empty box of surgical tape cartridges, wipe my hands on my cammies.

"Aye, sir."

"Take her hand."

"Yes, sir." Reaching for the woman's hand, I notice she isn't a woman at all, but a girl.

She's at least eight months pregnant, but it's clear she's just a girl, no more than twelve or thirteen, her brown skin beaded with sweat. She squeezes my fingers, her eyes wide.

"Corporal," Lieutenant Harris says, "tell her everything is fine."

He douses her belly with an orange iodine solution.

I smile at her. "Todo está bien."

I hold her hand while Lieutenant Harris and the two corpsmen work on her, trying not to see the blood, although the scent of it is in my nostrils, in the back of my throat. I know the smell. After my mother died of leukemia four years ago, the smell lingered. It was in my clothes, my hair, in the bathroom we'd shared, even though when she died she hadn't lived with me for almost a year. I sat in the prison hospital with her six days, tending to a nosebleed that just wouldn't stop. That last day the stench was unbearable, like she was rotting from the inside out.

On the bed, the girl's breathing grows faint, her grasp on my hand loose. I squeeze it. She is drenched in sweat now, her lips chapped.

"What's your name?" I ask in Spanish, but she doesn't respond.

Lieutenant Harris holds up her baby, a boy, but he doesn't cry. He hands him off to one of the corpsmen.

The girl glances at her baby. "Chu-rile," she says, a word I don't recognize.

"Is that your name?" I ask.

She coughs, tries to shake her head. "Ghosts," she says, before releasing my hand.

#

I signed the papers to Baker Act my mother at 3 a.m. on the Saturday of my eighteenth birthday. After they took her, I borrowed a neighbor's car and followed the police cruisers to the Citrus House. The clinic was four miles from our trailer park in West Hialeah, and I already knew the way. I double-parked in the ambulance lane, rushed into the lobby as they tried to control her. She was pushing and kicking and threatening to set me on fire in my sleep. She swore she would never forgive me. She swore I was not her daughter.

It took three cops and two nurses to wrestle her onto the linoleum floor, to sedate her and lift her onto a gurney with four-point restraints. I wasn't sure if I'd imagined a bed with restraints. Handcuffs maybe, since I was used to her run-ins with the cops. But not this. She'd been here twice in the last couple of years, and I'd never seen her restrained. It seemed like something out of a horror movie, like straightjackets or electroshock treatment.

The sedatives started taking effect even before they finished strapping her in, and as they wheeled the gurney into the hallway, she lifted her head and looked at me. I expected her to spit at me, to curse me, to describe how she'd slit my throat and watch me bleed to death, grind my bones into dust afterward. That I was used to. But not the silence, not the pleading look in her eyes.

"Don't do this to me," she said.

That was all she said.

As they wheeled her past the double doors into the ward, I stood in the hallway and held myself, but said nothing. I was certain that this wouldn't be the last time. We'd be back here three, four times in the next year probably. I was sure of it.

That was the last time I heard my mother speak, on the morning of my eighteenth birthday.

Less than a year later she was gone.

#

We never learn the girl's name. We try to find the father of the baby, a family member, anyone who can tell us something about her, but no one comes forward. There are now just six women left in the village, but none of them seem to know her. I mention her last words, ask about Chu-rile. What language is it? I want to know, but they wave me off, refuse to hear any more, forbid me to repeat the word. The women insist that the girl must be buried, that she must hold her baby in her arms. She is not to be burned with all the other dead. They give me beads to place around her neck, rosemary sprigs that must be tossed into the grave with their remains.

Lieutenant Harris insists that we just burn the bodies, but I tell him we should honor the women's wishes. I can't stomach the thought of burning a newborn, or his mother, her small body. He orders me and Ramos to bury them behind our camp.

We take turns digging in silence, passing a bottle of sugarcane rum back and forth, wiping the sweat off our faces with our forearms. After a while, Ramos throws his shovel on the ground, pulls off his skivvy shirt. I keep digging.

"No one should have to bury a baby," I say. I can tell he's thinking about his wife, his baby boy who will be born in a couple of months. During moments like this, when Ramos has that distant look, I'm reminded that I have no one to think about back home. No one to send me care packages filled with clean socks and magazines and Gatorade and baby wipes.

"It was the water," Ramos says. He takes a mouthful of the rum and sets the bottle down. "They were drinking straight from the river before we came."

"Really?"

He nods.

We lower the body bag into the ground. I picture the girl's sweaty face, the baby in her arms.

"This whole place," Ramos says, "it smells like death."

I toss the rosemary over the bodies. Romero, the women called it. We cover them with dirt.

#

They say there are ghosts in the jungle. The children see them often, hear them calling, follow them through the trees, down to the river. The women say it's as if the ghosts were dropped along with the bombs. What else can you expect with so much suffering, so much death?

The women say that many of the children are motherless now, that they should be watched. That children who are not watched will run off into the jungle in search of ghosts and will never again be children. It has happened before, the children taken, and the next time they were seen they were almost ghosts themselves, wielding the weapons of war. Handguns, rifles, machetes.

#

The bombing moves further south every day. Transient troops use our camp as a stopover. So many of us coming and going, I never know when I'll see some of these guys again, except for Corporal Ramos, who's on fire watch with me every other night. While most of the camp is asleep in their tents, the two of us stay up shooting the shit, or talking about home—how odd it is that Ramos and I are both from Miami, how we enlisted the same year, the same month, but just met last year, before getting deployed to Iraq.

Ramos and I are standing watch one night, smoking Newports in the clearing behind the field hospital, when I spot someone in the jungle. Standing in the darkness, just standing there, a figure among the fallen trees and giant ferns, looking right at us.

"Ramos," I say, taking my eyes off the figure for just a second. When I turn back, it's gone.

I raise my rifle, scan the brush ahead, then freeze, listen for footsteps in the thicket of the downed trees. On my queue, Ramos tenses up, drops his cigarette and aims his rifle, stepping forward slowly, checking the perimeter. I follow closely in formation, shine my beam across the clearing.

"You hear something?" he asks.

"No." I'm not sure if I heard anything, but I definitely saw someone. "There was a guy, though. Just standing there."

He takes one last look around, lowers his rifle. "Probably one of the villagers."

"You didn't see him? You looked right at him." I lower my rifle, but keep my eyes trained on the tangle of vines and bushes and trees at the edge of the clearing.

He turns back toward the field hospital. "All I saw was darkness."

The rest of our watch is uneventful, until we're relieved by Lance Corporals Yurei and Aparicio. We head for our separate tents, but I lay awake listening to the sounds of the night.

I used to listen to the traffic outside my window back in Miami. During those weeks my mother spent in the Citrus House, I barely slept. And afterward, when she was transferred to Dade County Jail after stabbing another patient in the neck with a pencil, I would chain smoke in bed, listening to the trailer park warfare. The couple in the next trailer would hurl plates and shoes and tables at each other, fights that would spill out into the street at two, three in the morning, and would usually end with one of them being hauled off in the back of a squad car.

A few weeks after we got to Camp Fallujah, I told Ramos about my mother. Told him how I'd been thinking about enlisting even before my eighteenth birthday. How I'd considered leaving without saying goodbye. Seemed easier than visiting my mother in jail, and then prison. And how when she got sick, it started to feel like a dream, like I'd never be free.

After she was cremated, the Department of Corrections sent her ashes in the mail. I got a card in the mailbox telling me to pick up the package in the post office.

"That's horrible," Ramos said.

But I wasn't looking for sympathy. "It was a long time ago."

In my tent, I swat at mosquitoes for hours. In Iraq, we had camel spiders the size of Volkswagens. In Campo Verde, we have mosquitoes that fly through walls and pick up small children. When I can't take it anymore, I pull away the netting over my cot and head out.

I feel my way to Ramos' tent in the dark. He's awake and doesn't seem all that surprised to see me. He pulls off his shirt, and I'm glad I don't have to endure the awkwardness of his rejection and then have to face him in the morning. Our faces are slick with sweat, our necks sunburned and covered in grime. My hair is knotted. We reek of motor oil and mosquito repellent and foot powder, and when he goes down on me, I'm sure he imagines his wife. I try to picture her face, but can't. All I come up with is the dark silhouette of a pregnant woman. I imagine he can't picture her either after being on deployment for so long.

All this time, I've been closer to Ramos than any of the other guys on my platoon, yet I've never even called him by his first name. "Jason," I say, just to hear what it sounds like.

He doesn't respond, doesn't look into my eyes or kiss me or even let me see his face. There is the sound of our breathing, our dog tags clinking against each other, the faraway spray of gunfire in the night, the rustling of dry foliage somewhere in the jungle. He will feel guilty in the morning, and he will tell me all about it, since I have become the one he goes to with his guilt, with his loneliness, with his fear. For a moment, I long for the same thing, something to feel guilty about, someone waiting for me back home, ready to start living the life I deliberately left behind. But there is no one.

#

During our last week in Iraq, Ramos and I were on a convoy sent to deliver supplies to a platoon in Tikrit, when we encountered some wreckage blocking the road. Parts of an old Toyota HiAce van were strewn about, but we couldn't find any other cars. We were in the first Humvee, so Ramos and I scanned the area. We figured the van hit a roadside bomb. We found pieces of the driver scattered on the sand around the van, and inside, the limbless, burnt torso was still strapped to the seat with the seatbelt.

A few paces off the road, I could see the dark figure of a veiled woman kneeling in the desert, like a phantom. PFC Wilkins covered us from the gun turret as we approached the woman. We'd heard plenty of stories of Marines fired upon by women and children they'd passed on the road. But she needed help, and we didn't know how long she'd been out there. As we got closer, we realized she'd been praying before the body of a little girl sprawled out on the sand. The girl was long dead—the fire had already stopped burning. I pulled my canteen off my utility belt and held it out for her, but she wouldn't take it.

I unscrewed the cap, took a sip to show her it was okay. I took another step, bent further to give her the canteen.

"Please," I said, my hand extended.

She started crying. I didn't know what to do, so I kneeled down next to her, keeping my distance, but she would not take a drink. She rocked herself back and forth, looking me right in the eye. I felt exposed there, my hand extended, as if I'd been the one to do this to her, to her daughter, to the man whose remains were scattered all over the road.

And then, in her eyes, I saw that she meant to die in the desert next to the girl, probably her daughter.

Ramos drove the rest of the way to Tikrit, and I couldn't shake the image of the woman kneeling in the desert, of the little girl, couldn't shake the dread I felt walking away from them, even though the corpsmen had arrived with food and water before we left, even though they'd make sure she wouldn't die of exposure. And I thought about my mother.

Ramos kept looking at me. "You alright, Vega?"

"The day I pulled the card out of the mailbox," I told him, "the day they sent my mother's ashes—"

"Yeah?" He kept one hand on the steering wheel, but his eyes locked on me expectantly, like he was really listening.

"I packed some clothes into a duffle bag and took off," I said. "I never made it to the post office."

He didn't say another word until we reached Tikrit.

#

In Campo Verde at dusk, the mosquitoes come in swarms. We lie in our cots under the mosquito netting, our side arms under our pillows. Some of the guys pretend to read Hemingway when they're really jerking off to hand-me-down copies of *Penthouse*. Most of the Marines sleep in one large DRASH tent, except for officers, noncommissioned officers, and women. In my case, I get a four-man tent to myself until the other women Marines arrive or until they decide to move me with the female corpsmen, whichever comes first.

I'm smoking in my cot when I hear footsteps outside, scattering dry leaves. I reach for my side arm.

"Vega, you in there?" Ramos calls out. He pulls back the flap, steps inside. "You sleeping?"

"You know I never sleep." I lift the mosquito netting over my head. He hands me a bottle of sugarcane rum.

"Where do you get this stuff?" Ramos manages to find liquor anywhere we go. He pulls out a few packets of strawberry Kool-Aid and drops them on my cot. I know they're for my benefit—he doesn't need his rum flavored.

"No watch tonight," he says.

I tear open one of the packets, pour the powder into the mouth of the bottle.

"Rum punch," I say. I down some of it, pass it back.

We take turns drinking the stuff, smoking Ramos' Newports and not saying much. There was a time when the two of us could sit around without exchanging any words, when we could just enjoy each other's company, but something changed after that first night. The air around us is heavy, humid. My nails dirty, ragged, my hands dry. The hands of a mechanic. I wonder how Ramos sees me, if he could ever be with a woman like me.

"We need to talk," he says.

"Is that what you came for? To talk?"

"Sure." He kisses me on the neck, cupping my breast over the skivvy shirt. I feel the heat of him against me, and wonder if he's ever let himself imagine a future where there is just the two of us.

I pull his hand away. "I thought you wanted to talk."

He jerks back, straightens himself out like he's considering what to say. "Sometimes I'm confused."

I take a swig from the bottle. "You're just drunk."

"That's not what I mean." He swats at a mosquito, scratches at the stubble on his face. "Sometimes I think we might die in this jungle."

"Nobody's dying," I say.

He breathes deep, then exhales. "I love my wife."

I don't know how to respond to that.

"I love my wife," he says again, then kisses me anyway.

We kiss like teenagers, tasting like sugarcane rum and cigarettes. I let him do whatever he wants with his hands, waiting until the last possible moment before pulling them away.

"Please," he says.

"Maybe we should stop," I say.

He takes a deep breath, then lights another cigarette. I rest my head on his shoulder, close my eyes.

#

When I wake a few hours later, it's dark and raining and I don't remember falling asleep. Ramos is snoring, face down on the ground next to my tiny cot.

"Hey," I say, shaking him. "You gotta go. If we get caught, there's gonna be trouble for both of us."

He gets to his feet, rubbing the sleep from his eyes.

"Don't forget *this*," I say, handing him the half-empty bottle.

"I wanted to tell you something," he says. "But I didn't want you to think it was the liquor."

"Yeah?"

"Sometimes," he says, "when it's just you and me, when no one else is around, and I see how strong you are... Sometimes I think I could love you." He doesn't wait for my reaction, just ducks out of the tent into the dark.

I go after him, not caring who might overhear us. The camp is quiet except for the rain, the tree frogs and crickets screaming in the distance.

I pull him by the arm. "I'm sorry, but what exactly do you expect me to do with that?"

But I don't wait for his response. The rain is a slow drizzle now, droplets pelting me in the face, but I can see, clearly, that there's something in the trees.

"What is it?" he asks, and I think he must read it on my face. There, at the edge of the tree line, right at the entrance to the trail we use to hump back and forth between our camp and the river. She is watching us. Her baby boy in her arms. The girl we buried behind our camp.

#

The women have many stories about the jungle and its trails leading to the river, but they say these stories are to be protected. They will not share them with the other Marines, would rather keep them for Ramos, and for me. They say the Loogaroos are human by day, but at night they shed their skin and transform into demons, haunting the women, calling out to the children. They say it's better to drown the children in the river, better than leaving them to wander aimlessly through the jungle, to one day return and find that their brothers and sisters are now the enemy. They say the military brought these ghosts, that Ramos and I are like the ghost-children, that we were taken. And what's worse, we don't even know it.

#

It's harder to be with Ramos after that night, after seeing the dead girl. Maybe I'm afraid of the villagers' stories, or that he'll confess that while I saw the girl, he saw only darkness. It's hard to see him out in the open, to stand watch with him at nights. But when we're alone in my tent, things change, the tension between us is almost tangible. Sometimes we fuck without words. Hard one night, his hand tangled in my hair, the stink of our bodies thick. The next night soft, his breath against my face, the two of us in tears, and I can feel that he is almost mine. Almost.

We don't venture out into the jungle in the dark, but during daylight hours we check out the perimeter, look for tracks in the dirt. None of the other Marines have seen anything, and the corpsmen mostly stick to the field hospital.

417

One morning we're on the river slopes, Ramos cranking the generator for the Water Purification Unit, and me, knee-deep in mud as I place the strainer in the water.

"Don't give it too much slack," Ramos calls out.

I tie the float to the strainer, give the rope just enough slack to let the water in without it touching the bottom. And then I notice it, up the river, tangled in branches and debris.

"Is that..." I start to ask, but when Ramos takes off running toward it, I know I'm not seeing things. It's a body. A child.

By the time I get to them, Ramos has pulled him from the river. We start CPR. The boy's lips are blue, his body cold. He is six, seven at most. There are no visible wounds, no gunshots, or blood anywhere.

"It's no use," Ramos says. "He's cold."

We take the boy back to camp, following the same track we've been using through the jungle. Ramos carries him in his arms. I walk in front of him, rifle ready, finger on the trigger. There is no sound coming from the jungle, no wind in the trees, no bird calls. Only the smell of wood, plants, earth, all of it half destroyed by the bombs and the fires, soot and ash everywhere.

The villagers, all of them men, surround us when we get to camp. We explain how we pulled the boy from the river, how we tried to revive him. We ask about his family. Only one of them steps forward. Kofi. Something stirs in my stomach when I notice his nose is still swollen and he has deep black circles under his eyes.

He takes the boy from us, holds him against his chest, tells us there is no family. The men shoo us away, not interested in our explanations or our offers to help, letting us know that even though the boy belongs to no one, he belongs to the village.

I watch Kofi cradle the boy in his arms, carry him away. I search the crowd, the faces, looking for the women, but they are gone.

"Let's go," Ramos says. He pulls me by the arm, just like he did that day in the desert on the road to Tikrit.

Later, when the women return to the village, I will deliver the news of the boy. I will tell them how sorry I am, offer to help with the burial. I will expect them to weep, pull the hair from their heads, wailing. But the women will go on with their day as if the boy never existed, back to the washing and the cooking, back to breastfeeding their own babies.

#

After speaking with the women, I find Kofi behind our camp, digging, the boy's body wrapped in a brown sheet from the field hospital. I consider helping. I'm not sure why I can't. Maybe I can't look him in the face, can't stop thinking of him outside the latrines, lying on his back. I keep seeing the woman kneeling in the desert, will see her until the last day of my life, and I know it isn't my burden to bear. There is one thing I know: war is made by men.

No one comes to the boy's burial. No one claims him except for Kofi. He takes it upon himself, maybe because he knows that when he dies, there will be no one to do the digging, no one to leave flowers over an unmarked grave. When it is my time, no one will come for me either.

Ramos approaches from behind me, and together we watch. I take his hand. I think I should say something, ask how he's holding up maybe. I think about saying his name, Jason, just to hear if it will become more familiar each time I say it, but somehow I know it will always sound like a stranger's.

GREEN SYMPHONY

JACQUELINE JOHNSON

I am the water's daughter
longing to know her hidden ways.
Always curious I swim uncharted waters.
Ancient mirror reflects my truth.

Thin bands of God's green, dried leaves
Mixed with loam of several generations.
Wild fields of corn, white sage and lavender.
A flock of blue jays, arcs of bird wing.

Angels in the mist, incessant
Cacophony more urban each second.
Silence then sound of the open road.
All around bivouacs, tributaries

a wild, rushing thin. For miles
green symphony fills my eyes.
Yet the water rules here,
her muddy residue coats my feet.

Unpredictable mingling of wind and water
Her rhythm slow, rippling silver, mischievous.
At the water's edge I hesitate almost fearful.
In up to my shoulders, hair glistening.

I am the water's daughter unable to deny
pull of ivory half moons, seasons; to resist
music and currents of waves centuries old.
Her unruly, imperfect many sided child.

Here I know exactly who I am,
fecund, stubborn and always in trouble.
Out of bounds at last,
I kick into the deep brown waters.

MAAFA TO MAMI WATA

HEATHER 'BYRD' ROBERTS

1526 - We were one. Then two. Then twenty million
trudging to coast. Bounded by ironhorse
shoes. Waiting for splintered lips.

We were seized counter clockwise.
Directed east. Cramming Savannah with chattel
and contracted weapons for new world.

We were crumbles. Bartered bodies slathered
plague. We were choking from plague. Swallowing
traded pearls and gunpowder for new world.

We were water spirits' daughters waiting to be taken
Home. We were drowning in vomit and menstrual seeds
and traded textiles and rum for new world.

We were high-pitched screeches across ocean. Wails
penetrating sonar. Awakening snake, wool-like hair,
and gapped teeth. World of seas lured Savannah into deep.

Mami Wata receive us from maji.
Let statues from prows plunge.
Take us Home.

Back to bottle caps and brown. Warm.
Bursting of Ugali and goat. Jollof rice
and ginger. Puff Puff, meat pies, and Fufu

smashing in Mami's burnt left hand. Back to
plucking jumbo mangos raining with spice. Back to
harmonious coil picks and mirrors. We waiting

on veil to disintegrate shackles and dust ocean's bottom.
Fuse legs to make fin. Gallop gills across bruises.
Twist indigo and alizarin crimson to safety. We

free now. Our breasts float. We gyrate to sacrificed skins
in the name of rejoicing. We giggle with fish now.
This is best family reunion

after flotsam. After dive or flop or bones
snapping in half. We sail
underwater.

TROUBLE THE WATERS:
TALES FROM THE DEEP BLUE

CONTRIBUTORS

Maria Osunbimpe Hamilton Abegunde is a Memory Keeper, poet, healer, an ancestral priest in the Yoruba Orisa tradition, and a daughter of Osun. Her research and creative work respectfully approach the Earth and human bodies as sites of memory, and always with the understanding that memory never dies, is subversive, and can be recovered to transform transgenerational trauma and pain into peace and power. Abegunde's research on the power and roles of women in the Egungun (ancestral) society in Itaparica, Brazil laid the foundation for her memory-work *The Ariran's Last Life*, as well as her current commissioned works for the ancestral masquerade series, including the collaborative community exhibitions *De/Coming, Keeper of My Mothers' Dreams,* and *Sister Song: The Requiem.* She uses poetic inquiry, contemplative practices, and ritual to explore historical and sexual violence, especially in the US, Brazil, and South Sudan. Her poems have been published in numerous anthologies and journals, including *Jane's Stories, Kenyon Review, Massachusetts Review,* and *Tupelo Quarterly.* Essays/book chapters have been published in journals, including *North Meridian Review, FIRE!!!, Journal for Liberal Arts and Sciences,* and the book *ASHE: Ritual Poetics in African Diasporic Expressivity.*

Linda D. Addison award-winning author of five collections, including *The Place of Broken Things* written with Alessandro Manzetti, & *How To Recognize A Demon Has Become Your Friend,* the first African-American to receive the HWA Bram Stoker Award® and recipient of the HWA Lifetime Achievement Award. She has published over 360 poems, stories and articles and is a member of CITH, HWA, SFWA and SFPA. Addison is a co-editor of *Sycorax's Daughters,* an anthology of horror fiction & poetry by African-American women. Her site: www.lindaaddisonwriter.com.

Nanna Árnadóttir is an Icelandic writer and journalist living in the Danish countryside with her family and full-figured cat. Like many of her ancestors she has spent most her life living abroad. Her work is rooted in family lore and Nordic magical realism. She has been published in *The Guardian*, *National Geographic Travel*, *The Independent* and *The Reykjavík Grapevine* to name a few. Her first novel, the pulpy and queer, *Zombie Iceland*, was published in 2011.

Story Boyle's hair is perennially green, on account of being part river troll... or part gardener, depending on which day you ask the question. They studied undergraduate anthropology, work as a professional bookseller, and live in the Boston area with two elderly cats, a relatively young potted lime, a partner, and not enough book shelves. Their fiction has appeared in *PerVisions*, *Aliterate*, and *On Spec*.

Maurice Broaddus is a community organizer and teacher, his work has appeared in magazines like *Lightspeed Magazine*, *Beneath Ceaseless Skies*, *Asimov's*, *Magazine of F&SF*, and *Uncanny Magazine*, with some of his stories having been collected in The Voices of Martyrs. His books include the urban fantasy trilogy, *The Knights of Breton Court*, the steampunk works, *Buffalo Soldier* and *Pimp My Airship*, and the middle grade detective novels, *The Usual Suspects* and *Unfadeable*. His project, *Sorcerers*, is being adapted as a television show for AMC. As an editor, he's worked on *Dark Faith*, *Fireside Magazine*, and *Apex Magazine*. Learn more at MauriceBroaddus.com.

Adrienne Maree Brown is the author of *Pleasure Activism: The Politics of Feeling Good*, *Emergent Strategy: Shaping Change, Changing Worlds*, *We Will Not Cancel Us* and *Other*

Dreams of Transformative Justice, Holding Change: The Way of Emergent Strategy Facilitation and Mediation, and the co-editor of *Octavia's Brood: Science Fiction from Social Justice Movements.* She is the cohost of the *How to Survive the End of the World* and *Octavia's Parables* podcasts. adrienne is rooted in Detroit.

Christopher Caldwell is a queer Black American living abroad in Glasgow, Scotland. His work has appeared in *Uncanny Magazine, Strange Horizons,* and *Fiyah* among others. He is an Ignyte Awards finalist, Clarion West Alumnus, and a recipient of the Octavia E. Butler Memorial Scholarship. He is @seraph76 on twitter.

Jaquira Díaz is the author of *Ordinary Girls: A Memoir.* She is a recipient of a Whiting Award in non-fiction and two Pushcart Prizes, an Elizabeth George Foundation Grant, and fellowships from The MacDowell Colony, the Wisconsin Institute for Creative Writing, *The Kenyon Review,* Summer Literary Seminars, the Tin House Summer Writers' Workshop, the Virginia Center for the Creative Arts, the Ragdale Foundation, and the Bread Loaf Writers' Conference. Her work appears in *The Best American Essays 2016, Rolling Stone, The Guardian, Longreads, The Southern Review,* and *The FADER,* among other publications. A Writer in Residence at the Summer Literary Seminars in Tbilisi and Kenya, she is a Visiting Assistant Professor at the University of Wisconsin-Madison's MFA Program in Creative Writing, and Consulting Editor at the Kenyon Review.

Rylee Edgar has been writing all her life, mostly to impress her friends. She lives on horror movies, coffee, and baked goods. She lives in Georgia with her husband, son, two dogs and one grumpy three-legged cat. In 2013, she graduated with a Bachelors

Lyndsay E. Gilbert is a hopeful YA author from Northern Ireland. She lives by an ancient castle looking out to sea. Her interests are reading, writing, science fiction and fantasy, horror, music, playing the fiddle, movies, fairytales, cats, dogs @lyndsayegilbert on Instagram.

Andrea Hairston Andrea Hairston is a playwright, novelist, and scholar. Aqueduct Press published three of her novels: *Will Do Magic For Small Change*, a *New York Times* Editor's pick and finalist for the Mythopoeic, Lambda, and Otherwise Awards; *Redwood and Wildfire*, winner of the Otherwise and Carl Brandon Awards; *Mindscape*, winner of the Carl Brandon Award. Aqueduct also published *Lonely Stardust*, a collection of essays and plays. "Griots of the Galaxy," a short story, appears in *So Long Been Dreaming: Postcolonial Visions of the Future*. A novelette, "Saltwater Railroad," was published by *Lightspeed Magazine*. "Dumb House," a short story appears in *New Suns: Original Speculative Fiction by People of Color* edited by Nisi Shawl. Andrea has received grants from the National Endowment for the Arts, the Rockefeller Foundation, the Ford Foundation, and the Massachusetts Cultural Council. Her latest novel, *Master of Poisons,* came out from Tor.com and is on the *Kirkus Review*'s Best Science Fiction and Fantasy of 2020. *Redwood and Wildfire* will be reissued by Tor.com in 2022, and *Will Do Magic for Small Change,* and *Mindscape* thereafter, with new fiction works also forethcoming on Tor.com in between. Check andreahairston.com for updates. in 2022. In her spare time, Andrea is the Louise Wolff Kahn 1931 Professor of Theatre and Africana Studies at Smith College and the Artistic Director of Chrysalis Theatre.

Jacqueline Johnson is a multi-disciplined artist creating in both poetry, fiction writing and fiber arts. She is the author of *A Woman's Season*, on Main Street Rag Press and *A Gathering of Mother Tongues,* published by White Pine Press and is the winner of the Third Annual White Pine Press Poetry Award.

Her work has appeared in: *"Revisiting the Elegy in the Black Lives Matter Era,"* Routledge 2020, *The Slow Down,* American Public Media, October 16, 2019 and *"Pank: Health and Healing Folio,"* 2019. Ms. Johnson has received fellowships from the New York Foundation of the Arts, the Mid Atlantic Writers Association's Creative Writing Award in Poetry and MacDowell Colony for the Arts. She has received fellowships from Cave Canem, VONA and the Black Earth Institute.

Recent publications include: *Show Us Your Papers*, Main Street Rag, The Langston Hughes Review and Zora's Den. Works in progress include: *This America*, poetry and *How to Stop a Hurricane*, a collection of short stories. She is a graduate of New York University and the City University of New York. A native of Philadelphia, PA., she resides in Brooklyn, New York.

Jamey Hatley is a Memphian. Her writing has appeared in *Callaloo*, *Memphis Noir*, *Oxford American*, *Torch*, and elsewhere. She has received a Prose Fellowship from the National Endowment for the Arts and a Rona Jaffe Foundation Writers' Award. She was the co-founder of the Center for Southern Literary Arts. She received the inaugural Black Filmmaker Fellowship for Screenwriting to develop her feature screenplay, *The Eureka Hotel*, selected by Barry Jenkins. Her short film, *Always Open, the Eureka Hotel* debuted at the 2019 Indie Memphis Film Festival.

Kate Heartfield writes science fiction and fantasy, including the Aurora-winning novel *Armed in Her Fashion* and the Nebula-shortlisted novella *Alice Payne Arrives*, along with dozens of stories. She is the author of *The Road to Canterbury* and *The Magician's Workshop*, both of which were shortlisted for the Nebula in game writing. Her next novel is *The Embroidered Book*, a historical fantasy coming in 2022. A former journalist, Kate lives near Ottawa, Canada

Nalo Hopkinson was born in Kingston, Jamaica, and also spent her childhood in Trinidad and Guyana before her family moved to Toronto when she was sixteen. Her groundbreaking science fiction and fantasy features diverse characters and the mixing of folklore into her works. Hopkinson won the Warner Aspect First Novel contest for *Brown Girl in the Ring*, as well as the John W. Campbell and Locus Awards. Her novel *Midnight Robber* was a *New York Times* Notable Book and she has also received the Spectrum, Sunburst, Campbell, and Prix Aurora awards. Her short story collection, *Skin Folk,* was honored with a World Fantasy Award. Hopkinson has also edited several anthologies, including *So Long Been Dreaming: Post-colonial Science Fiction & Fantasy*,

Mojo: Conjure Stories, and *Whispers from the Cotton Tree Root.* In 2021, Nalo Hopkinson was named the 37th SFWA Damon Knight Grand Master for her contributions to the literature of science fiction and fantasy. Hopkinson taught in the Creative Writing department at the University of California, Riverside and writes *House of Whispers* for Neil Gaiman's new *Sandman Universe* series. In 2021 she joined the UBC School of Creative Writing as a professor. Visit her website at www.nalohopkinson.com.

Danian Darrell Jerry, writer, teacher, and emcee, holds a Master of Fine Arts in Creative Writing from the University of Memphis. He is a VONA Fellow and a Fiction Editor of *Obsidian.* Danian founded Neighborhood Heroes, a youth arts program that employs comic books and literary arts. Currently, he revises his first novel, *Boy with the Golden Arm.* As a child he read fantasy and comics, as an adult he writes his own adventures. His work appears in *Apex-Magazine.com, Fireside Fiction, Black Panther Tales of Wakanda,* and *The Magazine of Fantasy and Science Fiction.*

Naila Moreira teaches at Smith College and has been writer in residence at the Shoals Marine Laboratory, Maine, and Forbes Library, Massachusetts. Her second chapbook, *Water Street* (Finishing Line Press, 2017) won the New England Poetry Club Jean Pedrick Prize, and she has published poetry and essays in literary journals including the *Cider Press Review, Connecticut River Review, Terrain.org, Poet's Touchstone, Cape Rock,* and a range of others. Her debut middle grade novel, *The Monarchs of Winghaven* (Walker Books US, 2022), is forthcoming.

Pan Morigan is a Canadian/American author of surrealist fiction and a singer/composer. Her story, *Severed Fruit* was recently published in *The Magazine of Fantasy and Science Fiction.* Her anti-real play with original music, titled *I Sing Earth* debuted at Hallie Flanagan Theater, Smith College. She edited *In Jerusalem and Other Poems* by Tamim Al-Barghouti for Interlink Books. As a vocalist/songwriter, she toured globally with novelist Andrea Hairston, composer Adele O'Dwyer, and vocalist Bobby McFerrin, among others. In collaboration with Andrea Hairston, (as music director of Chrysalis Theater,) she created and performed music and lyrics for over

30 original plays. She worked as a composer and musician with directors, Wang Dao, (*Golden Lotus,*) and Helen Suh, (a Bunraku version of *Riders to the Sea,*) among others. Pan wrote and produced a recording of original songs titled, *Wild Blue,* (hear at <u>panmorigan.com</u>) She produced a song collection/radio program for Public Radio International, *Castles of Gold, Songs and Stories of Irish Immigration.* She's a recipient of a Massachusetts Cultural Council Fellowship in music composition, a New England Foundation for the Arts Meet the Composer Grant, three composer residencies at Blue Mountain Center, and grants with Chrysalis Theater from the Ford Foundation and the NEA to produce Chrysalis Theater's inter-cultural, multi-disciplinary theater works. Pan is currently finishing a series of four interlocking novels.

Susana Morris is a queer Jamaican-American writer based in Atlanta. She is the co-editor, with Brittney C. Cooper and Robin M. Boylorn, of *The Crunk Feminist Collection* (Feminist Press 2017), co-editor, with Kinitra D. Brooks and Linda D. Addison, of *Sycorax's Daughters* (Cedar Grove 2017), a short story collection of horror written by Black women, and co-author, with Brittney C. Cooper and Chanel Craft Tanner, of the forthcoming young adult handbook, *Feminist AF: The Guide to Crushing Girlhood* (Norton 2021). She is passionate about Afrofuturism, Black feminism, and climate change.

Ama Patterson was an elegant writer who delighted in unexpected metaphors, haunting characters, and startling storylines. Her short story, "Hussy Strutt," appeared in *Dark Matter: A Century of Speculative Fiction from the African Diaspora,* and "Seamonsters" appeared in *Scarab,* edited by Sheree Renée Thomas and in *Trouble the Waters: Tales of the Deep Blue* edited by Sheree Renée Thomas, Pan Morigan, and Troy L. Wiggins. Her short fiction is included in *80! Memories and Reflections on Ursula K. Le Guin* edited by Karen Joy Fowler and Debbie Notkin (Aqueduct Press). Ama also wrote *Finding Your Inner Goddess: A Journal of Self- Empowerment; Zen and the Art of Haiku* with Chris Paschke; *The Lost Art of I Ching [With 64 Card Set]* with Marian Morton; and *The Essential Guide to Astrology Kit* with Pauline Southard. Her writing has been characterized by *Publishers Weekly* and other reviewers as "gorgeous and tough" and "unbearably poignant."

Cecilia Quirk is a queer writer and part-time medieval lady based in Melbourne, Australia. She writes speculative fiction stories with a focus on atmospheric world-building, surreal magic, and complex characters. *The Weaver's Tale* is her first foray into folklore. You can read her fantasy short story *Scattered Souls* in *Aurealis* magazine.

Heather 'Byrd' Roberts is an award-winning Chicago-based poet, creative catalyst, educator, and author. Her first chapbook, "Mahogany: A Love Letter To Black," is her 14-poem calling card. It is an invitation to discuss Blackness and our relationship to this country, each other, and how they intersect. Byrd's work focuses on the intersectionality between form and freedom. Her work unlocks the opportunity for unheard voices to be heard. She is dedicated to inspire and transform lives through creativity. Byrd's work has appeared in *CAGIBI*'s journal, *Sixfold*, *Expressions from Englewood*, and other literary journals. She is the 2019 National Artist of the Year, 2020 Best Storyteller, and the 2020 Fringemeister. Her favorite words are balloon and bubble. To join her on her journey, follow her on Facebook & Instagram @blubyrdsworld, and visit www.byrdsworld.com.

Shawn Scarber is a North Texas author, a graduate of Clarion West, and works in the field of artificial intelligence. His short stories have appeared in anthologies and magazines.

Betsy Phillips writes about politics and history for the *Nashville Scene*. She has also written for the *Washington Post*. He book about the integration-era bombings in Nashville, *Dynamite Nashville: Unmasking the FBI, the KKK, and the Bombers Beyond their Control* is forthcoming from Third Man Books. Her research on the sculptor, William Edmondson, was featured in the

New York Times. She has contributed an essay "Perverse Incentives," to *Greetings from New Nashville: How a Sleepy Southern Town Became "It" City* (2020) and an essay about the grave markers carved by William Edmondson to the catalog of his 2021 Cheekwood Exhibit. Betsy's fiction has appeared in *Apex Magazine* and *The Magazine of Fantasy & Science Fiction*. "Mother of Crawdads" was first published in a Third Man Books chapbook, *Jesus, Crawdad, Death* (2018). Her short story "Frank" was made into an award-winning short film. She is currently working on an afghan.

Rion Amilcar Scott is the author of the story collection, *The World Doesn't Require You* (Norton/Liveright, August 2019). His debut story collection, *Insurrections* (University Press of Kentucky, 2016), was awarded the 2017 PEN/Bingham Prize for Debut Fiction and the 2017 Hillsdale Award from the Fellowship of Southern Writers. His work has been published in *The New Yorker,* and in journals such as *The Kenyon Review*, *Crab Orchard Review*, and *The Rumpus*, among others. He lives in Annapolis, MD with his wife and two sons.

Henry Szabranski was born in Birmingham, UK, and studied Astronomy & Astrophysics at Newcastle upon Tyne University, graduating with a degree in Theoretical Physics. His fiction has appeared in *Clarkesworld, Beneath Ceaseless Skies, Daily Science Fiction, Diabolical Plots, Constellary Tales, Kaleidotrope* and *Fantasy For Good: A Charitable Anthology*, amongst other places. He lives in Buckinghamshire with his wife and two young sons. Contact him at henry@szabranski.com or follow @henryszabranski.

Sheree Renée Thomas is an award-winning fiction writer, poet, and editor. Her work is inspired by myth and folklore, natural science, and the genius of the Mississippi Delta. *Nine Bar Blues: Stories from an Ancient Future* (Third Man Books 2020) is her debut fiction collection. She is also the author of the hybrid collections, *Sleeping Under the Tree of Life* (Aqueduct Press 2016), longlisted for the 2016 Otherwise Award and honored with a *PW* Starred Review and *Shotgun Lullabies* (2011). She edited the World Fantasy Award-winning groundbreaking anthologies, *Dark*

Matter (2000, 2004) and is the first to introduce W.E.B. Du Bois's science fiction short stories. Her work is widely anthologized and appears in Marvel's *Black Panther: Tales of Wakanda* edited by Jesse J. Holland, *The New York Times,* and *The Big Book of Modern Fantasy* (1945 – 2010) edited by Ann & Jeff VanderMeer (Vintage 2020). She was honored as a 2020 World Fantasy Award Finalist in the Special Award – Professional category for contributions to the genre and is the Editor of *The Magazine of Fantasy & Science Fiction,* founded in 1949 and Associate Editor of *Obsidian: Literature & Arts in the African Diaspora*, founded in 1975. She also reviews new books for *Asimov's*. Sheree lives in Memphis, Tennessee, near a mighty river and a pyramid.

Marie Vibbert is a computer programmer and author from Cleveland, Ohio with over seventy short fiction sales, including eleven appearances in *Analog* and three in *China's Science Fiction World*. Her work often reflects her blue-collar background, growing up with a single dad who was a laborer. Her debut novel, *Galactic Hellcats*, came out in 2021, and is about an all-lady biker gang in outer space rescuing a gay prince. Learn more at www.marievibbert.com or follow her @mareasie on Twitter.

Mateo Hinojosa is a mestizo Quechua Bolivian-American storyteller based in California. Specializing in channeling collective voices and visions into creative expression, he has facilitated collaborative cross-cultural storytelling workshops and audiovisual productions with Native American youth, Argentine transgender prisoners, and climate justice activists. His feature documentary, *Spectacular Movements*, was co-created with young Aymara actors reviving the spirits of the recent Bolivian revolution with theater and street interventions. As Media Director at The Cultural Conservancy since 2013, he has produced numerous documentaries, community education experiences, and the *Native Seed Pod* podcast. He is also director of the production/education company, Woven Path.

Jasmine Wade is obsessed with the ridiculous, and oftentimes traumatic, trials of growing up. Her short stories have appeared in *Drunken Boat, TAYO Literary Magazine, Lunch Ticket, The*

Copperfield Review, and others. Her work is also included in the anthologies *Little Letters on the Skin* and *Running Wild Anthology of Stories, Volume 2.* She has won the 2016 Edward P. Jones Short Story Contest and was a finalist for the Hurston/Wright Founding Members Award for College Writers and the Tu Books New Visions Award. She is currently a PhD student in Cultural Studies at the University of California, Davis.

Troy L. Wiggins is a writer and editor living in Memphis, Tennessee. Troy is co-editor of the World Fantasy Award-winning and Hugo nominated *FIYAH Magazine of Black Speculative Fiction* and a co-editor of *Trouble the Waters: Tales of the Deep Blue* (Rosarium). His short fiction and essays have appeared in *Long Hidden: Speculative Fiction From the Margins of History, Expanded Horizons, Memphis Noir, Uncanny,* and *Fireside Fiction Magazine.* You can follow his musings on race and nerd culture at <u>afrofantasy.net</u>, and follow him on Twitter <u>@TroyLWiggins</u>

Elle L. Littlefield is an Afro-Mississippi writer, editor, and professor, a regular contributor to creative and literary projects in the "MemphisSippi" area. A regular contributor to creative and literary projects in the "MemphisSippi" region, she works to document and preserve Black vernacular and culture from the American South. A two-time Callaloo Fellow, she holds an MFA from Sarah Lawrence College. She has served as editor and creative director for *BG Memphis Magazine,* and as Assistant Editor *Hieroglyph.* In 2021, she co-curated the Afrofuturist virtual exhibition *Curating the End of the World: Red Spring,* the third installment of the series by Black Speculative Arts Movement (BSAM) hosted by Bill T. Jones' New York Live Arts and Google Cultural Institute. Currently, she serves as Assistant Professor of English and Fine Arts at HBCU Rust College in Mississippi, and as a Contributing Editor at *Obsidian: Literature & Arts in the African Diaspora.* You can find her on Instagram @d_ellellfield and on Twitter @ElletheVeil.

Gina McGuire is a wahine kupa 'ai au (Native Hawaiian woman), currently pursuing doctoral work on coastal ecology and wellbeing through the lens of Hawaiian healing practice. She holds master's degrees in Creative Writing from Lancaster University and Tropical Conservation Biology from University of Hawai'ias well as a BA in International Relations from Stanford University. Gina grew up in the rainforests of Hawai'i Island listening to the rain dripping down through the native canopy and ferns, as hō'ailona (signs) of those who have come before. She is passionate about writing for Indigenous peoples and places.

TROUBLE THE WATERS:
Tales from the Deep Blue

Permissions